James Harris, Daniel Owen

Rhys Lewis, Minister of Bethel

An Autobiography

James Harris, Daniel Owen

Rhys Lewis, Minister of Bethel
An Autobiography

ISBN/EAN: 9783337117566

Printed in Europe, USA, Canada, Australia, Japan

Cover: Foto ©Raphael Reischuk / pixelio.de

More available books at **www.hansebooks.com**

RHYS LEWIS,

MINISTER OF BETHEL:

AN AUTOBIOGRAPHY.

By DANIEL OWEN.

TRANSLATED FROM THE WELSH

By JAMES HARRIS,

EDITOR OF " *The Red Dragon*," *the National Magazine of Wales;*

AUTHOR OF " *The Bar Sinister*," " *Polly Morgan, Pit Girl*," " *Herbert of Glaslyn, a Story of the Eisteddfod, the Chapel and the Coal Mine*," &c., &c.

LONDON: SIMPKIN, MARSHALL AND CO.

WREXHAM: HUGHES AND SON, 56, HOPE STREET.

PREFACE.

It has long since struck me that there are more things in Welsh literature than are dreamt of in the average English reader's philosophy. One of the best of such things, in its own particular line, that I have come across, is the story of which I here present a not very rigidly textual translation, my aim having been to act as the author's interpreter rather than to cling, with undeviating fidelity, to the extreme niceties of a literal rendering.

For the word "Seiat," in the original, I give "Communion;" a very beautiful word, in itself, which I trust will prove acceptable. The "Seiat" is as peculiarly a Calvinistic Methodist Church institution as Calvinistic Methodism is peculiarly a Welsh Nonconformist denomination. Originally, no doubt, a corruption of the English word "Society," "Seiat," has, by long user, acquired a special signification for which "Society" would now furnish but a meaningless or absurd equivalent; as, I think, the English reader who takes the trouble to try the word in the text will at once see.

There is, I know, one objection to "Communion;" but, after weighing it against the many objections which exist to each and all of the other words suggested, I had no difficulty in discerning the side of the scale which kicked the beam.

Slips, I fear, the book is almost bound to contain, the exigencies of publication, in view of the holding of the National Eisteddfod of Wales at Wrexham, having demanded a high pressure rate of work such as I did not at first contemplate.

I am sure, however, that that large English public to which I appeal, will be no less indulgent to me than the comparatively limited Welsh one has been before which the author made his first appearance; and that, as he was, so shall I be, given the chance of successive editions in which to rectify my mistakes.

THE TRANSLATOR.

Cardiff, *August 20th,* 1888.

CONTENTS.

CHAPTER.   PAGE.

    INTRODUCTION   7

  I. BIOGRAPHY   9

  II. MY BIRTH   11

  III. EARLIEST RECOLLECTIONS   13

  IV. EVAN JONES OF GWERNYFFYNON, HUSBANDMAN   16

  V. THE CHILDREN'S MEETING   22

  VI. THE IRISHMAN   27

  VII. THE TWO SCHOOLS   33

  VIII. UNDER INSTRUCTION   40

  IX. CHURCH MATTERS   47

  X. THE SUBJECT OF EDUCATION   56

  XI. WILL BRYAN ON THE NATURE OF A CHURCH   ..   64

  XII. ON THE HEARTH   73

  XIII. SETH   81

  XIV. WILL BRYAN   92

  XV. THE BEGINNING OF TROUBLES..   100

  XVI. THE DAY OF TRIAL   110

  XVII. FURTHER TRIALS   122

  XVIII. THOMAS AND BARBARA BARTLEY   131

  XIX. ABEL HUGHES   139

  XX. THE VICAR OF THE PARISH   149

CHAPTER.		PAGE.
XXI.	CONVERTS	158
XXII.	A VISIT FROM MORE THAN ONE RELATION	169
XXIII.	BOB	180
XXIV.	REMINISCENCES, SAD AND CONSOLATORY	192
XXV.	AN ELEGY IN PROSE	204
XXVI.	DEGENERACY AND AN APPARITION	214
XXVII.	DAYS OF DARKNESS	226
XXVIII.	MASTER AND SERVANT	237
XXIX.	THE CLOCK CLEANER'S ADVICE	250
XXX.	THE POACHER	263
XXXI.	DAVID DAVIS	278
XXXII.	THE MULTITUDE OF COUNSELLORS	290
XXXIII.	MORE OF WILL BRYAN	304
XXIV.	THOMAS BARTLEY ON COLLEGIATE EDUCATION	318
XXXV.	TROUBLOUS	332
XXXVI.	A WELL-KNOWN CHARACTER	344
XXXVII.	THOMAS BARTLEY VISITS BALA	359
XXXVIII.	A FORTUNATE ENCOUNTER	378
XXXIX.	WILL BRYAN IN HIS CASTLE	390
XL.	THE AUTOBIOGRAPHY OF WILL BRYAN	405
XLI.	THE FIRST TIME AND THE LAST	417
XLII.	THE MINISTER OF BETHEL	427

RHYS LEWIS,

MINISTER OF BETHEL.

AN AUTOBIOGRAPHY.

INTRODUCTION.

THE Minister of Bethel has now for some time been peacefully reposing beneath the turf of the valley. In his day he was reckoned a wise and an unassuming man, those best acquainted with him being wont to say there was more in him than was seen on the surface. Although as a minister of the Gospel he was "a public character," as it is called, he was always averse to making a parade of himself. As a preacher he was not popular, chiefly because he could not sing, which was a great drawback. Nevertheless, he had at all times something to say which was well worth the listening to; and I have heard men of mature judgment aver that his sermons, were they printed, would compare favourably with the best productions of the Welsh pulpit. Indeed, the few things from his pen which appeared in the *Tractarian* were attributed to Dr.——, and were read with avidity. In those days, writers' names were not appended to their productions in that valuable quarterly. Even if they had been, probably no one would have gone to the trouble of reading the contributions of Rhys Lewis.

His pastorate was, on the whole, a happy and a successful one. It must be admitted, however, that this was but an accident of the situation, due chiefly to the fact that the majority of the Church to which he ministered were possessed of a good deal of common sense and just a little of Christian feeling.

Although he could be pleasant and sociable enough in company, he always preferred the seclusion of his library. There were times when, forgetting himself, he indulged too much this love of solitude, and on more than one occasion the deacons felt compelled to call his attention to the neglect of his public duties. He occasionally suffered from lowness of spirits, and it was thought by some people that something weighed upon his mind, the nature of which not even his nearest and dearest friends were cognisant of. Others, again, attributed the cause to a disordered nervous system. Possibly the following history, of his own composition, may throw a little light upon the question which of the two suppositions was correct.

The Minister of Bethel died in the midst of a useful career, and whilst he was yet comparatively young, without a single blot upon his character. Recently, while under direction of the executrix, arranging the books of the deceased, preparatory to their sale, I lighted upon a bulky M.S., which, on examination, I found to be autobiographical. Thinking there might be something of interest in it, I obtained permission to take it home with me, where, as soon as I found leisure, I gave it a careful perusal. Apart altogether from the fact that the writer explicitly says so (as will be seen hereafter), the order and context of the M.S. make it obvious that he did not intend it to be printed. So pleased, however, was I by the perusal that I asked consent to publish the work, which I now give to my readers in the hope that they will derive from it a satisfaction equal to my own. At the same time, I feel that some apology for its appearance is necessary. The opening chapters are childish and frivolous, although harmless. They are, however (so I believe), faithful to Nature, and reflect the feeling and experience of a great many. As the history proceeds it gathers strength and solidity. Furthermore, it will be found to contain descriptions of some remarkable old characters, worldly and religious. For obvious reasons, I have changed the names of the author and others who are referred to, which is all the liberty with the text I felt I had the right to take. Lest the reader should meet with anything in these pages not exactly to his taste—as, for instance, that free treatment which sometimes borders on the profane, or an over minuteness of description—I must ask him to bear constantly in mind the fact that the author did not write his history with a view to its publication.

CHAPTER I.

BIOGRAPHY.

In my time I have read many biographies, and I can neither measure nor value the amusement and instruction I got thereby. There is, possibly, quite as much genius—sense, at any rate—in biography as there is in any branch of literature, for the reason, it may be assumed, that the author generally knows something of his subject, which is not always indispensable in other directions. At the same time, however ably and faithfully the biographer may describe the public character of his subject, we are frequently grieved to think how little he knew, after all, of the inner consciousness of the man. We feel also, how well it were with the biographer, and with the reader likewise, had he been able to put questions to the man long lying in his peaceful grave. It is here that autobiography has a great advantage over biography ; although, on second thoughts, I fancy a life-history written by another, and not by the subject himself, is the more trustworthy after all. True, there are facts and feelings at the command of the man who writes his own life, which another, let his talent and fidelity be what they may, can never obtain. Nevertheless, when one writes his own history, and is at the same time conscious of the fact that it is to be published, he becomes the prey of diffidence, of a fear lest others may think he has over-estimated himself; the consequence being that he does not claim for himself the character and station which would unhesitatingly be assigned him by another.

I have many times thought I should like to have an accurate memorial of the life of an ordinary individual like myself. In all the biographies I have read the subjects were great and remarkable in some way or another, had moved in circles I could never enter, and had passed through circumstances to which I was wholly strange. And although I knew it to be possible it was these considerations which made the memoir worth the writing, I, at the same time, felt how delightful it would be to read the history of a commonplace man—one who had moved in circles and met with experiences similar to my own. Are there not thoughts and feelings that were never given utterance to simply because they were commonplace, in the same way that many of Nature's beauties remain unnoticed because they are everywhere met? Is want of loveliness the reason why the daisy has not attracted the attention of the florist, and kindled the enthusiasm of the bard? Or is it because the flower is seen in every field, and trodden upon by every cow? Did the robin redbreast and the gold-finch begin to descant upon the beauties of Nature, the modest primrose would come in for a goodly share of their praise, although it is but the untrimmed hedge-row which the flower adorns. I am inclined to think the man was never born of whom the honest life-history would not be interesting. Are there not, in every career, circumstances worth the chronicling, thoughts of the heart to which neither their owner nor anyone else has given voice? I have often fancied that one great difference between the common man and the uncommon was that the latter could give expression to what he thought and felt, while the former either could not or would not attempt to do anything of the kind. What made me think so was this: — When reading some eminent author, or listening to leaders of congregations, I instinctively perceived they were saying nothing wholly new to me, but merely that they were able to give form to, and set forth in words, that which I myself had either felt or thought previously, but which I was wholly unable to express; in other words, that they were able to read those heart-secrets which I had for years been trying in vain to spell. I was already conscious of the possession of such thoughts and feelings; but they were asleep, or rather napping, and all the masters did was to knock at the door of the sleeping apartment, with such effect that its occupants rubbed their eyes and sprang up.

I have a mind to write the history of my own life, not for others, but for myself; certainly not for print, but rather as a help to self-communion. I know well enough there is no fear of any one's writing my biography after I am dead. A hundred years hence no one in this world will know more about me than if I had never been. With thousands upon thousands of my contemporaries, I shall be reposing peacefully in the silence of oblivion. And yet I do not like the thought of this; although, what help is there, since it is the fate of all of us, the common people? Why is man so unwilling that his name shall be forgotten after his death, when nor remembrance nor forgetfulness can do him either good or evil? The dead, I imagine, derive quite as much satisfaction from the stone which marks their resting place as do those tender friends who placed it there. Their bones lie easier with a memorial overhead! Immortality! hast thou aught to do with this?

I want to write my own history, I say; but not, thank Heaven, to print it, for were that the case, I should not be then, as I am now, able to tell the truth, the whole truth, and nothing but the truth, because I should have the reader to study as well as myself. Rhys! what have you to say for yourself? Be sure you tell the truth. This I shall do, and should either friend or relative meet with my writing, be it known to him that I have not one word thereof to withdraw.

CHAPTER II.

MY BIRTH.

WHEN first struck with the notion of writing my own life I thought I should be able to do so without help from any living soul. How foolish of me! I see at the outset I must depend entirely upon the testimony of others with respect to the earliest portion of my existence; and, inasmuch as I am determined to stick to facts, I shall confess that I do not remember anything of the occasion when I first came into the world.

In view of this failing of memory, I think I can wholly rely upon the evidence of my mother. She told me, more than once, it was between two and three o'clock in the morning, on the 5th of October, 18—, that I first saw the light of a halfpenny candle. Whether because I felt offended at the poverty of the preparations made for my arrival, or that it was for some other reason I seemed so cross and yelled and screamed so, the two female neighbours who were present at the time were quite unable to determine. They, anyhow, made up their minds that I was an inconsiderate, unfeeling little wretch for making such a noise, aware as I was, or ought to have been, that my mother was so ill that morning. Of this much I am certain, I was not consulted at all upon the occasion, and it is possible that is what made me so ill-tempered and unreasonable—which, of course, is only surmise, and not to be set down as sober fact. If I were not perfectly sure that my mother never told the thing which was untrue, I could hardly believe myself to have been at that period of my life, as I nearly am now, bald-headed and tooth-less; that my nose, commonly considered Roman in shape, was not only flat, but like the new moon had its two ends turned up, and that so fleshy was I that there were holes in my elbows and knees, where there are now, goodness knows, nothing but protruding bones perceivable.

I do not remember, either, a time when I could not, or was not tolerably ready to walk; but my mother told me, for all that, that I was altogether averse to the process once, and did nothing but lie on my back, crying and kicking, unless I found someone to carry me. Although possessing no recollection of it, I regret having been guilty of so much misbehaviour. I marvel to think three years of my life should have passed which I know nothing of from memory; and if those who were best acquainted with me during that period, and in whose truthfulness I could rely, were to bring the very worst accusations against me, I should have nothing to do but believe them. Could I at that time have had reason, memory, feeling? Was I but a lump of living clay? If so, whence came reason, memory, and the like to me?

One thing I possessed, I know, from the testimony of my mother—and I fear I possess it even yet in too great a degree—namely, the spirit of mischief. I broke, so she told me, a great many things; and I know she told the truth. I smashed the few ornaments she owned; I scratched the faces and pulled the hair of divers of my relations and neighbours. I dragged one young girl's earring right through her flesh, causing the blood to stream down upon her shoulder. I squeezed the life out of three young kittens, and committed a number of other atrocities, such as it is not pleasant to have to admit, even to one-

self, although I am not conscious of any guilt on their account.
What surprises me most is that everyone should have been so
taken with me, and behave towards me as if I had been a source
of profit to everybody, when, in reality, I was good for nothing at
all, and not only that, but a source of worry and trouble. My
mother lost much of her sleep on my account, and was scores of
times obliged to get up in the middle of the night to dose me
with Cinder Tea. Upon occasion I used to cry for hours
at a stretch, and inasmuch as I had taken it into my head not to
talk for a matter of two years or so, no one knew what I cried
for. And yet, for all that, I heard my mother saying she
would not take the world for me—even when I screamed my
loudest.

I grew up a great lump of a fat fellow, considering I lived
almost entirely on milk; but, my weight notwithstanding, my
neighbours used to compete for the pleasure of carrying me.
It seems that I liked being without teeth, because when those
parts of me began making their appearance I became very
troubled in spirit, so much so that I experienced a falling off in
flesh. I have been told that so greatly did I give way to bad
temper on their account that I fell, ultimately, into convulsions.
How mad it was of me! Would to heaven I were to experience
the same ailment *now*. There is, however, one advantage in
being as I am at present; no one is able to throw anything in
my teeth.

Well, enough of the period of which I have no recollection. It
is with much greater pleasure that I turn to a time I know
something about from personal experience and memory.

CHAPTER III.

EARLIEST RECOLLECTIONS.

I BELIEVE, nay, am certain, that one of the first things I remember is going to chapel with my mother. I am not sorry
my earliest recollections should be associated with the chapel.
Dear old chapel! Many an imprint hast thou left upon my
memory; and upon my conscience too, I trust. Whether it
was the first, or the second, or the twentieth time I went there,

or divers times which have fused themselves together in my memory, which created so deep an impression upon me, I cannot now determine, but sure I am that, taken in my mother's hand to chapel, I remember finding the journey a very long one, and insisting upon being carried the greater part of the way. It was a Sunday night, very probably; the chapel being full, and lighted up, not with gas as now, but with candles. The crowd frightened me, and I burst out crying. Mother, I recollect, placed her hand upon my mouth, nearly smothering me, and it was not until some one near us gave me a Nelson ball that I was comforted. Where have those famous sweetmeats gone to? There is nothing like them in these days. Is it I or the sweetmeats that have changed? The ground floor of the building was very different then from what it is at present. It was open, rows of backless benches running across it, and a few deep seats being ranged around the walls. In the centre there was a large stove, surrounded always by a crowd of children with faces red as a cock's comb. Most likely the season was winter.

I remember the Big Seat, the Singers' Seat to its left, and Abel Hughes, with his velvet cap, stationed under the pulpit, going about every now and then to snuff the candles. I shall have something more to say concerning Abel directly. The pulpit was built against the wall, so high up that it reminded me of the swallow's nest left under the eaves of our house during the previous summer. It puzzled me how "the man" (so I styled him) who was in the pulpit could have climbed thither, and what was his object in doing so? Was it a habit of his, and did he ever get a fall in descending, as I did more than once in coming downstairs? Did someone carry him down, as my brother Bob used to carry me?

I wondered greatly no one had a word to say but "the man in the box," and still more that he should have so much. I understood not a word of it all with the exception of "Jesus Christ," and I fancied at first *he* was the "Jesus Christ" whom my mother so often spoke to me about. I was expecting him every moment to stop talking; but in vain. After he had spoken a long time, according to my reckoning, he put on a fierce look, flushed in the face, and shouted loudly. I made up

my mind then that he was not Jesus Christ. I fancied
him to be "giving it" me rather badly—what for I did not
know; but he looked at me so often that I knew well enough
it was to me he was referring. So thinking, I began to cry
again, and had to be half suffocated a second time, and given
another Nelson ball before I ceased my noise.

I looked about me, upstairs and down, and wondered at seeing
so many people in the gallery. Were they in the habit of
sleeping there? How did they get beds enough? I found the
chapel darkening, and the man in the box looking smaller, and
appearing to retreat farther and farther away from me, although
he kept on shouting, higher and still higher. I felt myself
gathered to my mother, and suddenly—in profoundest slumber
—lost sight of everybody and everything. I don't know how
long I slept; but they had great trouble in waking me, despite
the singing of the congregation. I liked the singing much
better than the sermon, feeling, in some way I could never
explain, that I understood it. By this time the man in the
pulpit had sat down. He was wiping the perspiration from his
brow, and tying a great cravat loosely about his neck. Seeing
Abel Hughes mount the pulpit steps, I concluded he was
going to bring "the man" away upon his back, just as brother
Bob used to bring me downstairs at home. Great was my disappointment at finding him stop mid-way and saying something
to the people, which I subsequently learned referred to the Church
progamme for the ensuing week. The greater part of the congregation then left, but my mother and divers others remained
behind, and the chapel doors were shut. This made me think
we were never going home again, and I began to cry once more.
Mother however told me, "in her deed," we should go "just
directly," and that pacified me a little. Thereupon I saw the
man who I imagined had been belabouring me descend from
the pulpit. I watched closely his progress, fearing he would
have a fall. He got to the bottom safely. After this I saw
Abel Hughes lift the linen cloth which covered something in
front of the Big Seat, fold it neatly, and put it on one side. I
wondered at the sight thus brought to view. What lovely
vessels! The man who had spoken at such length rose,
advanced towards them, said something further about Jesus

Christ, and began to eat of the broken bread placed near. I thought he was taking supper, and that having tasted one bit and one drop only, the meal was not to his liking. To my great surprise I saw him take up the broad, carry it about, and give everybody a morsel. Feeling very hungry myself, I reflected that despite his treatment of me, he was a decent person after all. My mother, when he came to her, took a bit up from the plate. I, too, held out my hand, but he refused me. Feeling mightily offended with him, I burst out crying afresh, and for about the sixth time that night. It was clear now that the man owed me some grudge. Mother had great difficulty in soothing me. When the man came round with the cup, I hid my face under her cloak, so as not to have to look upon him, nor he to have the chance of refusing me a second time. What with the darkness of the night and these insults of the preacher, I became very cross and ill-tempered, my mother being obliged to carry me all the way home.

How fortunate it is that this history is not intended for publication! Were it otherwise, I should not have been able to narrate what I have narrated; so simple is it and so childish, though true; and, though possibly new to literature, yet not so to the experience of here and there a reader.

CHAPTER IV.

EVAN JONES OF GWERNYFFYNON, HUSBANDMAN.

CARRYING back my mind to the period of childhood, how wonderful the reflection that I am still the same being, spite of all the changes that have taken place in my thoughts and inclinations! Comparing the child to the man, how unlike and yet how like they are! I would not for the world deny my personality, nor change my consciousness for that of another. I have frequently stopped to pity the river Alun at the point where it loses itself in the Dee. From Llanarmon-yn-Iâl down to Cilcain, through the Belan, along the vale of Mold, how brave and bright and beautiful it looks! But on nearing Holt

its face changes, the sorrow being plainly depicted upon it of
its pending absorption by the Dee. I do not know how other
men feel, but as for me, I am happy to think I am ever the
same being, and I would not for anything it were otherwise, for
is it not that way madness lies? "He is beside himself," goes
the saying, does it not, when we speak of one who has become
insane? Well, I am happy in being able to cast back my
memory and, following the course of my life through its various
epochs, circumstances and views down to the present hour, to
reflect that I am individually still the same. And I am even
more happy to think that, when taking the leap, I cannot tell
how soon, into the great world of eternity, I shall even then be
my former self, and that my identity will not, like poor old
Alun's, be lost in another. How strange and wonderful! At the
end of a thousand ages I shall still possess the same consciousness that I did when walking in my mother's hand to chapel!

But to return to my childhood. If I am to tell the truth—as
I have resolved to do—I must confess that I did not at all relish
going to chapel. The service was much too long for me. It
was not always I was able to sleep through it, and when awake
nothing pleased me but the singing. While the preacher talked
on and on for ever, as I thought, I suffered intolerable pain in
the legs, and it was as much as mother could do to soothe me.
Mother was a Methodist of the Methodists, and clung fast to the
faith and traditions of the fathers. Blessings on her! One of
her most sacred beliefs was in the necessity of a strict observance
of the Sabbath. I dared not as much as talk of play, or look at
a toy on the Lord's Day. I was obliged to sit still and look
serious at a time when I had not the slightest notion of the
difference between one day and another. Did I become restless
or sportive, mother would say Jesus Christ was angry with me,
and that I should never go to Heaven, but would, instead, be
thrown into the "burning fire." This grieved me greatly. I
could not for the life of me make out how, if Jesus was as fond
of little children as mother said he was, he could be so rigidly
averse to my playing on the Sunday. At last I hated seeing
the Sabbath approach, knowing I should be sure to offend Jesus.
On one occasion I asked mother what sort of a place Heaven
was? She replied, in an endeavour doubtless to adapt herself

B

to my understanding, that it was a land wherein all the inhabitants kept everlasting Sabbath. My countenance fell upon the instant, and I told her emphatically I would never go there. O! the blow it gave her! I see, now, her dear face darkening, and the tears coming into her eyes. I threw my arms around her neck, and said I *would* go to Heaven for her, my mother's sake, only I hoped that Jesus Christ would let me play just a little bit when I got there.

Poor old mother! with the best intentions in the world, she set about my religious training in the most awkward way that could have been devised. Dear old mother! Ignorant and uneducated thyself, thou wert yet, to my mind, the best mother in the world. I doubt not but that thy prayers in my behalf, have, in some measure, been answered. Now at the age of man what would I give for one look at thy countenance; for one more chance of atoning for every ill word I have spoken, and every act of disobedience I have committed towards thee? Dost thou know the many trials and temptations I have undergone since the day when we escorted thee to the cold churchyard? How I have marvelled that not all my disobedience, not all my wickedness, ever lessened by one single grain thy love for me. I have met with many a faithful friend since, but not one who loved me like thee—who didst love me more than thine own life. Cold is the world, and strange without thee. I have no one left who understands me, no one who can enter into my feelings, like thee. Before I write another line, let others think what they will of me for so doing, I must pay one more visit to the "rough stone and double-lettered" which covers thy last resting-place.

My Sunday School reminiscences are confused and indeterminate. I am sure, however, of this much—that it was not there I was taught my letters. I do not remember ever being put to learn the A B C; either I must have known the alphabet intuitively, or, what is more likely, mother must have taught it me at some period of which I have no recollection. I am quite certain my first teacher was Evan Jones, the Gwerny-ffynon husbandman, and equally certain it was from a little book, something like the Primer of these days, he gave me my lessons. What makes me so sure about it is this: that it was as "A b, Ab," I used to speak of Evan to my mother, that being my lesson—a b, ab; e b, eb; o b, ob, &c.

A decent old fellow was Evan Jones, who on the Sunday, wore a blue coat with bright buttons, and breeches with leggings of grey. We were six or seven in Evan's class; and his method of imparting instruction was to take one of us upon his knee and give him a lesson whilst the rest indulged in play. After a lesson each all round, Evan considered he had done his duty, and at once proceeded to take a nap. Whilst so occupied—his chin sunk deeply into his vest, and the great coat collar almost level with the top of his head—I reckoned, not once nor ten times, the whole of the buttons on his clothing. I remember at this very minute their exact number. If I took oath to anything, I would take it to this, that it was seven buttons he had on each legging, five on the knees of his small clothes, four on each side of his coat, with two behind, and seven upon his waistcoat. Evan had an enormous watch—in these days they would have called it a timepiece—which he carried in his breeches pocket. I asked my mother once, why Evan did not wear his watch in his waistcoat pocket after the manner of the gentlemen up at the Hall. Her answer was that it was a great sin to wear a watch in the waistcoat pocket, and that no one ever did so but those who had not "felt the rope." I did not know at that time what "feeling the rope" meant; but I fancied it must be some tremendous and incomparable means for the making of a good man. So fond was I of Evan Jones that I cannot describe my satisfaction ever afterwards at the fact that it was in his breeches' pocket he kept his watch instead of in his waistcoat. Attached to Evan's watch was a bit of black ribbon, attached to that again being a white shell, an old coin, and a red seal.

We, the boys of the class, felt a burning desire to get that watch into our hands. One warm Sunday afternoon Evan had discharged his duty as usual, and fallen into a profound sleep. We knew this to be the case from his loud snoring, which we had never previously heard. Here then the long looked for opportunity had come! Will Bryan, the oldest of us, volunteered his services, and to this no one had any objection. The watch was abstracted from the sleeper's pocket, and handed round for inspection, each lad in turn putting it to his ear. The class was located in the highest corner of the chapel-loft, known as "Gibraltar," and was consequently a somewhat secluded spot. Evan's watch had twice made the circle of the class, and was in my hand. We were putting our heads together how best to return it to its original home without disturbing the owner, when a voice thundered above us the words, "What are you up to here?" In my fright I dropped the watch, smashing the glass to atoms; simultaneously our teacher jumped up as though some one had stabbed him in the small of the back. The thunderer was Abel Hughes, our superintendent, whose velvet-cap-surmounted head was peering angrily over the top of the seat. Our teacher was too unnerved to take notice of his watch.

"Is it sleeping you are, Evan Jones?" asked Abel severely.

"No—meditating," was Evan's sheepish reply.

"Meditating indeed! Meditating; and your class playing with your watch, eh? I must bring your case before the Teachers' Meeting, sir," sniffed Abel, and away he went in high indignation.

While Evan was taking in the situation I began to cry—a business I could always get through very effectively. No one had touched the watch since it fell from my hands. Evan looked at the damaged article and at me alternately, after which he picked it up, wrapped it in his handkerchief, and placed it in the breast pocket of his blue coat. Seeing the great distress I was in, he took me upon his knee and—although I knew he believed me guilty of the whole mischief—said soothingly, "Never mind, sonnie; it is'nt much after all."

I have thought since it was some sort of a fellow-feeling of guilt which made Evan so wondrous kind. Anyhow, the kindness only made me cry the more, and by the time I got home, my eyes were swollen to an extent which made it impossible to conceal the story from my mother. All she said to me was, "Well, we will see to-morrow."

She was as good as her word. She *saw;* and I *felt.*

I do not know for certain whether the case of Evan Jones, of Gwernyffynnon, was brought before the Teachers' Meeting; but I have every reason to believe it was, because always after that, when Evan settled down for a nap, he strictly charged us to be on the look out, and to be sure to wake him up on the approach of Abel Hughes; to which instruction we were ever faithful. I remember well that, as a class, we regarded Abel's prohibition of Evan Jones's nap after each had been given his lesson, as an act of unpardonable arrogance and tyranny.

Were this history to be published some one would perhaps be found to say, "How much better the teachers and the arrange-ments of the Sunday School are now than they were then." Possibly so. Evan Jones was only one of many such; but taking his virtues with his failings into account, he was as good a teacher as most of those of our day. Young though I was when he died, I have a two-fold respect for him. It was under him I learned to read. I have by heart many of my mother's sayings concerning him, as for example:—"A man is Evan with the root of the matter in him." "Evan Gwernyffynnon is greater on his knees than he is up-standing." "Evan knows well what it is to feel the cord." "A man of secrecy is Evan Jones." "Had Evan as much learning and money as he has grace, he would have been a Justice of the Peace long before now, and the occupant of the Hall would be but a beggar in comparison." These maxims of my mother, and many others like them, were as Latin to me at the time, and it was only in the course of years I came to understand them. It is a pleasure to call to mind the days when I was studying my mother's classics. As already intimated, I have every reason to believe that Evan Jones, despite his faults, was a fine character, and one who had proved the great things of our religion. Whilst in his class, I considered his habit of sleeping through a portion of the service more of a virtue than of anything else, because it gave us children a chance of play. When I call to mind the fact that he was compelled to work hard for a livelihood, and to get up at five every morning, I can excuse him from the bottom of my heart. If I go to Heaven I shall search for him, in order to thank him for all he did to me. But how silly of me! I keep thinking of Evan in Heaven in breeches and leggings and a blue coat. I cannot picture him otherwise attired.

CHAPTER V.

THE CHILDREN'S MEETING.

In the days of my boyhood, one of the most precious of religious institutions was the Children's Meeting, or according to the common name with both young and old, the Children's Communion. It was invariably held once a week, summer and winter; and I think I can certify that not a lad nor a lass, whose parents were church members, but was regularly present at it, unless prevented by ill-health. Let anyone be absent for two nights in succession without sufficient excuse, and Abel Hughes would, as sure as the world, call the father or mother to account at the next Church Meeting; and unless a satisfactory reason were forthcoming, a public rebuke would be administered for the neglect. What a falling off there has been in this matter since! It is almost impossible in these times to keep together a Children's Meeting for a few weeks during the winter months. And what if the parents were publicly called to account for neglecting to send their children thither? Fancy for a moment reproving Mrs. Dowell, of "The Shop," whose children are not seen once in four times at Church Meetings. Save us! Were anything of the kind to be attempted, it is doubtful whether she or her children would ever again come to chapel, let alone to Church Communion. But were Abel Hughes now alive, he would have called Mrs. Dowell to account, and many another Mrs. too, be the consequences what they might. Of a certainty, he would have told them that the Church of England was *their* place, and that the sooner the better they went there. Have all the race of honest elders died out? I am bound to admit that many of them were outspoken to the verge of rudeness, but, for all that, they possessed a probity and a sincerity standing out in strongly favourable contrast to the present generation of bland and velvety religionists.

As soon as I could recite the verse, "Remember Lot's wife," I had to sail off to the Children's Communion, under convoy of Will Bryan, who was some years my senior. In connection

with my history I shall often be obliged to refer to Will Bryan
—sometimes with pain. Perhaps it would have been better for
me had I never seen him, although at one time I thought he
never had his equal in the world. I was dreadfully slow at
learning a verse, and on that account, "Remember Lot's wife"
had to serve my turn for some score of occasions, a fact, by the
way, of which my mother knew nothing. She took care to
teach me a fresh verse for every meeting; but by the time I got
there the verse would have taken wing, and nothing would be
left me under the circumstances but to fall back on "Remember
Lot's wife." I well recollect, beginning more than once the
recitation of a fresh verse, as for instance, "This is a faithful
saying, and worthy——;" at which point I broke down, and
was forced to conclude with the inevitable "Remember Lot's
wife." I was such a small boy that this shortcoming was for a
long time overlooked, and it was not until the other children
began to call me "Lot's wife" that I gave over mentioning the
lady.

My constant repetition of this well-known verse gave
occasion to the conductors of the meeting to make it the subject
of frequent discourse, and I fancy I knew all about Lot's wife
that there was to be known, long before I was five years old.
Anyhow, I am not aware that my views with regard to the
Sodomites, the angels, the fire, the brimstone, Lot and his
family, the pillar of salt, Zoar, &c., have undergone much change
since. Thus was Scripture history instilled into our minds unconsciously. I am almost certain that Biblical knowledge was
much higher and more perfect in the youth of those days than
in those of this "enlightened age." Not long since, I happened
to ask the son of Mrs. Frederick Dowell of "The Shop," who
is quite fifteen years old, "Who was Jeroboam?" And his
answer was that he believed him to be one of the apostles. I
have reason to fear that there are many religious people's
children nowadays who are not one whit more advanced than
Solomon Dowell.

What zeal and devotion did John Joseph and Abel Hughes
display with us children, to be sure; despite the fact that the
last-named was an old man—old when I first remember him.

John Joseph was quite in his element teaching us to sing such refrains as

"O, that will be joyful,"

and

"Never-ending shall the sound be
Of those glorious harps of gold."

In contrast to this would Abel Hughes be seen soberly and seriously listening to our verse-recitals, and commenting upon them—as seriously, I say, as if the Day of Judgment were the morrow. We, children, liked John Joseph better than we did Abel Hughes, because when Abel was not present, John would use the tuning fork; and we were delighted to see him strike it on the stove, place it to his ear, shut his eyes, set his neck awry to catch the sound, and hum two or three notes before we began the singing, although we did not know in the world what high and awful purpose these means were intended to accomplish. It would not have been well for John Joseph to have gone through all this ceremony had Abel Hughes been present. I saw him once attempt it, but Abel promptly told him to keep such things at home, they were not in keeping with the house of God. What if Abel were alive now? What if he were to hear a man from the Big Seat announcing that such and such a tune was in the key of Lah, and one or two dozen people shrieking each against the other, "Doh, soh, doh, soh?" Of a truth he would say that religion was going to the dogs, and I fear that some unsettlement of his senses would have resulted. So do circumstances change in less than a single generation!

Abel Hughes was most particular as to beginning and ending the Children's Meeting punctually at the appointed time. We knew to the minute when he would arrive in chapel. I well remember mother praising Will Bryan for calling for me in such good time for the meeting. Little did she suspect that our early departure was made with a view of playing hide and seek in the gallery. Will managed somehow or other to find out that Abel always began the meeting by his watch, and finished it by the chapel clock. One night, all being in their places expecting Abel's arrival, Will told us he was going up into the gallery to move the clock-hand half an hour forward; and with the words he went. We were in the greatest trepidation lest Abel should come in and catch him. Will had hardly reached the clock seat and touched the hand, when Abel made his appearance. Will dived down on the instant. Our hearts went throbbing painfully, for Abel Hughes was not a man to be trifled with. While Abel was offering up the prayer with which he always began a meeting, and had tightly closed his eyes, everyone of us availed himself of the opportunity of opening his own, and looking up in the direction of the clock seat. We were simply astounded at Will's daring. We saw him, after he had moved the hand, coolly rest his elbows on the balustrade, and gave a wink first at one and then at the other, all round. He next went fumbling in his pockets, and taking out a handful of crumbs, deliberately dropped them down upon old Abel's head. Whether it was that Abel was so absorbed in his devotions, or because he wore a velvet skull-cap, and could not consequently feel the downpour, I know not, but he did not seem in the least to heed the infliction.

John Joseph happened to be absent that night, and the meeting therefore was somewhat flat. Very imperfectly did the boys recite their verses—their thoughts were in the chapel loft with Will Bryan, whose head kept popping into sight every now and then. Each time we caught a glimpse of his face it wore a grin, which showed the owner to be enjoying himself immensely. I verily believe he was the only one of us all whose heart was not quaking with fear. Time and again were we reproved by Abel Hughes for our indifferent verse-recitals, and for so constantly turning our eyes towards the clock, as if we were in a desperate hurry to get away. Little did he know that it was not at the clock we were looking, but at the hair on Will Bryan's crown. Serious though we contrived to appear, Abel Hughes at length grew tired of the effort to direct our minds to the lessons. He looked up at the clock, and expressed his great surprise to find how fast the time had flown. At this juncture the door opened, and Margaret Ellis, the caretaker entered, with a sad complaint as to the early coming of the children to chapel simply for the sake of play, and of the frightful row they kicked up.

Abel asked her who the culprits were.

"Hugh Bryan's son is the worst of the lot," she replied. "He has been more than usually bad to-night."

"My good woman," returned Abel, "you, like myself, are getting old. Will Bryan has not been here at all to-night; although that is somewhat odd, for he is a faithful attendant as a rule."

"Do you think, Abel Hughes, that I don't know what I am talking about?" asked Margaret, stiffly. "Did I not see him with my own eyes, did I not hear him scampering up and down the chapel?"

"Rhys," said Abel sternly, and looking me straight in the face, "did Will Bryan accompany you to the meeting, to-night?"

Spite of myself my eyes wandered up towards the clock seat where Will stood shaking a warning fist at me. I would never have dared to open my lips after that, and luckily there was no need to, for caretaker Margaret caught sight of Will's head as it ducked down into his hiding place.

"Abel Hughes," she cried, "He's in the clock seat now; I saw him this very minute."

We fairly trembled with fear as Abel, backing himself against the Big Seat, took a look up at the gallery. For the life of him, however, he could not see Will.

"Bring that bad boy down, Abel Hughes. He is there for certain," said Margaret.

Abel Hughes, agitated to the very soul, made for the gallery. My heart got into my throat as I watched him approach the clock seat. Before he could reach the spot, however, Will sprang into the next seat, and the next, and thus springing reached the top of the stairs, down which he went, it seemed to me, at a single bound, nearly upsetting Margaret, who tried to intercept him at the bottom. Will was well on his way home before Abel, poor old man, could look around. Whilst caretaker Margaret was expressing pretty freely her opinion of the boy's character, our revered old teacher was doing his best to regain his self-control. So shocked, however, was he that he dismissed us without prayer. All he could do was to enjoin us to go home quietly, like good children, and not to follow the example of

William Bryan. Abel proceeded at once to complain to Hugh Bryan of the unseemly conduct of his son, and next morning I heard the latter say he never got such a licking in all his life, as the one his father gave him over night.

The foregoing episode is so simple and so childish in its character, as not to be worth narration except to one's self. And yet I remember a time when I used to look upon the occurrences of that night with as much weighty concern and seriousness as ever Wellington did upon Waterloo. It was a great night in my young life. In my foolish simplicity I admired above everything Will Bryan's pluck and daring. I honestly believed the world did not contain his fellow. At this time I cannot help perceiving in Will's conduct on that occasion the seed of what has subsequently developed into a great tree.

Pity, Will, pity thou didst not give ear to the serious counsel of Abel Hughes and John Joseph at the Children's Communion. Hadst thou done so, thou would'st have been very differently situated to-day. Rememberest thou, from thy present place, how Abel used to advise us to keep from even the appearance of evil, and show us the peril of walking in the ways of the ungodly. Dost remember, also, how earnestly he prayed for us, and committed us to the care of Him whom he had found a Faithful Guide and Mighty Saviour? If thou dost remember it—and I have but little doubt on the subject—then thy reflections, methinks, can be none of the sweetest.

CHAPTER VI.

THE IRISHMAN.

My experience, probably, is not different to that of other people who endeavour to trace back the beginnings of things. How difficult it is to lay hold of the beginning of anything in my own history! For instance, when did I first learn that there was a closer tie between me and my mother than between me and some other woman? When did the idea of a God first form itself in my mind? When did I come to learn that I was a separate being? When did the notion of personal responsibility,

of sin and of a future world, become part of my consciousness?
&c. In the effort to hark back upon a particular point as the
beginning of these and similar notions, I find that I have
been mistaken, that the goal is farther off than ever; and
following it up, I at last lose it in the Un-beginnable. I do
not know how to account for this. Does the memory not
register the beginning of things in the mind? Must the beginning have happened for a particular space of time before the
memory can receive any impression from it? Or, are the
beginnings and the memory of them contemporaneous? Has
every idea a man may happen to be possessed of been existent
in the soul since its creation, only in a state of torpor from
which circumstances awaken it; or is it some adaptability
that the soul possesses for receiving impressions which by
constant accretion become deepened until they at length form
themselves into ideas?

At the time I am endeavouring to revert to, I think I must
have been about six years old, and my brother Bob about
eighteen. Bob, in my estimation, was a great strong man; it
being sufficient proof to me that he was able to carry me upon
his back without the least trouble. He was a collier; and no
one ever admired a brother more than I did mine when I saw
him coming home, clogs on feet, and lamp in hand, with a face
as black as the chimney. Up to that period I fancy I did not
know how mother, Bob and myself obtained our livelihood.
I then, or very shortly afterwards, came to understand that
none of the good things of this world could be got without
money—a truth which, to my sorrow, I have proved a thousand
times since. The means, possibly, by which I got the knowledge were my constant requests to my mother for this thing
and for that, and her reply that she had not the money wherewith to buy it. An occasion of great interest to us was that on
which Bob brought home his wages. We would all three sit
about the fire; Bob emptying his pocket into mother's apron,
and she reckoning the money many times over. To me
the sum had so large a sound, that I wholly failed to understand how mother could say she was without money. I noticed
that in the counting she sometimes looked pleased, at other
times serious, at all times thoughtful. I surmised she must be

wondering to find herself in possession of so much wealth. Poor innocent! Had I but known it, she was simply planning and puzzling her head how to lay out the few shillings in her apron to the best advantage, how to be able to pay everybody his due. The amount of Bob's earnings borne in mind, what a splendid Chancellor of the Exchequer must my old mother have been! She and Bob, when the counting was over, would indulge in a lot of confidential talk, of which all I could make out were the words "rent" and "shop." I came to look forward to pay day with eagerness; because my mother, after receiving the money, would go to the shop for food; and so, for one day at any rate, we had enough to eat. How few are they, as is best, who have experienced the exceeding pleasure of having enough to eat! I am thinking none can know that pleasure save those who, like myself, can tell what it is to have gone short of food. Short, did I say? Yes, without any! But to that I shall have to refer again.

As I have already intimated, Will Bryan and I were great friends, and I cannot help connecting with him the creation or the stirring up of thoughts and ideas within my soul. Particularly do I remember how I used to envy Will Bryan. His father kept a large shop (so I thought it), in which there was an abundance of everything. Will had potatoes and meat every day for dinner; I had brewis only. Will frequently had new clothes; for me there were ever and always my brother Bob's old ones re-made by mother. Will got a penny every Saturday to spend; I never saw the colour of one save when Bob was emptying his pocket into mother's apron. But what made me look upon Will as the happiest lad on earth, was the fact that he owned a real live little mule. I did not know of anything in the whole wide world I so much wished to possess as a little mule like Will's. And I was not the only one who envied Will his happy lot; the feeling was common amongst those of the same age as myself. Will himself was not unconscious of his superiority to us all. If any of us happened to offend him, the heaviest punishment he could possibly inflict was to forbid us to come anywhere near his mule; this, as a rule, being quite sufficient to bring us repentant to his feet. In virtue of this little mule, Will tyrannised over us most unmercifully, so much

so (I remember the occasion well), that at one of our gatherings
when somebody happened to stray from the subject, he gave
orders that nobody, without his permission, was to say a single
word of any kind that did not concern the mule. And there
was nothing left us but to submit in silence. Now I think of
it, what a number of people, of every age and station, have I
come in contact with who make capital out of their little mules!

I should never have mentioned this matter, had it not been
that Will Bryan's little mule was the means of rousing or of
creating an inquiry in my soul. I remember on one occasion
thinking over and envying the happier lot and superior advantages enjoyed by Will, and trying to account for the
difference, the conclusion I came to being this—that Will had a
father, whilst I had none. Why was I without a father?
When I put the question to my mother, she became agitated,
and the tears sprang into her eyes, but instead of saying a word
in reply, she tried to draw my attention to something else. I,
however, pressed the question, and asked moreover, whether my
father were dead?

"Yes," she answered, "your father, poor, child, *is* dead—in
sin and transgression."

Mother frequently used a Scriptural simile. I did not understand this one, but I took her to mean that my father had been
put down the "black hole," as I at that time called the grave.
The reflection made me very sad for a while, but the sadness
speedily passed away.

Some time after this—I cannot be particular to a month or two
—I remember mother had been to the shop, because it was pay
night, and we had just finished a good supper. All three were
gathered round the fire, I, at any rate, feeling exceedingly comfortable, whatever might have been the case with mother and Bob.
Mother always permitted me to remain up an hour or two later
on nights when Bob received his pay. I cannot convey in words
the mighty satisfaction and happiness this staying up late
afforded me. Thinking what very little things were those which
brought me so much happiness in my boyhood, I am grieved to
the heart to find that it was not possible to remain a boy for
ever. We three sat by the fire, I say; it was winter, and the
night was cold and stormy. I occupied my own little stool

listening to the wind roaring in the chimney and whistling through the keyhole. I felt very sleepy, but made desperate efforts not to close my eyes lest mother should send me to bed, and my privilege of remaining up late on the following pay night be thereby forfeited. I was just on the point of surrender when I heard some one knock at the door. I became wide awake at once. Before time had been given to open, there came in a repulsive looking fellow, who shut the door and walked straight to the fire without saying a word. Directly I saw him, I made up my mind that he was a bad man. He was ragged and dirty, and his clothes filled the house with an unwelcome odour. Even though I heard him speak Welsh I felt certain he was an Irishman. I used to think that all the dirty, ragged ones must be Irish. He had no sooner made his appearance than my brother Bob, white in the face and trembling in every limb, jumped to his feet. I knew from Bob's attitude that he wanted to collar the intruder, and pitch him out—a task he could easily have accomplished, the man being puny and weak, while Bob was well-built, supple, and strong. Mother discerning Bob's intention, tremulously begged him to refrain.

I thought I had never seen such another ugly dirty lout as this stranger, and I marvelled at his impudence in coming thus into our house. Never had I known mother so profoundly agitated, and making such efforts at self-control, uttering the while something to this effect: "James, I have told you many times you are not to come here. I never wish to see you again."

The stranger pretended not to hear her. He tried instead, by tender words, to make friends with me, whom he addressed by my own name. I wondered greatly how he knew it, and recoiled from him as from a serpent. At length he took hold of me and tried to put me on his knee. Fairly driven wild, I struck him my hardest with my little fist right in the face, Bob, at the same time, dragging me from his clutches. Mother asked him once more to leave; but he refused to go, whereupon Bob again jumped to his feet to pitch him out, and was again prevented by my mother. I grew perfectly savage at her interference. The Irishman, as I called him, asked for food, which, to my surprise, my mother placed before him. He ate at such an unconscionable rate, that I at one time thought he would never give over. I begrudged him every bit he put into his mouth, and I knew my brother Bob did the same, because I sat upon his knee, and felt his limbs to be in a constant tremble of anger.

When, at last, he had done eating, the Irishman coolly drew up to the fire, just as if he meant to settle down for the night. Mother begged him once more to go away, but this, he said, he would not do, unless she gave him money. To my utter astonishment, I saw her hand him some. Bob flew into a passion, and I heard him angrily telling mother she was mad. He wouldn't go into the mine, he declared, to toil and sweat, if his hard earnings were to be given to a drunken thieving scamp in this fashion. I too, was highly incensed at the idea that mother had given the Irishman more money than would have sufficed to buy me a little live mule like Will Bryan's. Young as I was, I sympathised greatly with her, the impression being left upon my mind that the stranger had some secret influence over her, and that she could not help herself in what she had done. Bob's bad temper had not the slightest effect upon the Irishman, who, after he got the money, seemed more than ever determined to stay the night. He lit his pipe, and began undoing his boot laces.

Bob, losing all patience at the sight, sprang to his feet, opened wide the door, took the Irishman by the nape of the neck, flung him as if he were so much carrion, out into the street, and barred the door. All this took only a quarter of a minute to do. I was clapping my hands with joy, when seeing my mother had swooned, and was dying, as I thought, I grew nearly wild with grief. Bob having sprinkled water over her face, she came to herself, and began to cry, Bob and I mingling our tears with hers for a while. Drying her eyes she held confidential converse with Bob, of which I could very well make out that the subject was the Irishman, whom they alluded to as "He." Spite of earnest question and inquiry, directed both to Bob and mother, I entirely failed to find out who the stranger was. All the answer I got was, that he was a bad man, and that I must never speak of him to anybody.

Well would it have been for me had I acquired no better knowledge of him subsequently. Providence, however, ordained

it otherwise. Is it not this "Irishman" who has been the bane
of my existence? Is it not he who has dropped wormwood into
my sweetest cup? How different would my history have been
but for him! When my friends have thought me blessed and
happy, he, like some spirit of evil, has blighted my every enjoyment, and sat upon me like a nightmare when I should have
been at rest.

CHAPTER VII.

THE TWO SCHOOLS.

I HAVE thought that every man has formed some opinion, however true or false, concerning himself—that is to say, his personal
appearance, his abilities, physical and mental, and his social
status. To put it in another form, every man has some idea of
his own importance; although it is not at all times that he will
communicate this idea to others. As a rule he keeps such
matters to himself. And there are, doubtless, sufficient
grounds for his conduct. It stands to reason that the man himself knows himself best, and that it is he who is the best fitted to
form a correct judgment on the matter. If he is a man of parts,
he dare not say so for fear of lowering himself in the estimation
of others, and of appearing smaller to their minds than to his
own. It is only one in a million who has the assurance, like
the Apostle Paul, fearlessly to announce his superiority over
others, although the proportion of those who believe in their
own superiority is much greater. So brightly doth the beauty of
humility shine before men, that even honesty is obliged to veil
its eyes in her presence. How great must He have been who
could make such revelations, set up such claims for Himself
without tarnish either to His meekness or His modesty.

It is commonly supposed that greatness and humility should
go together; yet there is room to think that what men call
humility is very often but another form of wisdom, or rather
strategy. Picture to yourself Dr. —— in midst of the Association, addressing his hearers after this style:—"Well, my

c

dear brethren, you know I am greater than you all, that I can
write a tract or compose a sermon better than any of you. In
a word, you know, that for culture and natural ability, I am as
good as a dozen of some of you, and better than any two of your
best." What would the brethren say? Would they not stare at
each other, and would their looks not convey a plain hint that
the speaker was going off his head? And yet, who knows better
than the speaker himself that that which I have just put into
his mouth is true in every word, although he would not take
the world for saying so. The really great man feels he can
leave it to others to form an estimate of him without any
guidance of his own, the probability being that they will rate
him only too highly, and he prefers that they should err in this
direction than in any other. In neither great nor small men is
there too much readiness to set others right who evince a
tendency to value them at more than their proper worth.

Speaking from personal experience, I can say that the con-
ciousness of inferiority is an uncomfortable one; and this is
possibly the reason that the small man, on every occasion, en-
deavours to show all of himself there is to be seen, and that to the
best advantage. This tendency is observable in other animals
besides man. The other day I saw two cocks upon a dunghill—
a great Cochin China, long-shanked and high-crested, and a pert
little dandy bantam. The one looked listless and easy-going;
but as for the other, how he thrust out his breast, and standing
a-tiptoe, held head and tail so high that they nearly touched
each other. In clear note he crowed and crowed again,
attempting, it struck me, to pick a quarrel with the Cochin,
round whom he circled, saying, after his own fashion: "Don't
you see my breast and tail? You haven't a tail like this one."
Cochin, for a while, pretended not to notice him, but at last he
too crowed, although with note so much like a groan that I
fancied he must be commiserating the dandy upon his diminu-
tiveness. I do not know whether it is the Cochin and the Bantam
who imitate men, or it is the latter who imitate the former; but
there is certainly some resemblance between them. This, however, is what I was going to ask, "Rhys, what measure hast
thou taken of thyself? There is no one here to listen, so thou
can'st answer honestly and without much danger of being

thought either conceited or hypocritical. Thou art a preacher, the pastor of a flock, thou rhymest occasionally, and contributest at times to the periodicals. What station dost thou occupy in thine own eyes?" Well, putting my foot upon the neck of pride, I shall answer honestly, without deceiving myself, there being nobody about to hear.

He who knows everything knows that in those matters I ought and deserve to be great, namely, religion and the proof of things spiritual, I am painfully small. And the more I have to do with things divine and eternal, all the more do I feel the grip of earth upon me, all the heavier do the weights become which hold me down. But that the promises of Holy Writ were so strong and emphatic concerning the power and grace of the Saviour, I would long since have sunk into despair under the load of a depraved heart and a guilty conscience. My prayer, from the depth of that heart, is that He may strengthen me in the faith.

With regard to my personal appearance, I know there is nothing attractive about it, and I have often wondered at the reflection that some one, at some time, had a tender regard for me, as I shall have occasion to refer to later on. I have many times envied that charm of manner possessed by "Glan Alun," which made everybody forget his person. Dear man! I prefer thee to a hundred of these comely and smart, but soulless ones. At the same time I try to believe there is nothing repulsive in my appearance. Can it be that I am mistaken? Be it as it may, I should be more than pleased were I Thomas John, and were it possible to possess his remarkable soul. After all, a fine and commanding presence is a great thing in a preacher, and he who climbs the pulpit without one is always at a discount.

In the matter of natural tendencies—well, yes, there is no one here to listen—I think I excel some of my brethren. And they know it or, at any rate, ought to. I would not for the world tell this to anybody, and if anybody were to say it to me, it is certain I should protest; and that, maybe, is reckoned for humility in me.

As to the amount of knowledge I possess, it is neither here nor there. Indeed, there are in the church here mere youngsters, who, in some directions, know a good deal more than I do; and I am sore put to it very often to prevent them from understanding as much. Take geography for instance, I know next to nothing of that valuable science; and when some of these same youngsters happen to question me upon the subject, I am forced to tax my ingenuity to the utmost in order to conceal my ignorance. It would never do to let them know how ignorant I, a church minister, really am, because, the boys, poor things, believe I know everything. I have various ways of getting out of difficulties of this kind. When a question is asked me which I do not know how to answer, I invariably direct it to a lad in the class whom I think able to do it for me, and if I fancy he has answered correctly, I bestow upon him a nod of commendation. But if a question be asked which neither I nor any one else in the class can answer, then I endeavour to impress upon the minds of my scholars the importance of everyone's reading and investigating for himself, the knowledge thereby acquired being of much greater value to them than any they would get by my answering the question off-hand. I add that the question will be borne in mind until the following meeting, when I shall expect every one of them to be able to answer it. Meanwhile I hunt up the information for myself. Of course no one knows all this, and the wise would not blame me even if they did know it, because were I to admit my ignorance before the boys, it would detract greatly from my pastoral usefulness.

What occasioned the writing of so long a preface to the present chapter was my thought of the misfortune it is, for a preacher more particularly, to be deprived of the advantages of education in one's early youth. He is constantly stumbling against something he ought to have learned in school when a boy, and he can never aspire to the position and the usefulness of those who have received a thorough elementary training in their childhood. When I was a boy there were only two day schools in the town of my birth. One was kept by a gentleman of the name of Smith, whom I remember very well. Mr. Smith was the great oracle of the town. He was looked up to by some people with an admiration bordering almost upon worship. He was believed to be proficient in at least seven languages, and he was said to utter words which no one else could understand. I heard my mother declare that Mr. Smith and Dic Aberdaron were the two greatest scholars the world had ever seen. Whatever my opinion may, by this time, be with reference to the accuracy of my mother's judgment, I know that I implicitly believed in it then. I would pull up in the street when Mr. Smith passed by, and look after him with an indescribable awe. He was a tall, thin, grey-headed personage, wearing black clothes and spectacles. I think he was the only one in the town at that time who allowed the hair to grow under his nose. Mr. Smith's was looked upon as a very superior sort of institution, and none ever thought of sending their children there save the gentry and the well-to-do. I remember associating some great mystery with the green bags in which his scholars used to carry their books.

I have reason to believe that mother would never have thought of sending me to school to Mr. Smith, even had her circumstances permitted it, because she considered him irreligious. She had a variety of reasons for forming this opinion of him. For one thing, he went to the Kirk on the Sunday instead of "professing religion;" or, in other words, he frequented the Church of England instead of going to chapel. The "English Church" and "Religion" were two words very far removed from each other in my mother's vocabulary. Then again there was his habit of taking a stroll on Sunday afternoons instead of remaining at home pondering over the Word and the Doctrine. Moreover, she had heard from an old maid-servant of Mr. Smith's that he had in his house a "Devil-raising Book," which he was constantly reading "after dark." There could be no doubt of the correctness of this story, because one night Mr. Smith left the book open upon the table, where the girl saw it next morning. Thoughtlessly she drew near and tried to read it, but not one syllable could she make out beyond the single word "Satan," and before she had visited the room a second time the book had disappeared. It happened that the girl did not know a word of English. As additional proof, mother recollected very well that Mr. Smith was in Parson Brown's company when the latter visited Ty'nllidiart to lay the spirit there, and shut it down in his tobacco box. Hereupon my mother came to this conclusion:—that if Mr. Smith, who was not a parson, was able to help Mr. Brown, who was a parson, in the work of laying spirits, he could not be any stranger to the work of raising them either. But mother's principal reason for believing Mr. Smith to be irreligious was, unquestionably, the fact of his wearing a moustache. Nobody could persuade her, she declared, that the man who had proved the great things of religion could possibly allow the hair to grow upon his upper lip. She had never seen any one deserving the name of Christian who wore a moustache. What would Mr. Elias and Mr. Rees have taken for wearing moustachios? A wisp of hair near the ear was a different thing entirely. As I have said, these considerations, even could my mother have afforded to send me, proved an unsurmountable obstacle to my going to school to Mr. Smith. And besides, my mother did not believe in higher education. I heard her say, more than once, that she never knew good to come of over-educating children, and that too much of this sort of thing had led many a man to the gallows. "As to the children of the poor," she would remark, "if they are able to read their Bible, and know the way into the Life eternal, that is quite enough for them."

The other school was kept by one Robert Davies, or, as he was commonly called, "Robin the Soldier,"—a well-set, fleshy man, but somewhat advanced in years, who had spent the prime of life in the British Army, where he distinguished himself as a brave, intrepid warrior. He returned to his native village minus his right leg, which he had left behind him in Belgium, a pledge of his zeal and fidelity in his country's cause, whilst campaigning against "Bony." Robert supplied this deficiency by means of a wooden leg, of foreign growth but his own shaping, and tipped with an iron ferrule. Upon his departure from the army the Government then in power deemed it incumbent upon them to endow him with a pension of sixpence a day for the rest of his life, in recognition of his valuable services as a soldier, and as a substantial recompense for the loss of his limb; for which reasons Robert used to address his wooden leg as "Old Sixpenny." For some weeks after his return from the army, he used to be regularly asked out by old friends to supper for the sake of hearing him give an account of his battles, and

all he had seen and heard abroad. Robert, however, speedily
got to the end of his tether, and his stories gradually grew to
be a good deal staler than his appetite, so that at last the only
place they were tolerated was the taproom of the Cross Foxes,
to which Robert became a constant visitor.

The income from the wooden leg being barely sufficient to
meet the weekly calls of the Cross Foxes, our old Soldier
speedily found himself in straightened circumstances. But
relief was not long in coming. Providence found him an
opening as toll-gate keeper, in which situation, for a season, he
fared sumptuously every day. He grew sleek-looking, and self-
satisfied, and doubtless would have continued to do so, had not
the turnpike authorities happened to discover that it was not
Robert who kept the gate, but that it was the gate which kept
him. In solemn conclave they came to the conclusion that this
was not the original intention of the trust, some of them
happening to be self-willed and hard-hearted, going the length
even of insisting that the tolls should be restored to their
intended use; and Robert was obliged to leave in consequence.

Parson Brown was wondrously kind and charitable towards all
his parishioners, especially the orthodox. And inasmuch as
the old soldier was one of the " dearly beloved brethren," and a
devout man—that is to say, one who went to church every
Sunday morning, to bed every Sunday afternoon, and to the
Cross Foxes every Sunday night,—Mr. Brown took an especial
interest in his welfare, and was the very first to suggest to him
the advisability of setting up school.

"Robbit," said Parson Brown to him in broken Welsh—so I
heard mother tell the story—" Robbit, you scholar, you able to
read and write and say catechism—you start school in old empty
office there—me help you—many children without learning
hereabouts, Robbit; you charge penny week, make lot coin,
live comfortable, I do my best to you. You, Robbit, have been
fight for the country, me fight for you now."

Fairplay for Mr. Brown, he had a warm heart, and he never
rested until he had set Robert on his feet, or rather on his foot,
in this matter of starting a day school.

Soldier Robin's school was an old established institution before
I got of age to be able to go to it. How my mother came to

send me there my memory is not sufficiently alert to furnish the details. Sure I am that no burning desire of mine towards education gave the inducement. I am pretty positive, also, that it was not because mother was satisfied of Robert's religiosity. The likeliest reason I can think of at the moment is that Mr. Brown had used his influence with mother in the matter. Although believing Mr. Brown had never proved "the great things," she entertained, I know, a very high opinion of him as a philanthropist and neighbour. The only thing which reconciled me to the notion of going to school was the fact that Will Bryan was already a member of that valued institution. I remember very well a consciousness that I was doing a great work by going to school, and that I deserved some sort of tribute for my self denial. Now I have observed, in reading biography, that seldom incommemorate in the life-history of the author is the day upon which he first went to school. That day is fresh in my memory, and I recall it and its occurrences, not as my predecessors have done, for other people's diversion, but for my own, who am the only one, probably, who can find diversion therein. Perhaps it will be better if I take another chapter in which to relate that day's doings.

CHAPTER VIII.

UNDER INSTRUCTION.

SHOULD this history happen to fall into the hands of any of my friends when my head will have been laid low, and should they go to the trouble of reading it, I know they will wonder why I have lingered so long over matters that are trivial and unimportant. Here have I devoted seven chapters to the brief period comprised between my birth and the day I first went to school. Had I sent this to one of the periodicals the editor would, doubtless, have long since lost patience and would have urged me to move a little faster, or else to knock the history on the head. It is here the advantage comes of writing for one's own diversion, and not for that of the public. The man who goes

an errand walks straight ahead, along the nearest road, at the
rate, say, of four miles an hour by his watch. But he who takes
to strolling about the old country of his birth is blind to mile-
stones; he climbs over hedges, wanders about the bushes, goes
bird-nesting, gathers nuts and blackberries, sits upon the moss-
banks, or lolls by the riverside, all oblivious of the fact that he
has such a thing as a watch in his pocket. Give me the latter.
What a liberty is mine! I have no one to call me to account for
writing a preface to every chapter, if I choose; there is no
necessity for re-casting sentences which may happen to read a
little stiff and rugged, nor for asking myself what will the reader
say of this thing or of that.

I was thinking, only to-night, of all nights in the year, of
David Davis, our elder here. A God-fearing man, and an
oddity, one of the faithful of the old school who would not de-
viate from the rules of the fathers to the extent even of brushing
his hair back from his forehead. I have a great respect for his
sense and for his prejudices. I know David Davis has a high
opinion of me, and it may be that is the reason I think so
highly of him. Indeed, when I come to consider it, I find that
this is the rule by which I take my measure of the brethren
generally. If I get to know that such and such an one
happens to think highly of me, I somehow, despite myself,
come to the conclusion that there must be something in that
man. And so the contrary. I remember the time when I
thought rather highly of the brother who keeps the Post Office;
but when I came to understand that he was not of the same
mind with regard to myself, he at once fell in my estimation,
and ever since I can only think of him as one with a serious
failing, although I cannot lay my finger upon that failing.
What if David Davis knew me to-night to be doing anything so childish as writing the history of the day I first
went to school! I fear me I should go down in his eyes.
Luckily he knows nothing about it. I often find myself doing
some things and refraining from doing others, all for the sake of
David Davis. In conversation with him, I have frequently
been tempted to indulge in a joke, but out of respect for the old
man I have refrained. A while ago I had a great longing to let
the hair grow upon my upper lip; but I instantly remembered

David Davis—the thing would be impossible without giving
him offence, and I have regularly shaved as a consequence. It
is because David Davis knows not what I do that, for my own
diversion, I wish to give a detailed account, concealing nothing,
of the day I first went to school.

It was a Monday and winter. Will Bryan called for me
betimes, and was particularly enjoined by my mother to take
care of me. Will hinted on the way that it was not at all
unlikely I should have to fight one or two of my school
fellows. It was not a pleasant thing to do, he knew, but such
was the custom always with a new scholar. He, however,
would take care to be at my back to see I got fairplay. The
hint was anything but a consoling one, chiefly because I was
conscious that my talents did not lie in that direction, and also
because I perceived the possibility of the occurrence, did it take
place, coming to my mother's ears at home, and to those of Abel
Hughes at the Children's Communion. I was ashamed to admit
as much to Will Bryan, and so I told him I should act
according to his instructions; indeed I would not for anything
have crossed him, he stood so high in my estimation.

The "Office" in which the old soldier kept school was a
long, narrow structure, round which ran a rough and crooked
bench connected with a desk which leaned against the wall. I
noticed, among one of the first things, that of this desk there was
hardly a square inch on which the knife had not carved some
kind of pictorial design, figure, or name. At the other end,
close to the fire, stood the master's desk, through the base of
which there was a good sized hole, made (I afterwards found),
for the convenience of the master's wooden leg, which he thrust
through whenever he sat down. Upon my entrance, I saw
what to me was a new and wondrous sight. Some of the boys
were mounted on the desk, some on other boys' backs, "playing horses," and galloping about the room, while others were
heaped on the floor, wriggling about like eels in the mud.
One lad who was lame, and carried a crutch, was mimicking
the master, at whose desk he sat with the crutch thrust through
the hole in imitation of the wooden leg, and yelling, all to no
purpose, for silence. The scene changed every minute; everybody shouted at the top of his voice with the exception of one

boy, who standing on the desk near the window, divided his
attention between the play and the direction from which they
expected the appearance of the master. A curious feeling
came over me. I thought I had come amongst a lot of very
wicked children, and if mother had known the sort of beings they
were, I should never be sent there again. On the other hand,
I fancied this was the best place for fun I had ever seen. The
dominant feeling, however, was one of strangeness and a painful shyness, now that Will had left me to myself and eagerly
joined in the play. While thus affected, I saw the lad who was
on the look-out place two fingers to his mouth, and give a
clearly sounded whistle. In a twinkling every boy, panting
and blowing, was in his proper place. I knew very well I must
be looking foolish enough, standing like a statue all alone near
the door when the Soldier came in. He passed me by without
taking upon him that he had seen me. He seemed agitated,
and looked fiercely about him. I understood directly that the
sentinel had not been quick enough in giving the signal, and
that the master had heard the deafening disturbance. He
walked up to his desk, and drew forth a long stout cane. Each
lad shrugged a preparatory shoulder while the old Soldier went
the round of the school, caning all, cruelly and indiscriminately.
I was the only one who escaped even a taste, and I was the only
one who burst out crying, the chastisement having terrified me.
The other boys appeared too well-used to the proceeding to
mind it. The last of them having received his allowance, the
master returned to his desk, put up his hands and said, "Let
us pray," after which he slowly repeated his Paternoster, the
boys following. I subsequently learned that some of the wicked
ones, in the midst of the general clatter, had uttered words very
different from any to be found in the Prayer, thereby eliciting
the low laughter of those who were within hearing.

Prayer ended, the old Soldier in a voice of command, cried,
"Rivets, my boys," a synonym used every Monday morning
for "Pass up with your pence." The lad who had come away
without the customary copper had to hold out his hand and
receive thereon the tingling imprint of the cane, which sent him
dancing back to his seat, squeezing his fingers between his knees,
or under his armpit, or shoving them into his mouth, or

shaking them as if he had but just drawn them out of the fire. This was the general result which a slap with the cane produced, but more especially if there had been no opportunity for spitting upon the palm, and placing two hairs crosswise thereon. In passing, I may mention that the boys had an unswerving belief in the spittle and crossed hairs as a charm against the smart. My own opinion, after many trials, is that there is not much good in the practice. It was not often a lad cried after one slap on the hand; but if he got two slaps or three he was entitled, by common consent, to set up a howl without danger of being considered a coward. I invariably cried after one slap. I was a noted crier, and could not help it.

But to return; after Will Bryan had taken me to the master, and the latter had entered my name in the book, and received my penny—which I remember well to have been quite hot from the tight clutch I had kept, lest I should lose it—I was requested to go to my seat, where I should be told directly what my task would be. I had the privilege of sitting between Will Bryan and a boy named Jack Beck.

The latter, without any beating about the bush, asked me had I a ha'penny.

I replied I hadn't.

Could I tell when I should get one? He knew a shop where there were heaps of things to be had for a ha'penny. He knew the shopwife, and I would get almost as much again for my money if he were with me.

Will Bryan told him to shut up, or he would repent it, adding a broad hint that if he didn't I would be sure to give him a thrashing. Little did I think at the time that Will was such a cunning young rascal.

Beck observed that to thrash him was something more than I could do.

Will asked me if I was afraid of Beck?

Although feeling quite otherwise, I replied boldly that I was not.

"Very well," rejoined Will, and before five minutes were over, the news had been whispered into every ear in the school that a fight was to come off between Rhys Lewis and John Beck.

My conscience, a tender one, grew troubled at the mere

thought of such an occurrence, but it would never have done to
tell that to Will, who kept pouring into my ear a number
of directions proper to be observed by way of preparation
for so important an occasion. I had been taught by my mother
at home, and by Abel Hughes at the Children's Communion,
that fighting was a great sin; and my conscience was afire at
the notion of doing battle with a boy who had never said a scurvy
word to me, and towards whom I had no sort of enmity. I
tried to comfort myself with the reflection that if the affair came
to mother's ears, she might look upon it a little more leniently
from the fact that my opponent was a Churchman, for I knew
she entertained no very high opinion of Church people. I
trusted, therefore, she would consider the thing as a sort of
accidental collision between Church and Chapel.

For about an hour it did not appear to me that there was any
work going on in the school. The old Soldier, during the
greater part of the time, had his head down, occupied either in
reading or in writing, while the boys, although their books were
open before them, kept up an incessant murmur. I knew
perfectly well it was I and John Beck who were the subjects of
conversation. Did the talk become a little loud, the master, at
the top of his voice, would shout "Silence!" and for a few
minutes silence would ensue. At a quarter to eleven o'clock,
the word was given us to go to play, whereupon all jumped
to their feet and rushed out like a drove of sheep through
a gap. My heart beat fast at the thought of what was about to
take place. I hardly knew where I was before I found myself
in the yard standing up to John Beck. I did my best under the
circumstances, although I did not know how I got on, my eyes
being most of the time closed, not from my antagonist's blows,
but from fear. For all that the combat did not last long, and
I rejoiced greatly when I found that everything was over and
that I was the victor. I believe to this day that I was helped
by Will Bryan. I don't know whether I felt the prouder that
the fight was over, or that I had come out a conqueror and
whole-skinned, when the authoritative voice of the Soldier,
calling us into school, struck terror to my heart. It was clear
that he had seen the whole transaction. I heard several of the
boys muttering in concert that it was the son of the woman who

cleaned the Church, nicknamed the " Skulk," who had carried the news to master, and the threats were legion that were launched at his head. On the return to school Rhys Lewis and John Beck were called up to the desk to give an account of their stewardship. It was a fearful moment, but Will Bryan rose equal to the occasion. He came up to the desk, unasked, to give testimony, and declared unflinchingly that it was Beck who had challenged me and struck me first. This was emphatically denied by Beck. Another witness was called who, happening to be an enemy of Beck's, confirmed Will's evidence, whereupon the old Soldier, saying that inasmuch as this was the first day I had been at school, he would let me off unpunished, but as for Beck, he should receive three strokes with the cane, one for fighting without reasonable cause, one for taking a beating from his opponent, and one for denying the accusation which had been brought against him.

I sympathised sincerely with Beck. He was hoisted, poor chap, on the back of the stoutest lad in school, denuded of his clothing at a particular part of the body which I did not then care to see and do not now care to name, and had inflicted upon him the punishment prescribed.

The old Soldier prefaced each stroke as follows:—"This is for fighting without a reasonable cause" (whack!) "This is for coming vanquished out of the fight" (whack!) "And this is for denying the truth of the accusation brought against him " (whack!)

In subsequent days I heard the same formula repeatedly gone through, which is why I remember it so well. It was a sermon of exceptionally direct applicability and influence, this one of the old Soldier's, which was doubtless why he delivered it so often. In his turn I saw every boy but one of the whole school dancing and shouting from its effects, although not for joy. That boy was Will Bryan. Be the old Soldier's humour what it might, he could never get a cry out of Will, who thus became a hero in our eyes, and the very embodiment of bravery. It seemed to me that the lads, as a whole, enjoyed immensely the flogging of poor Beck, which I considered very cruel of them, seeing none knew but that he himself might be the next to come in for similar treatment.

A heavy load of guilt was laid upon my conscience on account of Beck's punishment, and I was in great haste to go to bed, so that, as I had been brought up to do, I might ask forgiveness for the day's transgression. Fortunately the affair never came to mother's ears, and for all I know Abel Hughes never heard of it, either. Nothing particular happened that afternoon. I am positive I got no more than one lesson—and that was one in spelling—the day I first went to school; and I don't much fancy the other boys got any more. Speaking generally, I can certify they all got more canings than lessons. One thing happened that day which eased my conscience very considerably, and which is a source of great comfort to me, even at this moment. When I went home to dinner a relative of mine gave me a half-penny for my pluck in going to school. I lost no time in informing Jack Beck of the happy occurrence, and in making a covenant of peace with him. He, on his part, accompanied me to the shop where the prodigious ha'porth was to be had, and got the greater share of the purchase, so that the sun did not go down upon our wrath. In my innocence I fancied that things having ended so happily, there was no necessity for me to pray for forgiveness before retiring to rest. And I did not. As far as I can remember them, the occurrences of my first day in the school of Soldier Robin were such as they are here narrated.

CHAPTER IX.

CHURCH MATTERS.

THE other day I had the pleasure of paying a visit to the British School of this town; and on remarking its excellent order, the good and useful instruction imparted, the strict yet easy discipline, and the clean and happy appearance of the children, I could not help calling to mind the immense disadvantages I laboured under in the school of Soldier Robin. My blood boils within me this minute at the thought of his hypocrisy, his stupidity, his laziness, and incomparable cruelty. To do justice to the narrative, I am bound to say something farther about him in the present

chapter before turning to something more important; and after
that I shall bid him farewell for ever, unless, indeed, I am
compelled to give testimony against him in some day to come.
I trust, however, he will find forgiveness, even as I expect the
same.

The old Soldier's most important business was taking our
pence, and the next, in point of diversion, the breaking of a
good stout cane on our backs and hands every week or nine
days. This rough treatment was no secret to our parents; but
they, in their ignorance, considered it necessary to our good.
We boys looked forward to our sharp discipline with the same
regularity, though not with the same appetite, that we did to our
meal time. As far as I can recollect, none of the boys, any
more than myself, cared the least bit for learning, while he, to
whom our instruction was entrusted, cared less. He seemed to
me, at all times, to derive greater pleasure from our failure to
say our lessons, than from our success, because it gave him an
excuse for our castigation. He expected us—if he expected at
all—to learn without help from him. I often thought he felt
disappointed if we happened to master the lesson in spite of him.
He never attempted to create in us a love of knowledge and a
desire to excel; on the contrary, what he did create was a dislike to every kind of learning, and an unnatural itching in every
lad for strength sufficient to thrash him in return, a pleasure
which, I am sure, every one promised himself, once he "became
a man." I remember well how, after a sore beating from
him, with fretful back and heavy heart, I would look at his
wooden leg and occupy my mind with guesses at the number of
Frenchmen he could have killed when fighting against Bony.
Jack Beck used to say he had heard it was three hundred.
Will Bryan put the figure much higher, adding that nothing
would give the old Soldier greater pleasure than to kill
the whole lot of us, and that he would do so too were he not
afraid that he would be hung for it—in which opinion we all
concurred. And it really needed no great effort to believe this;
because of the diabolical rage depicted in his face when he was
engaged correcting a boy—his jaw distending itself, the veins of
his forehead swelling and becoming black, and the whole
countenance horrible to look upon.

He had a marvellous faculty of changing the expression of
his features. I remember seeing him more than once in this fit
of fury when Parson Brown put in a sudden appearance. Mr.
Brown was a corpulent, easy-going, kindly man, who never
thought ill of his neighbours, particularly if they were Church
folk. I saw him, I say, coming suddenly into school when the
old Soldier had his fit on, and the face of the old hypocrite
changed in a twinkling into an expression almost heavenly.
On such an occasion he would call one of us up to repeat the
Catechism or a Collect, and when we had done, would stroke
our heads most affectionately. Parson Brown would congra-
tulate him upon his labour and success. " You do deal of good
here, Robbit," he would say, " You be paid for all this again."

Should any of us happen, in Mr. Brown's presence, to look
displeased, or to give any indication of the fact that we were
not perfectly happy—woe to us when the good man's back
was turned. Indeed, whether we were industrious or idle, the
effort it cost the old Soldier to appear gentle and benign, and
the tax he put upon his villainous propensities in Mr. Brown's
presence, brought about such a reaction immediately Mr.
Brown had left, that his temper became worse than ever.
Occasionally some one ventured to complain to Parson Brown
that the Soldier behaved cruelly towards the boys. The
reverend gentleman would then come to school, and talk the
matter over with the master, who would call up, maybe, the very
lad in respect of whom he had been accused of cruelty. And
then, before Mr. Brown's face, he would ask the victim, his eye
containing a plain intimation what the answer was to be: "Am
I not a kind master?"

It were not well with that boy if he said otherwise, and so Mr.
Brown would be satisfied that the complaints were only so much
idle gossip after all.

And yet Soldier Robin's school had its advantages, or what
we boys considered to be advantages. Every Friday afternoon
the old warrior would select two of us to be his servants for the
following week. It was the servants' duty to clean the school-
house, light the fire, and run errands. Under the latter head
were included frequent journeys to the Cross Foxes to fetch the
Soldier's beer—always without the money. Until one got used

D

to it, this latter was a very unpleasant business, because old Mrs. Tibbet, the ale wife, chid us at a frightful rate, and made it a point of showing the messenger, each time, the amount of the old Soldier's indebtedness, scored up, in chalk hieroglyphics, on the back of the cellar door. She was a fat old woman, the same size all the way up, was Mrs. Tibbet, with a perpetually purple face, arising, some people said, from constant protestation that she never as much as touched a drop of intoxicating drink. The boys cherished a very high regard for her for taking the same view of the old Soldier's life and character that they did. I remember well the gusto with which she used to deliver her opinion of his failings, whilst pointing to the reckoning on the cellar door, which he would never, she declared, be able to pay. I heard Will Bryan once make the remark to her that the old Soldier had another and much larger reckoning than that, which, also, he would never be able to pay.

"What!" exclaimed the old woman in great alarm, "has he an account anywhere else, then?"

When Will explained that it was to the great reckoning of the Day of Judgment he was referring, she cooled down at once, and said, "O! well, between him and his business as to that. Every one of us must go to his Answering, and all will have justice done them. If he pays what he owes me he may take his chance afterwards."

The servants' most unpleasant duty was that of lighting of the school-house fire, because they were obliged to hunt for brushwood for the purpose, as the hedges round about bore witness. I remember very well one morning when we were without a scrap of wood to start the fire, Will Bryan asking me, in all seriousness, if I knew whether the master was in the habit of taking his wooden leg to bed with him, and could we possibly manage to steal it?

"Ah!" said Will, "what a beautiful blaze it would make."

In fancy, I still see his face brightening with satisfaction at the bare idea of the thing. Poor old Will! He never had the chance of putting his wish into execution.

But as to the advantages of which I spoke. Whilst acting the servant, one was never asked to as much as look at a book, and was wholly exempt from punishment, no matter what the

mischief he may have committed during his period of ministration. Indeed, it was said that the master, on one occasion,
actually smiled upon a servant. I cannot vouch for the truth
of this, for I never once saw a smile on his face save when Mr.
Brown was present. In view of these tremendous advantages,
we were always found on Friday afternoons waiting like mice
to hear whose lot the comforting ministry would fall to on
the following week. Seldom did it come to Will Bryan's turn
and mine, for the reason that our parents were chapel people,
and that we ourselves hardly ever went to Church except when
distributions of cake took place there. It was our visit to
Church on one Good Friday morning which put an end to the
term of our stay in the school of Soldier Robin; and after I
have described that event, I shall, as I have said, bid this
particular Pharaoh an eternal farewell. In contemplating the
circumstances I am about to relate, I hardly understand my
feeling with regard thereto. I have a sort of guilty consciousness for my own mischief, while, at the same time, I am unable
to repress the inward chuckle which will arise when I remember
the part I played. If the feeling is a sinful one, I hope I
shall be forgiven for it. Though it contain the chronicle of
my own wickedness, it is impossible I can pass over such an
occurrence, inasmuch as it has an important bearing upon my
history, and was the cause of terminating that modicum of day-
schooling it was thought best I should receive.

It was a Good Friday morning. There being no service at
the chapel, and the weather being too wet for us to go out to
play, Will Bryan and I went to Church with the rest of the
boys. I had no notion Will had any but an innocent object in
going, and he never opened his mouth to me on the way. He
feared, possibly, if he made his intention known to me, I and he
would not have agreed about it. In the old Church there was
a great square, deep-seated pew, capable of holding twenty or
more youngsters, set apart for the accommodation of Soldier
Robin's scholars. The door once shut upon us we were not able,
on account of the depth, to see even Parson Brown in the
pulpit; neither could any of the congregation see us. The seat
next to ours was long and narrow and here sat the Soldier, all
by himself, that he might overawe the children and keep them

well in order. For the schoolmaster's greater comfort, Mr. Brown, conformably with his usual kindness, had caused a hole to be bored in the partition, through which the wooden leg might be thrust when its owner sat down. The schoolmaster's comfort was not the only purpose achieved by this means. The timber extremity protruded into the boys' pew "to the end" that they might be perpetually reminded of the fact that he whom they feared was near them, though unseen. So were they kept within the bounds of decency.

Shortly after the service began, I found Will gazing contemplatively at as much as was in sight of the wooden leg. Next behold him taking from his pocket a length of thin, but strong cord, the running knot on which showed clearly that his was no unpremeditated plan. He got upon his knees and gently slipped the knot round the tip of the timber toe, handing me the other end of the cord, with the whispered words: "When you feel a bite, keep your hold of the line,"—referring to the leg as if it were a fish. I dared not disobey. It was not long before I got my bite. As is customary in Church, the congregation rose to their feet, and the Soldier tried to do the same. We heard him fall back in his seat like a lump of lead, in which position we kept him during the whole of the service. At first he bellowed and roared like a bull in a net, but his voice was speedily drowned by the mighty tones of the organ. Will and I held on to the cord until we were blue in the face, none of the other boys giving us any assistance, with the exception of Jack Beck, who, without waiting to be asked, rolled up his sleeves and seconded us splendidly. The greater number of them enjoyed our mischievous trick to such an extent that they were obliged to hold their sides with laughter, and stuff their handkerchiefs into their mouths to prevent themselves from screaming. Others looked on in fear and trembling, thinking only of the consequences. The Church cleaner's son was the only one who seemed actually displeased. When the service was being brought to a close, Will ordered John Beck to take out his knife and cut the cord within a foot of the leg. Beck having done so, Will instantly whipped the remainder into his pocket, observing, "There he is now, like a hen which doesn't come home to lay," alluding, doubtless, to the custom of tying a string to a hen's leg, so that her owner might be able to tell where she deposits her eggs. Will told us to file out leisurely, and with a sober face. We were going, slowly and seriously according to the word of command, when we noticed Parson Brown, on his way to the vestry, looking over the edge of the Soldier's pew.

"Holloa! Robbit," we heard him saying, "I thought you not in Church to-day."

We did not wait to see or hear any more. Will Bryan, however, assured us that, on looking back, he saw the reverend gentleman pressing his handkerchief to his mouth, the nape of his neck and his ears being as red as fire, Will believed from laughter on discovering what it was that had kept the Soldier invisible. And this was not unlikely; for a merry old soul was Mr. Brown.

We had a very bad time of it thence till the following Monday morning. When we became aware of the nature of the atrocity we had committed, we entertained no sort of doubt but that the "Skulk" would give the master the fullest particulars of all that had taken place. Many were the conferences between Bryan, Beck, and myself; but we could not see any way of escape from the punishment we so richly deserved. Monday morning came, and with it the necessity for going to school. Indeed, Will appeared only too eager to go, for he called for me much earlier than usual. I sometimes fancied he wanted the business over and done with; at others, that he had some scheme in hand for evading it, he appeared so particularly reserved and thoughtful. As for me, I was so terrified that my legs would barely carry me; and Beck felt the same. Seeing us so dreadfully frightened, Will said as we were going through the school-house door, "Cheer up, boys; it will come off better than you fear it will." I did not see how he could hope for anything of the kind, but his words confirmed me in the notion that he had formed some plan for our rescue. All the boys were in attendance, and, for once, silent and still, as if in anxious expectation of our arrival. When we had taken our seats, Will planted his eyes straight in the face of the "Skulk," who, blushing to the roots of his hair, turned away his head. All understood what that meant, but nobody said a word.

Presently the silence was broken by the soun i of the Soldier's
wooden leg pegging away towards the school. The boys
glanced at Bryan, Beck, and myself, with looks of pity and
concern. I cannot describe my feelings when the fierce face of
the master made its appearance, and when I noticed that, the
instant he came in, his glance shot straight to the spot where
Will and I were sitting. Still I had some faint hope that Bryan
had a plan of escape. The old warrior, as Will called him, went
at once to his desk and said prayers as usual, the responses of
the boys being weak and half-hearted this time. No sooner
had he pronounced the "Amen," than every eye was directed
towards him, and I saw him take from his desk a stout new
cane. He turned up the cuff of his right coat-sleeve, spat on
his hand, and glaring, tiger-like, at Will Bryan, advanced with
quick step in his direction. Instead, however, of making the
usual preparatory shrug, Will jumped to his feet. The Soldier
pulled up and ordered the "Skulk" to lock the door, and guard
the outlet. But Will had no thought of flight. Although his
lips were white and trembling, his eyes shot fire, and he never
once took them off the Soldier. This defiant attitude made the
master hesitate one moment, but the next he moved on again,
his face looking ghastly from rage. When within a couple of
yards of Will he raised the cane to the level of his head, for the
purpose of a stroke, but before it could descend, Will, with one
bound, had laid fierce hold of the wooden leg, a sharp pull at
which, and a butt with the head in his stomach, sent the Soldier
to the ground like a log. The bump of that skull against the
floor still sounds as plainly in my ears as if it had only occurred
at the moment of writing. Will turned upon his heel and walked
leisurely towards the door, of which the " Skulk " tremblingly
handed him the key—and in this he was wise. In passing out
Will beckoned us to follow. I refused, because, for the first time,
I believed him to be a bold bad boy. Hundreds of times since
have I repented that I did not take the hint. Beck, wiser than
I, ran off for dear life.

For a while the Soldier lay dazed and stunned, although not
altogether helpless. I never saw, before or after, a man with a
wooden leg trying to get up off the ground. I can imagine it
to be one of the most stupendous of feats. Up the warrior got,

however, without help from any one, looking like an ox in the shambles, which the butcher has made an unsuccessful attempt to knock down. He snorted through the nostrils audibly. I saw at once the folly of not running out after Will, and sprang to my feet with the intention of rectifying my mistake. It was too late. The next minute the cane was cutting and slashing me in all directions—over the head, the neck, the back, hands, legs, in short, the whole of my body. Dark night fell upon me, and I lost all consciousness. I do not know how long I remained in that state. On regaining my senses, I felt as if in a dream, and was utterly unable to move from where I lay. I fancied the school to be empty, and yet I heard some one moaning as if in the agony of death. I thought at one time the moans were my own, and that, deserted by all, I had been left there to die. Managing, after a desperate effort, to turn my head, I saw, standing terror-struck near the open door, two or three of the boys, of whom Jack Beck was one. I called to him, and he, finding I was alive, ran up and helped me into a sitting posture. Every joint and bone of me seemed parting asunder. To my astonishment I found the old Soldier stretched on his back, with pallid face, and my brother Bob, in working clothes, and black as coal, kneeling upon his chest, and, it seemed to me, deliberately throttling him. To my shame I must admit, being bound to tell the truth, that I shouted with all the strength which was left me, " Give it him, Bob." Finding from this that I was alive, Bob let go his hold, came over to me and began to cry. Seeing I could not walk, he took me upon his back, and away we went, leaving the Soldier to recover himself whenever it pleased him. It would appear that Beck, after making his escape, stayed at the door to listen and to see how it fared with me. He quickly made out that I was "catching it." Who should come by, almost directly, but my brother Bob, on his way home from the night shift. Beck shouted to him that the old Soldier was killing me. That was enough. Bob rushed into the schoolroom, and, I have heard the boys say who were eye-witnesses of his sudden entrance, with face as black as the chimney, that they thought for certain he was the Evil One come to fetch the old Soldier. Bob caught the master beating me whilst I was wholly insensible, sprang upon him like a madman, and brought him down with the same suddenness that he had been brought down a few minutes previously. It was in this position I found them when I came to myself.

That was not the end of the business. Bob and I and Will Bryan were members of the Children's Communion, and it was impossible an occurrence of this kind could be passed by unnoticed. But inasmuch as I shall have to make reference to divers of the good old fathers who were connected with the church at that period, I will take another chapter in which to narrate the history. Had I intended it for publication, I would have written in greater detail my account of Soldier Robin's school, so that the lads of these days might see the enormous increase and improvement that have taken place in schools and schoolmasters during less than half a generation.

CHAPTER X.

THE SUBJECT OF EDUCATION.

I REMEMBER perfectly well what was passing through my mind whilst being carried home upon Bob's back after that unparalleled flogging I had received at the hands of the old Soldier; and it was this: "Shall I receive another beating from my mother, I wonder, on her coming to hear of my wickedness?" I put the question to Bob, who assured me I would have no need of another beating for a twelvemonth at the least. Wounded though I was, the reflection that the punishment was over brought its happiness. My mind ran upon Bryan and Beck. Poor fellows! Punishment was still awaiting them, if not at the hands of the Soldier, at those of their parents, for certain. True, I had been made a scapegoat for them in the school, but that was all over now, and I was more fortunate than they. Has not this been my experience at every period of life? Does not the small trial awaiting me loom larger in my eyes than the great trial passed? It never occurred to Bob to ask me what I had done to deserve so severe a thrashing from the

master; but that was the very first question put me by mother on my entrance into the house. Never in my life having concealed from her the truth, I told her, weeping, the story of the tying of the wooden leg in the Church. I could not help noticing that Bob enjoyed the narration immensely. Mother, however, was differently affected, and it was with difficulty that Bob managed to save me from another beating. On examining my body and seeing the great red weals which covered it, her tone changed wonderfully, and she gave other evidence of her close kinship to me.

I remember, as well as if it were yesterday, looking upon myself as one who had come through much, and feeling a sort of satisfaction that I had scars to show, which enlisted the sympathy of my mother. But I wondered she blamed so little of the Soldier. I do not wonder at it now, because her purpose, doubtless, was to impress my mind with the fact that I had deserved my chastisement. She told me I was a naughty boy, and wept, I then thought, for my wickedness; although I am sure by this time it was for my bruises. She said many things which I cannot now call to mind. Of these, however, I am certain:—"That there was sense even in soldiering; that there was a difference between beating a child and battling against Bony; that a wooden leg was but a wooden leg after all." But the most cheering words which greeted my ears were those in which she declared I had had quite enough of schooling; that I had been under instruction for well nigh a whole year, and that it was high time I set about doing something. Neither once nor twice had mother told us that too much learning spoiled a child, and had led one here and there to the gallows, adding that she had never had a day's schooling herself, save at the Sunday School, and that not a penny had been spent on the education of my grandfather and grandmother. Still they knew "what was what," had found the truth, were blameless in their lives, respected by their neighbours, and had died in peace.

Mother was a woman of strong feelings, and remarkably free of speech. She must also have had an excellent memory, because she invariably clenched her words with a passage of Scripture, or a verse of Vicar Pritchard's, or the Bard of Nant's, although not often from the latter without the addition, "It is a great pity Thomas never found grace." Upon this particular occasion she directed Bob's attention and my own to divers of the Proverbs of Solomon, hurrying on her cloak and bonnet the while, and then going out. Bob looked through the window in order to see what direction she took. and said, "Rhys! mother, mark you, is going over to put the old Soldier through his drill. Let us have that story of the wooden leg once more."

I went over the story a second time, and, I must admit, it came much more easily now my mother was absent. Hardly had I finished when she returned, looking calmer than when she left the house, but much more serious and troubled. After she had taken off her cloak and bonnet, sat down and wiped her eyes with her apron, the following conversation took place—that is, in substance, and, as far as I can recollect it, in words, too.

"Bob," said she, "without saying anything of the trouble I have had with your father, this is the saddest day I have lived to see. I had hoped better things of you, things tending to salvation. I thought you would have been a bit of a succour to me. But whilst I fancied that the good seed prospered, behold the tares appearing. An enemy hath done this."

Mother, as I said before, would often use a Scriptural idiom. Bob, although a chair was close by, squatted, collier-fashion, on his haunches, leaning his back against one of the supports of the mantelshelf.

"Well mother, what's the matter now?" he asked. "The enemy, otherwise Satan, is always troubling you; and one might think, from your talk, that the old fellow never found time to think, or take notice of, anything or anybody but ourselves, for nothing ever happens in our history from morning till night that you do not see the devil's hand in it. For my own part, if such is the case, I think it about time now he gave somebody else a turn. I have no great liking for his company, and I don't care if he heard me say so, either. Besides, I can't see what there is in our family to require that particular attention on the Devil's part which you are in the habit of attributing to him, and it is my opinion that he must neglect a good deal of his business with other people quite as deserving of his notice as we are; for, clever as he may be, he is but finite after all."

"Bob," said mother, "I am sorry to hear you speak so lightly of matters of such weight. We are not without knowledge of his devices who goeth about like a roaring lion seeking those whom he may devour. That which I have greatly feared hath come upon me. I have, over and over again, said that this newspaper, half of which is lies, would be sure to prove your ruin, and yet you must have your head constantly inside it, instead of reading your Bible. When I was a girl we never heard of a newspaper save up at the Hall, and with some few of the uncircumcised Saxons—an idle, pleasure seeking, fox hunting lot. No one who set store by his soul ever thought of reading anything but the Bible, Bunyan's "Pilgrim's Progress," Charles's " Bible Dictionary," and Gurnal's book. But now, forsooth, everybody must have his newspaper, and his English book, of which no one understands the contents. And what is the result? Why, a generation of people who have not the fear of God before their eyes, who are under no dispensation, who are proud, and ostentatious, thinking more of finery than of salvation, knowing more of every thief than of the thief on the Cross, and of every death than of the Death which was life unto the world. Those are the fruits for you, Bob."

"You err, mother," returned Bob, "those are not the fruits of reading newspapers, but the fruits of a depraved heart. You remember the Apostle says, 'Give attendance to reading.'"

"So he does, my son; but to reading what? Not the newspaper, but Holy Scripture, which is able to make us wise unto salvation. And the same Apostle also says, ' Meditate on these things, and in these things remain;' but how is it possible for you or anyone else to remain in the things when you have your nose in the newspaper everlastingly? Beware, my boy, beware!"

"The world goes ahead, mother," remarked Bob, "and it is no use your thinking that things should remain as they were when you were a girl."

"Goes ahead!" said mother, in a loud voice, "yes, fast enough, but whither, pray? Nearer heaven? I don't know. Are the means of grace better relished now than they used to be? Is there more of hearing of the Gospel, and of following in the footsteps

of the ministers of God's Word? Do you, in these days, see the
people in harvest time leave their labour in broad bright day
to go and listen to the stranger? Hardly. They'd much
rather go to concert or competition meeting to stamp their
feet and shout 'Hooray!' and 'En-koh!' after some comic
song than go to sermon to cry 'Hallelujah,' and 'Glory to
God,' for free grace. If that is what you call 'going ahead,'
give me 'going back,' say I, Bob."

"At the period you refer to," returned Bob, "the Gospel was
new to Wales, and people naturally took greater interest in it;
but by this time we have been long accustomed to the truth,
and let us hope there is none the less of real religion in the land."

"New! Do you know what you are talking about?" asked
mother, in a bit of a temper. "Is the Gospel not as new to-
day as it ever was to those who feel its need.

'Some new virtue in that dear death shall ever come to light.'

Glad tidings of great joy the Gospel is, and always will be. No,
goodness help us all at the end of a thousand ages, if it is
'long accustomed' we are to be. I am surprised to hear you
speak like that, you, a lad who have read so much. The Gospel
was not a new subject—Wales was acquainted with it time out
of mind—but it was the people who had got a new heart,
new spirit, new relish for it, through reading the Word,
prayer to God, and an outpouring of the Holy Ghost. But now,
as I have said, people read the paper instead of their Bible, and
have a greater taste for concert and eisteddfod than for the
means of grace. And there is no room to expect a blessing and
an increase in the ministry while things remain as they are."

"You must admit, mother," said Bob, "that there is a
greater hearing of the Word, that we have more chapels and
opportunities of religious exercise, and more preachers of the
Gospel now than ever. At the time you speak of, there were
but a few poor folk connected with the cause, and our preachers,
as a rule, were but plain men, ill-informed, and uneducated.
Nowadays our best and most respectable people are religionists,
while our ministers, for the most part, are men of refinement
and culture."

"You have spoken truly, Bob," replied mother. "There is

more of hearing, and we are thankful for that, but the question is, is there more of believing? There is room to fear—I hope I am mistaken—that religion in these days has become more of a fashion than a matter of life. Many, I fear me, come to chapel, not to see the Saviour, like those wise men of old, but to be seen of others; and our congregation is often more like a flower-garden than like people who have come to listen to the Gospel. 'Poor folk,' it is true, were those who joined the cause at the commencement, as I have heard your grandmother say, and as I myself have to some extent seen. But they, look you, were rich in grace, and heirs of the life eternal. How many can you name of these spectacled people, as you call them, who are noted for grace and piety, and a terror to the ungodly of the neighbourhood? Do you ever see the drunken and the idle skulking off to their holes when a spectacled one comes in sight, as I have known them do before the ' poor folk ? ' And as to these fine chapels, they are very convenient, I admit; but, do you know what, I have often feared—I hope I am wrong—there will be more of rejoicing in heaven over the barns and the dwelling-houses than over them. You ruffled me a little, Bob, by speaking so slightingly of the old preachers. You too, I see, like many others in these days, have learned to think meanly of God's servants of old. 'Plain and uneducated' they were, it is true, but don't you call them ignorant in my hearing, it's best for you. They had been taught the way to heaven, Bob; while as to the Bible, they had that at their fingers' ends. And where can you find their equal in these days ? "

"Nothing was farther from my mind, mother," said Bob, " than speaking disrespectfully of the old preachers. They were pious, holy men, without a doubt, but they wouldn't do for these days, when education has made such strides, and congregations are so much better informed than they were at that time."

"Wouldn't do!" mother said, raising her voice. "Wouldn't do for whom, do you think? They did for God then, and surely to goodness they ought to do for us now. Wouldn't do, indeed ? Nothing would please me better than to see one of them given the chance. Were old Llecheiddior permitted to visit us once more, you should just see the racket there would be here

directly. Do you know what? One of the old preachers would
set a congregation afire, spectacled folk and all, in the time it
takes a whole waggon-load of these students to fumble for their
pocket handkerchiefs.

"You have always gone against the 'Students,' and indeed,
against education generally, mother," returned Bob. "But it
is not meet for you to kick; the best men we have are splendid
scholars, and do all they can in the interest of education, particularly the education of preachers. And what would have
become of us by this time but for our learned men, some of
whom you yourself think very highly of?"

"I gone against learning, Bob! No, name of goodness. But
I will say this much, that it is not necessary to give a lot of
education to poor children; and that it is not learning that
makes a great preacher; else Dick Aberdaron, the greatest
scholar the world ever saw, would have made the best preacher.
But goodness help him, with his cats and his filth. Education
is all well enough where it is wanted, and if sanctified by
grace, but a curse, otherwise, to my way of thinking."

"Paul, your great friend," observed Bob, "was a great
scholar, and he would never have done what he did unless he
had been."

"How can you prove that?" asked my mother. "That he sat
at the feet of Gamaliel does not show he was a great scholar.
Don't you fancy, even if you do understand polikits, you understand your Bible better than your mother. It was the conversion on the way to Damascus that made Paul great; before
then he was great in nothing except as a persecutor, and you
and I would never have heard of him but for that. And I'll
tell you another thing: it was but a poor price Paul put upon
worldly knowledge; and had they wanted to make him a
Doctor or a Mister of Harts, he would have told them directly,
'I never took it upon me to know anything save Jesus Christ,
and him crucified.' A thousand times better to him the title
'Paul, servant of the Lord,' than 'Doctor Saul of Tarsus.' Do you
know what? I have no patience hearing you and others talk of
education, education ever and always, just as if education could
make main and mountain, and was a good enough substitute
for the grace of God. Education, for all I know, teaches some

people not to respect their elders. Grace of God does nothing of the kind—that I do know."

"What are you alluding to, mother?" asked Bob.

"You know very well what I am alluding to, I warrant me. Is it the newspaper, the general enlightener, that taught you to beat an old man who lost a limb by fighting for his country? Bob, I am astonished that you, a boy who never got a day's schooling, should thus bring disgrace upon the cause, and shame to the face of your mother. Go and ask the old man's pardon at once, for shame to you."

"Ask his pardon—Never," said Bob. "Even if I was a little hasty, I did nothing but my duty by him, and if ever again I see the old Soldier or any one else, were he as big as a house, beating Rhys as mercilessly as I saw him being beaten to-day, I am not his brother if I do not then what I did just now, should it be in my power. It is so nature teaches me."

"It is not depraved nature that should govern you, my son," said mother mournfully, "but the new birth. The Word says distinctly you should be 'no striker.'"

"A verse for a bishop, and not for a collier, mother," remarked Bob.

"Bob," returned my mother, "your heart has become hardened. I never thought those English books and newspapers would have had such an effect upon you. I am glad now, although I did it in a bit of a hurry, that I called with Abel Hughes to tell him the story before anyone else had the chance, and induced him to come and speak to you in Communion to-morrow night. If other people wish to conceal their children's disobedience and wickedness, I do not. Pray for grace, my son," and, burying her face in her apron, she began to cry—a proceeding which always put an end to the controversy, as far as Bob was concerned.

Although still broad daylight, I was sent to bed to be healed of my wounds. Unable to sleep, I fell to musing and pondering over one particular expression which mother had used to Bob—"the trouble I have had with your father." What could that mean?

CHAPTER XI.

WILL BRYAN ON THE NATURE OF A CHURCH.

I PASSED a day and a night in bed, for the healing of my wounds, but was very little better when I got up. I felt as though I had been sleeping in starch, so stiff were my limbs when I attempted to move. But for all my pain, the thought that I had "finished my schooling" was more than sufficient to sustain me under the trial. Mother looked low-spirited, and I noticed that she frequently sighed. I fancied I knew what was troubling her, and was stricken to the heart with grief to think it was my wickedness which had brought it all about. Still she did not reproach me, and the only difference in her demeanour towards me was that she was silent and serious. She never as much as asked me how I felt, lest, I imagine, that should make me think the severe whipping I got was anything but what I richly deserved. And yet I knew very well she much desired to find out.

I think, if I am not deceiving myself, that I had in me, even when rather young, a certain quickness in understanding broad hints and signs, and that, to some extent, I possess the faculty still. I perfectly recollect that when a neighbour came to our house, my mother, so that I might not understand the conversation, would speak in parables, observing to her friend, that "little pigs had long ears," and thinking, in her innocence, that I could not tell what that meant. But I knew very well that I was the little pig, and was always fairly able to follow the dialogue, although she thought it was Latin to me. She fancied I did not see her that morning furtively watching my attempts to move. The fact was I could read her heart as plainly as if she carried it in her hand. Oh! how unworthy was I of the care, the solicitude, and the love that heart contained towards me! I did not know at the time what it was that weighed most heavily upon her mind. It was the knowledge that circumstances demanded the infliction of church discipline upon her sons.

In the course of the day, I got to know that Will Bryan and John Beck were hanging around the house anxious to see me.

Whilst mother was looking after a loaf in the oven, I stole out, and in a corner of the garden my two companions and myself had a long confidential chat. On comparing notes, I found that our proceedings in the Church and at school were known to all the neighbourhood, that Bryan and Beck had had a thrashing from their parents, which, as they themselves admitted, was not worth talking of in the same breath as mine from the master. This admission made me think once more that I was one who had "come through much," and I began to consider myself a kind of hero. I learned further that neither of my friends had been to school that day, that Beck had got permission to stay at home until his father found an opportunity of speaking with the master, but that Bryan, though distinctly ordered off to school by his father, had been "playing trowels." In the course of conversation I made two remarks which had a great effect upon the boys. One was that mother said I had had quite enough of schooling. Both stared enviously and incredulously at me, as though they could not possibly comprehend how such happiness could fall to the lot of any human creature. After numerous manifestations of astonishment, Bryan, addressing me, said, "Rhys! I would be willing for the old Warrior to tie my hands behind my back, make me stand an hour on one leg, and then to break a new cane across my shoulders, if the gaffer there (meaning his father), would but say the same thing to me."

Beck gave a nod, which signified that for the same reward he would be perfectly willing to undergo the same ordeal. Not less was their wonder when I told them that Bob's case, my own, and Bryan's would be brought before Communion that very night. Beck, being a Churchman, could not clearly make out what "Communion," and "brought before Communion" meant, until after will Bryan had given him the explanation following. Will had a special gift of definition with respect to anything which he fancied he himself understood, and it was in this way he defined for Beck the nature and object of Communion.

"Do you see, Jack," said he, "Communion means a lot of good folk who think themselves bad, coming together every Tuesday night, to find fault with themselves, and run each other down."

E

"I don't understand you," said Beck.

"Well," said Will, "look at it in this way: you know old Mrs. Peters, and you know Rhys's mother here—it is not because Rhys is here that I say it—but everybody will tell you they are a couple of good, pious women. Well, they attend Communion, and Abel Hughes goes up to them and asks what is on their minds. They reply that they are a very bad lot, guilty of I don't know how many things, Mrs. Peters very often crying as she says it. After that Abel Hughes will tell them they are not so bad as they think, give them a piece of advice, repeat a lot of verses for them, and then move off to some one else, who will carry on in the same way, and so the whole round, until it gets to be half-past eight o'clock, when we all go home."

"There is nothing of that sort in the Church," observed Beck. "We have no 'Communion,' and I never heard anyone of us run himself down."

"That is where the difference between Church and chapel comes in," said Will. "You Church people think yourselves good when you are bad, while chapel people think themselves bad when they are good."

"You don't mean to tell me," said Beck, "that all who belong to Communion are good people, and that all who belong to the Church are bad?"

"All," returned Will, "who take the Sacrament in chapel are good people, although they think themselves bad, and all who take the Sacrament in Church think themselves good, while more than half of them are bad. There is the old Soldier—you know very well he takes Sacrament on Sunday morning, just to please Mr. Brown, while every Sunday night he goes boozing to the Cross Foxes till he is too blind to see his way home again. Did he belong to chapel, look you, he would get the kick out pretty sharp. But when did you see anybody broken out of Church?"

Beck was not a ready controversialist, and so Bryan went on with his exposition of what was meant by "being brought before Communion."

"You see," he said, "when any one belonging to Communion does wrong—even they, you know, are not perfect—someone else must needs go to the elders and split upon him;

and next Communion, after that, Abel Hughes will call him to
account. If he should be badly off, like William the Coal, Abel
makes him come up to the bench before the Big Seat; but if he
is a swell, like Mr. Richards the draper, Abel goes up to him."

"Well, and what does Abel do with the man? Take him to
jail?" asked Beck.

"No danger," was Will's reply. "Abel will inquire into the
business, and invite one or two of those present to say a few
words. If the sinner is repentant, and, like William the Coal,
lays the blame on Satan, saying he will never do it again, they
forgive him, but if, like Mr. Richards the draper, he won't say
anything at all, they refuse him the Sacrament for three months
or more, or even break him out of Communion. There is not
much harm about the thing, you know, but it is a bit of a
bother. I would much rather not go to Communion to-night;
only I must, or there will be a row over yonder."

Though younger by some years than Bryan, I looked upon
Communion as something much more important than this.
Mother had taught me to do so. But, for that matter, Will
looked lightly upon everything, and that proved his ruin. To
proceed, however. Beck's last words made a great impression
upon me. They were these:—

"Boys, I like the order of the Church better than the order
of the chapel. All who belong to Church can do just as they
like, without anyone to call them to account. Each minds his
own business, which is the best way too, I think."

Bryan was usually a zealous advocate of chapel, but it was
clear that he was disposed to agree with Beck upon this point;
so by way of conclusion he said:—

"This is how it is, John: it is more comfortable in the
Church, but more safe in the chapel."

As far as my memory goes, this was the first discussion I
ever heard on Church Government, and it left a deeper impression on my mind than many an one heard later between persons
of greater importance and assertiveness. I, at any rate, could
not look on church discipline in the same light that Will
Bryan did; and great was my anxiety at the thought of going
to Communion that night.

The time of going arrived; and seeing Bob getting himself
ready, Mother did not think it necessary to speak to him on the
matter. She and I started together towards the chapel, but
after we had taken a step or two she turned back, and I heard
her say, " Bob, don't be stiff to-night, I beg of you; " and we
then went on our way.

Recalling that Communion, I cannot help thinking of divers
of the old characters, who have, by this time, to use Mrs.
Tibbet's phrase, " gone to their happening." There's Abel
Hughes, of whom I have said something already. A God-fearing man, firm in the faith, and strong-minded, was Abel. His
one fault, as far as I am aware of, was his severity. There was
harmless Hugh Bellis, gentle, tender-hearted man, who always
wept during sermon, eager for the forgiveness of all, no
matter what the sin committed. The least religious-minded
would admit Hugh to be an exceedingly pious man. There was
Edward Peters, precise, and careful about the books, but
crabbed, and unpopular with the children, because he would
not allow them to leave in the middle of the service. Never a
word did he speak in public, save in connection with the collections and the seat-money. A good man at bottom, who had
the confidence of the church. There was Thomas Bowen the
preacher : lively, zealous, impulsive, constantly making mistakes and apologizing for them. There was Mr. Richards the
draper, a proud, showy person, at all times pushing to the fore,
and with everybody desirous of keeping him back. There was
William the Coal, poor, small of body and of mind, soft, and
easily persuadable. He was called William the Coal, because
some member or other of his family had, time out of mind, sold
coal by the penn'orth. Every winter, when work was slack,
William was constant at Communion ; but when spring came,
he would take to drinking over-much, and be excommunicated
in consequence. He was forgiven many a transgression because
he was not considered quite like other people. I heard mother
say that William had the root of the matter in him, but that
trunk and branches were too weak to withstand the cross-wind.
I was of the same opinion, for William, every time he prayed,
would shed tears, and to my boyish mind, everyone who wept
while praying must be a very pious man indeed, a notion which

sticks to me still. There was John Lloyd, too, of unpleasant memory: tall, thin, sharp-featured, coarse-skinned, and fidgetty; diligent in the "means," and always finding fault with something or somebody. "The Old Scraper," Will Bryan called him. He was a shocking miser, on which account he never came under church censure, for his love of money prevented him from getting drunk, or frequenting forbidden places. He set a rigid face against tea meetings, concerts, and every gathering to which the token with the King or Queen's head was a passport. He was always great on economy, and the necessity of making provision for the future. His concern for spirituality in religion was something tremendous, and he doubted, very often, there was too much talk of money and of preaching for money. Mother tried to believe that he, too, had the root of the matter, but she feared it was worm-eaten somewhere, with the result that his leaves had become soured. Yes, there is Seth also, the witling youth, of whom I shall have to speak hereafter, as of one whose story marks an epoch in my life. And there were many others I might name, a few of whom will come under notice again.

There was an unusually large gathering at Communion that night. Hardly anyone had stayed away. I have noticed that the news that some is to be disciplined is always an effective means of bringing the friends together. There is something in the good of a nature similar to that which prompts those who are differently constituted to go and see a man being hanged. Will Bryan and I sat next each other in the midst of the children, and I marvelled to find him so thoroughly unconcerned. The meeting was begun by Thomas Bowen, whom I carefully listened to for any reference he might make to myself. But he made none. Whilst Thomas was praying, Will whispered in my ear, "If they ask us anything, let us say, like William the Coal, that we'll never do it again, and they are sure to forgive us." Will said a great many other things, but I was too much occupied to notice them. The verse-recitals of the children were taken by Abel Hughes, who, when it came to Will's turn and mine, passed us both by without asking us for ours. The storm had evidently begun, and although I held my head down, I knew that all were looking at me, and felt

their eyes burning right through my velvet jacket. Glancing
under my brows, I saw Will, with head up, looking about him
wholly unabashed. After Abel had done with the children,
Thomas Bowen said a word in general, and then invited Hugh
Bellis to speak. Hugh made some observations on the Sunday's
sermons, expatiating forcibly upon the blessing he had received
therefrom. Thomas Bowen, upon this, asked whether anyone
else had anything to say upon the same subject. After a while
Edward Peters got upon his feet, and reminded the brethren that
the quarter's seat money was due. Then there was silence, and a
consultation between Abel and Thomas Bowen. I heard the
former say, " You do it, Thomas," to which the other replied,
" No, you do it, Abel."

I see Abel, velvet cap on head, get upon his feet, looking
serious and agitated. I would have been glad were I able to
chronicle the words of that true and honest man just as he
delivered them, but I cannot. I remember his saying something of an "unpleasant circumstance," of "children of the
Communion behaving like the children of the world," of
"scandal brought upon the cause of religion," of the "necessity
of enforcing church discipline," and so forth. He spoke at
length and with severity, winding up by naming brother Bob,
me, and Bryan, as the offenders.

Abel having sat down, John Lloyd observed that the church
wanted to know from its officers what had been the nature of
the transgression.

" Hark at the old scraper," said Will in my ear.

Abel replied that he believed our transgression was well
known to John Lloyd and everyone else then present, and that
it would not be wise to repeat the circumstances. Thomas
Bowen here rose suddenly to his feet, and said something to the
following effect :—

" My brethren, children will be children, and we should all remember that we were children ourselves once. I am very sorry
for this business. Abel Hughes has done quite right in calling
attention to it, but what can we do except give these poor lads
a word of advice ? Remember, my brethren, I am not speaking
of Robert Lewis now, he is of age and sense ; but as to William
Bryan and Rhys Lewis—they are young and unreflective ; and

well-behaved, decent lads they are, too. Who recites his verse
better than William or Rhys? It is a great pity the boys should
have done wrong. Have you anything to say William, my
son?"

"I'll never do it again," replied Will.

"Good boy," said Thomas. "Are you sorry for what you
did?"

"Yes," said Will, at the same time giving me a pinch in the
leg, which made me cry.

"And do you say the same thing, Rhys?" queried Thomas,
adding, "but there, we have no need to ask Rhys anything,
his face is bathed in tears already. Abel Hughes, do you hear
what the boys say? They are sorry for the thing, and they'll
never do it again. What could we ourselves do better than
repent us of our fault, and resolve not to commit such another.
What are we to do with the boys, Abel Hughes?"

"Do what you like with them," replied Abel savagely.

"Well, brethren," said Thomas, "we cannot do better with
these boys than give them a word of advice and send them
away, inasmuch as we have another and weightier matter to
attend to."

Thomas Bowen having given us a kindly word of advice, told
us to go home like good children. No sooner had he spoken
than the youngsters rushed out for the fastest. I had just
passed the doorway when Will Bryan caught me by the arm,
and gave me a "right wheel" down the side of the chapel. I
felt offended with him, and asked him why he had pinched me
so sorely in the chapel?

"To make you cry, you silly," he replied. "I knew very
well you hadn't a word to say for yourself; so crying did the
job, you see. Didn't I tell you they would let us off? But we
must find out what becomes of Bob."

In the side wall of the old place of worship was a door opening upon the steps which led to the gallery, through which
Margaret of the chapel-house used to enter for the purpose of
opening and shutting up the building, and which was consequently not locked on this night. I divined Will's purpose
instantly, but nothing was left me but to follow him, for he had
some strange influence over me which I could not withstand.

Will softly opened the door, and closed it in the same manner. In the darkness he whispered, "take off your clogs, and put them there on that side; I'll place mine on this, so that we shan't make any mistake when we come down." I did so, and heard Will say, "Now up we go as soft as mice." And up we went, on all fours, Will leading the way, until we reached his favourite spot, the clock seat. There we sat out the whole hearing of Bob's case; and I could, I think, repeat the pleadings almost word for word. But to what purpose? The occasion is too painful for me to linger long over it. Words were spoken there sharp as sword-thrusts, particularly by John Lloyd, with whom I grew furious, because, let Bob's offence be what it might, I knew him to be a hundred thousand times a better man than Lloyd. Bob might have been wrong in setting upon the old Soldier as he did, but he did it in order to prevent a greater wrong to me; and I knew him to have so large and feeling a heart that he would sacrifice his life, not for me alone, but for any one whom he saw being wronged. As for John Lloyd, he had a love for nothing but money, and had a heart no bigger than a spider's. And yet this was the man who slavered his dirtiest over Bob that night! I am afraid I have never forgiven him, believing, as I do, it was his insulting words that made Bob so stiff-necked. I knew my brother could have borne the sharp, stern reproof of Abel Hughes, and that Thomas Bowen's loving expostulation would have soothed the wounded heart of him, but the poisoned darts of a narrow-minded hypocrite like this made him hardened and obstinate; and we heard him proclaim before all Communion that he had nothing to repent of.

Never shall I forget that half hour in the clock seat. I was annoyed with Bryan for his unseemly behaviour. While Bob's cause was being argued, Will was cutting his name with his pocket knife on the seat, and passing remarks on the various speakers; doing so, too, in such a loud tone of voice that I constantly found myself begging him to be quiet, for fear we should be discovered. I felt so much for Bob that I could not help crying, observing which, my companion asked sarcastically whether I had the toothache. It appears strange to me now that my impressions of several people in that Communion wherein I was brought up, should have been formed whilst I

sat in the clock seat. I had seen, for some time, what the end
of the business was going to be, and fell to thinking of the
dreadful blow it would give my mother, who had never dreamt
that Bob would be excommunicated. But nothing else could
happen, with Bob declaring he would do the same thing again
under the same circumstances. Will Bryan, whilst occupied in
the work of carving his name on the seat, observed several times
that Bob was "missing it." "If he only did like William the
Coal," he continued, "put the blame on Satan, and say he'd
never do it again, it would be all right; but if he goes on like
that, he is sure to get the kick out." For all his light-headed-
ness, before a few minutes were over Will proved himself a true
prophet. Thomas Bowen did his best to get Bob to admit that
he had been to blame, but could not succeed. Abel Hughes did
the same, with the like result. The officers of the church were
bound to do their duty. Abel Hughes got up to take the vote
of excommunication. The old man's voice trembled, and the
words stuck in his throat, as he did so. The usual sign of
assent was given, and Bob was no longer a member with the
Calvinistic Methodists. Almost simultaneously Abel sank to
his knees, and in prayer prayed, if man ever prayed in his life.
I have wondered hundreds of times that the supplication on
Bob's behalf was never answered.

Would the Church have excommunicated Bob had it known
the consequences of the act? I hardly think so.

CHAPTER XII.

ON THE HEARTH.

WHATEVER other gifts I may be deficient in—and they are
many—I fancy I have cause to be thankful for a good memory.
Indeed, I would not have begun this autobiography had I not
been conscious beforehand that its writing, in my hours of
ease, would be of greater pleasure than of labour to me. In
turning up one circumstance after another in my history, I find
each with its family and relatives rising again in living form
before my mind. Similarly, when looking over an old packet

of letters, every letter has its unwritten associations, here and there a letter making one think of others which have been reduced to ashes by fire, but which cannot be burnt out of the memory. Some are read with a sense of satisfaction, others bring painful recollections, others stir up our whole nature, awaking feelings and ideas we had thought lost for ever, but which had lived on, hidden away in the caverns of the mind and the crannies of the memory.

Although I register the night of brother Bob's excommunication among the dark nights of my life, it is not without its bright side. The occurrence made me meditate seriously upon the nature of religion, and what it was which constituted the importance and sacredness of church membership. I already had some sort of notion that there was a great difference between religious people and "people of the world," as my mother called them; but I am afraid it came to no more than this—that the former partook of the Lord's Supper once a month, did not get drunk, or curse and swear, and that the latter, not belonging to Communion, were at liberty to commit any sin they chose. But somehow, that night, I got to doubt this view, and began to think that something more than the one I have named went to make up the difference. Without being able to bring myself to believe that he would, I asked myself would Bob, now that he was no longer a church member, get drunk occasionally? Would he curse and swear, now and again? Would he give over reading the Bible and other good books, and kick up a row in the house like Peter the potman? I questioned, also, whether Bob, out of Communion, would be a worse or more wretched creature than John Lloyd in it. That, too, was quite as impossible, to my mind. What was it, then, which made a man religious? The occurrence, moreover, made me form a high opinion of my mother's piety. Possibly it was the conversation which ensued between her and brother Bob which caused me thus to regard her. I will try and reproduce this conversation as accurately as my memory will serve. Of course mother did not know I had heard the whole of the inquiry into Bob's case, and it wouldn't have been well had she found out that I and Will Bryan had stowed ourselves away in the chapel-loft. When all went in a body to chapel, the last to leave the house would hide the door-key under the water-tub, so that the first to return might gain a speedy entrance to our castle. That was one of the family secrets. As it was I who, of necessity, must be first home on this night, I hurried along and just managed to be for a couple of minutes seated before mother came in. Although nearly out of breath, I endeavoured to appear as if I had been expecting her for some time. I told her she had been very long coming. "Every wait is a long one," was all her reply, made as she hung her blue cloak and great bonnet on the nail behind the door. Bob must have taken a turn with his companions after leaving Communion, because supper had been some time prepared before he came in. After long waiting, he made his appearance, looking sad and dispirited. He sat down without a word, and took up a book to read. It was not without much coaxing that he came up to the supper-table, and I speedily saw that neither he nor mother made much impression upon the food. Having had a great load taken off my mind, so far as the discipline of the church concerned me personally, and reflecting that it would be a pity such good provision should go to waste, I did my best to put as much of it out of sight as I could. Supper over, Bob again took up his book, and mother drew her chair nearer the fire. I knew from her manner that she meant to start a conversation. She had a habit, when gathering her thoughts together, of pleating her apron.

"Well, my son," she presently said, "this had been rather a bad night in your and my history. Poor as I am, I would rather than a hundred pounds if what took place to-night hadn't happened."

Bob, who spoke a little more grammatically than mother, said in reply :—

"I do not see, mother, why you should look at the matter in that light. It will make no difference in my conduct. Being in Communion does not guarantee a man's salvation, nor being out of it his perdition."

"Rhys," said mother, turning to me, "you had better go to bed."

"Directly," said I, laying my head upon the table, and pretending to sleep. I am not sure I did not snore. Such a sly young fox was I! My behaviour threw both off their guard.

"Bob," resumed my mother, "I trust you do not mean what you say. You have been saying so many things of late, since you've taken to coddle with these old English books, that it's difficult for me to think you do."

"Mother," said Bob, whom I heard putting his book down, "you know very well there is no deceit in me, and that nothing in the world is so hateful to me as hypocrisy. I, a thousand times, prefer being expelled from the church for telling the truth, to being suffered to remain in it by showing myself mealy-mouthed, and speaking the thing I neither believe nor feel. I know my excommunication must be a sad blow to you, mother, and for that I am sorry; but the church having chosen so to deal with me, I have nothing in the world to say."

"What! my son," exclaimed my mother. "Do you set no store by church membership?"

"I do not," was the reply, "if I must buy that membership by double-dealing. You have never yet heard me talk about myself or complaining, but you know very well that neither my father nor you once thought of giving me a day's schooling. I was allowed to grow up ignorant of all things save those of the Bible. I was sent into the mine at an age when I ought to have been at school, and I was an experienced collier before I was sixteen. Directly I became sensible of my want of education, in my spare hours I set myself, with all my energy, to learn English, and that without help from any living soul, and with you constantly complaining that I wasted the candles. To say the least, I have been as faithful at chapel as any of my own age. I have been a teacher in the Sunday School since I was seventeen. I am not praising myself, but you know that since the bother with my father, I have worked hard, and done my best to keep a home for you and Rhys; and what would have become of you had I gone away? You know I never in my life spent a penny in dissipation, and that all the money I could scrape together was devoted either to buying books or subscribing towards the church. Besides this, I have endeavoured, for years, to impart to my brother all the knowledge I possessed, so that he, if possible, might become something better than the poor collier I am myself. Seeing that brother oppressed and beaten most unmercifully, I did what anyone with a grain of humanity in his composition would have done—I rushed on the oppressor and rescued the oppressed, as David did the lamb from the lion's jaws. But this, in Communion's sight, was a great sin, especially in that of some of the members, who, doubtless, must feel very happy now that they are rid of a depraved creature like me."

"Do you know what?" said mother, "your words have much the sound of self-righteousness. You make me think of that man who began the prayer meeting in the temple of old. You have his tinkle about you, to a T. There is as little of the publican ring in your voice, now you are at home, as there was in it in Communion. What has come over you, tell me? You have shown a wonderful stiffness of late. Pray for grace, my son; pray that you may feel the rope, and see your filthy rags. Brought before your betters at the Quarter Sessions it would be all right to talk of your virtues; in Communion before the Great Judge, the less you speak of them the better, save by the names wherewith Paul baptized them—"dung and loss." Do you know, Bob, I have suspected for some time that there were notions forming in your heart which you never found in the Bible; and that has cost me many a sleepless night."

"You, mother, know me best, of all people," said Bob feelingly, "and I must be bad indeed, when my own mother can entertain so poor an opinion of me. I, no doubt, am the biggest scamp in the neighbourhood. Well, be it so."

"No, my son, not so, either," said mother. "As a good son to his mother, there isn't your superior in the six counties. I never had any trouble with you in that way, and I am very thankful to you and the Great King for your kindness in working so hard to keep a home for your mother and brother. It is of your soul I am speaking now. It matters little whether I have a crust or not; but it matters everything, my darling boy, that your soul and mine should be under the dispensation of the Spirit of God. Blessed be His name, He never gives me rest, and I believe He means to make something of me. O that

I had room to think He spoke also unto you! To see you so little affected by your excommunication breaks my heart, my poor boy. Without are the dogs—without are the tempest and the storm. You have gone out from the circle of the covenant and the intercession; you have lost the shelter, my dear Bob."

"It was the church that decided whether it was within or without I should be; it was the church that repudiated me, not me the church," replied Bob.

"No, my son," rejoined my mother. "It was your own doing entirely, and you ought to be ashamed of it. It was your refusal to repent and admit your sin which made the church expel you. How often to-night, did Thomas Bowen beg, and you decline, to own your fault and ask forgiveness? No, to the church your excommunication was a very painful matter; but what else could you look for if you did not repent? It is useless your expecting forgiveness of God or man without repentance."

"I can't fall in with the opinions of old-fashioned people, when my own run counter to them," said Bob. "What do you think Mr. Brown, the clergyman, said to me to-day, when I mentioned the matter to him? Why, he laughed at the whole thing, and expressed a hope that the licking I gave the old Soldier would do him good."

"Bob!" cried mother, not a little warmed, "don't you talk of the great doctrines of the Gospel as old-fashioned, in my hearing, it's best for you."

"I did not do so," observed Bob.

"You did something very much like it," returned mother. "Repentance, you'll find, is a fashion you will have to 'fall in' with, or you'll never enter into the Life. It is a fashion, Bob, that has made thousands conquerors to all eternity. But I'll tell you when it will become an *old* fashion: when the summer hath ended, and the harvest of the soul shall have gone by. Many will be found turning to the old fashion when it is too late. Pray, my son, lest you be one of them. As to Mr. Brown, I don't think much of him. A nice one he is to guide our youth. If I wanted something for my soul's good I'd never go to him, for, most likely, I should find him out in the fields a-rabbit shooting. Every respect to Mr. Brown as a good neighbour, but well was it said, by Thomas of Nant, of him and his sort. Although Thomas was not all that he should be, still he hit it off at times fairly well :—

> 'Praised and reverenced, worthily,
> O'er all men the priest we see ;
> But none more accursed than he,
> If God-guided he not be.' *

Would that Mr. Brown had half the spirit of the old Vicar of Llandovery. This is what the Vicar would have said to you, if I remember rightly :—

> 'Repent, sinner, while you may,
> Thou wilt harden with delay ;
> Lest thine heart should hardened be,
> Here and now, O ! repent thee.
> To the faithful and repentant,
> God is ever gracious, constant ;
> To the odious, stubborn, perverse,
> God a cruel is and fierce.' *

And your conscience knows whether it is Mr. Brown or the old Vicar who is in the right."

" ' Every respect,' to use your own words, to the old Vicar," returned Bob ; " but I do not believe that God is ' fierce and cruel ' at any time, much less towards me for what I did to the old Soldier. The Bible teaches me that ' God is Love.' "

" What ! " cried my mother. " You are surely not going to contradict the good old Vicar, who knew his Bible a thousand times better than you do, hundreds of years before you were born ? You never spoke a truer word than that ' God is Love.' But for that, good-bye to the life eternal and election by grace, as I heard Mr. 'Lias say on the Green at Bala—blessed be his memory ! Who could speak better—better, indeed, who, a quarter as well as Mr. 'Lias—of

> 'The love we see to-day
> All other love out-weigh.'

---

* For the benefit of the purely English reader, let me mention that these renderings are as near the originals in rhyme as they are in reason.—
TRANSLATOR.

But had you heard him hold forth God's justice and wrath towards the wicked, it would have made your hair stand on end. If you are going to cherish notions of that kind, Bob, I'd as lief have Wesley as you, every bit. No, my son, the vicar is quite right—God is ever displeased with the ungodly, and that you know, better than I can tell you."

"I have neither the spirit nor the desire for a discussion with you, mother," remarked Bob.

"I'm not so sure about that," replied mother. "More's the pity, it is only too much spirit, by a good deal, you have got as a rule. I had some secret hope it was a fit of obstinacy that had come over you in Communion, and that your heart was better than your tongue after all. But I see I've been mistaken, and I see, moreover, I've been to blame for not having long ago remonstrated with you upon your condition. I have nothing now left but to pray, my son, that God's Spirit shall visit your soul. Well," she added, with a sigh, "there is greater need now, than at any time I can think of, for a revival of religion that will bring the proud spirit of people down and the people themselves to their religious duty."

"When He cometh," said Bob, "He will have much more to do than that. He will have a great heap of miserliness and niggardliness—which now pass under the name of economy— to clean out of the churches. Hypocrisy, narrow-mindedness, want of Christian charity—now designated sanctity, exactitude, and zeal for church discipline—will come under the same disguises then as they did to meet me to-night. But on that day—if ever it arrive—it will be revealed that some of those folk who clamoured loudest for my expulsion, are cankered and rotten with worldliness and filthy lucre, that they sell Jesus Christ for thirty pieces of silver every day they get up out of bed. When that visitation comes, of which you speak, I shall expect to find myself amongst a numerous company which I shall be ashamed to recognise."

"You leave out one thing," said my mother. "On that day everybody will have his hand upon his own heart-plague—not picking out the motes in other people, and indulging in his own self-justification. Peter, look you, did not think of pointing to Judas's betrayal as a reason why he should not repent for his denial. No, he went out and wept bitterly, and I would like to see a little of the same spirit in you, my son."

And at this stage mother began to cry, a proceeding which, as I have already observed, had at all times the effect of putting an end to the argument on Bob's part.

Having given full vent to her feelings, mother caught me by the collar and shook me sharply, little thinking I had been wide awake the whole time—a fact of which she never became aware. After going to bed, I mused a great deal over what I had heard, especially the references to my father. But that night passed like every other. Mother's appeals had not much effect on Bob. After his excommunication it was seldom he spoke of religious matters, or of the chapel, although he continued his attendance. In the house he kept very quiet, almost always reading, and never ceasing to impart all the knowledge he was possessed of to me. What would I give to-night had I nothing more unpleasant to relate of him?

CHAPTER XIII.

SETH.

As intimated, I must say something about the witling youth, Seth, whose acquaintance marks an epoch in my history. A remarkable character was Seth. I do not recollect when I first got to know him. I have milked my memory without obtaining from it anything but—Seth, the same in stature, appearance, age, and disposition always. If someone asked me when did I first see the crab tree near our house, and could I tell the different changes that had taken place in the form of its branches, I should be obliged to answer in the negative. The one particular incident I remember in its history is, that the owner of the Hall ordered it to be cut down. And when the hard-hearted woodman applied his axe to its roots, making the chips fly, and the tree came tumbling down to earth, I felt as if I had lost a dear old friend. It furnished me, now and then, with a crab, which, though it set my teeth on edge in the eating, was sweet

F

in the absence of something better. This is about all the notion I can form of the size and history of that crab tree up to the day it was cut down. It is much the same with regard to Seth. Up to the time of his death his history presents but one period, with nothing in it but Seth: a fresh-complexioned youth, inclined to be tall, thin, and bony, with a slight stoop of the shoulders, a little bit of a chin which almost lost itself in the neck, a mouth nearly always half open, small, blue, meaningless, if rather merry eyes, a somewhat irregular nose, a forehead retreating almost into line with the crown, which was high, narrow, and jutted out over the long nape.

Simple, harmless folk were his parents, who lived in a trim little cottage a little way out of the town. Thomas Bartley, the father, was by trade a shoemaker, or, more strictly speaking, a cobbler, for he never made shoes. Neither he nor his wife, Barbara, was reckoned to belong to the class of knowing ones. Indeed, both were usually looked upon as not being altogether square-headed; consequently—Seth. Neither knew a single letter of the alphabet; neither ever went to Church or chapel, except once a year, on the day of harvest thanksgiving. I heard Thomas, more than once, say that in his younger days he attended Sunday School regularly for four or five years, and he believed that, had he stuck to it a few years longer, he would have mastered the A. B. C. I heard him boast, also, that he had several times been to hear John Elias, Williams of Wern, and Christmas Evans; but when asked what sort of preachers they were, his unvarying answer was: "Save us! they were rough uns—awful rough!" These two old fogies, Thomas and Barbara Bartley, were wondrously innocent and happy. Thomas's besetting sin was a tendency to take God's name in vain, although, one might fancy, it was not from any want of reverence that he did it. He would not for a great deal, have done any work on the Sabbath, and would not have expected a blessing had he been guilty of such a thing. But he saw no harm in spending hours every Sunday, with his pipe in his mouth, watching the pig feed, and calculating how long it would take to become fit for the knife, what it would weigh, would it be advisable to make black puddings and brawn, should he keep or sell the offal, to which of his neighbours was

he under obligation to send a bit of spare-rib, and so forth.
Thomas thought it no harm in the least that he and Barbara
should spend the Sabbath talking of things like these, but he
wouldn't for the world have worn his leather apron an hour on
that day. My brother Bob was very fond of taking his shoes to
be mended to Thomas Bartley, for the sake of drawing the old
man out; and I have seen him laugh till the tears came when
relating to my mother the queer notions he had learned during
some of these visits. Mother was frequently troubled with
rheumatism, and I remember she had a bad attack on one
occasion just as Bob had returned from a visit to Thomas. Bob
told the following story as one of the old shoemaker's latest, and
although my mother was never, at any time, fond of fun, she
could not repress a smile at the natural way in which Bob
mimicked old Bartley's method of speaking.

" How's your mother, Bob?" asked Thomas.

"Very bad, Thomas Bartley," replied Bob. " Suffers very
much from the rheumatis, you know; sleeps very little from
the pain."

" —— save us! Save us!" said Thomas. "D'ye know, Bob,
I don't und'stand that Great King, look you; don't und'stand
Him, at all. A woman like your mother, who never did anything in the world agenst Him, to be plagued like that always,
always. Don't und'stand Him, 'deed to you."

" You think too highly of my mother, Thomas Bartley,"
remarked Bob. " She finds fault with herself very often, and
fears every day she will not be saved in the end."

" Not saved in the end! What's the matter with the
woman? I never in my life heard anything wrong of her; did
you, Barbara?"

" Not I, name o' goodness," said Barbara.

" Of course not," said Thomas, " and nobody else, either.
But look here, Bob, you're a scholar, and Barbara and I have
often thought of asking you, only we always forget—Does'nt
the Book say there'll be a lot of us saved at the last?"

" It speaks of a great multitude which no man can number,"
replied Bob.

" To be shwar! Did'nt I tell you, Barbara? The talk these
ignorant people make! It's my belief, look you, Bob, if we are

honest and pay our way, and live somethin' near the mark, we
shall all be saved. Don't you want soles as well as heels for
these? They're beginning to go, you know; better have them
vamped too."

Many similar things did I hear Bob relate. But it is of Seth
I was speaking. I have often heard of people who have been so
unfortunate as to come into the world *non compos mentis*, as the
saying is, that they have in them some craft and cunning
beyond other people. But there was nothing of this in Seth.
I believe him to have been perfectly harmless, and I know he
had a heart of wondrous love and tenderness. Whatever was
asked of him he would do, if it were in his power, and everything he had was shared with someone else. To me, his heart
seemed always in the right place; but, poor fellow, his head was
always wrong. Of a truth, he was in sense but a child, although
in size a man. Whatever thoughts might have flitted through
his brain, his power of expressing them was of the poorest;
his talk was childish, and his words were few. Everybody in the
neighbourhood knew Seth and respected him, on account of his
affliction, presumably. Even all the dogs, in town and country,
knew Seth, and wagged their tails at him. Seth never passed
one of them without patting its head, and giving the creature,
after his own fashion, the heartiest greeting. Now I think of
it, he had one special gift—that of remembering the names of
dogs, horses, and other animals. He did not spend much time
at home. Somehow he was happier everywhere than in the
house of his father and mother. Did I happen to rise early, I
would be sure of seeing Seth. Did I stay out late, Seth would
cross my path at some point. Was there anything on in the
town, one of the first I would see at it was Seth. Did a house
take fire, or a haystack, there was Seth also. At every
preaching meeting, concert, and lecture, Seth made one of the
congregation; he was free of every place, asked for a ticket by
no denomination or sect.

He attended all the services at our chapel regularly, listening
attentively to every word, although nobody imagined he understood the least bit of what was said. I have reason, by now, to
doubt the accuracy of the general verdict. I remember many
times watching his countenance while the minister was speaking,

and seeing a gleam of intelligent enjoyment steal across it. The gleam was but a transient one, it is true, and on vanishing left the face vacant and expressionless as before, but it gave the countenance an appearance sufficiently differing from the ordinary one to attract my attention. When asked what the preacher had been saying, he could remember, or at any rate, could reproduce, nothing but the name Jesus Christ. There is reason to believe that he thought highly of every preacher, for nothing gave him greater pleasure than the holding of a preacher's horse, or showing him where the chapel was. When either of these things fell to his lot, he would relate the circumstance to his companions with great gusto. Although Seth, as I have remarked, was in age and size a man, his associates were children always.

He came to the Children's Communion regularly, and recited his verse as the children did. It was the one verse always: "Jesus Christ the same yesterday and to-day, and for ever." Mother, myself, and others tried in vain to find out who had taught it him. It was as if the words had grown up with him, and so filled his mind that there was no room for any other. It being the same verse he was always repeating, Abel Hughes, I remember, passed him by on one occasion in Communion without asking him for the recital, seeing which Seth broke out into bitter lamentations, and would not be comforted. We, children, being very fond of Seth, the greater part of us joined him in the crying; I, as I remember well enough, was tear-shedding at a particularly beautiful rate, for it did not take much, at any time, to make me cry. Although Abel, as I have already said, was a determined, self-possessed man, I never saw him in such a fix. He pulled the strangest faces, and could not, for the life of him, utter a word. Presently he attempted to soothe Seth's grief, but in vain. I knew Abel felt sore for what he had done, and as some sort of atonement for it, he rewarded Seth next day with a hymn book, to the complete healing of the latter's wounds. That hymn book was the only thing I knew Seth refuse to share with another. Nothing would have bought it of him; he carried it to every service, opening it towards the middle during the singing, and almost always holding it upside down. Seth had noticed that some kind folk would show their page to those near them who had not caught the number of the hymn; so he, on the slightest sign of hesitation in anyone, would go straight up and show his open book, as if he were quite sure of the place.

Seth behaved very strangely at times in chapel, and in a manner which must have been trying to a strange preacher. The congregation, being well used to it, did not notice him. He would rise up suddenly, put his foot upon the bench in front of him, rest his right elbow upon his knee, and, chin in hand, would never take eyes off the preacher. Seeing Will Bryan, and myself, and others taking down the text and the heads of sermon, he would now and again show a great desire to imitate us; and some wag or other having furnished him with a large square of white paper and a long stick of pencil, there would Seth be seen holding the paper in his right hand, and the pencil in his left, waiting, with anxious face, for the preacher to give out the text, when, full of business, he would scribble his sheet with the strangest characters ever seen. But he soon tired of this work, and returned to his old form of an unbroken stare into the eyes of the preacher. Remembering his demeanour, and also that he at all times sat right opposite the minister, I have wondered that he did not upset the gravity of more than one of our visitants. Seth possessed something very much like the spirit of worship. I heard Margaret of the chapel-house relate that she generally found him waiting her to open the door, and that directly she had put the place to rights, and turned her back, he would walk into the Big Seat, take up the Bible, and utter a low peculiar sound, as if reading. He would then go upon his knees, and say no end of things, nobody knew what, even if he knew himself. As soon, however, as some one put in an appearance, Seth would desist, and softly direct his steps to his accustomed seat.

Seth and I were great friends; not because we were of like minds, I trust. At times, when mother refused to let me out to play, I used to see Seth lingering about the house, for hours at a stretch, awaiting my release. I do not know what made him take so much to me, but sure I am, it always distressed him greatly to see me put upon by some of the other boys. Remembering his delicate health, I am ashamed to think how often he was horse for me. Altogether, I am certain he must have carried me scores of miles, and that quite uncomplainingly. Given a halfpenny or a penny, which happened frequently, he never failed to consult me as to what he should do with it, my invariable advice being—spend it. But I must hasten on, inasmuch as I have something more important to say regarding my connection with the lad.

I noticed one day that Seth looked very ill, coughed badly, and cared nothing for the play; although he made no complaint. Indeed, I never did hear him complaining. Next day Seth did not leave the house. The day after, I went to look for him, and found him in bed. On my entrance into his room, he looked wildly at me; then, his countenance brightening, he held out his hand, and cried "Rhys!" A few minutes later he lost all recollection of me, and began calling me by strange names. He talked on incessantly, but I could not make sense of anything he said. In vain did his mother try to keep him quiet. He sat up in bed, and pointed with his finger to an empty corner of the room, as if he were seeing something there, he could not tell us what. His look frightened me; and with a heart almost breaking with sympathy for him, I slid quietly down the stairs. In the kitchen I found Thomas Bartley, pacing to and fro, in heavy grief. The first thing he asked me was, did Seth recognise me. My decisive answer cheered him greatly. Presently, however, his sorrow returned, and he observed, "The doctor says he's got the fever, Rhys! Save us! Save us! Ask your mother, my lad, to pray a bit for him. Save us! What if I was to lose him!"

Had Seth been the greatest genius in the world, his parents could not have been more concerned about him. My friend continued in the same state for days. I visited him daily— sometimes twice a day. Will Bryan and I were all of his old companions who were admitted to his room. It was seldom he recognised us. I forget whether it was the eighth or the ninth day of his illness that Will Bryan came to our house late at night with the news that Seth had "altered," and that he was calling for me. Although it was nearly bed-time, I got my mother's permission to go and see him. On the way, Will said to me, "I fear, look you, that Seth is going to clear out;"

by which he meant that Seth was on the point of death.
Although speaking in this manner, Will was perfectly serious.
When we reached the house, Thomas Bartley gave us cheerful
greeting, and told us Seth was much better. My heart leaped
with joy at hearing this. We went softly up the stairs. Old
Barbara and a female neighbour were sitting by the bedside,
looking secretly pleased.

"He has been asking for you for some time," said the neighbour to Will and me.

Seth lay perfectly still, with a cheerful smile upon his face,
which also wore a look of strange beauty. One who did not
know him would, as far as appearances went, have said he was
perfectly intelligent. Will and I were struck dumb nearly at
seeing him so little like his old self. I should have mentioned
that Seth always spoke of himself in the third person. For
example, when going anywhere, he would not say "I am
going," but "Seth is going to such and such a place." And so,
in every circumstance, he would speak of himself as if he were
some one else. We, his companions, had adopted the same
style of speech in conversation with him. After Will and I had
entered the room, Seth, holding out a thin white hand to us,
and greeting each by name, requested his mother and the
neighbour to go down into the kitchen, which they immediately
did. When we had the apartment to ourselves, I bent over him
and said, "Seth is better."

"Yes, Seth is better," he faltered.

"Does Seth want to say anything to Rhys?" I asked.

He gave me a cheerful, bright, intelligent look, which reminded me of one of those gleams I have spoken of as
occasionally stealing across his countenance in chapel. Then he
repeated the verse I had heard hundreds of times upon his lips
in the Children's Communion: "Jesus Christ the same yesterday, to-day, and for ever." There was something in the recital
which made me think it came, not from the tongue, but straight
from the heart. He continued to gaze at me as if he expected
to be asked something else. I did not know what to say to him.
Presently I murmured, "Seth'll get better directly."

"No," said he, "Seth 'ont get better. Seth never agen play
with Rhys. Seth go to Abel's chapel no more. Seth's goin'

away, far away, to—to," and he pointed with his finger upwards, as if he could not find the proper word.

"Heaven," suggested I, but that was not the word he was
seeking, for he presently gave the sentence in its entirety:

"Seth's going away, far, far, to the great chapel of Jesus
Christ."

That was poor Seth's idea of Heaven—"the great chapel of
Jesus Christ." I had for some time noticed that Will Bryan, who
stood behind me, was breathing in short gasps, as though he had
caught a cold. In school I had seen the old Soldier break his
cane to pieces over Will's back without as much as a tear or a
cry from him; but this hearing of our innocent old companion,
Seth, talk of dying, and of going afar, was more than Will could
stand; and, to use his own expression, he "cleared out" down
the stairs, leaving me alone with Seth. When Will had gone,
Seth looked about him, and seeing that no one but he and I
were present, said:—

"Rhys'll pray."

I understood the request at once, but did not know what to
do. I had thought that no one should pray with the sick but a
preacher. He re-iterated, with greater earnestness of look:—

"Rhys'll pray."

I could not refuse. I was glad by this time that Will had
gone away, fearing he might jeer at me for it afterwards. I fell
on my knees by the bedside, and prayed as best I could. I do
not now remember what were the words I used, but I know I
asked Jesus Christ to make Seth well again, after which I got
into a mist, and had to fall back upon the Lord's Prayer.
When asking Christ to restore my friend to health, I knew the
prayer came from the bottom of my heart. At this juncture I felt
Seth's thin light hand resting upon my head. He kept it there
while I was repeating the Paternoster. I waited a little to see
if he would take it away, but he did not. It got to weigh more
and more heavily upon me, and grew cold, cold, sending
a strange indescribable shiver through my very soul. I gently
removed the hand, and, trembling in every limb, rose to my feet.
Seth's eyes were wide open, and had in them a far-away look,
I thought. I spoke to him, but he made no reply; I called
him by name, but he was at too great a distance to hear.

Before me was but an empty tenement, clean and bright though the windows were. His harmless—I had almost said sinless—soul had taken flight, to use his own words, "far away, to the great chapel of Jesus Christ."

When I realised the fact that he was dead, I set up a great loud cry, and, next minute, his mother and the neighbour were by my side. I shall not try to describe the scene, although it was one I can never forget. It would be cruel to attempt a picture of the wild uncontrollable grief of parents who had strength neither of mind nor of religion to sustain them under so severe a trial. I hastened home with a heavy heart. It was a goodish distance from Seth's house to ours, and I was obliged to traverse it alone, Will Bryan having left some time before me. It was a bright moonlight night, the sky being cloudless, and the shining stars appearing sunk into immense distance. I fancied the moon to be gazing steadfastly at me, and the stars beckoning ceaselessly upwards. The more I looked at them, the harder they seemed to look at me. I asked myself had Seth gone past them yet, or was he only on his way thither? How long would it take him to get to heaven, and would he reach there before I reached home? together with a host of similar questions. It appears strange to me, by this time, that something should have got into my head that night that I was to become a preacher. Whence the thought came, or who sent it, I know not; but I date from that night my desire to become a preacher. Was it the hand of witling Seth upon my head at the moment he was hanging between both worlds that first consecrated me for the work? My sermons are sorry enough, so often, that many people would believe me if I said that such was the case.

But I am digressing. I had two or three fields to cross on my way home. My path, too, skirted the Hall park. Although fairly brave, considering I was but a stripling, I must confess I was not without my fears on that night. I hurried along, however, using every effort to keep my spirit up. When I got to the wood, I saw something in human shape sitting on the hedge, right by the side of the path I was to take. I started, and my heart began to beat so violently that I could fancy I not only felt, but heard its throbbings. It was late at night,

and it required as much nerve to retreat as to advance.
Summoning up all the courage I possessed, I advanced at a
rapid rate. On nearing the man, I found he had a gun in
his hand, and concluded that he was the game-keeper at the
Hall, whom I knew well. All my fears vanished on the instant.
The moon was by this time behind the wood, so that I could
not see things clearly. When within a few yards of the man, I
said, in a loud voice, "Good night, Mr. Jones." I was
answered in harsh, unpleasant tones.

"Wait a bit, Rhys Lewis! Don't walk quite so fast, for fear
you might drop across some of your relations."

I stood stock still, and saw it was not Mr. Jones, but some
one else, who carried an old-fashioned double-barrelled gun.

"Don't be afraid," the stranger went on, "I shan't shoot
you *now*, if you do as I tell you. Take a seat by the hedge
here, so that I may have a talk with you."

I tremblingly obeyed. I fancied I ought to know that voice;
but then the appearance of the man was wholly new to me.
When I had taken my seat in the manner ordered, the man laid
his gun to rest against the hedge, so close to me that I could
see the glitter of the yellow caps upon its nipples. Without
another word the man charged his pipe, and struck a match.
In the glare of the flame I instantly recognised that face, and
nearly fainted with terror at the sight. Confronting me were
the ugly, villainous features of the dirty, bad fellow, whom I
saw coming into our house late at night some years previously,
and whom I had dubbed "the Irishman." A considerable
change had taken place in him since then. For one thing,
he appeared sturdier by a good deal. He began to question
me, closely and authoritatively, concerning mother and Bob, and
especially about the owner of the Hall and his game-keepers. I
kept back nothing, fearing him so much that my clothes stuck to
my skin with cold sweat, and he seeming much diverted by my
fright. He kept me there a long time, some of the words he
let drop having the effect of opening my eyes to our family
history. I had had my doubts previously; but now I saw
clearly through the whole. The Irishman, for that was the
only name by which I knew him, was busily questioning
me, when, in the very midst of a sentence, he suddenly

paused. He snatched up his gun, and, taking his pipe from his mouth, paused to listen attentively. The silence was simply oppressive. Next minute he gave a vigorous pull at his pipe, as if fearing the fire would go out, and then took to listening attentively once more. I fancied I heard footsteps advancing quickly along the path by which I had come. The Irishman drew his hat down tightly over his head, and I heard, at no great distance off, a low signal whistle. Without saying a word, my strange companion jumped to his feet, cleared the hedge at a bound, and disappeared into the wood. Simultaneously I, like a frightened stag, was diminishing the distance between that spot and our house. A bullet would hardly have overtaken me. On reaching the highway, I stopped to take breath, and heard first one gun-shot and then another, followed by shouting and a disturbance. I proceeded quickly along, and almost directly met my brother Bob, to whom, briefly, I related what had occurred. He, on his part, warned me not to say a word to mother or anyone else on the subject, adding, that the time had now come when I ought to know that which had hitherto been kept from me, and that he would tell me all when we were in bed. He fulfilled his promise, and I his command, for, from that day to this, I have never mentioned a word to any living soul of what took place on that night near the Hall park.

Said I not appropriately that Seth's acquaintance had formed an epoch in my history? How much more, by the morrow, did I know about my family; and, let me hope, how much better a boy had I become!

CHAPTER XIV.

WILL BRYAN.

SETH's funeral was the first I ever was at, and such have been the changes introduced in connection with this ceremony during the last thirty years, that I have thought it might not be uninteresting to note a few facts in relation thereto. About that period the more enlightened Methodists of ———shire were teaching the people to abolish the silly custom of beer-drinking at burials. I was in Thomas Bartley's house on the eve of Seth's funeral, when Abel Hughes paid a visit to the mourning family. Abel endeavoured to draw some useful moral from the sad occasion, and it was evident that Thomas and Barbara Bartley were touched to the quick under his instruction. But directly Abel alluded to the practice of drinking beer at funerals, and expressed the hope that Seth's parents were not going to perpetuate it, Thomas raised his head, and, with a look of displeasure, remarked: "Abel Hughes, you don't think I am going to bury my son as if he were a dog, do you? No, there will be bread and cheese and beer for all who come, if my eyes are still open."

Abel seriously argued the point with him, but without avail.

"No, no, Abel Hughes," he declared, "even if Seth wasn't like other children, I aint going to bury him with a cup of tea" —wiping his eyes with his coat sleeve.

He was as good as his word. When Will Bryan and I went there, early on the morrow afternoon, we saw upon the table half a cheese, with a knife by its side, a loaf of white bread, a good-sized jug, full of beer, a number of new pipes, and a small plate containing tobacco. We were received by Thomas Bartley in person, whose first word to us was:—

"William, put something to your mouth; Rhys, put something to your mouth."

As for me, I did not feel anything the matter with my mouth, and I fancy Will felt no differently, for I noticed him staring at Thomas Bartley, who, finding we did not know what he meant, cut a chunk of bread and cheese, and filled a small glass of beer for each of us. I marvelled how Will Bryan could drink the stuff without pulling faces. I had great difficulty in swallowing my portion, of which the effects became speedily known to me. I felt myself, all at once, on wonderfully good terms with everybody. I fancied my hands had grown remarkably fine and large, and I had a great desire either to sleep or laugh, I could not tell clearly which. I knew that neither the one nor the other proceeding was proper at such a place, and, strongly exerting myself against the influence of the glass, refused to put anything more "to my mouth." Divers of our old neighbours,

who had arrived before us, were enjoying their pipes. Several
more came in after us, Thomas Bartley greeting every one
upon his entrance with the same words: "Put something to
your mouth," whereupon the new-arrival would walk straight
to the beer jug, pour out a glass, and cut himself a bit of bread
and cheese. Everyone kept his hat on, and each in turn spoke
of this, that, and the other thing, which had no sort of connection
with Seth's death. Nearly everybody smoked and expectorated
upon the floor, which was somewhat thickly strewn with white
sand. The jug was many times replenished. The man who
last helped himself placed the glass opposite him who sat on his
left, and turned the handle of the jug in the same direction.
When anyone forgot to do his duty within a reasonable space of
time, someone else, more impatient than his brethren, would cry:
" Whom does the handle point to?" which was a signal for the
man towards whom the handle pointed, either to drink up, or
turn the handle toward his neighbour. This business went
on for an hour and a half or two hours, until here and
there a member of the company had taken about as much as he
could comfortably hold, and had undergone a considerable
change of countenance. I remember, to this day, the tailor,
James Pulford, a little, talkative fellow, with a face that was
ordinarily as pale as death, but which was, on this afternoon, as
rosy as any farm labourer's I ever saw.

A few minutes before we turned out for the churchyard, two
men came in from the next room, with pewter vessels in their
hands, something like those now used for administering the
sacrament, only larger, and with handles ornamented with lemon
peel. One contained what was termed "mulled ale," but
which might have been more properly called "boiling ale;"
and the other "cold ale," both being highly spiced. Directly
these vessels made their appearance, every man took his hat off,
and in the midst of a silence like the grave's, the cup-bearers
went around, serving out both kinds of drink in exactly the same
manner, and with almost exactly the same seriousness, as we
administer the Lord's Supper. What it all meant I did not, and
do not, to this day, know. This ceremony gone through, all
put on their hats again, and resumed the conversation. Shortly
afterwards, David the Carpenter took a plate round, the men con-

tributing a shilling, and Will Bryan and I sixpence a-piece, that
being the customary proportion. I ought to have said that Abel
Hughes came in a few minutes before the time for "raising the
body," as it is called, and that when Thomas Bartley asked him
to " put something to his mouth," he declined—which greatly
offended Thomas Bartley. When the time came for starting, it
was found that not one of those who had come to the funeral
was accustomed to pray in public, with the exception of Abel
Hughes, but the refusal to " put something to his mouth," had
so annoyed Thomas Bartley that the latter would not ask his
services. I saw him speaking in the ear of David the Carpenter,
who was a very worldy-minded man. When the body was laid
upon the bier, every man dropped his hat over his ear, as if
listening to something the article had to say. The women from
the other apartment hurried to the windows, and looked
through, holding pocket handkerchiefs to their mouths; David
the Carpenter fell on his knees beside the bier, and rattled
through the Lord's Prayer at express speed, just for all the
world as if he were counting a score of sheep.

Then came the procession to the cemetery. Will Bryan and I
walked on either side of Thomas Bartley, I carrying the ever-
greens, and Will the gravel for the adornment of Seth's grave.
In Church, while Mr. Brown was galloping over the Burial
Service, I noticed that several of those present had fallen into a
deep sleep, among the rest being James Pulford, whose nose
was neatly disposed along his waistcoat. At the termination of
the service at the grave, David the Carpenter ascended a tomb-
stone, and, on behalf of the family, thanked the neighbours for
their kindness in coming to the funeral, adding that Thomas
and Barbara Bartley wished to express the hope that, at some
day not far distant, they would have the opportunity of returning a similar compliment to each one, and that the father of the
departed desired they should all meet at the Crown, now the
service was over. After the bedecking of the grave, those
present, Abel Hughes, Will Bryan and myself, excepted, made
straight for the Crown. Will would have gone too, but for fear
of a row at home. While we were in Church, a houseful of
women took tea with Barbara, my mother being one of the
invited. I do not know what went on at the Crown, but some

hours later I saw Thomas Bartley returning home between two neighbours, and although they were all pretty quiet over it, I fancied there was some disagreement between them as to which side of the road it was best they should walk on. Shortly afterwards, I heard James Pulford go by our house singing:—

"On Conway's banks, once on a time."

Were all this put into print, some people would doubtless wonder and disbelieve; but others, I know, would bear testimony to the accuracy of the description, and say that its fault is its brevity, and that it does not convey the whole truth. I have refrained from noting all the unseemly things which took place in connection with Seth's funeral. Of a mercy, what a reform there has taken place by this time. And there is yet room for more. If the beer has been banished, tea and coffee, beef and ham, have taken its place. When strangers from a distance attend a funeral, it may be proper, no doubt, to make provision for them. But what reason can be given for all the junketing that is now seen on such occasions among the neighbours. Some poor families will prepare a costly feast, and that simply for the sake of people who live close by. The maintenance of such a foolish custom is a cruel hardship towards the poor, and unseemly in the last degree, I should fancy.

Seth buried, there remained to me but one bosom friend only —Will Bryan; and the conviction constantly forced itself upon me that our acquaintance was not to continue long. Will had an open, kindly heart, and a lively, daring spirit; but, day by day, the consciousness strengthened in me that he was not a good boy. He spoke contemptuously of the strict rules of Communion; and it was but rarely he called people by their right names. He had a nickname for nearly everyone he knew. John Lloyd, as I have observed, he called "old Scraper;" Hugh Bellis, the deacon who wept during sermon, "old Waterworks;" Thomas Bowen, popular with the children, "old Trump;" Abel Hughes, who wore knee-breeches, and had thin legs, "old Onion." He had an "old" to every name. He never mentioned his parents save as "the gaffer yonder," and the "old pea-hen yonder." I have observed that truly did my mother say there was some serious defect in that lad's character who was in the habit of calling his father "gaffer," "governor," and the like. I do not deny but that this aptitude for finding descriptive names for people would have been a special talent in Will, had it been turned to right use. Some of these satirical designations have stuck to their owners to this day; but it would be ill were I or anyone else to specify them. I did not take any particular notice of this tendency in Will until on one occasion he referred to my mother as "the old Ten Commandments." This offended me greatly, and Will perceiving I did not like the name, never used it again. Thinking the matter over to-day, I cannot help seeing some appropriateness in the designation, for my mother was ever and always giving us commandments of some sort, and charging us to do this thing or that. When I reflect that my mother was a woman of some penetration, I rather wonder she should have permitted me to associate so much with Will Bryan. On second thoughts, however, I see nothing in the world to wonder at. I never, in my life, knew a lad who had such a knack of putting himself on good terms with everybody. His impudence, his handsome, cheery face, his bold, brave bearing, his musical voice, and smooth, witty tongue, were weapons which he used to some purpose always. He understood my mother to a nicety. I heard her, more than once say, when low-spirited, that a visit from Will would half cure her. I have seen her smile, and obliged to use a strong effort not to laugh outright, at some of those pleasantries of Will's for which, had I used them even in the self-same words, she would have boxed my ears. I know she often felt she put up with too much of this kind of thing in Will, and, as a salve to her conscience, she would give him bits of good advice in return. Let the following conversation serve as an illustration of many such:—

"Will, my son, you'll do a deal of good or of harm in this here world. I hope to goodness you'll get a little grace."

"There's plenty of it to be had, isn't there, Mary Lewis? But I never like to take more than my share of anything, you know."

"Don't talk lightly, Will; you can never get too much grace."

"So the gaffer yonder says, always; but it is'nt a good thing, you know, Mary Lewis, to be too greedy."

G

"And who's your ' gaffer,' pray ? "

"The old hand, you know—my father," replied Will.

"Will," said my mother, severely, "I charge you not to call your father ' gaffer ' and ' old hand' again. I never, in my life, knew good to come of children who called their father and mother ' him yonder ' and ' her yonder,' or ' the old hand yonder' and ' the old woman yonder.' Don't you let me hear you call your father by any such stupid names again, you mind, now."

"All right," said Will. "Next time I shall call him Hugh Bryan, Esquire, General Grocer and Provision Dealer, Baker to his Royal Highness the Old Scraper, and ——."

Before he could finish his story he had to bolt, mother after him, weapon in hand. For all his mischievousness mother was never angry with him. "He's a rough 'un, that boy," she would often say. "If he got grace, he'd make a capital preacher." A remark of this kind made me a little jealous. She never told me I would make a preacher, although that had become the chief desire of my life by this time, and I knew Will Bryan never intended to be one.

I do not think mother regarded Will as anything worse than a mischief-loving lad, until he began brushing up his hair from his forehead, or, as it was then called, "making a Q. P." When she saw a white parting upon Will's head, and signs that he oiled his hair, his fate was sealed for ever. It troubled me much to think my mother should take this innovation so seriously, because I thought Will looked splendidly in his " Q. P.," and I longed for permission to imitate him. I was quite tired of my mother's fashion of cutting my hair, which was to clap a large butter-basin upon my head, and shear around the edges until my head looked for all the world like a haycock newly thatched. I saw there was no hope of improvement upon this method; especially in the light of the following observations, made by my mother to Will Bryan, directly she saw his " Q. P.":—

"Will, my son, I used to think you a good lad, for all your foolishness. But I see the devil has found the weak spot in you, too."

" What's the matter now, Mary Lewis? I haven't killed anybody of late, have I ? " asked Will.

" No, I hope not," replied mother. " But then you ought to kill the old man."

" Whom do you mean, Mary Lewis? Is it the gaffer yonder? No, name of goodness; I shan't kill the old hand. What would become of me ? I should starve."

" No, Will, it is'nt your father I mean, but the old man who is in your heart."

" Old man in my heart! There is no old man in my heart, I'll take my oath."

" Yes, there is, Will, and you'll come to know it some day."

" But when did he get in there, Mary Lewis ? " asked Will. " He must be a very little 'un—less than Tom Thumb."

" He was in your heart before you were born, and he's bigger than the giant Goliath," replied mother. " And unless you take a smooth stone from the river of salvation, and sink it deep iu his forehead, he is sure to cut your head off with his sword."

" But how am I to drive a stone into his forehead, if he is in my heart ? " said Will. " And being there, how can he cut my head off with his sword ? "

" You know who I'm talking of, Will," said mother; " it is the old mau of sin, I mean."

" O ! now I understand you. Why don't you speak plain, Mary Lewis ? But isn't there sin in the hearts of all of us, according to the old—father yonder ? "

" There is, my son," said mother; " and it breaks out in your head, in the shape of that silly ' Q. P.' "

And, at this juncture, my mother attacked fluently and unsparingly, the evil habit of brushing the hair off the forehead. Will felt the rebuke, and walked almost haughtily away.

" Rhys," said my mother, after he had gone, " don't you have much truck with Will Bryan from this time out. Pride has taken possession of his heart. I'm surprised Hugh Bryan should permit such a thing. If Will were son of mine, I'd cut his hair in a jiffey, that I would. There he is, I know, looking at himself in the glass, every day, to feed his vanity. Thank Heaven, there never was a looking glass in our family till your brother Bob brought one here; and I could have wished in my heart that that had never crossed my door-step. Your grandmother used to say that people, by looking in the glass, saw the Evil One, and I can easily believe it. I don't know what'll come of the rising generation, unless there is a speedy revival."

And mother sighed from the bottom of her heart.

CHAPTER XV.

THE BEGINNING OF TROUBLES.

SAID my mother to me one day:—

"You are getting to be a big boy, Rhys, and, as things are, I can't afford to keep you running and romping about any longer. Your brother began work in the mine long before he was your age, and younger boys than you are earning their bit every day, I warrant me. But what you are fit for, I don't know, and can't think of. It is a hard case you should be carrying your head in the wind at this age, and your mother no better than a widow, if as good. You are not strong, that is plain enough, or it is to the colliery you should go, straight away; you are not scholar enough for a shop-keeper, and even if you were, I have no money to give you a start. How I could raise five or ten pounds to apprentice you, I don't know. Even if ten shillings were to get you into the best shop in the town, I couldn't tell where to turn my head to look for them. And yet, you must think of doing something for a livelihood. Your feet are nearly on the ground, and, like the dog, you wear the same suit Sundays and weekdays. If you earned only enough to keep yourself in clothes, it would be something. Food is so dear, and your brother's wages are so small, that as much as I can do is to make both ends meet, and scrape an occasional penny towards the cause. And you'd wonder greatly if you knew how much I am obliged to moither and scheme to keep things straight. As Thomas of Nant says :—

' It's a deal of skill gets Will to bed.'

If this strike they talk of in the work takes place, I really don't know what'll becomes of us. I only hope we'll have the means of living honestly, whatever happens. Up to now, thanks to the Great Ruler, we have been able to pay our way remarkably well, though obliged to live hard. But I never saw good come of keeping children too long without setting them to work; it only brings them up to mischief.

"I don't dispute but that I could persuade James Pulford, the tailor, to take you on. But he is an unmannerly, good-for-nothing man, who often gets drunk; and I fear your soul would not receive fair play, which is the main thing after all. I would rather see you a godly chimney sweep, than an ungodly clerk of the peace. Perhaps, you'd tell me, the children would be calling after you,

' Tailor, tailor tit,
Clogs on your stockingless feet.'

Well, let them. That would break no bones in you. You'd have a dry back and a trade at hand always. I'd rather see you a tailor than a farm-servant. The weather or some other thing stiffens and freezes the souls as well as the bodies of people of that sort, I'm thinking; and being always in the company of animals makes them very much like animals themselves. I never in my life saw a set so listless and with less of the man in them, as one of the brethren used to say. These farm-servants are somehow like slaves. They are too shy to raise their heads, save in the stable, or on the day of turning for the best. How I pitied them the night I was at Vaenol! It was cold and wet, and when the men, poor things, came in to supper, with not a dry rag about them, they went to that long table, you know of, near the window, far from the fire. There were some half a dozen of them, I should fancy; and they came into the house softly, and sat on the benches each side of the table, with their heads hung down, and their eyes looking up under their brows, just as if they had been thieving all day instead of toiling hard in muck and moisture. And not one of them spoke a word. All I heard was the sound they made in eating pottage, and even that finished in a crack. For about a quarter of a minute or so they watched, from under their brows, the eye of the husbandman, and when he gave the signal, there came a bit of a noise of moving feet and benches, when out the poor wretches went in a row. I pitied them from my heart. They did not look like men, somehow. I reflected at the time that two of them were members of the same church as Mr. Williams their master, one of the two, Aaron Parry, being an extraordinary man in prayer. I was very sorry to see such a distance kept between master and man. I'll never believe the Saviour likes a thing of that kind.

"But this is what I was going to say:—I wouldn't for the world see you become a farm-servant. I almost begin to think your brother Bob was right, and that a little learning always came in handy, only not too much of it. If you'd had a bit more schooling, I shouldn't mind a feather asking old Abel to take you into his shop. He wouldn't, surely, after all our acquaintance, have refused. But I may as well say no more about that. Thomas Bowen told me, coming from Communion, it was high time you were taken into full membership, and I should like to see you coming forward, if you have properly considered the matter. You have mastered the chapter from the *Preceptor*, I know, and have learned, a long time since, those portions of the Gospels which give an account of the ordinance of the Lord's Supper. But it is necessary, my son, you should pray that your mind be bent in the right direction, lest you be found unworthy. I wish from my heart to see you apprenticed to the heavenly calling before you are apprenticed to a wordly one.

> ' 'Tis better youth the yoke should wear,
> Than worlds of empty pleasure share.' "

She said a great many things in addition; indeed mother was quite capable of going on in this strain all day long. It was plain that the time had come when I must think of earning my bread. I was older in the head, and knew more of mother's affairs and troubles than she suspected. My heart burned with a desire to help her. We all three depended entirely upon Bob's earnings, but these, hard though he worked, were barely enough to keep him in proper food and clothing. The coal market was pretty brisk, but a swarm of officials and overseers—greedy, rapacious strangers—pocketed, ate and drank up all the profits of the Red Fields Colliery, while the poor workmen and their families were half-starved. Bob, who was one of the oppressed, had for some time past been chafing under the infliction, and it was obvious that his righteous indignation, long pent-up, would, one day, burst its bounds. I learned from some of the colliers' children that Bob was a person of considerable influence with his fellow-workmen; that he had taken the chair at a meeting, held a short time previously, to consider the advisability of asking for an advance of wages, and that he had made a capital speech. I felt proud of him, and not without cause, for he had taken great pains with me. Never did he tire of guiding me in my studies, and I am more indebted to him than to any man living for the direction my life has taken. True, after his excommunication, he never spoke to me of religion or on religious subjects, unless I first spoke to him. But whatever other knowledge he could impart to me, he, to the best of his ability, did. He made me promise solemnly, more than once, that I would never become a collier, even if I was obliged to go out to beg. Likely enough it was the insufferable tyranny and arrogance he himself had experienced which made him ask this of me. But he need not have been so insistent; I never had the slightest inclination to go to "the work." Bob's daily complaints of the hard labour and the oppression had created an unconquerable disgust in me towards employment in the coal-mine.

Besides this, I was secretly cherishing the desire to become a preacher, and I fancied it must be a long way from the pit's bottom to the pulpit. The notion might have been a foolish one, but I thought it was easier climbing the pulpit from any place than from a coal-pit. Not a living soul knew my predilection, and I have no fear now that anyone will get to know. I have completely failed to explain to myself, or find out, the moving cause of my wish to become a preacher. I should have been glad to hear the experiences of others, if there are any, who have been similarly situated. I admit that the motive was not the right one, namely, the desire to do good, and the conversion of sinners from the error of their ways; for that, at the period of which I am speaking, had not yet entered my mind. I am strongly inclined to believe it was some sort of admiration of the order that possessed me, unless it was something worse, namely, a proud ambition. I remember picturing myself a great, portly, pulpit-filling personage (which I never have been), preaching with a zest, with people listening for very life, talking about me, and praising me, when the sermon was over. I would be doing my history an injustice if I were to say that I knew nothing of religious impressions. After all the trouble mother had taken with me, it would have been a miracle almost had I remained unimpressed. I was cognisant, long before this time, of serious moments, of the fear of sinning against God, and dying the death of the wicked. But I cannot, in any way, account for the irrepressible desire I felt, and that whilst I was yet a mere lad, to become a preacher. I am sorry, even to this day, that I did not confide to mother what was lurking in my heart, not only because she would have given every welcome and encouragement to the desire, but also because I feel that I deprived her of the greatest joy and pleasure I could have extended to her in her bitter troubles. I know I could not possibly have better filled her cup of happiness than by disclosing my determination to, one day, become a preacher. But I kept it all locked up in my own breast. I am not flattering myself, nor relating any but a simple fact, when I say that I was, at that time, more thoughtful than my associates; and although touched to the quick by Will Bryan's ridicule, when he called me "the holy one," I was conscious of a hidden purpose which he could neither understand nor in the least sympathise with. I took the greatest interest in every preacher, and never tired of talking about the order to any one who would talk to me.

By constant application, and with Bob's help, I had become a better scholar than mother took me to be. I could read and write, both Welsh and English, tolerably well. Induced by John Joseph, at the Children's Meeting, I had, for some time, been in the habit of taking down the text on Sundays, with as many as I could of the heads of sermon. I remember being

very angry with some preachers because they did not divide
their texts, and very pleased with William Hughes of Abercwmnant, because his heads of sermon were pretty much alike,
whatever text he took. They were usually three in number,
and ran somewhat as follows : —

I. The object noted.
II. The act attributed.
III. The duty enjoined.

I often foresaw and wrote out these divisions during his excrdium,
and before he had named them. The old preacher had one
habit for which I often wondered he had not been called to
account. Towards the end of his sermon he always said, "One
other word before I finish." He would speak a hundred words
or more. He would next say, "One word again, before I leave
you," and go on for five or ten minutes. A third time he would
say, "One other word before I take my departure," and we were
sure of a long speech after that. I thought it strange that he,
a preacher, should not be called to account for telling stories.
Will Bryan would often make such conduct his excuse for saying that which was not true. John Joseph used to praise me
for being able to repeat the heads of sermon—which pleased
me greatly. About this time John established a class for
teaching young men the elements of music and grammar,
which speedily grew into one for competitive recitations, essay-
writing, and religious controversy. It had many members, but
I am afraid to name them, lest I should be obliged to go into
their histories. Will Bryan was a member, but it was not often
he took part in our public gatherings. His favourite business
was to poke fun at our mistakes and shortcomings—a business
he pushed to an extent which made him odious to the majority
of the young men, who resolved, if they could do so anyhow, to
get rid of him. Will was the only member who brushed his
hair away from his forehead; and at a properly-convened
meeting a resolution was passed that no one should be a member
of that Society who was found guilty of "making a Q. P."
Will was consequently expelled. He cared nothing for that.
To avenge his disgrace, he nicknamed us "The Society of Flat-
hairs;" and, like the rest of his nicknames, this one stuck to us

as long as we were in existence. Our minds received impressions which were never obliterated, and there was created in us a taste for things religious, which we could never be too thankful for, by these meetings.

Shortly after Will's expulsion from the society, his name and mine were brought before Communion as candidates for full membership. Our applications were submitted by Thomas Bowen, the preacher, who was at all times zealous in behalf of the youth of the church, and particularly careful they should not be left too long out of full membership. He was constantly urgii.g parents to press home the matter to their children's minds, and duly to prepare them for such an event. On the other hand, Abel Hughes would speak of the circumspection necessary in, and the danger of, the reception into full membership of those who were not of ripe knowledge and experience. Preacher and deacon being thus at opposite extremes, occasionally squabbled over the point. Thomas Bowen had long been talking of my coming forward, while Abel Hughes advised they should take time and go slow. In the end Thomas Bowen conquered, and so one night we were called up to the bench in the centre of the chapel, for examination. I and others of the same age were anxious to be admitted, but Will Bryan would have preferred being left alone. Doubtless he feared the examination, for he had taken but little interest in religious questions, although in natural ability he was far above us all. If I remember rightly, we were six in number, and I sat at one end of the bench, while Will Bryan, unconcerned as usual, sat at the other. Abel Hughes got up and began the examination with me. He was rather hard on me, but I pulled through better than I expected. I knew from Thomas Bowen's voice and manner that I was answering satisfactorily, for he smiled, threw his legs about, one over the other, nodded to Hugh Bellis, and muttered, " Ho! " " H'm! " after each reply, as if he meant to say, " Not so bad, really." Abel proceeded with the two lads next me, with the same satisfactory result. He then sat down, and invited Thomas Bowen to take the remaining three. Thomas Bowen got up, thrust both hands into his trousers' pocket, assumed a satisfied look, and, addressing the deacon, said, " Well, Abel Hughes, have you been pleased? Tell me, was I not right, in thinking the boys were quite fit to be received? Have I not said so for months? But we will proceed."

And he did proceed, with the fourth youth and the fifth. He did not, I thought, put such difficult questions as Abel Hughes had done, and the answers came quite easily. After an answer he considered rather a good one, he would turn to Abel with a significant look, as much as to say, "What do you think of that, Abel? Will it do?" Presently it came to Will Bryan's turn. Said Thomas to him, "William, my son, you're a little older than the rest of the boys, and ought, in my opinion, to have been admitted long ago; but there are people here who believe in taking time. I will not make my questions hard for you, although I know, were I to do so, you could answer them well enough. Will you tell me, William, my boy, how many offices appertain unto the Lord Jesus in his character as a Mediator?"

"Three," replied Will.

"Hah!" ejaculated Thomas. "'Three!' Do you hear, Abel Hughes? Three! Had Dr. Owen himself been here, he couldn't have answered better. These boys know a great deal more than you think, Abel Hughes. The Children's Meeting, and that other one, have not been held in vain, you see. The boys have listened and observed more than we imagine, I assure you. I have always said this. Yes sure, 'Three.' Well, William, my son, will you name them?"

"Father, Son, and Holy Ghost," said Will.

A titter went through the chapel. Thomas Bowen looked as if some one had hit him with a hammer over the back of the neck. He sat down, in shame and chagrin, and fixed his gaze upon his boot-tips, uttering not a word save "H'm!"

"Go on, go on, Thomas Bowen," said Abel, eagerly.

Thomas pretended not to hear him.

I do not know whether it was mischief or ignorance that prompted Will to answer as he did, because he was wag enough and careless enough for the one thing or the other. Abel Hughes evidently believing it was not possible Will could be so ignorant as the answer implied, spoke sharply to him, and by way

of punishment, submitted to the church the proposition that
we five should be received into full membership, leaving Will
out until his knowledge and experience had matured. It was
unanimously carried.

Will did not care a jot for what had happened. Directly we
left the meeting he laughed heartily, and declared he did not
want to become a full member, adding, "It was a good job the
old hand and the old pea-hen weren't in Communion to-night."
I felt now, more than ever, there was some serious defect in Will's
character; and yet I loved him greatly. Hardly were we out
of chapel before he took hold of my arm, saying, "Let us go to
the Colliers' Meeting." I did not as much as know that
such a meeting was to be held, but Will somehow knew of
every public gathering that took place. Seeing no harm in
going, I went with him. It was an open air meeting. The
night was a lovely one in summer. On approaching, I heard a
great noise, and shouts of "Hear, hear," and "Hooray!"
There were many hundreds present. I cannot express my
astonishment when I found it was my brother who was addressing the crowd. My heart gave a jump. I believed everything
he said to be perfect truth, for it never entered into my head he
could be mistaken. Will and I pushed to the front, Will
shouting "Hear, hear!" before he could catch a word of what
was spoken. Never shall I forget my brother's appearance.
He stood upon a high mound, with a number of the principal
colliers at the Red Fields Pit about him, and a tremendous
crowd below. He held his hat in his left hand, and had his
right extended. His eyes glowed like lamps in water, his lips
trembled, his face was deathly white, and formed as strong a
contrast to his beard and hair as if it had been a snowball set in
soot. I remember wondering why Bob's face was so pale, while
preachers' faces were so red, when speaking. I know, from his
appearance, that every joint, bone, and sinew of him were
agitated right through, and I thought to myself what a splendid
preacher he would have made, if he had not been expelled
Communion for that trifling fault of his. I had never heard him
speak in public previously, and wondered where he got all those
words which dropped so fluently from his lips. His audience
laughed, groaned, vociferated. They were entirely in his hand.

I think I could reproduce all I heard of his address; but to what purpose? Well would it have been for him had he never said a word that night. His subject was the injustice and hardship suffered by the workmen, by reason of the arrogance and incapacity of the officials. He proved, to the satisfaction of those who heard him, that the "Lankies" knew nothing of Welsh mining operations, that they oppressed the men, and ruined the masters by their conduct. At the conclusion of the speech there were loud cheers, in the midst of which I ran home to tell my mother what I had seen, and what a capital speaker Bob was.

Mother sat before the fire, pleating her apron. On my entrance, she looked up at me with a pleased expression, and complimented me on the way I had passed my examination. I, on my part, hastened to tell her all about Bob—what a splendid orator he was—how the people had shouted their applause, and so forth. Instead of rejoicing at the news, as I expected her to do, her face assumed a serious look, which was wholly inexplicable to me.

"Well, well, she said, with a heavy sigh, "the sweet is never without the bitter. Something tells me that trouble will come of this. The day of trial is at hand. Oh! for grace to say nothing rash!" And she fell into a deep study, in the course of which she kept on pleating her apron and looking steadfastly into the fire.

I was sorry now I had told her the story, although I could not comprehend why it should have vexed her to such an extent. I went to bed thoroughly dispirited, chiefly because I did not understand the reason of my mother's sadness. The night was far advanced when Bob returned, and although I could not, from my bed, make out what was said, I heard hot words between him and mother, in the sound of whose voices I fell off to sleep.

How true were my mother's fears! While the most reckless and extravagant of sinners were reposing peacefully on down that night, in the midst of plenty and luxury, with a whole continent between the wolf and their doors, and whilst I was sleeping heedlessly on my bed of straw, the trouble my mother had prophesied was already stalking to and fro before our cabin door, ready to seek admission, yea, even though he knew that inside there was at least one who feared her God above many. And that God knows she never spent six hours of her waking life without sending Him a prayer!

CHAPTER XVI.

THE DAY OF TRIAL.

IT is with melancholy recollections I pen this chapter; and were it possible to give a faithful history of my life, leaving out all mention of what is narrated herein, I would do so. But I cannot. Now, in cold blood, and at an age better competent to form an opinion, it is possible I do not entertain the same notion of the occurrences I am going to relate that I did at the time they took place. However, it is in their original aspect I must try to describe them.

Red Fields was one of the principal works of the neighbourhood in which I was brought up, and gave employment—reckoning the boys—to some hundreds of people. If I remember rightly, the owners were English to a man. At one time "all things under the earth" were managed by a simple, honest Welshman, named Abraham Jones, a deacon with the Congregationalists. He was a cool, strong-minded man, possessing great influence with those under him. Whatever dispute arose amongst them, it only wanted Abraham Jones to arbitrate, and everything was settled at once. The secret of his influence lay in his special aptitude for perceiving the location of the mischief, and the entire confidence everybody had in his honesty and his religious character. He proved himself, at all times, a sincere friend of the workman, knowing well what it was to have been a workman himself. With him it was a matter of conscience to keep his eyes open to the welfare of the employers who paid him his salary; but that did not prevent him from bearing constantly in mind the comfort and the safety of the men whom he saw every day toiling and sweating in the midst of danger. He was considered one of the most expert practical colliers in the country, and, during his management, everything went on smoothly and without any hitch or disturbance worth the mention.

He laboured under one great disadvantage in his connection with his chiefs: his English was so imperfect that, in consultation with them, it appeared at times as if he were not perfectly straightforward in his story. And he vexed himself greatly on that account. He had lately got to notice that one or two of the directors deligted in putting him through a course of minutest interrogatory with reference to the work; and although he had nothing to fear in that direction, the difficulty he felt in explaining himself often placed him, he thought, in a rather unpleasant position. So sorely tortured had he been by these cross-examinations that he felt neither disappointed nor grieved when, one day, at a meeting of directors, he was told it was best he should leave, they having found an Englishman likely to do the duties better, and also to be able to give a completer account of the state of the colliery. The words appeared to remove a great burden from his mind. In his jerky way he blurted out, with a breast which swelled a little as he spoke :—" Gentlemen, I am very pleased indeed to hear what you say. If he whom you speak of can keep the work going, as smoothly and peaceably, in the interests both of masters and men for six months, as I have done for six years, then indeed he must be a very clever man." He thereupon took up his hat, made a polite bow, and went out. He often used to say afterwards that he believed he got help from above to speak English when taking leave of his employers. On his return to work, and communicating the news to the men, there were mourning and tribulation not a little. Here and there a collier would have given vent to his feelings in language which was not altogether parliamentary. But in Abraham Jones's presence all such words had to be gulped back again after they had ascended to the lips, the effort to do so bringing tears to the eyes, which, trickling down the checks, left a clean white streak on each black face, to show how pure was the feeling which had produced them. It was hinted and pretty plainly spoken by the men that it was no want of ability or of faithful service, on Abraham Jones's part, which caused the directors to invite him to resign, but the anxiety of some of them to find a place for a hard-up friend. Whether right or wrong, this belief prejudiced the men against the new manager long before they set eyes on him. And his appearance and acquaintance, so far from lessening, deepened their dislike towards Mr. Strangle, for that was the gentleman's name. He was a middle-aged personage, fat-paunched and blustering, who carried in his own person all the roughness, the slovenliness and ignorance of his tribe at Wigan. His speech was coarse and uncouth, even the uneducated smiling to hear him say "Ah" for "yes," and "mun" for "must." His speech, however, was but a trifling drawback compared to his insufferable self-importance and inconsiderate behaviour towards everybody about him. He was nicknamed "Bulldog," on the very first day he came to work, and really, on recalling his squab nose and wide jaw, I fancy that, had he chosen to claim it, no one would be found to deny his relationship with the species, except, perhaps, on the ground of his pretensions. If he were taken at his own word, he knew everything knowable, and never in his life made a mistake. To be brief, Mr. Strangle was a whole colliery in himself—main coal, haulier, bye-man, cutter, shelterer, shaft, chimney-stack, engine-house, boiler and all, especially the last. But Bob would say—and, of course, I believed everything he said must be right—that Abraham Jones's old flannel jacket was much more capable of managing the Red Fields works than was Mr. Strangle. The antagonism of the men was rivalled only by his own hatred of Wales and the Welsh. He delighted in snubbing the people, and in doing everything connected with the colliery in a fashion directly contrary to Abraham Jones's. The result was that he speedily drew the work about his ears, as the saying goes, and some hundreds of pounds worth of fresh timber had to be used to keep the place together. To sum up, because it would take me a long time to tell the whole story, the state of things got, at last, to be so bad that the tradesmen of the town, and the neighbourhood generally, went in daily fear of a strike at the Red Fields Colliery.

This was the state of affairs when that Colliers' Meeting was held, which I referred to in the previous chapter, and at which my brother Bob had made, what I considered to be, such a capital speech. Next day, whilst mother and a neighbour were conversing about the meeting, I got to know why she had been so much moved by my account of Bob's public utterances. It was from a fear that Bob would get himself into trouble. It was worth suffering a little hardship, she said, for the sake of peace. On the other hand, the neighbour thought it high time someone should speak up—the men's earnings were so small that it was impossible to maintain a family upon them. She had, however, warned her husband not to say a word, nor to make himself, in any way, conspicuous in the agitation. Mother made answer something to this effect:—

"So, Margaret Peters, you are anxious our Bob and others should do all the fighting, while your husband, Humphrey, and everybody belonging to you, like Dan of old, 'remain in ships,' and come in for a share of the spoil when the battle is ended. There is many a Dan in our days, as Mr. Davies of Nerquis, used to say."

Margaret did not know enough Scripture to understand the comparison, but she could see right well it contained a blow aimed at her. so she turned the conversation to something else.

How speedily were my mother's fears verified! When Bob came home from work that night he appeared unusually serious and thoughtful. After he had washed and taken food, my mother said to him, "Bob, I know by your looks you have some bad news. Have you had notice?"

"Yes," replied Bob. "Morris Hughes, James Williams, John Powell and myself, are to leave the work next Saturday."

"Well, and what are we to do now?" asked mother.

"Do our duty, mother, and trust in Providence," said Bob.

"Yes, my boy; but do you consider that you have done your duty? I gave you many warnings, didn't I, not to take so prominent a part in this business. [Mother's observation as to "Dan in ships" recurred to me.] I know very well you workmen have cause to complain, and that it is a shame for a mere Saxon to come around the country and take the place of a pious man like Abraham Jones, with whom there never was any bother. You are but young, however; and why did'nt

II

you let some one like Edward Morgan go talking and messing
in this matter—a man who has a house of his own, and a pig?
It wouldn't have made much odds to Edward if he got notice.
But I may just as well shut up now. It is too late to lock the
stable door after the horse has been stolen. The question is,
what'll become of us?"

"Mother," replied Bob earnestly, "it was not thus you
taught me. 'Do your duty, and leave the consequences to God,'
was one of your first lessons, and I intend to act upon it as long
as I have breath, not only because it was from you I learned
it, but also because I believe it to be a sound one. The notice is
no more than I expected. The few must suffer before good
can come to the many, and if I and others are made scapegoats
for the three hundred who work at Red Fields, if we are the
means of bringing about their liberty and their benefit, all well
and good. I have never spoken a single word beyond what
everybody in the work believes and feels to be true, although
others have shrunk from uttering it in public. As I have said,
someone must suffer for the many; it is the great principle of
God's government. Either the comfort or the life of one animal
is sacrificed continually to keep other animals alive. As Caiaphas
said, 'It is expedient that one man should die for the people, and
that the whole nation perish not.' The principle of the Sacrifice
on the Cross is practised daily on a small scale, and —— "

"Stop your nonsense," commanded mother sharply. "I
won't listen to you talking in such a fashion. Has your head
gone wrong, or what? Do you wish to compare the Death on
the Cross with your notice to leave the work, or anything else
on this blessed earth? Do you mean to tell me there is anything in that to resemble the sufferings of the Saviour? If you
do, you'd better pack off to the 'Sylum as soon as you can."

"Gently, mother," said Bob. "I need not tell you, who are
so well acquainted with the Acts of the Apostles, that I am not
the first who has been accused of madness on account of his
zeal. To allay your fears on this head, understand that
I mean to compare nothing to the Sacrifice on the Cross,
either for magnitude or intent, but solely for principle. If
there is no comparison between the finite and the infinite, there
is an analogy, and it is of the analogy I am speaking."

"Come, come," replied mother, "don't you go throwing your big words at me. Keep within the Scripture, and I'll follow you wherever you like; but none of your fine words, if you please. I'm sure 'analogy' is not a Bible word, and, as far as I remember, it is not in Mr. Charles's *Preceptor*, either."

"I know, mother," observed Bob, "that you have not read Butler's *Analogy* —— "

"Butler?" interrupted mother. "Don't talk of your butler to me! A pagan like him, who never goes to any place of worship but the Church, and who doesn't know anything but how to carry wine to his master. What do you mean by reading the butler?"

This was too much for Bob, who laughed outright, which annoyed my mother so much that he hastened to explain.

"It was not the Hall butler," he said, "but Bishop Butler I was thinking of, a great and good man. And this is what I was about to say, had you let me alone—a sacrifice is a covenant of life, blessing, and profit. Before it was possible for sinners to find life, it was necessary that the Son of God should sacrifice himself. ['There, now you're talking sense,' muttered mother to herself.] Before that life could be brought to men it was necessary that the apostles and a host of other of the world's best men, should suffer much, even to the laying down of their lives. And something of the same kind still takes place every day, only with this difference—that the least are sacrificed for the sake of the greatest. The cow, the sheep, the pig, and a host of other creatures, lose their lives so that you and I may preserve ours. And so in every state of being of which we have any knowledge. The like rule prevails in society. In fighting for the right, and against oppression, some of the heroes in the strife are sure of being trampled under foot and hurt by the tyrant, aye, even when he is in retreat. Some one must fight the battle of the Red Fields workmen before they are rid of their tyranny, and if I and my associates fall while sounding the battle-trumpet, let it be so; the call to arms has gone forth, we have justice on our side, and others, even though we do not, will reap the rich fruits of the victory which is bound to follow. With a little wisdom and determination, I do not doubt but that things will wear another face at Red Fields before

many months are over. All I fear is that the men will use un-
lawful means to attain their object. Many of them are utterly
devoid of judgment, and are governed entirely by their hasty
tempers. These, unless they have a wise man to lead them,
will do more harm to the cause than can easily be imagined.
But perhaps they will behave better than I anticipate."

Either my mother paid no heed to what he had said, or was
unable to answer Bob.

"Pray more, and talk less, my son," was the only remark
she made in reply.

The notice given my brother and the other men named excited
a deal of adverse comment at the colliery and neighbourhood,
and the following Saturday was looked forward to with the
most serious concern. Some feared a disturbance amongst the
workmen if the notice were allowed to take effect; others
fancied the masters had merely adopted a ruse in order to
frighten the men into silence, and that Mr. Strangle would
never dare to turn away the best and steadiest hands in the
colliery, unless he wanted to get himself into hot water.

Saturday came, and Will Bryan, I, and other youths, went to
the pit's bank about the time the men were expected to come
up, in order to see what would happen. Presently a couple of
police officers came there, seemingly on the same errand. They
were English, both. Almost directly afterwards, the workmen
began to ascend, a cage-load at a time, each contingent making
straight towards the office for their pay; only, instead of going
off home, as usual, after receiving their money, they settled down
upon their heels, in scattered groups, all over the bank.
Whether it was from accident or design, I know not, but Bob
and his associates under notice formed the last load. No sooner
did they make their appearance above the pit's mouth, with
picks tied up together, than, like a great goblin-host, the men
upon the bank sprang to their feet. Black face and ugly attire
notwithstanding, many were the warm and honest hearts in the
crowd, through which there ran a murmur. Bob and his companions went to the office, their coming out being awaited in anxious
silence. They had not to wait long. Wholly unconcerned,
apparently, the friends hoisted their picks upon their shoulders,
a sure sign that their notice had been insisted on. They were

immediately surrounded by their fellow-workmen, each inquiring of the other whether they had been paid off. Morris Hughes desired Bob to speak. He did so as follows—and I, who yield to no man living in correctly relating what I myself have heard (for if I am vain of anything, it is of my memory), bear most solemn witness that he never said a single word beyond those which I now reproduce:—

"My dear fellow-workmen," Bob began. "I and my associates have been paid off. We bid a last farewell to Red Fields, and turn our faces elsewhere to look for employment."

Before he could say any more some of the men began execrating the management, whereupon the two police officers interposed, with a request that they should go off quietly home. Both were unceremoniously thrust aside, and Bob was asked, with a shout, to go on. He accordingly proceeded:—

"We leave you with an easy conscience. We have done nothing wrong, and we trust no one will condemn us for publicly repeating the conviction we held in private, that we were unfairly and unjustly treated. You must now fight for your rights without help from us; but wherever we go to, your welfare and your success will always lie near to our hearts. I am not unconscious of the fact that there are before me scores of men older, wiser, and more experienced, than I; but permit me to give you a word of advice. Take care not to do anything of which you may be ashamed hereafter. Be led by the wisest of your number, and, in battling for your rights, do so as men endowed with reason, who are to be called to account hereafter for all your actions. I think, and my friends here agree with me, that your best plan will be to lay your complaints before the directors in person. In Abraham Jones's time, if there was anything for which we wanted a remedy, all we had to do was to place the matter before him, and it would be sure of careful consideration. But I fear it would be useless for you to appeal to Mr. Strangle, because ——"

Unfortunately, while Mr. Strangle's name was on Bob's lips, that individual came out of the office, and looked frowningly at the crowd. No sooner did he make his appearance than scores of throats opened out upon him, like a pack of hounds in full cry. A fierce rush was made towards him, and he was carried along the road leading to the railway station like a straw before the whirlwind. The two officers, with incredible pluck, endeavoured to protect and to rescue him from the clutches of the infuriated colliers; and so did Bob and others. But no sooner was he liberated from one swarm than another was down upon him. One of the peace officers, thinking—honestly so, no doubt—that Bob was the ringleader, drew his staff and struck him over the temple, felling him to the ground. Better had the blow never been given, for next moment both officers were stretched senseless by the roadside and Mr. Strangle was being hurried away with a speed which must have been exceedingly uncomfortable for so corpulent a man. I thought Bob had been killed, for he lay, to all appearance, quite dead upon the ground, with no one but Morris Hughes and myself to look after him. I cannot describe either my grief on thinking him dead, or my joy when, a few minutes later, he came to himself, and sprang to his feet.

"Morris!" he cried. "All our efforts have been in vain. These madmen have ruined the cause. We must prevent this, if it be not too late."

Both, followed by myself, hurried after the crowd. The effects of the blow were such that it was with difficulty Bob could keep up the pace, and when he took hold of Morris Hughes's arm—the latter being a young, powerful fellow—I saw his legs were giving way under him. Nearing the station we found that the crowd had doubled in numbers.

"Thank Heaven," cried Bob, "the train has not yet come in, and we may still be in time to stop the fools from sending Mr. Strangle away."

We put a best foot foremost, but we were within barely three hundred yards of the platform when we heard the workmen give a loud cheer.

"Too late!" said Morris Hughes, "if it's any odds."

"Odds?" cried Bob, slackening his pace. "I should rather think it was. We shall lose the sympathy of the country, we shall be looked upon as savages, some of these lunatics will be sent to prison, and punished for their folly. Everything is now spoiled, and I'm sorry from my heart I ever meddled with the business." And he burst out crying like a child.

The steam-engine whistled, loud and shrill, and the air was rent with demoniac shouts. The disorderly rabble next made a rush for the town. When they came to the spot where Morris Hughes and Bob were, they wanted, at any cost, to take my brother upon their shoulders and exhibit him as their hero. But Morris's strong arm restrained them.

"My friend can't stand it," he declared. "But if you choose to listen, it may be that he has a word to say to you."

The mob having signified its readiness, Bob ascended to the top of a hedge, and, leaning upon Morris Hughes's broad back for support, said:—

"My friends, ever since the beginning of this agitation for the advancement of your wages and the better governance of the Red Fields pit, I have taken a public part in it, and done my best to bring about an improvement in your circumstances. You know as well as I do that two or three of us, had we chosen to truckle to the masters, might have made ourselves a comfortable nest here. But then, you would not have been an atom the better off. After what has just taken place, I must tell you, even at the risk of being treated as you have treated Mr. Strangle, that I am ashamed of ever having had anything to do with you."

Bob was too much overcome to say any more, and the crowd separated, some swearing, others grumbling, others silent and thoughtful. It is but fair to state that there were amongst the unruly multitude who whisked Mr. Strangle off to the station and bought a ticket for him, scores of workmen who disapproved of the foolish act, but who were powerless to prevent it. Before my brother and I could reach home, mother had been informed of the whole affair, with additions, and we found her waiting us in deep agitation. However, she was mollified a good deal when Bob assured her that he had done his best to prevent Mr. Strangle's compulsory departure. At the same time, I could not fail to note signs of fear and uneasiness on the faces of both. Bob, who did not leave the house that night, was visited by three of the friends who had been paid off like himself, who spent some hours in discussing with him the probable consequence of the day's foolhardiness. Though mother said nothing, I could see that she had a presentiment of some coming evil. Bob's companion's having left, but little talk took place in our house that night. My brother pretended to read, but I noticed he did not turn the leaves of his book, and knew very well he did not give a thought to anything it contained.

Late at night, as we were about to retire, we heard footsteps approaching the house. Next minute a knock came to the door, and, before we had time to open, two officers of police came in. Mother's face grew pale, and I began to cry my loudest. Bob ordered me to desist, but it was with difficulty I could master my feelings. Bob, perfectly self-possessed, invited the officers to take a seat, which they did. Although never much in love with either of them, I must admit that they were a couple of very civil men, and that both considered their duty that night an unpleasant one. I was glad they were Welsh, because mother, in that case, could understand all they said.

"I think," observed Bob quietly, "that I know your errand."

"Well," said Sergeant Williams, looking towards my mother, "it is a disagreeable errand enough, Robert Lewis, we must say. But I hope all will come off right on Monday. Mrs. Lewis," he went on, handing Bob the warrant to read, in order to spare my mother's feelings, "don't be frightened, it is only a matter of form. We must do our duty, you know, and, as I have said, I hope everything will turn out right on Monday."

Mother said nothing, but the twitching of her mouth, and the lump in her throat, showed clearly the state of her feelings. Bob drew his boots on leisurely, and with the parting word, "Mother you know where to turn; my conscience is at ease," walked away with the officers. They had hardly gone twenty yards from the house, when I heard high words and a struggle. Despite my mother's efforts to restrain me, I ran out, and saw a desperate encounter going on between the officers and two strange men. One, a tall powerful fellow, knocked the constables about unmercifully. The other was but of middling size, but a perfect master of the work he had on hand. I had no difficulty in recognising the latter. It was the man who stopped me on my way home the night Seth died, and whom I had christened "the Irishman." I could not tell who the other was, but I thought he resembled Bob in build and gait, only he was older and stronger. Their intention, as far as I could make out, was to give Bob a chance of escape, but when they saw he did not avail himself of it, but, on the contrary, assisted the officers, both took to their heels. On my return to the house, and apprising mother of what I had seen, she got up and locked the door.

Neither of us went to bed. Much as I tried to repress my feelings, for mother's sake, and much as she tried to hide her trouble for mine, we were both repeatedly overcome by fits of crying in the course of the night. The morning broke—a lovely Sabbath morning. I saw the people, as they went by to their different places of worship, eyeing our cottage askance. Mother and I never once crossed the threshold, and I heard her repeatedly murmur something about "The day of Tribulation!" We ate but little. The day seemed as long as a week. Mother opened our big old Bible dozens of times, but, as soon as she began to read, her eyes overflowed, and she would fix them abstractedly in one long gaze on the same spot. I saw the people going home from morning service, but no one called. I saw them again going to Sunday School, and returning from it, but no one turned into our house. I felt sure some of our chapel folk would come to inquire for us after evening service; but no one came. In mother's words, "Nobody darkened her door throughout the whole of the day." We were anxious that someone should call, because we did not know how many had been taken to the lock-up, and mother feared lest Bob had been the only one. The clock struck nine and mother said it was best we should both go to bed and endeavour to get a little rest. But at this moment someone knocked at the door, and I, jumping up eagerly to open it, found—two deacons? No, but Thomas and Barbara Bartley, who told us they could not retire to rest without coming to see how mother got on in her trouble. Two visitors more unlike my mother in character and disposition it would have been almost impossible to imagine; and yet we were heartily glad to see them. It gave us an opportunity of pouring forth the grief which had been storing itself up within us for four and twenty hours. Thomas and Barbara had been to the Crown, where they were given full particulars of the business.

They stayed with us for several hours.   Recalling the confabulation, I think it was one of the strangest and most amusing I ever heard, although it did not appear so then.   And if it were not that this chapter is already too long, and that what I am going to relate in the following chapter weighs so heavily on my mind, I would record all that took place.   The visit was a great relief to us, and mother and I were able to sleep that night without much thought that still bitterer things were in store.

CHAPTER XVII.

FURTHER TRIALS.

HARDLY can I persuade myself that they are facts I am narrating, and not the creations of my imagination.   It was Monday morning, and mother had been for hours sitting, in deep thought, before the fire, pleating her apron.   I easily got permission to go down town to see what would become of my brother and the five other men who had been locked up with him.   The streets were full of people, anxiously waiting the opening of the police court.   I had not been in town many minutes before Will Bryan found me out.   He was always finding me out.   I speedily learned some interest was felt in me, as the brother of one of the prisoners, and, as regards some of the charges, the most important of them.   I met some friends of Bob, who asked how my mother was, and gave me each a penny.   Will said, "Take care of those pence; they'll come in right handy just directly."   I did not know what he meant, and was too much occupied to ask for an explanation; but I gave him the credit always of seeing farther than I.   Almost immediately afterwards, I chanced on other friends of Bob, and got more pence —making five in all.   Never in my life had I been so rich.   Will, who had a penny of his own, suggested we should amalgamate our funds.   I handed him over my five pennies, not caring a bit about them, in my grief, and having a boundless faith in Will's honesty.   No sooner was the money in his hand than he slipped into a shop where they sold pork pies.   I thought he was going to indulge in that particular delicacy, and had no objection to his doing so. When he came out I was disappointed at his showing me, in the palm of his hand, a silver sixpence he had got in change for the coppers, and which, with a knowing wink, he deposited carefully in his waistcoat pocket. I was thoroughly in the dark as to what he meant to do with the sixpence, and I am not sure I did not rather fancy that he purposed feeing an attorney with it to defend my brother. So little did I, at that time, know concerning the reasonable charges of that honest section of the human race.

I was resigning myself wholly into Will Bryan's hands, to do as he pleased, both with me and mine, when I noticed a considerable stir, occasioned by the appearance of the owner of the Hall driving rapidly towards the Court House. He was the principal justice of the peace. Before my companion and I could reach it, the spacious building was tightly packed, and hundreds besides ourselves unable to obtain admission. On each side of the door were two police officers—embodiment of authority—declaring positively that every inch of room inside was crammed full. "But," said Will, in my ear, "we are bound to get in." I did not see how he could hope for that. After a while the crowd shifted a little, and Will Bryan and I edged on into the neighbourhood of the officer's blue coat-tails. Almost directly, we were able to reach the door. Will was obliged to make more than one tug at the flap before attracting its owner's attention. All at once, the officer bent his head; Will spoke a few words in his ear, the officer opened wide his eyes, as if he had received a piece of astounding information, the two shook hands, and next minute Will and I had been let into the Court House, while hundreds of great strong men were struggling outside. But I knew our joint property had changed hands. The Americans talk of the "Almighty Dollar!" Tut! A book might be written upon the miraculous powers of a sixpence. Will had found out, even thus early, that the pass-word, the "open sesame," to all places was a sixpence. In the present circumstances, I felt that my friend had sunk our money to excellent purposes; and had it been six shillings, instead of sixpence, I should not have grumbled.

It became immediately evident that the officer had spoken no more than the truth when he said the court was filled to over-flowing. Will, however, did not find much difficulty in bringing himself and me into a position which enabled us to see and hear all that was going on. He drove me in front of him, like a wedge, into the heart of the crowd, and when he found a stoppage, he would, with an air of importance, say to those who were in the way, "Robert Lewis's brother; Robert Lewis's brother!" with which words, a speedy path would be made for us, just as if I was going up to give evidence in the case. There was simply no end to Will's scheming. I had heard that Mr. Strangle had returned to the place a few hours after he was packed off. He was one of the first I recognised in court, and surly and defiant enough he looked. The magistrates on the bench were Mr. Brown, the clergyman, and the gentleman from the Hall. As I have previously observed, Mr. Brown was a genial, kindly man; but the owner of the Hall was quite a different personage. The latter was huge, unwieldy, pompous, over-bearing, and merciless. One would think that everybody and everything had been created for his service; and it was the general opinion that, did the law permit him, he would un-hesitatingly hang a man caught killing a pheasant. His natural severity appeared to have been watered—or rather wined—too often, and, as a consequence, to have sprouted up through his face, which was of the colour of parboiled American beef and was ornamented (?) by a monstrous lump of a nose, wherein a kind of perpetual shiver was observable, and wherethrough its owner, when roused, would snort like a war-horse. Nobody ever discovered what other qualifications the gentleman from the Hall possessed for the magisterial bench, except that he was a rank Tory, a zealous Churchman, was very wealthy and always wore spurs, save when in bed. Even Mr. Brown dreaded him, and I myself had noticed that that pleasant, respected gentleman, in speaking to him on the road, always kept a dubious, wary eye upon those spurs, as if he feared their wearer might jump suddenly on his back and drive him to the ——, well, the place the wearer himself was speedily going to, more's the pity. The senior magistrate appeared that Monday morning to "be in his oil," as Will Bryan expressed it. To try

a lot of collier fellows was always a congenial task with him,
for he believed them all to be poachers. Those knew, who
wished to know, that but three of the six prisoners before the
bench had taken any part in the attack on Mr. Strangle.
Morris Hughes, John Powell and my brother had done all they
could to prevent such folly. But then Mr. Strangle and the
two police officers swore that these three were ringleaders in
the scandalous business; and, although neither overseer nor
constables understood a word of Welsh, they declared on oath
that Bob had instigated the attack, for, they said, they heard
him naming Mr. Strangle when the rush was made upon that
individual by the workmen. The prisoners had no one to
defend them—a fact chiefly due to my brother's obstinacy. He
would not have any one to defend him, he declared, and his
example was followed by the rest. The owner of the Hall
accepted the evidence of the officials with avidity; and nothing
was too bad for him to believe concerning the accused.

Having heard the witnesses, he asked, as a matter of form,
whether the prisoners had any defence to make. Of course,
three of them had nothing to say, for they were clearly guilty
of the offence with which they were charged; while as to Morris
Hughes and John Powell, they were not the most ready of
speech, particularly in English. After a second or two's silence,
Bob said that, speaking for himself, he was perfectly innocent of
the charge of taking part in the attack on Mr. Strangle. Not
only that, but he had done his best to defend the gentleman,
and it was this he was actually doing when he was struck by
the police officer.

"Do you expect the Bench to believe a story of that sort, after
all the evidence we have heard?" asked the owner of the Hall
with a contemptuous smile.

"I scarcely expect the Bench to believe anything I say,"
replied Bob, "for the reason that it is true. Were it of any
use, I could bring several eye-witnesses to testify to the fact."

"Several who were mixed up in the business, like yourself,
doubtless," observed the magistrate with a sneer. "If we
listened to you, you never did anything wrong, you never in
your life told a lie. But we happen to know something of your
history. You are one of those who want to make the masters

workmen, and the workmen masters. But wait a little! We'll
see directly how all this speech-making pays. We have heard
of you already, and we know your family, young man, before
to-day."

"My family has nothing to do with the charge now laid
against me," said Bob.

"We say it has everything to do with it," the magistrate
replied.

"If so, you had better fetch my mother here," said Bob.

"No," returned the magistrate, "we have quite enough in
you. We don't want any old women here."

"How should I know," retorted Bob, "but that you might
like to have another on the bench."

"None of your impertinence, young man, or you may have
to pay for it," cried the magistrate furiously.

Mother had many times advised Bob to learn how to hold his
tongue; but the task was too hard for him, his excuse always
being that his was a family failing. The owner of the Hall
having engaged in a brief consultation with Mr. Brown, who
listened to him in trembling deference, said:—

"The Bench do not see any necessity for a remand in this
case. The evidence is, to their minds, conclusive. They regret
very much that more of the scoundrels have not been brought
before them to receive their deserts; but the Bench are
determined to make an example of those upon whom the police
have laid hands. The Bench are determined to show that the
master is to be master, and that it is a workman the workman
is to remain. And the Bench wish to show that the colliers
must not take the law into their own hands, and that proper
people have been appointed to administer the law. And the
Bench are determined to show that the law is stronger than the
colliers, however numerous they may be. And so the Bench
are going to sentence five of you, namely, Morris Hughes, John
Powell, Simon Edwards, Griffith Roberts, and John Peters to
one month's imprisonment with hard labour, and Robert Lewis
to two months' imprisonment with hard labour, the Bench
believing him to have been the chief agitator. And the Bench
trust this will be a warning, not only to the prisoners, but to
others who ought to be in the same situation with them, who are

equally guilty with them, not only of creating a disturbance and breaking the law in this fashion, but also of poaching on gentlemen's estates."

As soon as sentence was delivered, there was a general movement in court, the noise of people's feet and the talk being so loud, that hardly could I hear myself sobbing—which I did to some effect. Will sympathised with me most sincerely and did his best to comfort me. So poignant was my sorrow that my friend was, for a minute or so, at a loss to know how to assuage it. Suddenly, however, a thought struck him. He handed over all he possessed to me, namely, his pocket knife, which, he remarked with emphasis, he gave me to keep for ever. I have the knife to this day; and although instrinsically not worth sixpence, I rank it with the mite of the widow and, valuing it as the sacrifice of a heart full of disinterested compassion, I would not for a good deal part with it.

The interest taken in the trial was manifested by the size of the crowd which had by this time gathered outside the Court House, unwilling to disperse without a last look at the prisoners, as they were being conveyed to the county gaol. I can answer for it that the majority of the Red Fields' workmen were sober, industrious, and moral; but amongst them, as it commonly happens in large works, there were a number of worthless characters, given to excessive drinking, the pity being that the best class often got blamed for their misdeeds. Several of these latter had, on the morning in question, been soaking about the public houses, and were not in the best of tempers on that account. But there, I see I am constantly slipping into detail, despite my promise to myself not to do so. How some of the colliers set fiercely upon the police who were conveying my brother and his associates to prison; how the assailants were arrested, tried, and found guilty; how the military were called out, were attacked and beaten; and how, under cruelest provocation, they opened fire upon the rioters, killing several, and so on, it does not concern me to narrate. I can say this much, when the disturbance was at its highest, the feeling of the majority, which included some men of reason and intelligence, was in favour of the colliers; but when things had cooled down, and opportunity was given of looking calmly at the circumstances, these same people were obliged to acknowledge the unwisdom and iniquity of the whole proceeding, and to view with apprehension the frightful lengths to which even sensible and religious men may be led when governed by their passions, instead of by reason and grace.

I remember that I was afraid to go home, because of the shock to mother's feelings which this shame would produce. I knew someone had already notified her of my brother's fate, and I feared it would be her death. But in this I was agreeably disappointed. Dear is the memory of that day to me, for the proof it afforded of what true religion can bring its owner in time of tribulation. Going into the house, I met, coming out of it, two female neighbours, who had been condoling with mother, on whose face I found signs of heavy weeping. The smile it now wore was as a rainbow in the clouds, after a heavy shower, and proved clearly that God had not forgotten his covenant with her. I think I can accurately recollect all she said to me that afternoon. Among other things, these :—

"Well, my son, it is getting worse and worse with us. Something tells me, however, that the light will come soon. The darker the night the nearer the dawn; the tighter the cord the sooner 'twill break. The Lord, I shall believe, has a hand in this. The furnace must, occasionally, be seven times heated before the form of the Fourth can come to sight. I never dreamt it would go so hard with your brother, but I think none the less of him, for all that has taken place. I know he is innocent, for he never told me a lie in his life. There are a hundred times worse than he now at large. From a child he was too ready with his tongue, and all the bother I had with with him was when he would be telling too much of the truth. He was a little too decided of purpose; that was why he left Communion. But he led a better life than many of us who profess. Who knows but that the Great King's design, through all, has been to bring him back, and to show him how he has lost the shelter and the defence."

I have noticed since, that the mother, when her son is overtaken by disgrace, as well as when he is overtaken by death, forgets his every fault and delights only in bringing up his virtues.

"It would be very difficult for me to believe," my mother added, "that Bob was not a Christian. If he is not in the house, he belongs to the family, I am pretty certain, and per-adventure it is from the far-off country of the prison that the yearning will arise in him for his Father. How did he look, tell me? Middling well? Yes? It's wonderful how he can take everything so composedly. I know what is uppermost in his mind, and that is, what'll become of us both, how are we to live, because there never was a lad who thought more of his mother, my poor darling!"

Upon this she burst out crying, a proceeding at which I helped. After quieting, she said :—

"Do they have a Bible in jail, tell me? They have? I'm glad to hear it; but, for that matter, Bob knows enough of the Bible to chew the cud upon, for two months, anyhow. What vexes me most is that I never had a look at him. It seemed a bit cold of me that I did not go to the Hall, but I could not for the life of me set out, somehow. Do you think he'd get a letter if we were to write? You do? Well then, I'll not sleep to-night until you've sent him a word. I'm glad you're a bit of a scholar, because I don't want all the world to know our affairs."

I was then obliged to set to and write a letter. At my mother's suggestion, I wrote it first on the unused leaf of a copy book, "For fear," she said, "we might want to alter it." The original is still in my possession, and perhaps I can't do better than finish this chapter with a transcript. There is nothing particular in its contents, what makes it precious to me being the proof it affords of my mother's acquaintance with the Bible. I give it exactly as she dictated it, with the exception of a few changes in the colloquialisms where the meaning is not quite clear.

"Dear Son,—I write you these few lines hoping you are quite well as it leaves us at present. I feel mixed and moithered very much, and I know you're the same. My complaint to-day is bitter—Job twenty third and second. But who is he that saith and it cometh to pass when the Lord commandeth it not—Lamentations, third and thirty seventh. I know very well you'll be troubling your mind about us as we are about you ; but I hope you know where to turn, as you said

I

I did when you were leaving the house on Saturday night. And call upon me in the day of trouble; I will deliver thee, and thou shalt glorify me—Psalms, fiftieth and fifteenth. If I'm not deceiving myself much, I think I've had a fulfilment of that promise to-day. Dear son, I fear greatly you will let your spirits go down and lose your health, because you've been wrongfully put in prison. Perhaps it'll be some comfort to you to call to mind those spoken of in Scripter who were wrongly put in prison like yourself, and the Lord showed afterwards that they did not deserve to be there. If you have leisure turn to the following :—Genesis thirty-ninth, Acts fifth, eighth and sixteenth. Remember also it was from prison and from judgment that He was taken—Isaiah fifty-third and eighth. You know the trouble I got with your father; the trouble to-day is very different. I'm pretty sure that even if you were a little amiss you were quite honest, and that your conscience is easy, as you said; and, if that is anything for you to think of, though you are in jail you're not an atom the worse in your mother's eyes, and I hope you're no worse in your Redeemer's eyes either. Same time, I much hope you'll now come to see you have offended the Man of the house by leaving Communion, and though I believe you're not at any time strange to the great things of the Gospel, I trust I shall see you, when all this is over, turning your face towards the shelter. Dear son, the wind is high and the waves are rising, but if through that we are brought to call on the Master to save us, all will be well. Read Luke eighth and the eighth of Romans. If Morris Hughes and yourself are put with each other, it'll be no harm in the world if you gave a tune now and then, as Paul and Silas did of old, and I know of no better verse for you than Ann Griffis's :—

> ' Living still, how great the wonder,
>   When the furnace is so hot ! '

You know how it finishes, and who can tell but that you'll get inspiration by singing of the Man whose fan is in his hand. I have a lot of things I would like to tell you; but I must come to an end. Keep your spirits up; two months is not much; it'll be over very soon. Pray night and day; if they stop you from reading, nobody can stop you from praying. In my mind

you were a good enough boy before, but for one thing; but
something tells me you'll be a better man than ever after the
present trouble. We wish to be remembered to you very
warmly. This in short from your loving mother and brother,

MARY AND RHYS LEWIS."

After I had re-written the foregoing, and read it to mother
many times over, I put it carefully into an envelope, and
addressed it. Mother made me write "Haste" on one corner,
and, inasmuch as she had not much faith in gum, she insisted
on the addition of red wax, which she sealed with her thimble.
When all was done, she appeared calm and resigned to the
decrees of Providence. The manner in which my brother's imprisonment affected our worldly circumstances, and marked an
epoch in my history will be shown in the next chapter.

CHAPTER XVIII.

THOMAS AND BARBARA BARTLEY.

ON looking back upon the time of boyhood, I become alive to
the fact that it went by without my enjoying but little of the
careless blithesomeness which falls to the lot of nearly every
lad, no matter what the station of his family. Even before I
got to know want or trouble at home, my mother's Puritanical
austerity set bounds upon my play, numbered my companions,
and limited my enjoyment. Some sort of knowledge of "the
Fall of Man," "the Two Covenants," and similar subjects, was
dinned into my head when I ought to have been playing
marbles. While those of like age were "hunting the hare," I
would be kept at home to learn portions of the great Psalm. No
wonder I was the worst at a game of any in Soldier Robin's school,
and that even the girls made fun of me. I would not, for anything I ever saw, say a disrespectful word of my mother, for I
believe her intentions to have been pure as a sunbeam. But I
fear that to her ignorance is to be attributed my bodily weakness, the sadness and the depression of spirit I am so subject
to, and which, by this time, sits as a disease upon me. Before

I could rejoice in the innocence of youth, I was being grounded in particulars of the estate my father Adam had left me, taught the ins and outs of my depraved heart, and the tricks and wiles of the old gentleman who goes about like a roaring lion. In a word, the dark side of human nature had been portrayed to me with all the hideous deformity my mother's gifts enabled her to bring to bear upon the work. The teaching had its effect; and, by this time, I do not wonder my companions got to call me "the old man."

I was thirteen when my brother was sent to prison; but it was not as a boy of that age I felt the shame and grief of the occurrence. It was no day-and-night's trouble, to be cured on the morrow by the cheerfulness of sportive comrades. Sorrow filled my soul and bred a worm in my heart that not even my faithful, merry friend Will Bryan could kill. I cannot easily describe my state of mind. It was a mixture of genuine sympathy with my brother in his sufferings, a deep conviction of his innocence and an increasing admiration of his character. I must confess to a wounded pride, a spirit of revenge, and a disposition to quarrel with the decrees of Providence. I know quite well that I was not in a proper frame of mind; because when I heard that, on the day following the one on which my brother and his associates were sent to prison, a frightful havoc had been played with the Hall owner's game, I felt delighted, although I dared not say as much to mother. The sense of vacancy to which my brother's absence gave rise was almost as painful as the circumstances which had occasioned that absence itself. Without him our home was like a body without a soul, the want of life affecting one as strangely as if he had been for hours in a mill, and found all its wheels coming to a sudden stop. I missed his manly presence, his resonant voice, and ready wit, and home was no longer home to me. Although she did not say so, I knew my mother felt the same. In the course of a single day the colour and aspect of her face changed. The remnants of its youthful bloom vanished, never to return; and beneath the eyes of blue did Adversity leave the imprint of his name in blackletter. Often during the day did she go to the door, looking out each time in the same direction, as if hoping against hope to see her boy return. So deeply convinced was she of his innocence and the injustice of his imprisonment, that I am not sure she did not rather expect some supernatural intervention for his release. I do not know whether it was force of habit, or something else, which made her, at meals, prepare for three of us; but I saw her more than once, as at tea time, laying three cups upon the table, and, perceiving her mistake, secretly putting one of them away again, thinking I had not observed her. I could note down many other little things she did, as showing her dreamy absent-mindedness. All my brother's belongings were laid under tribute to her condition. She would wipe the dust from his English books, against which she had been strongly prejudiced previously, and frequently turn the leaves, although she understood not a word they contained. I fancy I was perfectly cognisant of the state of her feelings, although I cannot now convey it in words. Hers was no surface trouble, but one reaching down into the depths of the soul and carrying with it a whole host of the painful associations. And yet it was not a hopeless sorrow that she suffered, either; but a sadness, rather, which seemed to span the distance from the abyss of affliction up to a firm faith in Him who rules over all. She read her Bible a good deal, and spoke cheerfully; but I knew it cost her a great effort to do so.

As on the preceding day, Thomas and Barbara Bartley were the first to visit us; and I felt very thankful for their kindness. As I have already remarked, they were a couple of simple, harmless old souls. They appeared to me to be wonderfully happy, always. In addition to being suitably matched as husband and wife, there was a similarity both of feature and mind between them. Whatever Thomas might say, Barbara, with a nod, would confirm; and whatever Barbara said, Thomas would seal with a "To be shwar." They were like two eyes on one string, at all times looking the same way. Small was the circle of their lives, and the amount of their knowledge about the same. Planting a potato patch and killing a pig, ten score weight, were the two poles on which their little world made its annual revolution. It seemed as if Providence, in drafting a scheme of life, had forgotten to set down trouble or trial against the names of Thomas and Barbara Bartley, with the exception of the death of their son Seth, and even that appeared as if it were a mistake, for it turned out a means of perfecting their happiness. Thomas had a great name as a mender of shoes, and was never short of work. He was also considered an excellent neighbour. He was not a total abstainer, but he never got drunk, save on special occasions, such as Whit-Monday, when his club walked. But even on those occasions, Barbara would not admit he was drunk—he had only "taken a drop." Both believed they had good hearts and that to live honestly was quite enough of religion. And they, doubtless, did live up to their professions, for it was never heard of Thomas and Barbara that they had "subverted a man in his cause," or of the first named that he had put bad work into a shoe. Theirs was not merely a cold and formal honesty, either. None so ready as they to do kindnesses, for which, it is probable, they took credit as for works of supererogation. In passing, I may say that I have, in the course of my short life, met with people of higher spiritual pretensions with whom it were well had their religion come up to that of Thomas and Barbara Bartley. But this is what I was about to relate—the two old folk came to visit us in our trouble, and we had a long talk, too long for me to repeat. Let the few words following serve as a sample of the whole. After they had sat down, said Thomas :—

"Well Mary Lewis, you be in a bit of a bother, ben't you ? I'm sorry in my heart for you."

Barbara gave a nod which meant "ditto."

"I am so, Thomas *bach*," replied my mother, "and I'm very much obliged to you for your sympathy. His way is in the sea, and His path in the great waters. Clouds and darkness encompass Him—but He knows ——."

"Hold on a bit, Mary *fach*," said Thomas, "you are wrong there. Isn't it to jail poor Bob's gone ? Not over the sea at all—not transported. You've got your head in the ash-pit over this, and you fancy things to be worse'n they are. Save us! The boy never went near the sea."

"I know that, well enough, Thomas. It's of the Great King's government I'm speaking," returned my mother.

"Ho! say so, Mary," said Thomas. "Barbara nor I can't read, you see, and so we don't know much about the Great King; and, to say the truth, we never speak of Him, 'cept by chance, when somebody dies or gets killed—for fear we'd make a mistake you know."

Barbara nodded, to signify her husband was quite right.

"I am sorry to hear that, Thomas," said mother. "We ought all to think and speak a deal about the Great King, inasmuch as it is in Him we live, move and have our being. This is how the Psalmist says, Thomas :—' My meditation of Him shall be sweet.' And in another place he says, ' Evening and morning and at noon will I pray and cry aloud, and he shall hear my voice.' And if we were more like the Psalmist, we would be nearer the mark, Thomas *bach*."

" Well in-deed, Mary, Barbara and I try to live as near the mark as we can; don't we, Barbara ?"

Barbara gave a confirmatory nod.

" I know that as far as living honestly goes, you are all right enough," said mother. "But religion teaches us that something more is wanted, before we can enter into the life, Thomas *bach*."

" But what can we do more than live honest, Mary ? I have a good heart, I'll take my oath, and I'd rather do a kindness than refuse, if it's in my power, wouldn't I, Barbara ? (Nod.) And I never bear anyone a grudge, do I, Barbara? (Nod.) And as to religion, I see you religious ones worse off nor anybody. Here's you, Mary Lewis, you have been professin' since I can remember you, and always talking about religion, the Great King, the other world, and things like that, but who has met with more trouble nor you ? One would think you'd had enough trouble with your husband, and here you are again, over head and ears in it. And there's Bob—one of the tidiest boys that ever wore a Blucher—when he came over to have his boots mended, always speaking of religion, and there he is to-day worse off nor anybody. I told Bob that if religion is a thing of that sort, I can't un'stand the Great King at all. I'm constantly seein' you in trouble, with your heads in your feathers."

"Religion does not promise to keep man from his trials, Thomas," remarked my mother. "And I don't know but what there may be a little truth in what you say, that religious people are oftener afflicted than others. ' Thou who hast shown me great and sore troubles,' says the Psalmist. ' In the world ye shall have tribulation,' said the Saviour. And Paul, in the Acts, says that 'we must, through much tribulation, enter into the kingdom of God.' The great thing for you and me Thomas, is that these tribulations so sanctify us that we are able to see the hand of the Lord in them all, and that we do not let our spirits sink in too much sorrow."

"'They do tell me, Mary," said Thomas, "there's nothin' better to rise the spirits than—what do they call it? The thing they sell in the druggist's shop—what's its name, Barbara?"

"Assiffeta," replied Barbara.

"To be shwar," said Thomas. "If you take a penn'orth of 'siffeta, a penn'orth of yellow janders drops, and a penn'orth of tenty rhiwbob, there's nothing in the world better for risin' your spirits, they do say. I never tried it myself—'twas a drop of beer I took for my grief after Seth, and it did me a power of good. I could cry very much better after it; and I shouldn't wonder if it did you good, too, Mary. Barbara wanted to put a drop in her pocket for you, but I told her you wouldn't take it—you religious folk are so odd in things of that sort."

"I hope, Thomas," said mother, "that I have, by this time, got to know a better receipt for raising spirits than anything sold in the druggist's shop or the public house. To my mind, Thomas, nothing but Gilead balm and Calvary ointment can raise the afflicted spirit."

"Very true. I hope it isn't expensive. The same thing 'ont cure everybody, and I always say so, as Barbara knows," was Thomas's reply.

"You don't understand me, Thomas," said mother. "What I mean is this—the only thing that can raise an afflicted spirit is the sweet and precious promise of the Bible, a knowledge of God in Christ, reconciling the world to Him without taking into account their sins, and a reliance of soul in the dear death on Calvary. I should have been glad had your son's decease led you and Barbara within sound of the Gospel, and had you sought consolation in its truths instead of trying to drown your sorrows in intoxicating and worthless drink, Thomas *bach*."

"Do you know what, Mary?" said Thomas. "If you only belonged to the Ranters, you'd make a champion preacher.

But I can't agree with you about the drink. You know more than me, I'll allow, but doesn't the Bible call it strong drink?"

"It does, sure," replied mother.

"So James Pulford, the tailor, says; and the Bible would never have called it strong drink if it didn't strengthen a man," declared Thomas.

"It is so strong that it'll knock you down, Thomas, if you don't take great care," mother observed, adding: "seriously, Thomas *bach*, isn't it time that Barbara and you should begin to think about your souls? You are getting old now, and do you never long to come and hear the Gospel? Don't you think it high time for you both to inquire after that Friend whom you and I will stand in need of before long, if we are not to be wretched for ever. I am making very bold with you, but you know it is your own good I have in view. My dear, good old neighbours, I have thought a deal about you, and tried to pray for you. How good the Great King has been to you! How well, how happy, what a comfort to each other you have been during the years! Will it not be a great pity, Thomas *bach*, if you are both left behind at the last. You would like, I know, to see Seth once again, and be with him evermore. Well, there is no doubt in my mind that Seth is safe in the midst of Heaven. 'The wayfaring men, though fools, shall not err.' Do you remember what he said to the boy here when dying—that he was 'going afar, afar, to the great chapel of Jesus Christ.' And he has gone there, sure to you. But then Seth came to chapel, Thomas; he never missed a service, poor dear! And although we took no notice of him, and thought he did not understand what was going on, Seth was making his fortune: he found the pearl of great price, which was worth his life to him. There are more pearls in the same field, Thomas; and you, my dear neighbour, must attend the means of grace, or you'll never go to the same place as Seth."

These last words had an electrical effect upon Thomas and Barbara. Thomas, overcome with feeling, stared straight into the ash-pit, great tears rolling down his cheeks and dropping upon his spotless cord trousers. Barbara rubbed her nose and eyes with her check apron, and it was with difficulty she restrained a sob when mother spoke of Seth dying. Mother saw the iron was hot, and set about in earnest beating it with that old sledge-hammer of the Scripture in the use of which she was so dexterous. To pursue the metaphor, she turned their hearts this way and that upon her anvil, until I fancied they had neither a side nor an aspect from which she had not struck a living spark. It is not because she was my mother that I say so, nor am I exaggerating when I say it, but I never knew her let an opportunity slip of giving a piece of advice, or a verse from the Bible to those whom she thought without religion, if she saw it would be of advantage so to do. As in the present circumstances, she forgot her own trouble in her eagerness to find some word likely to stick to the heart and conscience of one whom she fancied, to use her own expression, to be "careless about the welfare of his soul." When I consider how neglectful I myself am in this matter, I am ashamed to remember that I am my mother's son.

I had seen, for some time, that Thomas was growing very uneasy, and anxious to get away. Mother took the hint. Directly she ceased evangelising, Thomas gave a heavy sigh, and rose nervously to his feet, saying, in a half-choked voice :—

"Barbara, we must go home, look you. What have you got in the basket there ? "

Handing the contents to my mother, he said :—

"Champion stuff, Mary. Fed on taters and oatmeal. Never had a single grain. Don't mention it! Don't mention it! You're heartily welcome. Have you any taters in the house ? If you send Rhys over to-morrow, I'll give you a few of the best pink eyes you ever tasted. They eat like flour."

"Thomas *bach*," said mother, taking hold of his coat, "you've always been wonderfully kind; but be kind to your soul, now. Will you promise me you'll come to chapel next Sunday ? You'll never repent it."

Thomas cast his eyes upon the ground, and, after a second or two's silence, said : "Mary, if all the preachers spoke as plain as you, I'd come to chapel every Sunday. But, to tell the truth to you, I can't und'stand 'em—they always talk of something, I don't know what."

"Will you promise, Thomas *bach*, to bring Barbara to chapel with you? The light will come, if you only will," said mother, holding more tightly by the lapel.

"What do you say, Barbara?" asked Thomas.

Barbara having given a nod of assent, Thomas added:—

"Well, name of goodness, we'll come. Good night, and God be with you."

After they had left did mother set to admiring the piece of bacon? Not much! She had found a piece of something daintier by a good deal.

"I see it, Rhys! she exclaimed, joyfully. "I see it now! Bob was sent to prison so that Thomas and Barbara Bartley might be saved! 'His way is in the sea,'" &c.

Well, it was not of Thomas and Barbara Bartley I intended speaking when I began the present chapter, but I see "it is not in man that walketh to direct his steps" in this, as in other things.

CHAPTER XIX.

ABEL HUGHES.

It might be thought that all who have paid a little attention to men and their habits, have observed, among others, the three classes following. First, those who have once been almost entirely under the sway of the Devil and their own evil dispositions, but who, through some good fortune, have been brought under the divine influence of the Gospel, and have found mercy—"the former things have passed away, and behold all things are made new." Their passions are held in control, their hearts and course of life changed, and even their consciences, as it were, saying over of the Evil One, "he hath nothing in me." What a heavenly beauty distinguishes this section of my fellow men! Then again there is the other class, with whose hearts religion has something to do, and who themselves have something to do with religion, but the signs are palpable that the Prince of this World has something to do with them, also. On particular occasions the cloven hoof comes to sight. They appear as if both heaven and hell laid claim to them. And yet, when we hear them pray and tell their experiences, we are, like a jury trying a man for his life, very ready to give them the benefit of the doubt. The important thing for them and for me to remember is that there will be no doubt as to our characters in the great day to come. Then there is the third class: those who profess no connection of any kind with religion, but in whose mode of life there are, yet, a great many virtues. They are honest, straightforward, amiable, and obliging, kind towards both man and beast, and would sooner wrong themselves than wrong anyone else. Their innocence is as a remnant of the stuff from which our first parents were made. As already said, they are not religious in the accepted sense of the term, and yet there are many of religion's fruits growing upon them. They have not sullied their conscience with impious acts, nor read or thought enough to cause uneasiness and doubt, and so are pretty happy. To me, there is a great attraction about this class of people, and there have been times when I have envied their lot.

To this last category belonged Thomas and Barbara Bartley, but it was possibly their kindness towards mother and me in our trouble, which made me, in after days, look upon their like with interest and emulation. While we were in that family distress I have already described, I remember wondering greatly at the lukewarmness displayed by the officers of the church of which my mother was no obscure member, and comparing it to the ready kindness and sympathy of Thomas and Barbara Bartley. I could not help communicating what I had noticed to mother, who, however, would on no account have me entertain a poor opinion of our leaders. Conformably to her usual mode of speech, she said :—

"This is quite in the order of things, my son. There is something which causes the brethren to behave a little coldly towards us. Perhaps the Great Ruler is keeping the best wine until the last. If we are fit objects of succour, the Head of the Church will take care of us in His own good time."

I had not to wait long before finding that my mother was pretty near the right; for, early on the following morning, we were visited by our revered old deacon, Abel Hughes, of whom

I have already had occasion, more than once, to speak. Were it his biography, and not my own, I was writing, I should have a great many interesting things to tell about him. I flatter myself I have marched with the times pretty closely, considering my disadvantages. But somehow, old-fashione l notions, formed when I was a boy, will cling to me, spite of myself. I am almost ashamed to own them, but for the life of me, I cannot eliminate them from my mind. Were I asked by some young man from an English town for my views on this subject or that, I should give them easily and honestly; but underneath them all I know there would arise others of a very different kind, formed long ago, and impossible to get rid of. One of these is my notion of a church deacon. Is not Theophilus Watkin, Esq., of Plas Uchaf, who, by incomparable management of the world, made his fortune in a very short time, who lives and dresses in a style becoming his exalted station, who keeps a liveried servant and takes his wife and daughters in full dress to all the principal concerts—is not he an ornament to the big seat of the Methodist Chapel at Highways? Is he not liberal to the cause, generous to the poor of the church, does he not respect and hospitably entertain the ministers of the Word? True, he never goes to the Monthly Meeting, and is absent a good deal from Sunday School; but then we should remember his position, and the society in which he moves. He is zealous for the pastorate, and humble and self-denying at Church Meetings, where he allows the minister to do all the speaking. Is he not a worthy official, and a great acquisition to the cause? Yes, exceptionally so, and I feel proud of him. Again, there is Alexander Phillips ("Eos Prydain,") the hard-working young choir-leader, expert in the business of looking after the church books, ready at planning and getting up a concert, trim in appearance—is he not a very admirable man? He, too, is a little reserved in Communion, but it would be almost impossible the brethren could hold a tea party, or get up a competition meeting without the aid of his invaluable services. An agreeable man, fond of his joke, but of proper behaviour always. Take him through and through, he is of admirable use to the cause, and is considered by the multitude, myself included, a good deacon. And yet my antiquated notion will whisper to

me that they are not the men I have named who come up to the
diaconal standard. The type and pattern which this notion
persists in placing before my mind is to be found in Abel
Hughes.

He was a man of this kind: somewhat advanced in years,
wearing knee-breeches, dark coat and vest, a black kerchief,
tied several times about the neck, a broad-brimmed, low-
crowned beaver hat, the face clean shaved up to within half an
inch of each ear, whence depended a tiny lock, and the hair cut
parallel with the heavy brows which overlooked a thoughtful
face. This is one side of the picture. It has another: a man
strong in the Scriptures, well versed in, and an earnest enforcer
of, the teachings of the Gospel, loyal to Monthly Meeting
and Session, constant at service, of ready and original views,
inspiring and tear-compelling when upon his knees, whether at
prayer meeting or commencing service for the preacher; precise, almost to the point of harshness in the matter of church
discipline, but tender hearted and pious-dispositioned; blameless in life, an enemy of vain show and frivolity, one who
expected all who belonged to church, yea, even the children, to
behave seriously and with decorum. Such was Abel Hughes,
and it was he who first gave me a notion of the sort of man a
deacon should be, a notion which, however erroneous, remains
embedded in the depths of my consciousness. Reason disposes
me to believe that the model deacon is to be found between Abel
Hughes and some people who are called deacons in these days,
but who are no more than ministers' lodginghouse keepers,
or clerks of the church. In Abel Hughes, mother saw a man
almost without fault, and that, very likely, because her ideas of
the world and its ways, of religion and its doctrines, were about
on a level. Both deacon and member ate the same spiritual
food, drank the same spiritual wine, and frequently exchanged
notes on the subject of practical religion. In chapel, as at the
house, they were most unassuming and homely; and, after the
manner of old people, never addressed each other as Mr. and Mrs.

I know very well there was no one mother, in her trouble,
would have more wished to see than Abel Hughes, and nothing
would have pleased me better than to have been able to
chronicle fully the talk which ensued upon his visit. But I

cannot. Although I have an excellent memory, and had a
pretty long head, even at that time, I got to feel that the conversation was a very different one from that with Thomas
Bartley, and that much of it was above my comprehension. At
the same time, I am not willing to pass on without an effort to
commemorate at least a portion of the talk, for mother said
some things as to the value of personal religion which have
clung to my mind. When Abel entered the house, as usual
without knocking, mother gave him a look almost of hauteur;
but I perceived that there was a moisture in her eyes, and the
working of the corners of her mouth and throat showed that she
was obliged to summon all her energy to prevent herself from
bursting into tears. Abel held out his hand, and said:—

"Well, Mary, and how are you?"

"Wonderfully well, considering," replied my mother. "'I
am troubled on every side, yet not distressed; perplexed, but
not in despair; cast down, but not destroyed.'"

"I was certain, Mary," said Abel, "you knew where to look
for help, whatever your troubles were; otherwise I would have
come here sooner, very likely."

"Well," returned mother, "I hope I don't want much nursing.
I'm not like the woman of the 'London House,' Abel, who
stayed weeks away from chapel because the deacons did not
call upon her when she had a bit of a toothache. No, do you
think that, at my age, I haven't learned to walk? But it
would have been no harm in the world, Abel, had you come to
inquire for me a little sooner, especially after all the 'quaintance
between us; although, mind you, if you didn't come here for a
month I should not think any the less of you. Indeed Abel, I
feel almost thankful you didn't come, because if you had, I
should not catch the sight I did of the One

'—Who above every other,
  Through the whole creation wide,
Deserves the name of friend and brother,
  And who'll e'er the same abide.
Against man's hard lot forlorn,
Our Protector was he born.'

Joseph, you know, Abel, caused every man to go out from him before he made himself known to his brethren; and I rather hope that my present trouble is but a cup placed in the sack's mouth, so that I may be brought to know the Ruler of the country."

"I am glad to find you in the green pastures, Mary," said Abel.

"Where did you expect to find me, Abel?" asked my mother. "Not out on the common, surely? After all our religious professions it would be hard if we found ourselves without a shelter on the day of storm. If I am not deceiving myself—which I fear I very often do—I have, by this time, nothing worth talking of but the pastures. As you know, Abel, I am wholly without help, and worse off than if I were a widow The son who was my sole support has been sent to gaol"—and she buried her face in her apron, quite overcome by her feelings.

"There are in the Truth words like these, Mary," said Abel. "'I have been young, and now am old; and yet have I not seen the righteous forsaken, nor his seed begging bread. The Lord trieth the righteous, but the wicked and him that loveth violence, His soul hateth. Many are the afflictions of the righteous, but the Lord delivereth him out of them all. Light is sown for the righteous, and gladness for the upright in heart.' I am pretty certain, Mary, that light has been sown for you, though it be night with you now, and that you shall see it budding and sprouting in this world, even if you are not permitted to see it in full growth. Be of good comfort, trust in the Lord, and He will deliver you out of all your tribulations."

"I try to be so, Abel, as well as I can," said mother. "But hearing you speak, I can't help thinking of Thomas of Nant's words. Thomas, I know, was not religious, but he said a great many good things, and I think it was he who said this one:—

> 'Easy 'tis for the hale and well,
> The sick man to take comfort tell.'

Yet I feel very thankful to you for your cheering words, and I've been wondering and wondering why you didn't come here sooner, Abel."

"I did not give much thought to you, Mary," said Abel. "I was sorry to miss you from chapel on the Sunday, although I did not expect to see you, under the circumstances. Bob was not a member with us, although he was more like what a member should be than many of us. No one had a word to say against his character, and he was admittedly one of the best teachers in Sunday School. But these strikes are very queer things Mary. They have come to us from the English; they are not ours, and I fear they will do much harm to the country and to religion. We, as brethren, considered we ought to take time. Bob was one of the leaders, and of necessity so, because for understanding and the gift of speech he stood high above them all. Nobody doubts his honesty of purpose; indeed many of the wiser ones sympathised with the colliers in their agitation for an advance of wages and against the tyranny of their employers. But no one, with a grain of sense in his head, to say nothing of grace in his heart, could justify their attack upon the overseer, and hunting him out of the country. According to first accounts, Bob was one of those who were guilty of this act, and had I run straight hither to sympathise with you, someone would be found to say that we were no better than the agitators, the great cause would suffer, and the excellent name we enjoy would we calumniated. I am happy to tell you, Mary, that no one, by this time, believes in Bob's guilt, although he is suffering as if he were guilty. Men who were eye-witnesses of the whole transaction, and who can tell the truth as well as anybody, positively testify that he and John Powell strove hard to prevent the rash act. I have other good news for you. The men having resolutely refused to work under Mr. Strangle, the masters have paid him off and sent for Abraham, the former manager, who has entered upon his duties anew. The work will re-start to-morrow. For this we are indebted to Mr. Walters the attorney, who succeeded in getting employers and workmen together and in acting as interpreter and arbitrator between them. I understand that had this been done at first, the whole trouble would have been spared; because the masters have found out, by this time, it was not without cause Bob and his associates had complained against Strangle. So you see Mary, that things are not so bad after all."

K

" So, they'll surely let Bob out of prison now that they find he is innocent and that all he said was correct."

"No, I fear, Mary, we can't expect that. When the magistrates make a mistake, they never try to put it right. They are like the man who, having told a lie, thinks the best thing he can do is to stick to it."

" But is it possible," mother asked, " that Mr Brown, the clergyman, can go up into the pulpit to preach—if he does preach, too—of justice and mercy, after he has been upon the bench assisting the owner of the Hall in administering injustice ? "

" He'll preach—if, to use your own expression, he does preach, too—just the same, or perhaps better than ever, Mary."

" I'll defy him to preach any worse, Abel, if it was well I heard him," said mother. " But where people's consciences are, I don't know. I am very thankful it is with religion I am, and not in the Church of England."

The two proceeded, for some time, to talk about religion and its consolations. I could see that Abel's visit was a great blessing to my mother. She appeared happier, not the least of the things which made her so being Abel's declaration that no one now believed in Bob's guilt. Very soon, however, she and I got to know it was impossible to live on happy feelings. It was long to wait for my brother's release. Wages having been brought so low under Mr. Strangle's management, mother had nothing at her back on which to subsist. For about three weeks our friends were very kind to us; but as often happens in similar circumstances, time wore away the sharp edge of sympathy. Five weeks yet remained of Bob's imprisonment. Never shall I forget those weeks ! Either from pride, or some other reason, I never confided, even to my greatest friend, that I, at one time, experienced a want of food. I confess it now. I believe it impossible any man can realise such a situation who has not been placed in it himself. A state of perfect health with the stomach filled as with voracious lions with nothing to appease them, is one which I cannot describe; but I know, from experience, what it is to have been in it many times. Mother was not given to complain, and was possessed of a spirit of foolish independence, otherwise we need never have been in want. I, who had inherited her weakness, would not admit,

even to Will Bryan, that I suffered the pangs of hunger. I am
certain, however, that he guessed as much, because I saw him,
on sundry occasions, going into the house and bringing out a
great piece of bread and butter, or bread and meat. After a
bite or two he would pull a wry face, and say he had no appetite
and that he must throw the food away if I didn't take it. The
lions raged, and rather than allow him to do that, I would accept
it from him. Ah, Will! thou understoodest my proud heart as
well as thou knewest of my empty stomach!

Such small things as we were able to spare, mother sold,
taking care that the purchasers were strangers, always. She
was terribly afraid the chapel people would get to know we
were in such straits, for what reason I cannot tell, unless it was
the one I have hinted, namely, a spirit of independence or false
pride. I think she was guilty even of dissimulation on two or
three occasions, but I hope that under the circumstances it was
excusable. Once when we were without a single grain of food
in the house, and after a long abstinence, we went over to
Thomas and Barbara Bartley's, under pretence of congratulating
them on their coming to service—a matter to which I shall have
to refer again. I have no doubt whatever, in my own mind,
that mother rejoiced in her heart to find the two old folk had
begun to attend chapel; but there was some secret understanding between us that we should not be allowed to leave Thomas
Bartley's house without a capital meal. We went there three
times, on one excuse and another, and not once did we come
away fasting or empty-handed. The period is a painful one
to speak of, and I hasten on, leaving untouched many
incidents of distress which rise vividly before me as I write.
One, however, I cannot pass by without particular reference.
It was between breakfast and dinner times, that is with other
people, breakfast time and dinner time having no special
signification for us. We had not tasted a bit since the middle
of the previous day. Weak and dispirited, I tried to pass the
time reading. Mother sat by, still and meditative. Presently
she got up, put on her bonnet, and then sat down again for a
brief while. She got up a second time, put her cloak about her,
and, after a little musing, sat down once more. Evidently she
was in some deep conflict of mind. I heard her mutter some-

thing of which all I could make out was "meal" and "bread."
Hardly could I take in the meaning of the first word; as to the
last, I felt in no great need of it. After a minute or two she
rose resolutely to her feet and fetched, from the back room, the
recticule in which she used to carry things from the shop when
Bob was at work. I asked her where she meant to go to.

"Well, my boy," she replied, "it is no use in the world
moping about here. We can't hold out much longer, look you,
and they say it is the dog who goes shall get. I'll go far
enough so that no one'll know me."

I divined her purpose instantly, and became heart-sick at the
thought. Placing my back against the door, I declared, with a
loud cry, that she should not go, adding we could hold out
until the morrow at least. It did not take much to persuade
her. She put her basket by, and took off her cloak and
bonnet. Having given way a little to our feelings, I fancied my
hunger had entirely left me and that I could go for many days
without food. If there is one act of my life which affords me
more satisfaction than another at this minute, it is the one by
which I prevented mother from leaving the house, as described.
Had I let her go, my faith in God's promises would be less than
it is to-day. I cannot describe the pleasure which the reflection
brings me that, despite the hard pass we were brought to, she
was laid to rest without having ever gone out to beg. We did
not cross the threshold that day. The hours dragged slowly
along. When night came, we heard a loud sharp rap at the
back door of the house, and both got up to answer it. We
opened the door, but, there being no one in sight, we were about
to shut it again, when we saw something on the door-step. It
was a small brown-paper bundle, neatly packed. On taking it
into the house, I found my mother's name clumsily written upon
it. The hand-writing was not unfamiliar to me. The package
was, in one sense, like the heart of the sender—it contained a
great many good things which brightened the face of my
mother. And yet the mystery surrounding them made her
pause before putting them to use. Next moment, however, she
said:—

"David, look you, once, when in want, did eat of the shew-
bread, and the Saviour afterwards justified him for so doing.

And although we know about as much as the mountain-hurdle where these good things have come from, I don't think we shall be doing wrong in using them."

Inasmuch as she never asked me could I guess, I did not give her the slightest hint whence the package came. Had I done so, I question whether she would have touched the contents, for I strongly suspected that the sender had not acquired them honestly.

My noble friend! I know very well thou would'st have shared the last bit with me, and that, although thou did'st not afterwards mention that parcel to me, nor I to thee, I was as certain thou wert the sender as I am that it was from thy hand I received the bread and butter of the previous day.

CHAPTER XX.

THE VICAR OF THE PARISH.

I HAVE said that mother possessed a sort of foolish pride and independence of mind, and that had she been more pliable and clamorous, we need not have suffered much destitution. I fear I must confess, also, to seeing her once—only once—guilty of rudeness, and of speaking to a gentleman of position as if she were his equal, when in reality she was in want of the daily necessaries of life. I trust I shall be forgiven by those friends into whose hands this autobiography may fall—and the more readily because, by that time, the earth, a yard deep, will be covering my face—for believing that mine was the best mother in the world. But I should be dissembling, and unfaithful to my promise of telling the truth and the whole truth, did I hide her weaknesses. She was a woman of warm temper and strong feeling, and, I rather fancy, gloried a little in being a "plain speaker." My experience of such people is that, while they excel in straightforwardness, they run the risk of forgetting the feelings of others and of showing a want of that suavity and good taste which should adorn the character of every true Christian.

In a small, quiet place, the "Vicar of the parish," is at no time an inconsiderable personage. It often happens that there is a readiness, or an over-readiness, to acknowledge the importance of the fortunate occupant of the Vicarage. His irremovability from office has possibly a tendency to cause the Vicar, on his side, to receive, with a good grace, whatever of importance might be laid upon him, and sometimes a little more, just as he may be naturally inclined. Mr. Brown was no exception to the rule, and if there was a man in the town of my birth who was less respected than he deserved to be, that man was not Mr. Brown. He was a portly, double-chinned, genial gentleman, and although I would on no account insinuate that he "walked as men," still he was, in the literal sense of the word, "carnal." He bore about his person signs that his living, worth seven hundred a year, had not been without its blessings. And when I say that others were benefitted by his comfortable circumstances, I am paying his memory a tribute which it rightly deserves. Never was his ear heavy to the cry of the needy, nor his pocket buttoned against the poor and afflicted. In him the widow and the orphan found a kindly friend—especially if they attended Church. Although Mr. Brown, like everybody else, was obliged to remember that nearer is elbow than wrist, the wrist—that is to say, the poor Dissenter —was not altogether forgotten. When appealed to for help, if he could not see his way clear to contribute from his own purse, or from those legacies left him " as long as water ran," by the departed whose names appeared on the walls of the church, he would invariably say a good word for the applicants to some guardian or other, so as to secure them a few pence from the parish. If anybody wanted a letter of recommendation, it was to Mr. Brown he went for it. No town's movement, of any consequence, was complete if Mr. Brown's name did not figure in connection therewith. However severe their rheumatism, the shaking old man and the bent old woman, must doff the hat and curtsey to Mr. Brown when they met him. Those idlers and loafers who hang around street corners, whose means of living no man knows, when they saw Mr. Brown, ceased their funning, hid their cutty-pipes in their palms and touched their hats to him as he went by. There was some kind of winsomeness,

distinction, charm, I hardly know what to call it, about Mr.
Brown's manner at all times. I fancy everybody, at the time,
was as much capable of describing the thing as I am now. It
was something in the air which influenced all, aye, even the
Dissenters. I remember Mr. Brown once honouring a Bible
Society meeting with his presence. When he came in, never was
there such a clapping of hands and stamping of feet heard.
Some people, forgetting where they were, in the joy of the
moment, exerted themselves until they were fairly out of breath.
It is a fact that several Dissenters, to say nothing of Church
folk, shed tears of joy on the occasion ; the reason for such an
extraordinary manifestation of feeling, doubtless, being a
sincere respect for the good old Book, coupled with the knowledge that a gentleman of Mr. Brown's rank and position had
been secured as a patron for that Society whose object it is to
give

"A Bible to all the people of the world."

Mr. Brown said but little at the meeting (he never could without a book), but he was there, and that spoke volumes, a fact
which made some people, who thought they could read the
signs of the times, rather fancy that the millenium was not
far off.

For all this, Mr. Brown himself was an unassuming man, the
deference paid to whom would have made many another lose his
head. Even his warmest admirers admitted he had one drawback—he could not preach. His delivery was slow and painful,
but, like a wise man, he took care never, at any time, to tire his
hearers with verbosity. He had a habit, when in the pulpit, of
turning up the whites of his eyes, which was to some people
"as good as a sermon." Besides, his shortcomings in the
pulpit were made up, possibly more than made up, by the fact
that he was a justice of the peace, which character gave him an
influence over some whom he could never have reached within
the walls of the church. "Ned the Poacher," seeing him on the
street, would "make sly eyes" at Mr. Brown, and it was easy
to read in his face the consciousness of an unusual width of
pocket in the skirts of his velvet coat. "Drunken Tom," too
blind to see anyone else, would perceive Mr. Brown from afar,

and after a stagger and a glance through his half-open eyes, as through a mist, would make a desperate attempt to walk straight until Mr. Brown had passed. Had he not, in his magisterial character, come into contact with these gentry on Monday mornings in the County Hall, Mr. Brown's influence with them would have been *nil*. Not to be too minute, Mr. Brown was a man of considerable importance amongst all classes, and it was said of him that he feared no one but the owner of the Hall. I am forced to conclude that Mr. Brown was pretty much what he ought to be, or mother would never have esteemed him so highly; because, as I have more than once intimated, her prejudice against Church of England people was something awful. As to Mr. Brown, I heard her praise him many times, only she always took care to qualify the eulogy by the remark —"as a neighbour." It was "as a neighbour" alone she gave him a good word. In speaking of religion, she unhesitatingly expressed her fear that Mr. Brown had not "proved the great things." One observation of hers, with regard to him, I shall never forget. She happened to be talking to Margaret Peters. who was a Churchwoman, in praise of a Methodist preacher, when Margaret said, "Our Mr. Brown is a very good man, only he is not much of a hand at preaching." To which my mother replied :—"That's exactly the same, Margaret, as if you were to say James Pulford is a very good tailor, only he can't stitch." Margaret must have felt the force of the observation, for, as they sometimes say in the House of Commons, "the subject then dropped."

As might have been expected, the conviction and sentence of my brother Bob by Mr. Brown and the owner of the Hall, did not increase my mother's respect for the former. She considered the magistrates had manifested a want of judgment and an unpardonable haste. Whether it was his concern for us as his parishioners, or a consciousness of shame for the part he had taken in the trial, that brought the reverend gentleman on a visit to us, I cannot, for certain, say. Very willing am I to place the best construction upon his conduct and to believe that his motive was pure and praiseworthy. When I call that visit to mind, I become ashamed of the reception mother gave our visitor, especially when I consider the respect paid to Mr.

Brown by the generality of people. Perhaps I ought to say that, although Mr. Brown was Welsh on his mother's side, it was but imperfectly he spoke our old Cymric tongue.

"Good morning, Mrs. Lewis," said our vicar, panting for breath and wiping the perspiration from his red face and sleek, fat neck.

"Good morning," said mother stiffly, and without the least attempt at a curtsey, or as much as asking him to take a seat. But Mr. Brown sat, unasked, upon an old chair by her side, which, like all the rest in our house, was so terribly ricketty that I dreaded every minute it would give way beneath the unusual load now laid upon it, the more so because it was horribly uncomfortable, and creaked like an old basket.

After a brief, painful silence, Mr. Brown said:—

"Very fine day, Mrs. Lewis."

"The day is right enough, Mr. Brown. Were everything like the day, no one would have cause to complain," replied mother drily, and taking to that old habit of pleating her apron, which indicated always that she had something on her mind to which she wanted to give utterance.

"How do you get on, as things are now, Mrs. Lewis? Do you have enough food?" Mr. Brown asked, kindly.

"I get on better than I deserve, and have had enough food to keep body and soul together; although I have no one to thank for it but the One who feeds the young of the raven, who maketh his sun to rise on the evil and on the good, and sendeth rain on the just and on the unjust," was mother's answer.

"You say very good; you 'cognise the hand of the Great King," observed Mr. Brown.

"I hope I do," said mother, tartly. "But while recognising the Great King's hand, I can't shut my eyes to somebody else's hand also. Those wretched people of old who saw the hand of the God of Israel, knew something of Pharaoh's too."

"Yes, very bad man, Pharaoh, Mrs. Lewis."

"Bad enough," returned mother; "and though he was drowned in the Red Sea, his children were not, more's the pity. There is reason to fear that some of his offspring, and of Og's the king of Bashan, live to persecute God's people to this day, even though the Bible says that Og was utterly destroyed."

"You know deal of Scripture, Mrs. Lewis," remarked Mr. Brown, approvingly.

"I'm afraid, Mr. Brown," said mother, "that like many more, I know a deal more than I *do*. 'Blessed are they that do his commandments, that they may have right to the tree of life, and may enter in through the gates into the city.'"

"We must all try keep the commandments, Mrs. Lewis, or we never enter into the life," said our visitor.

"We must, as a rule of conduct," replied mother. "But we'll never enter into the life unless we do something more. I know this much of divinity, that we were shut out for ever on Sinai and that, if we wish to enter into the life, we must turn elsewhere for the foundation of our hope. That's what the Bible and Charles's *Preceptor* teach us. And I believe them, whatever the Common Prayer may teach. I say nothing about that."

"You chapel people know nothing 'bout Common Prayer. Common Prayer very good book, Mrs. Lewis; same as the Bible," said Mr. Brown.

"I say nothing about your Common Prayer, Mr. Brown, but I'll say this, that God's Book is the Bible, and I have no fear in saying, further, that the next book to that is Charles's *Preceptor*, and, if I were to live to a hundred, no one will change my opinion upon the point," declared my mother vehemently.

Mr. Brown, smiling at her simplicity, remarked:—

"Well, we'll leave it be so, Mrs. Lewis. I do like to see people zealous. But what I was thinking of was, how 're you getting along, now Bob's in jail? Do you have enough to eat, you and the boy here? Though you don't come to Church, I was thinking, Mrs. Lewis, to give a bit of—of assistance to you, or to get a little from the parish, till Bob comes back."

Mr. Brown spoke in a kindly tone, and I have no doubt that he sympathised greatly with mother and me in our distress. But his words touched a cord in mother's self-reliant nature which elicited a response I considered rude and altogether unbecoming towards a gentleman occupying a position and enjoying a respect like Mr. Brown's. I think I can remember, word for word, all she told him in reply.

"Mr. Brown," she said, "I know only of One who can give a bruise and heal it, who is able to cast down and raise up; so, if you came here thinking to put a plaister upon the hurt you gave, your errand has been in vain. A kick and a kiss I call a thing of that sort, Mr. Brown. After you had put my innocent boy in prison, it would be very difficult for me to take any help from you, let my distress be what it might. Perhaps you will say I am making bold, and so I am; but I must speak the thing which is on my mind; I'll feel easier then. I am surprised at you, Mr. Brown! I used to think well of you, as a neighbour; but, if it makes any difference to you, you have gone down ten degrees in my sight. I think I know with whom I am speaking; because, as Thomas of Nant said :—

'Praised and reverenced worthily,
    O'er all men, the priest we see;
But none more accurs'd than he,
    If God-guided he not be.'

And I don't much fancy, Mr. Brown, that God guides you when you associate and co-operate with a man like the owner of the Hall, who cares for nothing on this earth but his race-horses, fox-hounds, and furniture."

"Mrs. Lewis! Mrs. Lewis!" remonstrated Mr. Brown.

"My name is Mary, Mr. Brown. I'm but a poor woman, and I don't want to be 'mistressed,' if you please. But I tell you again—your place is not on the bench, hearing every cause, clean and dirty. A priest has quite enough to do to look after the souls of his congregation, if he has that work at heart, without meddling with other matters; and if I were queen, I would say to every priest, and preacher too, for that matter, as the Lord said in another case—and one which it would be well for you and I to think more of—'What hast thou to do to declare my statutes?' That I would. Paul, before his conversion, was on the way to Damascus with his pockets stuffed with summonses for putting good men in prison; but, after that great event, I warrant you he tossed them all over the hedge, and nobody ever heard of his sending anyone to gaol again; he had better work to do by a great deal. Another thing, Mr. Brown, I don't know how you can expect a blessing, or give sleep to your eyes, or slumber unto your eyelids, when your heart knows, by this time, that you have hurried an innocent lad to gaol, one who—and it is not because I'm his mother I say so—has a good deal more in his head than many who think themselves somebodies; one who, although, more's the pity, he does not now profess religion, has led a life against which no one can say a word. I have no wish to hurt anybody's feelings, but my son never, in his life, touched a drop of intoxicating drink, nor was he ever in the Red Dragon playing boogoodell, or whatever you call it. And although he was but a common collier, I think as much of him as other people do of their children who have been brought up in bordin' schools, and taught to frivol, and to feed their pride and fulfil the desires of the flesh; that I do. No one need have spoken to me of help from the parish, if you, Mr. Brown, and the owner of the Hall had not wrongfully imprisoned my son. I hope, still, to be kept from going on the parish, although there are many to whom it is useful. But as to going to Church, I never will. As you know, I've been there several times at thanksgiving services; but, I am bound to tell you, I never found anything for my soul there. Methodis' have I always been, and, by the help of God, Methodis' I shall always remain. I'll try and rough it, somehow, till my son comes back, without help of either parish or parson."

Mother delivered this address fluently, and with a withering scorn upon her face which I never knew it wear, before or since. Constant fear that the chair would give way under Mr. Brown, and deep shame for my mother's audacity, threw me into a great sweat. I was glad from the bottom of my heart to hear her put an end to her lecture. Mr. Brown seemed thunderstruck and wounded; and not without cause. But he was not the man to defend an act, though it were his own, if he thought it to be unjust. Mother knew him well enough to make bold with him in this. She knew, also, that if the belief were common in the town that Bob and his companion had been wrongfully imprisoned, no one could be more fully aware of the fact than Mr. Brown, who was never, at any time, a stranger to public opinion. Mr. Brown did not attempt to defend himself. When he got up to go I felt mightily relieved, because I was convinced, now, that the chair would not break. Before leaving, he said, morosely almost,—

"No one ever spoke like that to me before, Mrs. Lewis; and p'raps you'll want assistance from me yet."

"I don't deny the first, Mr. Brown," returned mother, "because I hope you never before put an innocent lad in gaol. It is no harm in the world for you to hear a bit of the truth sometimes, and I feel very much what-d'you-call-it after telling you what I have. But as to the other thing, namely, that I'll come to ask you, next time, I have nothing to do but trust in Providence; only, if I ever throw myself upon your good mercy, you may be sure that I shall have first tried everybody else in vain."

Mr. Brown left, fuming.

"I said nothing out of the way to him, did I?" mother asked, when he had gone.

I replied that I feared she went a little too far, and had hurt his feelings.

"Don't talk rubbish," she rejoined. "His skin is much thicker than you imagine. The Saviour and his Apostles spoke plainer truth, a good deal, to the High Priest than I did to Mr. Brown. I knew very well where I stood, and I'll defy him to send me a summons, big a man as he is."

That night, Abraham Jones, the overseer at the Red Fields Pit, came to our house to notify mother that good and constant work was being kept for Bob by the time he came home, and that whatever money she might stand in need of, meanwhile, was to be had, Bob to make re-payment from his wages as best he could. Mother having cried a little, and expressed her thanks, over and over again, gave Abraham—a zealous Congregationalist—particulars of the parson's visit, which diverted him greatly. On leaving, he handed mother a sovereign by way of loan. She looked at the coin on every side and from every angle, as one looks at an old friend whose face he has almost forgotten.

"'A good man showeth favour and lendeth,'" she said; "'he will guide his affairs with discretion.' Do you know what? I had nearly forgotten the sort of person our Queen was. I remember a time when I was right well acquainted with her. I hope we'll see each other oftener in the future. Long life and grace, both to her and her children, is the sincere wish of my heart."

CHAPTER XXI.

CONVERTS.

TIME passed, as it always does, bringing with it, as it always brings, not only its troubles, but its consolations. Through the kindness of overseer Abraham, our cupboard was no longer empty, the lions no longer raged within my stomach. The nearer the prospect of Bob's release, the brighter did my mother's face become. And yet I knew from her talk and demeanour that she was not without her fears for his appearance, for the effect of an unjust imprisonment upon his spirit, and a thousand and one other things which a careful mother troubles herself about under circumstances of this kind. John Powell had already come home, and although he could not give much account of Bob, the two having been confined apart, mother, by "pumping and stilling," had been able to extract enough from him to make her look forward with fear and anxiety to the day of my brother's return. Before that day came round, two things happened which cheered her greatly. Not to enlarge (as I sometimes say in my sermon, although I deliver myself of every word I originally intended), I will merely touch upon the occurrences.

The visits which our revered old deacon, Abel Hughes, paid to our house were of such common occurrence that I took but little notice of them, save on some special occasion like the one I have already chronicled. But I have good reason to remember one visit, about a fortnight before Bob came out of gaol. Mother and he had been conversing for some time; I, wholly heedless, being occupied in writing at the table near the window, for you must know I had not forgotten Bob's advice to apply myself to the work of self-improvement, so that I might not become a collier like him. My attention was suddenly arrested by Abel's saying to mother :—

"It is high time, Mary, for that boy to think of doing something, especially as matters are as they are with you now."

"I am of the same mind as you exactly, Abel," replied mother. "But what he is able to do, I don't know. He isn't strong, nor much of a scholar."

"But he is a big lump of a boy to be doing nothing, Mary."

"Exactly," said mother.

"I could do with a lad in the shop there, now, if I were sure Rhys would answer the purpose."

"The very thing I had been thinking of, dozens of times, Abel," said mother; "only I feared Rhys wasn't scholar enough. I knew he'd get fair play for his soul with you, and I fancy you'd have no trouble with him. He's a fairly good lad, considering. It's a very odd thing, Abel, but the older I get the more I see, with Bob, poor fellow, that a little learning comes in wonderful handy; only not too much of it—I'll stick to that."

"What're you doing there, Rhys?" queried Abel, coming towards me, and adding, "Do you know what? you write a very decent hand. Tell me, who taught you?"

"Bob," I answered timidly.

"Can you cipher? Can you do simple addition?"

I fear I smiled, almost sarcastically, in replying:

"I can do addition, subtraction, multiplication and division of money."

"What's he saying, Abel?" asked my mother.

"Oh! only that he knows how to reckon money," replied Abel.

"Rhys!" said mother, with a reproving look; "I never caught you in an untruth before. Do you want to break your mother's heart, or what? Haven't I had enough trouble already, without your going to tell a lie before my very face? The old saying is a true one, Abel: no one knows what it is to rear children. I tell you, honestly, I don't want to deceive you; but he has never had any money to handle. I'm surprised at you, Rhys, for saying such a thing to Abel Hughes."

Many of the old Methodists believed, I rather fancy, that laughter was not "becoming to the Gospel." I never remember previously hearing Abel Hughes give vent to his feelings in this particular fashion; and so unused was he to the business that his laugh was more of a cross between a screech and a groan than anything else. Laugh, however, he did.

"Don't disturb yourself, Mary *fach*," he said. "Rhys and I are only talking of the Tutor's rules for calculating money."

"Ho, say so! I never knew Mr. Tudor had any such rules, although I've heard he's got plenty of money, and that he takes good care of it, too. If he were to come here to reckon my money, he could leave his 'rules' at home, goodness knows. The children of these days know more than their parents, or they think so, at any rate. But as you und'stand each other, go on."

On we went, Abel questioning and I replying. Without flattering myself, I am certain Abel was astonished to find I knew as much as I did—I who had had such little schooling—and he admired Bob for the trouble he had taken with me.

"I hope Bob has taught him nothing wrong, Abel," remarked my mother. "They take so much to English, these days, that you can't tell what's taking place in your own house."

Abel assured her that Bob had been doing only good in teaching me these things; which, coming from him, was a sweet morsel unto her.

"I often quarrelled with Bob," said mother, "because there was too much book and slate going on, and too little of the Bible. I am glad, however, to hear you say that he taught the boy no harm; although I'll stick to it, there is in the youth of these days too great a tendency to neglect the Bible."

Not to amplify, as I have already said, the result of Abel's visit that night was an agreement between mother and him that I was to go on a month's trial to his shop, eating at his table, but coming home to sleep. This is one of the two things I referred to as bringing comfort to mother, as much comfort, I am certain, as many a mother has had on the appointment of her son to a post under government; a great element in such comfort being the reflection that my "soul would get fair play," as she expressed it.

The other thing which cheered her greatly was the fact that Thomas and Barbara Bartley continued to attend service, and that there was every reason to believe the Truth was, to some extent, working upon their minds. I have said that mother and I used often to visit Thomas and Barbara, and have intimated that there was a kind of understanding between us, during our

time of want, that we should not be permitted to leave our
neighbours' house fasting. I should, however, be doing
mother a great wrong if I let it be understood that this was her
only or her chief object. No, I think she felt as much interest
in their salvation as Paul did in that of his "kinsmen according
to the flesh." She watched carefully the manner in which the
couple listened to the Sunday's sermons, and on Monday
morning would visit them to know how much of the truth they
had comprehended and what effect had been left upon their
minds. I am under strong temptation to relate a few of the
conversations which occurred on these visits; but lest some
people should think I am over-drawing my mother's zeal and
devotion, I refrain. In the course of examining them, and
of explaining things, in the simple language of the truth, I
heard Thomas Bartley several times say :—

"It's a shocking pity you don't happen to belong to the
Ranters, Mary. You'd make an uncommon good preacher."

Our chapel friends understood, well enough, it was my
mother who had been instrumental in bringing Thomas and
Barbara to the means of grace. Great was their wonder and
joy to see two old folk, who, although living quite close to the
chapel, had spent their lives wholly heedless of religion, but
who, at last, gave their presence at every public meeting. "If
your brother's imprisonment," mother would say, "has been
the means of bringing Thomas and Barbara Bartley within
sound of the Gospel, and especially if it will be the means of
bringing them to Christ, I shall never repent of the bargain. I
much think, look you, that the truth has laid some hold of my
old neighbours' minds, and I shouldn't be a bit surprised to see
Thomas and Barbara come to Communion before Bob returns
home. I fancy I am about as good a Calvinist as anybody I have
met, but the devil must have farmed it badly with Thomas and
Barbara. There is in both good soil for Gospel seed; it has
none of the thorns and briars of envy and deceit, nor the reeds
and fens of fleshy lusts. In a manner of speaking, the spirit
will have less work there in making a new heart. Bob used to
talk a deal, as you know, of Thomas and Barbara's ignorance
and harmlessness, of which he made a lot of fun. Nothing
would please me better, when he comes home, than to be able

L

to tell him that both were saved. You may think I'm talking nonsense perhaps, Bob himself not being in Communion; but I can't help thinking—can't for the very life of me help thinking —that Bob is one of us. And something keeps telling me that he'll return to Communion directly. What is your opinion?"

I received, in connection with Thomas and Barbara Bartley's history, a lesson which I have never forgotten, namely, that those preachers whom some people term small are a much better blessing to a particular section of their hearers than those who are considered great. I remember that Thomas and Barbara received but little good from the ministration of the preachers whom my brother Bob styled favourites; while both would praise highly those whom he held almost in contempt. This pleased mother greatly, because she took it to verify her oft-repeated remark to my brother that everybody was not a Paul or a Peter, and that, although the fact had not been noted, many had been saved under Thaddeus, or the Master would not have called him to the work.

A few days afterwards, as we were at breakfast, mother observed: "This is the last Sabbath for Bob, poor fellow, to be in the house of bondage; thanks for it. And yet I'm almost afraid to see him come home, lest his spirit hath hardened under trial. I wonder who is to preach next Sunday? Were Bob home to-day I know he wouldn't care much for the minister. He was always disposed to under-rate William Hughes, of Abercwmnant. But I think William is one of the chosen, and I get a blessing from hearing him. Although we shall, no doubt, have to-day, as usual, as Bob used to put it, 'the object noted,' 'the act attributed,' and 'the duty enjoined,' it does'nt a bit matter; for William Hughes is sure to say something worth the hearing and the doing. Let us hope his Master will be with him, and that he will effect a conversion."

William Hughes kept his appointment. It is rarely a little preacher does not, except he be little enough to imitate the failings of a great one. I remember well the text that morning —'Turn ye to the stronghold, ye prisoners of hope.' I fancied everybody was thinking of my brother Bob when William Hughes was speaking of the prisoners. The old preacher appeared unusually spirited, and was listened to with the most marked attention. I have my notes of his sermon before me as I write. On looking them over, I find they contain the soundest doctrine; but, marvellous to relate, the ordinary divisions are not preserved. Possibly I was careless in taking down. They run thus:—I. *The objects noted—prisoners.* II. *The provision made by grace on their behalf—a stronghold.* III. *The duty enjoined—turning to the stronghold.*

I recollect mother helped the service to such an extent that I momentarily expected to hear her jubilating; as she did once under Cadwaladr Owen's ministration, at which Bob was so offended that he would not speak to her for two whole days together. I recollect, further, that Abel Hughes, towards the middle of the sermon, rose from his usual place under the pulpit, and posted himself in front of the Big Seat—a sure sign, always, that the preacher was saying something exceptionally good. Why I took such particular notice of our deacon's conduct was, possibly, because I had heard my mother say to him, more than once, after a rousing sermon : "Well, Abel, you too were obliged to come out of your kennel to-day." To me, a sufficient proof that William Hughes excelled himself on that morning is afforded by the imperfection of my notes ; my experience being that when a preacher speaks sluggishly I can take down nearly the whole sermon, but, if he has a swing and go about him, I forget my book and pencil and lose myself in what he says.

On coming out of chapel I found Thomas and Barbara Bartley waiting for mother. All three, engaged in earnest conversation, walked homewards together, Will Bryan and I keeping a little to the rear. Although it was Sabbath morn, I could not help telling Will that I was going apprentice to old Abel. Struck with surprise, and with a look of commiseration for my fate, he said,

"Good-bye, my hearty. This child (striking his chest), would sooner go apprentice to a roller-up or barber. You'll never more have any liking for play or laughter. From this time out you'll get nothing in the world but Communion and a verse ; and before this day month, I'll take my oath, you'll have been obliged to learn to groan like an Irishman with the toothache, and to pull a face as long as a fiddle. You'll be fit

for heaven any day then.　Rather than go 'prentice to the old
onion, this child (striking his breast again), would go footman
to the King of the Cannibal Islands.　I'm sorry for you Rhys;
but since the thing is settled—fire away.　This chap (striking
his breast once more), would sooner go oyster-fishing to the top
of Moel Fammau than go 'prentice to old Ab."

I knew Will was honestly speaking his mind, but having
told him I did not look upon my future in the same serious
light that he did. I was surprised at his reply.

"Listen here, old hundredth.　I think it about time we made
a preacher or a deacon of you, I'll swear."

Will little guessed I could desire nothing better than to be
made the former, were it in his power.　To avoid his gibes I
kept the reflection to myself.

On reaching home I found my mother humming a tune, and
although she was almost speechless, I never knew her to give
so many signs of inward happiness.　I imagined it was the
"stronghold," of which the preacher spoke, which made her
heart rejoice, but I don't remember that she said a word about
the sermon, beyond this alone—that William Hughes "had felt
his feet under him," which was her way of indicating that a
preacher had found inspiration.　At six o'clock that evening,
William Hughes had another successful meeting, of which my
memoranda are as follow:—

> TEXT:—"Come unto me, all ye that labour and are heavy-
> laden, and I will give you rest."
>
> HEADS:—1. The objects noted—Those who labour and are
> heavy laden.
>
> 2. The duty enjoined—"Come unto me."
>
> 3. The precious promise unto those who obey—"I will
> give you rest."

I do not remember anything in particular about the sermon.
In Communion, after service, Abel Hughes put the customary
question—"Is there anyone who has remained afresh?"
I wondered what made him ask, seeing he himself was looking
straight at two who had "remained afresh."　John Lloyd (he
whom Will Bryan had named "the Old Scraper,") in reply

said that which everybody knew already, namely, that Thomas
and Barbara Bartley had remained.

"Ho! will you have a word with them, William Hughes?"
said Abel, addressing the preacher, adding, "you must not
expect much from them; they have not been hearers for long."
He thereupon sat down beside the preacher, in whose ear, so I
have imagined, he whispered all he could, in half a minute,
tell about the converts. After some slight demur, the preacher
got to his feet and, with hands crossed upon his back, under
his coat-tails, walked, as if reluctantly, towards Thomas and
Barbara. As far as I can remember, the conversation which
ensued was somewhat after this fashion :—

"Well, Thomas Bartley," the preacher began, "I know
nothing about you, so perhaps you wouldn't mind telling us,
freely, a little of your history."

"I will, name of goodness," replied Thomas. "Father and
mother were poor people, and I was the youngest of three
children. There's none left 'cept me; and I don't know of
anybody belonging to us but one cousin down in England, if
he's alive. It's a dying-out sort of ——"

"I didn't mean you to give the history of your family," the
preacher interposed. "What I wanted to know was a little of
your own experience. What made you and your wife remain
behind to-night?"

"O! beg pardon," said Thomas. "Well, I'll tell you.
Barbara and I, for weeks past, have been thinkin' a lot about
comin' to Communion to you. Mary Lewis told us it was high
time, and that we could never do anythin' better. So, hearin'
you a-beggin' of us so earnestly this mornin' to turn to the
stronghold, we both made up our minds to stay to-night;
because we knew very well it was to us you was referrin'."

Barbara nodded her concurrence.

"You did well," remarked the preacher; "and I don't doubt
but that the friends here are very glad to see you. Very likely
you look upon yourself as a great sinner, Thomas Bartley?"

"Well, I'll say this much," replied Thomas, "I never nursed
a spite towards anybody, as Barbara knows; and I always try
to live honest."

"I am glad to hear it; it isn't everybody can say that much," Mr. Hughes observed, adding, " but we are all sinners, you know, Thomas Bartley."

"Yes, yes," said Thomas. " Bad is the best of us; but I'm thinkin' some are worse'n others."

" Can you read, Thomas Bartley ? " asked the minister.

"I've a grip of the letters, nothin' more; but I'm awful fond of hearin' others read," replied Thomas.

" It's a great loss not to be able to read; and it has got somewhat late in the day for you to think of learning," Mr. Hughes observed.

" I know I'll never learn, 'cause there's nothing quick about me, most the pity," said Thomas.

"Not having heard very much of the Gospel, Thomas Bartley, and not being able to read, you should be doubly diligent, in attendance on the means of grace from this time out," said Mr. Hughes.

"If we live," returned Thomas, "Barbara and I have made up our minds to come reg'lar to the means, 'cause the time passes better by half here'n if we stayed mopin' at home. To tell you the truth, Mr. Hughes, we find great pleasure in chapel, and if we'd a-known it sooner, we'd have been here these years; but no one ever asked us till Mary Lewis a'most forced us to come."

"What gives you such pleasure in chapel, Thomas Bartley ? " asked the preacher.

"Indeed, I can't tell you guzzactly, but Barbara and I feel much more what-d'you-call-it, since we've been comin' to chapel."

" Very good," remarked the preacher. " But what do you think of ' the stronghold ' I tried to say something about this morning ? "

" Well," replied Thomas, " I thought you spoke up nicely about it, only I couldn't catch guzzactly all you said. But Mary Lewis explained to us on the way home that Jesus Christ dyin' for us was the stronghold, and that trustin' Him for salvation was turnin' to the stronghold. I thought so too, only I couldn't speak my mind."

" Whoever this Mary Lewis is," observed the preacher, " she is pretty near the mark on that head."

"Yes, I warrant her. Mary is a real good 'un, sure to you, Mr. Hughes," rejoined Thomas.

It had been obvious for some time, so I heard mother say, that Mr. William Hughes did not understand his customer. After a moment's hesitation, he made one more attempt to bring Thomas to a point.

"Thomas Bartley," said he, "will you tell me what call was there that Jesus Christ should die for us?"

"Well, so far's I can make out," replied Thomas, "it was nothin' in the blessed world, only he himself liked it."

"But wasn't there anything in us which necessitated his dying, Thomas Bartley?" asked the preacher.

"Nothing at all, to my mind," replied Thomas. "P'raps I'm wrong, though; only I fancy no one told him to do it, and that he took everybody by surprise, as they say."

Mr. Hughes looked, once more, as if he had been pitched from his saddle. Turning to Barbara he said:—

"Well, Barbara Bartley, can *you* read?"

"A grip of the letters, same as Thomas," was her reply.

"Will you tell us a word as to your feeling?" said Mr. Hughes.

"Same as Thomas, guzzactly," returned Barbara.

William Hughes retraced his steps to the Big Seat, saying: "Abel Hughes, you know our friends here better than I do."

Abel got upon his feet. Although but a lad, I knew that if anyone could find out whether a spark of the divine fire had descended upon the souls of Thomas and Barbara, it was Abel. I never saw his like, I'm thinking, at probing the soul of a man, whatever reputation he bore.

"My dear old neighbours," said our senior deacon, in a voice trembling with emotion, "I need not tell you that my heart rejoices to see you making effort to turn to that stronghold we heard so sweetly spoken of this morning. I hope, and for that matter believe, that your intention was perfectly good in staying with us to-night. I, my friends, feel," he went on, turning towards the congregation, "that I have been severely reproved here to-night, and I trust we all felt the same, when Thomas Bartley told us that no one except Mary Lewis ever asked him and his wife to come to the means of grace. Let us be ashamed and repent. Well, Thomas Bartley, I'll try and talk so that you can understand me. Do you find any change in your disposition and mind, these days, different to what you used to, we'll say three months ago?"

"A great change, 'deed to you, Abel Hughes," replied Thomas Bartley.

"Well, tell us, in your own way, what it is," said Abel.

"You never met my worse at speakin', Abel Hughes; but before I began comin' to chapel, Barbara nor me never thought anythin' on the blessed earth about our end. But now there isn't a day goes over our heads that we don't talk about it. I think a good deal of what'll happen to us when we go from here — will Barbara and I be together, and shall we be comfortable?"

"That's right, Thomas," said Abel. "What do you think you must get here, so that you may be made comfortable after going from here?"

"Well," replied Thomas, "I can't tell you, guzzactly. But I'm thinking it's trust in Christ, as Mary Lewis says."

"Don't change your mind as to that, Thomas *bach*," said Abel. "You and I, and all of us, will be quite safe if we only trust in Him. You had a son, Thomas, who has gone to Him, without doubt. Seth, innocent as he was, got to know the Man; and I cannot wish you both, or myself, better than to be able to tell, as clearly as Seth did, where he was going to."

At mention of Seth great tears fell down Thomas's cheek, so choking his utterance that it was quite impossible to get another word from him. Barbara's check apron became wet with the same kind of moisture. Abel Hughes was a stern man, but he had a large heart; and when he wept, his tears, like summer rain, took effect on everything round about, save the rocks. So happened it this time, for he was completely overcome. Presently regaining his composure, he asked the church to signify its assent to the reception of Thomas and Barbara Bartley into membership. Before any hand could be raised, John Lloyd asked whether Thomas Bartley was an abstainer?

"Hark at the old Scraper," said Will Bryan in my ear.

Abel, without taking it upon him that he had heard John Lloyd's question, declared the Bartleys to have been duly admitted.

I sat near the Big Seat. After the preacher had brought Communion to a close, I saw Thomas Bartley go up to the chief deacon. Thrusting his hand into his pocket, he asked:—

"Abel Hughes, is there any entrance to pay to-night?"

"No, Thomas," replied Abel with a smile. "You'll have an opportunity of putting something on the church book by and bye."

"To be shŵar," said Thomas, and away he went.

CHAPTER XXII.

A VISIT FROM MORE THAN ONE RELATION.

HAD I known, before beginning to write this autobiography, it would swell to such a size, I am doubtful whether I would have undertaken the task at all. Behold me, at the end of twenty one chapters—some of them long and lean—only, as it were, just sharpening my pencil for a start. I have said so many things, of all sorts, that I do not remember whether I have previously described what I feel when writing every chapter, almost; namely that there is here too great an abundance of the "I," "my mother," and "my brother," of "said she," "said I," and "said he," which, if the work were published, would doubtless pall upon the reader. But what help have I? Having begun the work, I am not very willing to leave it unfinished, especially since I have not touched upon some of the principal events of my life.

Without flattery or false-modesty, the truth is, my brother Bob was a hero in the eyes of the Red Fields' workmen. Although in language, manners and habits he differed from most of them, yet I am perfectly certain that did they go to choose a king from their midst, Bob would have been elected monarch. It is a fact worthy of note that superior intelligence, and purity of speech and conduct will, sooner or later, win the admiration of even the most reckless and ungodly. Bob, since he was thirteen years of age, had been at work in the Red Fields colliery, and never an ear heard oath descend his lips. His fellow-workmen speedily got to know he was a reader, and, when meal time came round, he would be applied to for the news. He had an excellent memory and a fluent tongue, and while yet a mere lad he made glad the heart of many older than he, by the light of the Davy lamp deep down in the bowels of the earth. When he grew up to manhood he found himself one of the leaders of his fellow-workmen; and although, any more than someone else, he could not control a fierce crowd of colliers, still he was generally looked upon as their adviser. During the period of Abraham Jones's stewardship, it was to Bob he gave charge of the work in his absence. No wonder, therefore, that when Abraham regained office, my brother's former companions should look forward with interest to the time of his release from prison. Although it was only a few days since I had begun to "work" with Abel Hughes in his shop, the old man kindly gave me a holiday in order that I might greet my brother on his return home. He was expected by the mid-day train; and, from early morning, mother, nervous and agitated, busied herself cleaning the house and preparing a hearty reception for him.

"I have been a good while trying to make out," she said, "what we shall get the boy to eat when he comes. They tell me that too heavy a meal for one who has just left jail will make him ill. Now I think of it, Bob used to be wonderful fond of currant cake; and, so that he might have some delicacy which won't weigh too heavy on his stomach, perhaps a cup of tea and some cake would be just the thing. If you'll run to the shop for three penn'orth of the best flour, a ha'porth of carbonate of soda, and a quarter of a pound of currants, I'll be no time making it."

I was most ready to do my share of the work, my disposition, like Bob's, being somewhat favourable to the griddle. The tea things were on the table, the cake had been baked, the kettle had boiled and got cold again, many times over, long before the train was due. And I was at the railway station at least half an hour too early, Will Bryan, fair play for him, being there even before me. Very speedily, scores of stalwart colliers lined the platform, all with spirits and voices high. Some chucked me familiarly under the chin, others pulled my hair and ears—

with the best intentions of course—while others gave me
pennies. I preferred the last. Will Bryan looked almost
enviously upon my store, but did not ask me for any of
it, as he did on the previous occasion, when I thought he
meant to fee a lawyer to defend Bob. This time he seemed
puzzling himself to know what he should tell me to do with the
money.

"It's a great pity Bob doesn't smoke," he observed. "That
brass of yours would have done nicely to buy him a tobacco-
box."

With his failure to suggest anything else, I had half a mind
to condole. One remark he made I remember well.

"A collier who is taken to jail," he said, "has this advantage,
that they can't give him the county crop. I'll defy 'em to cut
his hair any shorter than it is already."

A great many other observations did Will let drop, which I
considered at the time to be the essence of wisdom. The crowd
of colliers who had come to meet Bob grew very large. I was
surprised at the absence from their midst of Bob's greatest
friend, John Powell. While I was thinking what a disappointment it would be to Bob not to find his old companion there to
welcome him, I heard the train approach. My heart began
beating rapidly ; Will Bryan made his mouth into a circle and
went imitating the engine. The bell rang, and the train came
in sight at a speed which I thought would make it impossible
to pull up. Pull up, however, it did. With the noise of the
steam which the engine let off, the throwing of coal on the fire,
the banging of boxes upon the platform, the opening and
slamming of doors, the rushing hither and thither of passengers
and other people, and the talk and chatter they made, the place
became one wild scene of noise and confusion. I looked in
every direction for Bob.

"All right," shouted someone, and away went the train
once more.

The colliers stared at each other with disappointment in their
looks. Will Bryan, running up to me, said, "A mare's nest.
Bob has not come."

My spirit sank within me, and hardly could I control my
feelings. The colliers tried to console me with the assurance

that Bob would arrive by next train, due three hours later.
I went home crestfallen. Long before reaching the house, I
saw mother in the doorway expecting *us*. On seeing me alone,
she fled inside. Her disappointment was sore. I told her the
colliers were certain he would come by next train. The cake
was left unbroken and the kettle, which had boiled dry, was
refilled. I went to meet the train a second time, and found a
greater crowd of workmen than before. I had a presentiment
Bob would not come by that train either. It turned out to be
true. By this time my own disappointment had lost its smart at
thought of the blow it would be to mother, whose heart-strings
had been strained to such a pitch of tension that I fancied they
must break at this fresh news. Nearing the house, I saw that
she was not, as on the previous occasion, standing in the doorway. On entering, I found she was not so much cast down as
I had anticipated.

"I knew he would not come; something told me so," she
said, before I had time to speak a word. "The furnace is not
seven times heated, even yet, it would seem. I know something has happened to him;" and burying her face in her
apron, she burst into tears.

I followed her example, and both of us presently felt better.
I do not remember that we ate a single morsel. Mother did
not care whether I went to meet the last train or not; but go
I did. On the platform this time were a number of the Red
Fields workmen who had been engaged in the pit during the
day. They appeared fresh washed, their faces being clean,
with the exception of a little shading about the corners and lids
of the eyes. I noticed, also, that great numbers of those who
had not been to work that day were half drunk. The train
came, but without bringing Bob; whereupon the last-named
section began cursing it, and almost everything else, but especially the two justices, Mr. Brown and the owner of the Hall.
Will Bryan tried to persuade me to wait a while before returning home, there being signs, he said, of a row worth the seeing
among the colliers. Finding his words were of no avail, at a
great personal sacrifice, he returned with me. Will was always in
his element in a row. Wherever there was a disturbance, there
also, if it were possible, was Will. At Soldier Robin's school it

was his whole delight to set the boys a-fighting. In connection with the chapel, again, he a thousand times preferred
accounts of a wrangling teachers' meeting to listening to a
good sermon. Ever since he began to part his hair and
"make a Q.P.," mother was very much prejudiced against him,
and was always putting me on my guard lest he should corrupt
me. Will understood this very well, and, whenever he visited
our house, he always took care to pull his hair down over his
forehead before coming in. This had an excellent effect on
mother, and I think would have uprooted her prejudices had
she not accidentally, in looking through the window one day,
caught Will going through this preliminary. She reproved him
severely for his hypocrisy.

But, after all, as I have previously intimated, Will understood my mother perfectly, and managed her with remarkable
skill. When it served his purpose he could, in his own way,
talk as religiously as herself, almost. I do not think she was
displeased to see Will coming home with me that night. She
had had a neighbour or two in to cheer her, and so, doubtless,
believed that Will was some sort of a support to me. When we
entered, we were both struck with her calmness.

"The old woman keeps up like a brick," said Will in my ear.

"I see," observed my mother, "it is bad news you have
again. But it's only what I expected. Something has
happened to him or he would have been home before now."

"Don't be down-hearted, Mary Lewis," said Will. "I
believe Bob will turn up from somewhere, just directly."

"You've no foundation for that belief, William," returned my
mother. "To-night, look you, I'm made to feel the words of
the wise man coming home to me: 'Hope deferred maketh the
heart sick.' And then Job, when he was in trouble, said,
'Thou washest away the things which grow out of the dust of
the earth, and thou destroyest the hope of man.' 'Where is
now my hope?' 'As for my hope, who shall see it?'"

"Well, but didn't the preacher say the other Sunday, Mary
Lewis," asked Will, "that it came right with Job in the end,
after all the humbugging he got, didn't he?"

"He did, William," replied mother; "and were I as trustful in my Redeemer as Job was, it would come all right with me too, look you."

"It's sure to come all right with you, Mary Lewis. You're as pious as Job was, I'll take my oath of it," observed Will.

"Don't presume and blaspheme, William," commanded my mother.

"I'm telling the truth, from my heart," returned Will. "You're as pious as Job was, any day he got out of bed. And, according to the way the preacher gave his history, I see you both very much like each other. Job had a bad wife and you've had a bad husband, and you've both stuck to your colours, first class; so I'm sure the Lord'll not be shabby in your case, in the end, either; you shall see if He will."

"I beg of you not to say any more, Will," said mother. "You ought to know I'm in no humour, to-night, to listen to any nonsense from you."

"Nonsense!" cried Will, honestly indignant, I am sure. "It is no nonsense at all. I'll bet you—that is, I'll take my oath—it'll be all right with you in the end. Didn't the preacher tell us about Job that the Lord was only trying him? So is He doing with you. He only just wants to show the kind of stuff there's in you."

"William," said mother, for the sake of turning the conversation, "were there many colliers at the railway?" ("Railway" was mother's name for the station.)

"Thousands upon thousands," replied Will.

"There you are again," observed mother. "There's only three hundred altogether in the Red Fields pit."

"Well, yes, in a manner of speaking, you know, Mary Lewis," rejoined Will. "I'm sure there was near a hundred there."

"Didn't one of you happen to speak to John Powell? What did he think about Bob's not coming?" mother asked.

"John Powell wasn't there," we both replied.

"Not there! John Powell not there!" exclaimed mother, in surprise.

"He was working the day shift," obesrved Will.

"Who told you that, William?" asked mother.

"No one; I only thought it," was Will's answer.

Mother fell to pleating her apron and musing. Presently she said,—

"William, you wouldn't be long running as far as John Powell's house and telling him, if he is in, I'd like to see him."

"No sooner said than done," said Will, jumping to his feet.

"It is very dark, William," observed my mother, following him to the door; "and it is almost too much to ask you to return. Rhys'll come with you to learn something from John Powell, so as to let you go home."

"Stand at ease, as you were!" cried Will in English. "If the darkness is very thick, I'll cut through it with my knife." And off he went.

"There is something very lovable and decent about that boy," mother remarked. "I can't, for the life of me, help liking him; only I'd like him better if he was a little more serious and spoke less English. I often fear he'll make you like himself; and yet I do not think there is guile in his heart. Why didn't you tell me John Powell wasn't at the railway?"

Although the time seemed long, Will speedily returned with the news that John Powell was not at home, neither had he been home during the day; on hearing which, mother fell once more into a deep study, so deep that she took no notice of what Will told me, almost in a whisper :—

"I called to tell the gaffer yonder I was going to stay with you to-night. We have lost some splendid sport. The colliers have been burning straw effigies of Mr. Brown and the owner of the Hall, and capital ones they were, too. There's been three battles, and One-eyed Ned has been taken to the round house, although he fought like a lion with the p'liceman."

Will rattled along with his story, but I was not in the humour to listen, and I have no inclination to repeat it here. Seeing me not interested he ceased, and, next minute was fast asleep, his heavy breathing filling the house and rousing mother from her reverie.

"William," she said, "it's time you should go home, my son."

"Not going home to-night; told the gaffer so," replied Will, who fell asleep again directly. Mother recommenced her apron-pleating, and looked thoughtfully into the fire.

I loved the silence. I don't know whether there is another like me, but I am thinking that my habit of spending hours at a stretch in the quiet of the night staring into the fire, with thousands of things which never had an existence and will never come to pass, running through my mind, is a legacy left me by my mother. Spite of every attempt to shake it off, it has clung to me to this day. Some nights I live an age in a few hours. Among other things, I have seen myself married to someone whose name I do not know. Our children fill the house with their clatter, they grow up and are sent to school, I try and train them as best I can, they give me all sorts of trouble, they leave home; at last their mother dies and I, a white-headed old man, am deserted of all save my crutches. I am cold and, the clock striking one, I spring to my feet with the remark that these are but vain imaginations, and I myself but a shivering old bachelor. I then run off to bed; but before closing my eyelids, I make a resolve that never again will I give my fancy rein, it being unprofitable, if not actually sinful, so to do. Next night I read till I am tired, and then say to myself, "Rhys, you had better, before going to bed, think over one or two matters, just for five minutes." No sooner do I say so, than I begin building castles in the air once more; I imagine great numbers of things, and fancy myself in one situation and the other for an hour, two hours, sometimes three! Away with such a practice! And yet I love it. Like the man who is a slave to strong drink, I hate the failing from the bottom of my heart, at the same time that I find the greatest pleasure in it, and am for ever resolving some day to shake it off.

But to return. As I have said, I loved the silence, to which neither Will's breathing nor the fact that something often rose to his throat as if it would choke him, did more than add. Mother and I exchanged not a word, but, so I have since thought, our fancies, though unconsciously, travelled side by side, so completely were our minds absorbed by the self-same object. I know not how long we thus remained, but I remember well fancying, a score of times, that I heard someone walking up the court-yard towards the house, the footsteps dying away within a yard or two of the door. At times I felt certain they were Bob's, and held my breath in expectation.

All, however, ended in silence. So sweet were these fancies that, as soon as I had finished with one I began upon another, and had I not found Will suddenly waking and mother springing to her feet, I would not have known whether it was in fancy or in fact that I heard someone knocking at the door, Before Will had awoke from sleep and I from dreams, to welcome Bob, mother had opened the door. But what a disappointment! It was the man I detested with all my soul, whom I heard saying to mother :—

" Well, Mary, how do you do, this long time ? "

He it was whom, when I first saw him, I called " the Irishman," and who stopped me near the Hall Park on the night Seth died. It was strange that at every critical juncture of my early life this man was sure to appear. I would as soon see him as see the Devil. Will perceived in an instant who he was, for he knew as much about him as I did, nearly, because, as intimated at the beginning of this history, I could conceal but little from my friend, who, on his part, never betrayed my confidence. Directly mother found out who our visitor was, she drew herself up, and I saw she had lost none of that pluck which she at all times showed when there was a real necessity for it. Standing before " the Irishman," as I called him, in such a fashion that it was impossible he could enter the house, except by force, she said :—

" James, I have told you many times I never want to see your face again and that you are not to come into this house."

Will played with the poker, and the Irishman thrust his head forward to see who was within.

" Isn't that Hugh Bryan's son ? " he asked, looking at Will.

" Yes," replied my mother.

" I thought so by his nose," observed the Irishman.

" What do you see about my nose, you kill-pheasant, you?" asked Will, hotly.

" William, hold your tongue this minute, is best for you," said mother.

I could read in the Irishman's face that nothing would have given him greater pleasure than to wring Will Bryan's neck, and that my mother knew, right well. Still toying with the poker and muttering his anger, Will said to me, softly, " Shall

M

I give him a downer?" I had only to answer "yes," and
Will would have used the poker on the instant. I, however,
told him to take care, for the Irishman was not a man to be
trifled with. Will, maintaining his grip of the poker, fixed his
eye upon that of the visitor as the chick does on the hawk
which is about to swoop down upon it, but with this difference,
that Will was not afraid of the onset. I knew from his look
that had the Irishman laid a hand on mother, or tried to force
his way into the house, Will would not have stayed to consult
us as to what use he should put the poker. Mother and the
Irishman were, by this time, speaking so low that we could
catch but very few words of what they said. I understood
her to be exhorting him, earnestly and threateningly, to go
away. I noticed him look towards Will, and heard him say to
mother :—"Can he hold his tongue after to-night?" I could
not make out my mother's answer, so softly was it given. All
of a sudden the two ceased speaking, and I saw the Irishman
peering in the direction of the yard and turning pale in the
face. Still, he did not move from where he stood. A moment
later we heard footsteps approaching the house. In that brief
space I saw before me a guilty conscience which shook and
paralysed its owner. Next minute, a hand was laid upon the
intruder's collar, he himself was hurled aside and a voice with
which those walls had not resounded for two months past was
heard saying :—

"Holloa, gamekeeper! what do you want here?"

I saw no more of the Irishman that night. Bob and John
Powell walked in, shutting the door after them. I will not
attempt to describe my mother's joy and mine, because I should
be ashamed to see it on paper. However paradoxical it might
appear, the way in which we two testified our happiness was by
a hearty cry. Thinking the matter over, I fancy Will's method
of exhibiting his feeling was much the more reasonable one.
He walked, or rather danced, round the kitchen, whistling :—

"When Johnny comes marching home, my boys,"

and running the poker up and down his left arm as if it were
a fiddle bow. Will had waltzed several times around before

mother noticed the ungodliness taking place in her house. When she did, she soon put an end to his pranks.

To my comfort I could not see that his imprisonment had wrought any change in Bob's appearance. His face wore the same calm thoughtfulness and determination it always wore, and there was nothing in his gait to indicate that he had lost a particle of his independent spirit. Hard labour was no new thing to him, and this, possibly may account for the fact. When mother came to herself, she viewed him over from crown to sole, and vowed that, like the youths of the captivity, he looked all the better for his hard fare. She then began an examination and enquiry. Upon her asking him how it was he did not come home by the mid-day train, John Powell made answer :—

"I am to blame for that. I got to learn that the workmen had determined to make a fuss and an exhibition of Bob, and knowing he would not like it, I went to meet him. I kept him back until everybody had gone away to bed. I am sure I shall catch it for what I've done."

When Bob came to ask the news, I expected one of the first things mother would tell him was that I had been apprenticed to Abel Hughes. But I was disappointed, and I am not sorry for it. The recollection of her words is a great comfort to me at the present moment, for they show clearly where her thoughts were domiciled, and what those things were which brought her heart its greatest joy.

"The best news on earth I have to give you, Bob," she said, "is that Thomas and Barbara Bartley have joined our church, and that there is every reason to believe them both to have been really converted."

"And fine fun there was with them," remarked Will.

"Don't you talk of fun in Communion, is best for you," said mother. "The two were a trifle comical, as you might expect, Bob; but, to my mind, the ring of a call was there, plain enough. And I have been thinking a good deal, my dear boys," she added, glancing around at us four, "of those words, 'the last shall be first.' It would be a hard thing, wouldn't it, if Thomas and Barbara, for all their ignorance and drollery, were saved in the end, while we children of the kingdom, were cast into outer darkness?"

Mother spoke much more in the same strain. I never remember seeing Bob so attentive to what she said; and unless there was something the matter with my sight, I fancy his eyes filled with moisture more than once. Mother was so absorbed in her theme that she forgot, for a while, to offer my brother and his friend something to eat. But it turned out that both had been feasting it somewhere before coming home, and mother at last was considerate enough to place the currant cake before Will and myself. I say it with a clear conscience: if Will and I, under every subsequent circumstance, did our duty as well and thoroughly as we did it when the currant cake was brought face to face with us on this particular midnight, Will would not be where he now is, and I would be a much better minister of the Gospel than I am. Mother ordered Will and myself off to bed. I felt perfectly happy, and according to Will's testimony, given the moment before he began to snore, the only trouble upon his mind was my refusal to allow him to give the Irishman "a downer."

CHAPTER XXIII.

BOB.

MONTHS went by. The work at Red Fields prospered under the management of Abraham Jones, who, by this time, had brought the place to order. Expenses were less and profits greater than when the "Lancie," as he was called, was overseer, while the workmen received a wage of which they could not complain. The unpleasant words "oppression" and "injustice" were no longer heard in our house, and Bob was wholly satisfied with his earnings. In a few weeks he paid off every farthing of the debt my mother had incurred during his imprisonment, and poverty and want were banished our cot. But was my mother happy? Bob's wages, as I have said, were more than enough to meet the family requirements, and mother was no longer compelled to puzzle her head about paying her way. To me it appeared that Providence smiled upon us, and that our troubles and trials were all at an end. One bitter thing, it is true, had a permanent place in our consciousness, though none of us ever made mention of it. But, by now, it had become an old story of which we took no account, save as we did original sin—something of which we could not shake ourselves free. As far as I could perceive, the prison had had but little effect on Bob's spirit, one way or the other. In his hours of leisure he read unremittingly, mother saying he would ruin his eyesight, for certain. He came, also, regularly to chapel as before; but, although earnestly pressed, he declined to take up again his class in the Sunday School. I must admit one other change in him—he never now read the Bible in our presence, a fact which troubled mother greatly, for she feared, for some time, that he did not read it at all. Generally he sat up after mother and I had gone to bed; mother regularly, after the device had presented itself to her mind, taking care to place the Bible every night in a peculiar position upon the table near the window, which enabled her to make sure, next morning whether Bob had touched it or not. So much was she comforted on perceiving that the Bible had been moved that it became her nightly habit to note its precise position on the table. Against this change for the worse in Bob must be placed his increased love and tenderness towards mother. He appeared more respectful in his demeanour, and more tolerant of her prejudices.

But was my mother happy? I am certain she was not. The bloom did not return to her cheek, nor did the black marks disappear from under her eyes. In the space of three months she seemed to have aged ten years. And yet I think the bloom would have come back, and the blackness beneath the eyes have gone thence, had Bob but said, "Mother, I feel very uneasy, and mean to offer myself to Communion next Sunday." But the words were never spoken. Often did my mother refer to the danger of tribulations, not merely leaving us where we were, but driving us farther from God, instead of bringing us gentleness of spirit, and making us consecrate and more religiously inclined. Bob quite saw the drift of her remarks. But

inasmuch as he persistently took it upon him that they did not
apply personally to himself, mother, one night, gave up
parablising, and pressed upon him seriously the duty of be-
taking himself once more to his religious professions.   His
answer, as near as I can recollect it, was in these words:—

"You know that it is not my fault that I do not profess. It
was not I who threw away profession, but the church who took
it from me. As far as I'm aware, there is nothing different
in me now from what there was when I professed, except that
I have been to prison; and that, I should think, does not add to
my fitness to profess. Were I to offer myself to the church,
the first question asked—or, at any rate, that ought to be asked
—me would be, have I repented the fault for which I was excommunicated? I should be obliged to reply that I have not
repented, never can repent it. Either the church or I, in that
case, would look like a ——. It is the church alone that is
responsible for my non-profession—if having my name on
Communion-book means profession. I believe, however, there
is a higher profession, and a far superior confession of faith.
There are men to be found—I do not say I am one, lest you
should tell me, as you did once, that I am self-righteous—but
there are men, I repeat, whose chief object it is to find out the
truth, from whatever direction it may come; men who are
constantly groping for the God of Truth, and who know what
it is to lose many a night's rest in eager, painful expectation of
the light. They know well what it is to be grievously wounded
by doubt and unbelief, and yet they will not give up searching
for the balm which is to heal them. I call these God's sons,
even though some of them have not their names on any book
of Communion. I have, as you know, a deep respect for
several members of the church as true-principled, piously-
disposed men, and, after their own fashion, strict disciplinarians.
But, to me, it does appear strange that they can see only one
kind of sin. Are Robert Lewis and William the Coal the only
transgressors? Can you explain to me why William has been
many times censured and John Lloyd not once? As far as I
know, there is not one who doubts William's innocence, poor
fellow. His besetting sin is a forgetfulness that his head is not
strong enough to resist the effects of more than two glasses of

beer, and that he has a tendency, after overstepping the mark, to fall upon his back, or lurch on one side—in which no one can, or wants to justify him. But is there, pray, any regulation by which a man can be called to account for avarice and parsimony? Are some men to be allowed to go on sowing the seeds of discord, persecuting their fellows, and blackening their characters, snapping like curs at their heels, living ever on envy and bitterness of spirit, always for killing and flaying preachers and deacons, merely because they *are* preachers and deacons? 'That thou doest do quickly,' said Christ to Judas, and Judas obeyed the command. But people like these can't come up even to Judas's standard. They sell the Master every day for thirty pieces of silver, but they do it leisurely, slowly, without haste, and without any sign either, more's the pity, of speedily hanging themselves and going to their own place. And yet it would appear there is no rule of discipline for folk like them. Has the church no punishment save for William the Coal and me? When William took too much drink, every letter in the regulations of discipline cried aloud for his expulsion, notwithstanding, as Will Bryan says, that he put all the fault on Satan. And when I happened to lay the Old Soldier on his back, on seeing him cruelly beating my brother, the spirit and letter of the rules demanded my expulsion also. It's nonsense I call a thing like that. In the great day to come —the day when will be revealed the secrets of our hearts—were I compelled to stand in either William the Coal's shoes or John Lloyd's, I know the ones I'd choose. As you are aware, I'm as strict an abstainer as anyone in church, and I think I grieve as much as any man over the evils of intemperance. But our God is not the God of temperance alone, is He? Is He not also the God of justice, love, magnanimity and meekness? The New Testament teaches me He is, pre-eminently so. But when did you see Abel Hughes—all respect to Abel; I believe he is a sincere Christian—when did you see him get upon his feet to move the excommunication of anyone for avarice, hard-heartedness and hard-facedness? Whom have you seen expelled for setting people by the ears? For persecuting his betters? For foul-mouthedness? No one, I'm sure. Not because there are none guilty of such sins; you know that as well as I do. Would that Paul lent me his authority and the mantle he left behind him at Troas! You should see directly that others besides William the Coal and myself were delivered over unto Satan."

Mother, quiet and self-possessed, heard him right through; at which I was greatly surprised, for I remembered a time when she would not have suffered him to go on in this way for half a minute without setting upon him fluently and unsparingly. Indeed had Bob dared speak as now some six months previously, I doubt whether, strong a man as he was, she would not have boxed his ears. Now, however, she listened attentively to every word he said, and were they the last he spoke from his deathbed, her face could not have been more serious and sorrowful. She appeared as one who had let go her every hope, as one who, cast down by despair, endeavoured to look calm and resigned in the face of doom. I was only a lad; but from childhood upwards my mother had drenched me with religious ideas and the terms of divinity, and I think I was then quite as competent as I am now to grasp the bitterness of her disappointment and her sorrow. I was able to follow and understand her words and feelings as she answered Bob in such sentences as:—

"Well, my son, I never expected to live to hear you talk like that; although I must admit having feared it was to this it would come. I have tried to listen to you carefully, fearing I should misunderstand and misjudge you. I can never tell you what my feelings were when you were taken to jail—wrongfully I know, thanks for that. But in the midst of many a night, when everybody else was fast asleep, I lay thinking of you, till I feared my heart would burst asunder before the morning; and I now fancy, if I'd not tried to believe your imprisonment was something in the Lord's hand to bring you back to the fold, that my heart would indeed have broken. Your words to-night have disappointed me much, and hurt me cruelly. It is evident your soul has gone into a far off country, and I much fear you will be left to yourself. I am loth to believe that God's Spirit does not wrestle with your mind. But remember, my son, there is a danger that you may vex Him, and that there's an end to the patience even of the

Almighty. You can never picture the state you'd be in were
He to say, 'Let him alone.' You spoke of some people whose
chief object was to find out the truth; and I understood from
your words that you put yourself in the same bundle with
them. But what truth do you mean? If it is the truth about
God, about sinners, and about eternity, I know you'll never
get that outside God's own Word. And here is what that
says:—'If ye continue in my word, then are ye my disciples
indeed, and ye shall know the truth. The secret of the Lord is
with them that fear him.' And the same Word says: 'He that
is not with me is against me; and he that gathereth not with
me scattereth abroad. Whosoever shall be ashamed of me and
of my words in this adulterous and sinful generation; of him also
shall the Son of Man be ashamed when he cometh in the glory
of his Father with the holy angels.' Who are the people you
talk about, who lose their sleep in searching for truth, but whose
names are not on the books of Communion? I'd like to know
them, 'cause I never saw anyone with the least grain on him
who did not belong to Communion. I can't make you out,
even if you can yourself. To speak my mind plain, I think it's
some notions you've got from those old English books that have
addled your head. I was sorry to hear you speak in the
language of the backslider when you were pointing out the
failings of those who profess. I thought you were above taking
shelter behind anything of that sort, and although I admit
there was a deal of truth in what you said, your conscience
must tell you a story of that kind 'ont hold water before the
judgment seat. Beware, my son, beware! I've no wish to
hurt your feelings, and I wouldn't for the world say anything
to drive you further astray, but really I'd like to hear more of
the publican ring about you. I, also, try to believe there is no
difference of condition in you since you have ceased to profess,
and I can't tell you how glad I am that you continue to come
to service regularly, and that you haven't given way to sin.
But I desire you to remember, my son, that when a shower
comes the rain is always heaviest under the eaves. There is no
verandah to God's house; so that if you are not inside, you
had almost better be out in the open. It is your own business,
my boy. In a manner of speaking, it is nothing in the world

to me; and yet it is something—as Mr. Hughes of Llangollen, says. I shall not be long with you—something tells me so. Between one thing and another I begin to feel that I am drawing near to some country, for in my soundings I find the fathoms getting fewer and fewer every day. But the ship would ride much more lightly could I cast into the sea my concern for you. Between one Euroclydon and the other I have been rather sorely tossed of late; but the Great Ruler has seen fit to show me a creek with a shore to it, more than once, and I have taken the hint that my soul shall not be lost. I have no desire to live to grow old, because I know I shall only be a drag upon you both. 'Although my house be not so with God' —you know who I'm referring to, and I hope God will visit the soul of him—'Yet He hath made with me an everlasting covenant.' Rhys, I really believe, is in a place where both soul and body'll have fair play, and if I only saw you, Bob, like you used to be, I wouldn't care how soon I was called away. The eternal world is quite new to me, and I do not know what change I must go through before entering it; but at present I can't see how I'm going to be happy, even in Heaven, without the knowledge that I have left my two sons zealous in the cause of the dear old Methodists."

Mother wiped her eyes with her apron which, according to her old habit, she began to pleat. While she was referring to her departure, which we never before heard her do, her words fell upon my ears, not as the complaint of the hypochondriac, but as the utterance of a prophet of God who was speaking the awful truth. My heart jumped to my throat. I looked at Bob, and found his eyes wet. As I said before, Bob was a most difficult one to move, once he had formed an opinion; but he had a remarkably tender heart, and his love towards mother was intense. Did the need arise, he would have died for her, any day. I noticed his whole soul was stirred, and that it was only by a great effort he could control his emotion. I fancy he and I felt like those disciples of old when Paul told them they should look upon his face no more. After a brief silence, Bob said,—

"I can't understand, mother, why you should grieve so much on my account, and especially why you should talk of dying and leaving us. You are no 'drag' upon me at all; and as long as I have health and strength it will be my chiefest pleasure to make you happy and comfortable. Why do you repine? Do you see any falling off in my character? What difference would it make in my condition supposing the church rose their hands, and Abel Hughes wrote my name on the book? I know you would not wish me to dissemble; and even if you did, I would never do so. It is as painful to me as it is to you that we cannot see eye to eye. But I say again— and you shall think, if you like, that I am self-righteous—that I hate hypocrisy with a perfect hatred. I cannot pretend that I feel, this way and that, if I do nothing of the kind. I know as well as you do that it is a privilege for any man to be a religious professor; but then the church has deprived me of it, and what help have I? Perhaps you will say I have transgressed? But I say no; for I will never believe that religion is antagonistic to the best feelings of human nature. If, to-morrow morning, I saw the strong chastise the weak, and knew myself to be stronger than the strong, I would make him show his heels to the sun that very instant, and would leave for work with a calm conscience that I had done nothing but my duty. Besides, you must admit that Heaven will have but a very scanty population if none are to enter it but those who have their names on the books of the Methodist Communion. I know you're not so narrow-minded as to think that."

"Will you answer me one question?" said mother.

"A hundred if I can," replied Bob.

"Good," returned mother. "If you answer two or three, to my satisfaction, I shall feel perfectly easy. Do you see yourself a miserable sinner eternally and hopelessly lost, on your own account? Do you see in the Lord Jesus Christ a perfect and sufficient Saviour? Do you feel that you must rely entirely upon his deservedness for your salvation? And is your conscience perfectly easy, as you say, that you are upon the path of duty?"

I saw from Bob's face that he had been squeezed into a corner. For some time he made no reply; mother meanwhile fixing him with her eye as if she meant to read his very soul.

" You know," he said presently, " that it is but few, even of
the professors, who can answer questions like those, clearly
and unequivocally ? "

" What am I to understand by 'unequivocally?'" she asked.
"Don't try to hide your meaning in words which are beyond
me."

" Well," replied Bob, " we'll put 'unequivocally' on one
side. I say again, it is but few even of the really religious who
are able to answer your questions clearly and without hesitation
or doubt. And I believe you hardly expect me to answer
them authoritatively. If I am able to do so after reaching
your age I shall be thankful. I do not want to conceal my
meaning from you, so I must confess it is in darkness I am,
up to now, and that I am but feeling the way. I can
honestly say I continue to grope, but spiritual truths appear to
escape me. I assure you that my soul's cry is—' Light, light,
more light!' At times I think I have it—from on high; but
it is only as a lightning flash, which leaves me in greater
darkness than before. At other times I get another kind of
light—from below; in following which I find myself among
the bogs and marshes, whereupon I become aware the light is
that of a corpse-candle. What am I to do? I am not willing
to shut my eyes and sit, despairing, in the dark. If I did that
I should be like Satan, of whom Goronwy Owen says that he

'Loves lurking in the great abyss.'

I do not love the darkness; I rub my eyes, stand a-tiptoe, and
crane my neck for some sign of morning. All I see, however,
is the night shaking out black sheets across the sideless
bed of truth. I had resolved not to say anything to you
about the state of my mind, for I knew it would pain you. I
am already sorry that I did not keep it all to myself; and yet
I could not, since you questioned me. I know you do not
understand me. To you who are ever living in the midst of
the light, my words seem mad; but I can assure you they are
the words of truth and soberness. I have gathered from your
talk, for some time, that you believe me to be careless with
respect to religious matters; but the Omniscient knows that I
am not so. And yet the future is utterly dark to me. I am

certain there is light beyond, somewhere; the thickness of the night assures me of that, to say nothing of the enjoyment I see you at all times taking in it. Why it is withheld from me I do not know. I, every day, go down into the darkness of the coal-pit, but there I have my lamp; when I try to delve in the world of mind and spirit, the darkness is quite as great, and my lamp goes out. What have I done, more than some other sinner, to prevent the dawn from breaking upon my soul? Perhaps you can tell me. I feel I am not as other people. I smile and laugh so as to be like my companions, but my heart is ever sad, my spirit ever weeps and makes moan. How can I laugh when I do not know the minute a mass of coal may crush me into yet deeper darkness than the one I am already in? Perhaps you will bid me pray; but are not the aspirations of the soul one constant prayer? And when I put my desires into words, they come back to me, saying, 'No reply.' O, wretched man that I am!"

Mother, with an effort at cheerfulness, said, "Well, my dear boy, I'm afraid you're in the melancholy. I used to think no one was troubled with that but the preachers of old, and I haven't heard of it troubling any of them since the time of Michael Roberts of Pwllheli. You are low-spirited, my son; you must take a little physic and a change of air. There's nothing in the world like it, they say. Sing a bit, my boy; I'll help you." And mother began, as best she could, the hymn—

"O Unbelief, how great thy pow'r!
A wound to me thou'st given;
Spite which I'll trust, to my last hour,
The greater grace of Heaven."

From that minute mother changed her tone and demeanour towards Bob. She spoke consolingly and encouragingly to him. But he only shook his head, as much as to say she did not understand him.

I think it must have been a fortnight or so after the foregoing conversation, that I was returning from the country where I had taken a shop parcel—my first months with Abel Hughes were occupied mostly in running errands. It was a lovely night, and I was well acquainted with the way, knowing every house, hedgerow, wall, gate and milestone. I fancied the trees gave me each a "Good Night" as I went past, as if to show that they rememembered me well since the time Will Bryan and I came birds'-nesting and nutting that way. Even at that early period I was, methinks, a bit of a dreamer, able to enjoy the romantic scenery and the profound calm. Ever since I can remember I have preferred the country to the town. I always feel that the noise and bustle of the town hinder one from hearing the voice of God speaking through nature. The night, because of its silence, has had a great charm for me. People would laugh, possibly, at the notion were they to read it; but true it is that I have often wondered why police-officers are not more refined and spiritual than other men. Think of the time they have for study, in God's air, in the deep silence of the night, "the blue glittering firmament," as John Jones, Talsarn, describes it, overhead, and all around wrapped in heavy slumber. What a glorious opportunity for communing with nature and with God, in the deep silence, unbroken by aught, save an occasional dog-bark at some farm house in the far-off distance. If it were not for the other duties connected with the office, I should like to be a policeman, for the sake of being out at night! But whither am I straying? I was, I repeat, returning from the country, fanciful and happy, thinking little of anything unpleasant awaiting me. On nearing home I saw numbers of people running towards the town. I hurried after them, and speedily overtook a lame old collier, making in the same direction. I asked him what the people were running for?

His reply was—"An explosion, my son, at Red Fields Colliery."

The words seemed to give me wings. My feet did not appear to touch the ground. I was lifted and carried along, as it were, by the whirlwind of fears which rushed upon my heart. Leaving the high road, I took a straight line for home, leaping walls, hedges, stiles, totally unconscious of any obstacle in the way. How selfish of me! I thought of no one but Bob. Was he amongst the injured? According to the time of day he should have been home, long before this, for his turn finished at seven o'clock. And yet it was only a few minutes

past seven now! Supposing Bob were burnt to death, what
should I do? Had the fire not touched him, how glad I should
be! But if it had reached his face—what a pity! Fancy
his having lost an eye—how ugly he would look! O, the
thoughts that ran through my brain as I devoured the distance
between me and a full knowledge of all! Very speedily I got
within sight of the house, and found Bob had come home.
But how? In a trolly filled with straw, supported by two men,
one on either hand of him. I was at his side in an instant. I
heard him groan, as they were carrying him upstairs. Mother
was deathly pale, but perfectly calm; Bob, black as the coal,
and charred to a cinder, lay quite still. His bright and
intelligent eyes had been burnt clean out of his head; and yet
he was alive. I would not have known him from all the people
in the world. The works' surgeon, Dr. Bennett, who was in
the room, shook his head as if there were no hope. I envied
him the great tear I saw stealing down his cheek, because, for
once, I could not cry. Trouble is sometimes so sharp and
severe that our usual tokens of it refuse their services from
very diffidence. So was it with mother and me at this juncture.
We could not weep. Someone, I forget who, having given him
a draught of water, Bob appeared to revive, and we heard him
distinctly say:—

"Mother!"

"Can you see a little, my son?" asked mother on approaching him.

She did not know that he had lost both eyes.

"Yes, mother," he replied. "The light has come at last.'

A second or two later he added, in English,—"Doctor, it is
broad daylight."

Next minute Bob had left behind him all the doubt and the
darkness to others and to me.

CHAPTER XXIV

REMINISCENCES, SAD AND CONSOLATORY.

ONE precious privilege of a rural district is that seldom any sudden catastrophe happens to plunge it into grief and sorrow. Not so with the neighbourhood of large works. There the morn sometimes opens its tender eyelids upon a scene already awake and bustling, smiles upon it sweetly, as a happy child upon the mother found by his cradle when he awakes. Droves of colliers may be discerned turning out of their houses, with lamps hanging from their belts. The patter of their clogs along the hard road and uneven pavement makes music unto the ears of some Welshwomen I have known, while it re-awakens the sorrow of here and there a widow, who comes to the door with one child in her arms and another clinging to her apron, and looks after the crowd, as if expecting John to return. If you observe, you shall see a well-built powerful man hastening out of his house, with a step of pride at the thought that he is going forth to labour for wife and children. Before he has taken many paces a tiny, bare-footed, bare-legged, half-dressed boy, not wholly clean, for there are remnants of last night's supper upon his round, fat face, runs after him; the father, in his hurry, having forgotten to kiss him before setting out. Reminded of his remissness, he takes the child up on his strong, broad breast, and, regardless of the mixture upon the cheek, gives him a sounding kiss, at which the mother, who by this time has got to the doorway, laughs right merrily. Is there one of them who dreams that that kiss shall be the last? The pit-engine— heart of the district—pulsates rapidly and regularly. The smoke of the great stack ascends in thick, black columns, straight to heaven, the morning being fair, and God—as I used to fancy when a boy—being in need of the smoke to make clouds with! Tram after tram, wagon after wagon, may be, found coming from the pit's head, laden with the best coal; the wagoner, knee-breeched, and with whip on shoulder, walking as if he had one foot in a furrow, and making furtive eyes at all he meets, to see whether they have noticed his well-fed horses, whose tails he took such trouble, the night before, to plait and tie with blue and yellow ribbon. Children play about the streets, make fun of the wagoner's thin shanks, and mimic his fashion of putting a "y" after his horses' names: "Boxer-y," "Blaze-y," and the rest. "Our man" pays no heed to them. All appear happy and contented, from the obese butcher—half asleep in his shop chair, in the interval between his customers' visits, and looking as if long poring over fat had made him, also, 'fit for the knife"—to the lean, sallow-faced cobbler, going homewards at a jog trot with an apron full of mending jobs. Although still early, the tidiest among the colliers' wives are already in Mr. Roberts's shop, looking out something nice for their husbands' dinners; for how can men work hard if they have nothing to their taste to eat? They earn good money, so why should they not have a few delicacies found them now and then? There is a thriving look about the business establishments, whose owners employ the morning's respite to remove the dust and put things in order. The ancient dame who keeps the toy shop is said to have an "old stocking." And what wonder? Watch the boys, of every age and size, going to school, and you shall see them, all of a row, slates slung over shoulder, scored with the previous night's home lesson—from the strokes of the boy, to the vulgar fractions of the stripling—all of a row, I say, flattening their noses against the window pane, and vowing each to have his toy with his next allowance of pocket money. Happy creatures!

But, possibly within the hour, the news will have run like wild-fire that there has been a "fall" underground, and that so many men have been killed; or that the water has broken in, and that so many have been drowned or shut up in the upper portions of the work. Lamentations, loud and deep, are heard all over the neighbourhood. The lad who, on his way to school in the morning, had looked forward to his father's assistance in buying a bat, finds himself, before mid-day, an orphan. The stalwart father, in the flower of health, whom we saw lifting his child like a feather upon his breast, for his morning kiss is brought home at night in a trolly, dead. Ye simple folk of Anglesey! What know ye of sudden heart-

N

rending visitations such as these? When, in long nights of
winter, ye sit warming yourselves by your coal fires—not
those of peat—remember that that which ye enjoy is often
bought with blood!

When the explosion took place at the Red Fields pit, which
caused the death of my brother Bob and divers others, there
was, of course, not a moment's warning; and the neighbourhood which, a few minutes before, was all peace and happiness,
was plunged into sore and indescribable sorrow. Every workman had his Davy lamp, so that how the accident happened no
one knew, and no one ever did know. It was not, however,
the why and the wherefore of the occurrence that troubled the
bereaved—amongst them mother and myself—but the results.
Mother lost a son who, since a mere youth, had stood her in a
husband's stead, upon whom she was wholly dependent for her
livelihood, and whom she loved much better than her own life.
I know she did not concern herself much about me; but there
was never a day, nor an hour of the day, that her soul was not
entwined with Bob's. As for me, I lost a brother of brothers, to
whom I felt indebted for nearly all I possessed in the shape of
learning. Even to this minute I feel certain I should be something wholly different to what I am but for him. If I
attempted to describe my grief at his loss I should make myself an object of contempt in these my reminiscences. I
envied mother, whom I saw holding up so bravely, whilst I
was but a worthless, inert mass. How precious now is the remembrance of her behaviour! Were all the works of the
Puritan fathers, and everything ever written on behalf of
Christianity, placed in one great pile before me, and could I,
by one single effort, comprehend the whole of their reasoning,
my mother's calmness and self-restraint in the face of this
terrible affliction would present an infinitely stronger argument, to my mind, of the truth and divinity of the religion of
the Gospel. Did she feel as deeply as other women bereaved by
this catastrophe, who screamed and became hysterical? She
did, and much more so, I shall believe. But she had some
hidden spiritual support to fall back upon which enabled her
to view the most direful calamity as but an indispensable verse
in the chapter of her life, without which the context could not

be made clear. It was not her physical strength which sustained her, for, to my sorrow, I perceived that that had for some time been rapidly declining. In her foolish fancy she had thought Bob the smartest, handsomest fellow in the neighbourhood, and suspected every girl who came to the house of having designs upon him. So dreadfully disfigured was he by the fire that she resolved, the moment his spirit fled, she would never look upon his face again. When his coffin was brought home (fearful object in a cot with no room in it to which to escape the sight!) mother gave the carpenter strict orders to screw it down at once. She was jealous lest a grim curiosity should lead someone to gaze upon the unsightly features. Is it not a fact that when those we love are overtaken by death—by sudden death more particularly—the failings and faults which were theirs when living retreat into the distance and grow smaller to the view? Memory does not care to look upon the departed ones save in their Sunday best. I was quite sure mother had prayed a deal for Bob, and had troubled greatly about his condition, although there was nothing in his conduct to need the intercession, with the sole exceptions of his taciturnity and the fact that he had not, for some time, been a member of the church. But now his burnt body lay at rest between four boards in the loft, she did not seem to concern herself in the slightest about the safety of his soul, at length far removed from all human aid. I remember well, after a silence of about an hour, occupied in pleating her apron and staring abstractedly into the fire, that she asked me: "What said he"—using the pronoun as if we had been talking of him only a minute previously—"What said he, tell me, in English to Dr. Bennett?"

"That it was broad daylight," I replied.

"And what did the doctor say?"

"That he was beginning to ramble," was my answer.

"I thought that was what he said; so Festus told Paul—'Thou art beside thyself.' 'The natural man receiveth not the things of the Spirit of God, neither can he know them, because they are spiritually discerned.'" And she added, as if to herself, "Ramble indeed! No fear of Bob's rambling. It was of the spiritual light he spoke—that for which he had been groping, as he used to say. 'And there shall be light in the evening!' Wonderful! Wonderful! Obliged to lose both eyes before beginning to see! 'For judgment I am come into this world, that they which see not might see.' I would rather than a good deal had he been professing; but I never considered him irreligious. Abel Hughes always said Bob had a better grain about him than the half of us. But what makes my mind easiest is his saying, a fortnight ago, that he was not careless about the things of religion, and that the cry of his soul was for the light. God has said, 'Yo shall seek me and find me, when ye shall search for me with all your heart.' 'I said not unto the seed of Jacob, seek ye me in vain.' 'Ask and it shall be given unto you, seek and ye shall find,' said the Saviour on the Mount. I shall not readily believe Bob to be lost. I hope I'm not sinning, but I feel so certain he is in heaven that, if I go there myself, as I expect I shall, and find him not there, it will be enough to destroy utterly all my happiness."

Well, there is nothing for me, at this moment, but to trust that my mother's faith was true. Some learned man, reading what I am about to say, would, doubtless, laugh at me. Let him laugh. But I believe that pious people, however ignorant they may be, possess some sort of spiritual perception, and receive, perhaps unconsciously, some kind of telegraphic communications from the eternal world, which are not permitted to the Godless or, if permitted them, not understood. I am perfectly well aware that this notion is incompatible with the knowledge of some able men in this (enlightened) age —an age in which religious people are often looked upon as old-fashioned, and the Bible is considered a harmless little book enough, the promise being hinted that the discoveries of science will shortly enable the boy at school to write upon his slate, between breakfast and dinner, all the mysteries of nature, the secrets of being, and the aspirations of the immortal soul.

Although my recollection of it is still fresh, I neither wish nor intend to linger long over the period when that which was mortal of my brother lay waiting to be taken from our sight for

ever. Were I to attempt a description of my feelings at the time, it might be regarded by some of those who took the trouble to read this autobiography as a want of taste in the writer. Although every family knows Death, yet is he at all times a stranger. He visits us unasked, and is never anywhere welcome. And the less welcome the more likely is he speedily to return. I know I am relating a not uncommon experience when I say that is a strange and wonderful occasion on which the body of a beloved one lies in the same house with us, and we are waiting the hour appointed by the custom of the country and what is considered propriety, for its conveyance to its last resting place. How difficult it is to realise that he who the day before, looked at us, spoke to us, ate, drank and walked about as we did, is now lying still and cold, dumb and deaf. How cruel it seems to leave him in a room all by himself. The season is inclement, and we have lit no fire. How hard! Does he think us unkind towards him? Would he so leave us? We know him to be—him —far away from us; and yet are conscious, all the time, that he is in the adjoining room; else why do we speak so softly, as if we were afraid to wake him? How slowly the hours drag! How unfeeling is that practice of shutting out the light of day, and making one night of the occasion, as if we had not night enough already in the soul! The gloom becomes oppressive, and the desire to get everything over grows strong. What! Are we in a hurry to bury him? O no; the dear one! But the time is long and cheerless. We try to read; the eye looks at the book, but the mind wanders off to some strange place. The slightest movement makes us listen, and listen eagerly. Our ear is strained in the direction of the next room. How like the sound of his well-known cough! Did he move? All is but fancy; the house is as quiet as the grave. We drop into a slumber of short duration and, on awaking, doubt whether we have not been in a dream. We go over the whole of the circumstances once more. Everything appears in a different aspect now. By this time life, wealth and fame have lost their charm for us. Vain are the things of this world in our sight; and we wonder how anyone can devote himself to matters earthly, particularly how he can laugh; forgetful that we ourselves, a few days previously, were guilty of the like conduct, and that in a short time to come we shall again be exactly as we were. The number of good resolutions we form; all to be sadly qualified, if not entirely forgotten in two months' time! Death is a black and hideous monster; but it throws some gleams of light on things even for the living. How much more so for him it takes away?

When death has ploughed the heart, and trouble has softened it, the evangelist and the man of counsel have an excellent opportunity of sowing the good seed, which then finds a "deepness" with ease. And though the earth should harden again, still the seed may some day sprout, and, breaking forth through its crusted covering, bear fruit, possibly a hundred fold. The visits of the chapel friends to mother and me in our trouble brought us a blessing and a comfort such as I can neither properly describe nor value. I recollect my mother saying that next to the priceless promises of Scripture and her faith in God as Over-ruler of all, she valued the cheering words of the religious brethren and sisters. They were not a few who came to comfort us, and not the least faithful among them were Thomas and Barbara Bartley; both so childish, so simple, and showing a sympathy so real and so genuine that it was impossible not to prize it. Mother could hardly help smiling at some of Thomas's artless questions, such as :—

"Mary, do you think Bob has told Seth yet that Barbara and I have come to Communion? That is, if they have dropped across one another, for there's such a crowd of them, isn't there?"

"For all I know, it may be he has, Thomas," replied mother.

"They'll light on each other some day, surely," said Thomas. "Two men will meet before two mountains, so they say."

After a minute's silence he resumed :—

"Barbara and I thought a deal about you last night, Mary, and we couldn't in no way see what on this blessed earth you are to do now, 'cept come to us to live. We have as much room as you want, and a hundred thousand welcomes, is'nt there, Barbara? We've made the place ready for you, and you two must come over to-night. You don't bury Bob till the day after to-morrow, and why should you stay here breaking your heart, eh Barbara?"

Barbara gave a nod.

"Your'e very kind and very neighbourly, Thomas," said mother; "but I can't for a moment think of leaving Bob by himself here; though 'tis all a fancy."

"To be shŵar," observed Thomas. "I never thought of that. No, no, honour bright; now I come to think of it, it would look a bit cold in you to leave him, 'specially since you've no fear. But we shall talk of that some other time."

"What have I to fear, Thomas? There is here but the poor body—the empty house."

"It was not to that I was referring," returned Thomas.

Mother guessed what he meant. Thomas knew more of our history than I was aware of. Mother nodded her thanks for his thoughtfulness, and said: "The door has a lock and a bar to it, Thomas."

"To be shŵar. But you must come over the day after to-morrow. We'll think no more of the bit of food you'll eat than of a chicken's."

The day after to-morrow came, but my reminiscences are dark and confused. I felt as if in a dream. Two impressions are left upon my mind, which I can easily read to-day, namely, that there were a great many people at the funeral, and that Will Bryan walked beside me, with a good-sized box-plant under his left arm and a bag filled with sand in his right hand. I have some faint recollection of hearing Mr. Brown's deep voice hurrying through the burial service, and a vivid one of Will Bryan on his knees by the grave-side sanding it, and planting it with box. Little did I then think how soon he would be at the same task again! Will was usually a very talkative fellow but, when feeling deeply for another, he was silent, always. He spoke not a word till we were half way home from the churchyard. I remember well his remark, which was:—

"Rhys, do you know what Bob would say if he knew Mr. Brown was going to bury him? He'd have used Bobbie Burns's last words—'Don't let that awkward squad shoot over my grave!' That's what he'd have said, I'll take oath."

Will was evidently thinking of Bob's wrongful committal to prison by Mr. Brown in his capacity of a justice of the peace, and was, doubtlessly, expressing my brother's feelings to the letter.

The reader—should I have one—will remember that Thomas Bartley was but a young convert. Old habits and notions, not strictly consonant to the religious profession, often showed themselves in him. Although ready and willing enough to renounce them, he could not do so without a bit of a wrench. On the day of Bob's burial, Thomas asked my mother whether she did not mean to provide a little bread and cheese and beer for the people, adding it was in the "Brown Cow," he thought, they kept the best beer, and hinting, plainly enough, he would take all the expense upon himself. While thanking him for his kindness, mother took pains to show him the unseemliness of the custom of feasting at funerals, and especially of bringing intoxicating drink to table.

"To be shwar, Mary," said Thomas. "You're the best judge. You know more of your Bible'n I do, and I always give in to you. But I thought it might look a little cold not to have a bit or a drop for anybody."

Mother met our good friends' wishes half way by permitting Barbara, on the return from the funeral, to provide tea, and to invite a few of her nearest neighbours to partake of it and to talk of the dead, a proceeding which eased Thomas's conscience not a little. The guests having gone and mother, I, Thomas and Barbara being left to ourselves, Thomas, after musing a while, said,—

"Now, Mary, you must pack out of this. Why should you stay here breaking your heart? People never do any good, living by themselves. You've no notion how comfortable we'll all be together. It'll save Barbara and I from coming over to hear you expounding. D'ye know what? It'll be as good as a sermon for us to have you yonder; and, as I've said, we shan't miss your bit of food any more'n if you were a chick."

"I don't know how to thank you enough for your kindness," replied mother. "But after your mention of a certain matter the other night, I have made up my mind to accept your warm-hearted invitation, on condition that I shall pay for my place as long as my money will hold out. I have a little put by; I

shall have a little more for the things here, and possibly that
may be enough to last me as long as I am with you."

"We'll settle all that again," said Thomas, filling his pipe.

I was fairly bewildered. I had never dreamt my mother
would stoop to receive a kindness, even from Thomas Bartley,
until circumstances absolutely compelled her to do so. I knew
that independence of mind and a dread of being a burden to
anybody were marked traits in her character. Barbara was
helping her on with her cloak and bonnet when the reason
suddenly occurred to me why mother had so readily accepted
Thomas Bartley's invitation.

It was her fear of our old visitor.

A few minutes later we were all four on our way to the
Tump, for so was Thomas Bartley's house called. I remember,
at this very minute, the order in which we travelled—not much
unlike a railway train: Thomas leading, like the locomotive,
the smoke from his pipe wreathing in the night air; I at his
heels, with mother after me, as passenger carriages; and
Barbara, who was somewhat stout, like a luggage van behind,
wobbling along pretty much as the tail end of a train does. All
four were silent, save when Barbara, who was troubled with
rheumatism, would groan, like the luggage van when its
wheels want greasing, and Thomas, like the locomotive, would
give a whistle in the form of: "are you coming, you women
there?" Of course, I am only describing the journey as I look
upon it now, and not as I looked upon it then. The thought
of leaving the old house in which I was bred and born, where
I had spent many a happy hour, and round which all my
memories gathered, filled my heart with sadness. This was my
first night from home. I had always considered the Tump a
model of cosiness and comfort, and our welcome to it was real
and unfeigned. But when I came to go to bed—the bed in
which Seth died, and which was much easier lying than
the one at home—such a heavy storm of regret for the old
house, for Bob, and for the old days, overtook me that I had to
hide my head in the bed clothes, and stuff the sheets into my
mouth to prevent myself from crying aloud. In the morning
mother saw by my swollen eyes how I had spent the night, and
a sob rose to her throat, but she choked it back before it found

utterance. I noticed Thomas Bartley making efforts to keep
us cheerful, and to divert our minds from our trouble. He
took us to the yard to see the pigs and fowls, talking ceaselessly the whole of the time. Mother paid great attention to
everything he said; but I knew she did not consider him
speaking to edification. He ran on something in this fashion :

"Mary, here's the best pigs I ever had to thrive. I wouldn't
give a fig for one as wasn't mischievous. These would eat the
trough if they didn't get their food in time. That one without
a tail is reg'lar master of the place. I always rear two—they
thrive much better—kill one and sell t'other. I never give 'em
India meal, 'cause the bacon when you put it before the fire'll
melt to nothing before it's done. Taters and oatmeal's the
best stuff for fattening a pig, if you want good bacon. You
may boil a little nettles now and then for 'em as a change.
There's nothing better for a pig's as lost his appetite than to mix
red raddle with his food. What's in grains, for a pig? Nothing
at all. D'ye know what, Mary, I'd never eat bacon if I had
to buy that American stuff. How can you tell what they
fatten their animals with out there? They say American
pigs eat those Blacks who die out in the woods; and I'll
b'leeve it easy enough. Holloa, Cobbin! are you there?
There's a bird for you, Mary! If that white feather wasn't in
his tail he'd be pure game. Look at his breast! Black as the
wimberry. I've seen the time, before I came to religion,
I'd have cut that cock's comb for him; but something tells
me it is'nt right, somehow; it's as if you were trying to
better the work of the Almighty. I don't find these game
hens great layers, only their eggs are more rich. Barbara
(with a shout), is breakfast ready? Right; we'll come
directly. Fowls pay very well, Mary, if they're well fed. Did
you ever see how fond you are getting of them already? They
look so well settled down when they hold their heads to one
side. Let's go into the house now, and see what the old
woman's got for us. I don't know how you feel, but *I* feel as
if I could eat a horse's head."

After breakfast I set out for the shop, and mother came to
send me a part of the way, in order to have a word with me in
private.

" I see," she said, placing a hand upon my shoulder, " that you are fretting. You must buckle-to, my son. We must both, look you, submit and not give way. *You* are but beginning life as it were; I am drawing towards the end. If you're a good and obedient boy—and I believe you will be— God will take care of you. Set to work to please your master, and by pleasing your master you will please God. I'll come, directly, to ask Abel Hughes to let you sleep at his house, because it won't do to impose too much upon our friends' kindness. You shall run over every evening, after shutting shop, to see how we are getting along, if you like. The only thing that troubles me is the fear of being obliged to ask for parish relief. But perhaps I shall be spared that, again. I have saved a little money, which may possibly last as long as I shall."

I, too, tried to say the thing which was on my mind, but the words stuck to my throat, and all I could do was to cry. My mother pressed my head to her breast and, when I had wept my grief away, dried my eyes with her apron, saying, "There! off you go now, and don't forget what I told you."

So I went; and so I did, I trust. On the road I could not help thinking of my mother's dread of going on the parish, and the reflection made me sorry that I was neither of age nor of position to support her. Only a few months had passed since she had spoken so freely and loftily to Mr. Brown, the clergyman, to whom she expressed the hope that she would never be obliged to seek help from either " parish or parson ; " and doubtless that little quarrel between her and the vicar was alive and bitter in her memory still. I was quite sure at the time that she would have much preferred throwing herself upon the mercy of that relieving officer general for all the children of adversity—Death—than stoop to Parson Brown. And I feared there was something in her voice and words that morning which showed that that had been her prayer.

CHAPTER XXV.

BEFORE bringing to an end what I consider to be the second epoch of my history, and before saying anything of the time I found myself alone and realising the fact that I had entered upon the battle of life, I must deal a little further with two or three characters who have already received no small notice from me—one of them more particularly.

During the whole period of my mother's stay with Thomas and Barbara Bartley she found a fostering care and attention at their hands as great as any she could have expected or desired. Her chief employment, as long as she lived at the Tump, was the preparation of the two old folk for admission into full church membership; and that was no slight task. It took her some weeks to coach them, as the saying is, before she felt sufficiently confident in asking Abel Hughes to call them forward for reception. When that took place, there was a deal of amusement in Communion. Their answers were simple and original, causing some to laugh, others to cry, and a few to laugh and cry, both. The limits I have set myself will not permit a description of the occurrences at that Communion. In answering some questions Thomas would look doubtfully and half in fear at mother, just as some lad may be seen watching his father while reciting his verse at church meeting; and he referred to her, more than once, in words, as an authority in doctrine. On the whole, Thomas gave pretty general satisfaction with respect to his knowledge and fitness for admission. Not altogether so well did Barbara pass her examination. It was very difficult to get more from her than that she thought and felt, "same as Thomas." Barbara clearly looked upon herself as a duplicate of her husband, and inasmuch as Thomas had answered aright, she seemed to think it needless wasting time with her. The two, as I have observed in a previous chapter, thought and acted exactly alike, with a unison and similarity such as that of two eyes on one string. Now I call them to mind, I am almost tempted to go a step further.

and to say that they had the same consciousness, and that there was more of identity than of individuality in them. They were like a clock with two faces, always indicating, to the minute, the same time of day. On the strength of Thomas's answers Barbara, like himself, was unanimously received into church membership, with all its privileges. The old couple went home that night arm in arm, close-joined as a double-kernelled nut, feeling excessively happy and magnifying the importance of the event. Mother had looked forward to the occasion with the greatest interest and anxiety, for she regarded Thomas and Barbara as special disciples of her own. And I know she took pleasure in the thought that her labour, instruction and prayers had not been in vain.

This was the last time mother was in chapel. As I have already intimated, her health had been for some time declining, and her strength failing her. " Between one Euroclydon and the other," to use her own words, she had been " tossed rather badly of late." Her end was hastened by Bob's sudden death. She saw that the staff on which she leaned was broken, and that she had neither health nor strength enough to earn her own livelihood. She dreaded being dependent upon the kindness of friends, and especially upon parish charity, for help ; and she seemed to me like one who had raised a finger at the King of Terrors, and beckoned him to her. Death had no sting for her, heart and contemplation having long since found a home on the other side. She was no money-lover; and I believe she looked upon the little she had saved when Bob was getting good wages, added to what was realised by the sale of the furniture of the old house, as the sand in the glass—the measure of her own life. Some kind woman—it is kind I have found all women towards the preacher—on a Monday morning before I return from an engagement, will boil me an egg for breakfast. Seeing her watch the sand in the glass always reminds me of mother. Even so did she watch the little money she possessed ; and the consciousness gradually grew upon me that with the last penny from her purse she too would take her departure. In her latter days she suffered but little pain. She went to bed to die much as you may have noticed a woman leaving the cold wind upon the railway platform for the shelter

of the waiting room, pending the arrival of the train, and
showing her face in the doorway, as if tired of the delay. Still,
like her former self, she remained calm and collected. Her old
Bible, loose-leaved, was always open by her side on the bed, as
if, to pursue the metaphor, she was constantly examining her
ticket. She died with spectacles on face.

Old mother, mine! I grieve to the heart that I am not a
poet. Did I possess the divine afflatus, I would sing thee
sublimest elegy—one which, whatever might be its shortcomings, would bear proof in itself that it had been wrought by
regret in the workshop of the heart. Yet, if I am not of
the elect of the bardic order, I am unwilling to pass on without
an effort to pay the tribute which is my due to thy memory;
though I am compelled to do so in plain prose. Is it something womanish, and a sign of weakness that one is over-fond
of his mother? Then am I womanish and weak. I know not
when I began to think of thee that thou wert the fairest, dearest, best of womankind. Going back as far as I am able, I
almost believe that this notion of thee was born into the world
with me; it has no beginning, I imagine, in my mind. It was
not the fruit of observation and reason; because, if so, it
might have been different. I felt nearer related to thee than
thou wast to thyself; and I am convinced that so did'st thou
feel towards me. Did I not know thy face years before I knew
my own? And were I, at this moment to look upon both our
faces in a glass, it is thine I should first recognise. A child in
thine arms upon the lake bank, it was thy face I knew and none
other, when thou didst direct my eyes to the shadow in the
water. What care, what trouble did'st thou take with me!
Before I could talk thou understoodest my wants and desires.
When I was ill there was no sleep or rest for thee; when well
and active, thy soul was full of delight. Thou did'st teach me
a language, thyself not knowing its grammar; and, for thy
years of labour in doing so, receiving not a penny in payment.
Our speech was the dear old Cymric; thou knewest none
other, nor believest its like to be in existence. Thou imprint-
est its letters upon my memory while my heart was yet young
and impressionable, so that I could not, even if I would, erase
them in after time. Sweet is the recollection, even now, that

one of the first lessons in syllabification thou gavest me was
"I, and e, and s, and u." * Thyself uninstructed, thy prejudices were many and strong. Hardly would'st thou believe
there was anything worth the mention outside the Welsh
language, nor any religion worth the name but amongst the
Calvinistic Methodists. Although one of the best read women
I knew, thou could'st easily have counted all thy books
upon thy fingers: The Bible, Charles's Lexicon, The Preceptor,
Hymnbook, Gurnal's Works, The Pilgrim's Progress, and
"The Welshman's Candle;" yes, and I must add two others,
namely, Roberts of Holyhead's Almanack, and Tom of Nant's
Works. Those were the entire contents of thy library; but every
book was black with thy thumb-marks, and hung down at the
corners like the ears of Moll of Glasdwr's old dog. The
volumes were not left long enough on their shelves to gather
cobwebs or dust; when the necessity arose thou would'st make
the leisure required for their reading and study. So did'st
thou furnish thy mind with their contents that thou could'st at
all times quote from memory ample portions of them to suit
the occasion. And thou wert as much acquainted with, and at
home in, the exalted discourses of the books of Job, Isaiah and
Revelations as thou wert in the fairs and fixed feasts of the
Almanack, with its doggerel prophecies :—

> "Snow for all,
> Towards the Fall."

Thinking of thy piety, I have wondered what pleasure thou
could'st find in the Bard of Nant, who was not·a man after
the Methodist heart. It was one of the inconsistencies of
human conduct, I imagine. I know thou would'st read with
a relish those severe buffetings which the noted old satirist
bestowed upon irreligious parsons and unjust stewards. Was
it Tom who created in thee such a prejudice against the Church
of England? I have room to think thou did'st believe that the
bard was converted before death ; certain it is I have heard

---

* A rhyming inculcation, upon the youthful mind of the sacred name of
the Saviour. The English reader will please pronounce: Ee, and eh, and
ss, and ee = Yessee (Jesus).—TRANSLATOR.

thee, dozens of times, repeat the following lines of his composition :—

> " My conscience, that captive maid
> Of wondrous grace, before me laid the startling story:
>> Greatest prophet thou they say,
> That sojourns in Samaria. Come, I implore thee,
>> Recover my leprosy clean.
>> No more do I prefer Abana and Pharpar,
> They're rivers impure, I ween.
> Give me of Jordan water—the Son of Man's, 'tis seen.
>> Nought e'er can flood my soul's dark dross,
>> Save Jesu's blood, who on the Cross
> Died, and was so sacrificed that, through his loss   [side
> We life might win, Lord, though we sin. Thy Son's pierced
>> Poured out its crimson tide ;
>> O precious blood ! shed not for woful world in vain, &c."

But the book thou wert most at home in, which thy mind revelled in, was the Bible. Never did'st thou tire of reading it, or of declaring its truths. Never did'st thou, for one single instant, doubt its inspiration, or that it was the real word of God. I remember, if Bob happened to drop the merest hint of a mistake in the translation of some verse, thy anger would be blown into a white heat. Partial though thou wert to the Rev. ——, wert thou not half offended with him when he said, in his sermon, that a few words in a certain place wanted altering a little? And did'st thou not tell Abel Hughes about him afterwards that thou feared'st much learning had made him mad? I know that one of thy chief reasons for not being over-fond of "the students" was that one of them, once upon a time, declared his text to read better in English than in Welsh; and I remember thee saying, hotly, thou had'st no patience listening to 'prentice preachers trying to improve upon the word of God. It was thy ignorance made thee speak thus, but mayhap thou hast got credit in Heaven even for that; it was thy zeal for the Bible, and thy love towards every verse and word in it, that made thee jealous of the least attempt to tamper with it. And what wonder ? Was it not the Bible, *as it is*, that was the foundation of all thy consolations ? Was it not its promises *as they are*, word and letter, that sustained thee in every trouble and affliction? Had anyone succeeded in shaking a grain of thy faith in its divine inspiration, all would have been over with thee. Thou had'st placed thy trust so entirely in its truths, and loved it so absorbingly, that I can easily believe Thomas Bartley when he said that, at the moment before death, he found thee gazing through thy spectacles at thy well-worn Bible, as if unwilling to leave it, as if anxious to take it with thee!

The circle of thy life was a contracted one; thou knewest nothing of the world, in the real sense of the term. Thou had'st no notion of its size, its bustle and its wickedness. Thy path was narrow, and its hedges were high; yet did'st thou succeed most remarkably in keeping the middle of it, without once, as far as I know, falling into the ditch. I am as certain that path led into life as that the little tributary, like the great broad river, leads into the sea. As thy way was, so was thy mind: narrow but just. Thou knewest, as well as any one, that the Saviour was a Jew according to the flesh, but thou believed'st, notwithstanding, that he was more of a Welshman than anything else. And in this thou wert right; for is not the faithful, of whatsoever nation, conscious that the man Christ Jesus is nearer related to his own race than to any other? And is not this clear proof of His fitness as a Saviour of *man*, wherever found?

Inasmuch as what I write about thee will not be read until I, like thyself, have gone over to the majority, I feel I can tell the truth about thee, without being hindered by diffidence or false-modesty. Thou wert endowed with strong instincts, above all with an excellent memory; and had'st thou received a good education in early life, I do not doubt but that thou would'st have been a woman of mark. Uninstructed though thou wert, it was seldom thou wert imposed upon. Yet wert thou deceived once, deceived grossly; a fact but for which this hand would not now be writing a summary of thy life's history; for its owner would have had no existence. Thou wert deceived by one who ought to have been thy guide and protector; who won thy heart and affections when thou wert a young girl—fair, methinks, also. Thou wert deceived by him

o

who should have been most faithful unto thee—thy husband.
my father. And this is not to be wondered at. He was, I
have heard, a sturdy, handsome man. He was irreligious.
He wished to speak with thee; but thou would'st have
nothing to say to one who had no religion. He attended
the means of grace; but to what end? At last he became a
member of the same church with thee. He could now hold
converse with thee, tenderly and religiously. Detestable
hypocrite! He was ready of speech like thyself, and in this
respect you were both well matched. O, how he envied the
preacher; and what pleasure he found in chapel! He was a
new man from thenceforth; but there was a legion of devils in
his heart. Thou gavest ear to him, yes! And ninety nine out
of every hundred girls would have done the same. Ye were
married, one lovely morning in May, amidst a shower of
presents and good wishes from thy friends. And after that—
ah, after that! God and thyself alone knew what thou
suffered'st, what trials thou did'st undergo! But of whom am
I speaking? Of my father—my own father. Wretch! When
thou died'st I rejoice that I had neither seen his face nor heard
his voice. One notable night in my history I caught one faint
glimpse of his form—only his form—in the darkness, in
company of another whom I hated with all my heart.

Dear old mother! What a mercy thou should'st have found,
while yet a lass, a religion of the best stamp. Thy husband's
vile ways and devilish disposition left thy faith in God untarnished! Under bruises from his cruelty—and the thought
that thou ever wert so makes my heart bleed—thou yet could'st
pray for him! Many a time wert thou unable to attend chapel
because of a "pair of black eyes." Inhuman scoundrel! My
flesh creeps, and my sinews tighten, when I think of all thou
suffered'st. How fortunate for thee, Mary Lewis, that his
wickedness developed to such a degree that he was obliged to
fly the country! He nearly made an end of thy life, many
times, without thought of escape, and without giving the
authorities any idea of his apprehension. But having once
come near taking the life of another, infinitely less worthy than
thee, all the country demanded his arrest, and every officer of
police burned with a desire to curb him. Thank Heaven! thou

heard'st of him no more; neither loved'st thou to hear mention of his name. Already have I referred to thy poverty and want, and all thou did'st go through consequent upon the imprisonment and death of Bob; but there was not, as far as I can tell, either shame, or guilt, or dishonour connected with these. What vexation, what sorrow and what hardship thou suffered'st before I came into the world, when thy house was the den of hard-hearted, reckless poachers, who neither feared God nor respected man, no living creature ever knew, nor thou did'st ever mention but sparingly. For all thou said'st to me, I should not have known the hundredth part of thy trouble. I had grown a biggish boy before becoming acquainted with anything definite about thy history, save what I had gathered from the hints and taunts of my enemies. The only thing I knew for certain was that in thy cupboard was a skeleton of some kind : and Bob was the first to enlighten me —in bed, on the night of Seth's death—after I had told him about the man who had stopped me near the Hall Park, and what he had said to me. I have many times asked myself the question was it possible thou could'st have had a spark of affection left for him who brought upon thee so much misery and shame ? O love of women ! Was it not about the last thing thou said'st to me before dying, " If ever you and your father meet, face to face, try and forget his wickedness and, if you have any good to do him, do it. He has a soul to be saved like you and me ; and it does not much matter, now, how he behaved towards me ; but it matters everything that he should be saved. If you should ever see him—and who knows but that you will ?—try and remember he is your father. I, myself, forgive him all, and endeavour to pray that He whose forgiveness is life everlasting do the same."

Well did Will Bryan, in his own way, speak of thee that, like Job, thou did'st "stick to thy colours, first class." Not soon would I come to an end did I relate every counsel and advice thou gavest me in thy last days. I do not forget there may be some one who will fancy that I have over-coloured thy virtues. The fact that thou wert my mother may make this possible. In this place I will chronicle only thy last words to me—those which were so helpful to me in after life :—

"If you are called upon to suffer in this world, do not complain, for it will make you think of a world in which there is no suffering. Do not make your home in the world, or dying will turn out to be a bigger job than you think it is. Prove all things by the word of God, yourself especially. Take the Bible as a weather-glass for your soul; if you lose relish for reading it, you may be sure there is no fair weather waiting you. Pray for a godly life, but do not expect to live old, for fear you may die young. Try and find a religion of which no one can have any doubt, and which you yourself will not doubt. One of the poorest things on earth is a sickly religion; it stops you from enjoying the things of this world, and does not help you to enjoy the things of the other. Get hold of a religion whose sheets will overlap someone else besides yourself. If you can be the means of saving but one soul, you will force your way farther into heaven after death than if you were worth a hundred thousand pounds and had done nothing of the kind. You have no room to expect a penny piece from any of your relations; but you can become the richest in the country in grace, if you try. Abraham would never have been heard of had he had no better property than camels. You will have three enemies to fight: the world, the devil and yourself, and you'll find yourself the hardest to conquer. In the battle, remember you have the whole armour about you — prayer, watchfulness and the Word of God. You're sure to lose the day if you do not take unto yourself all three. If you get strength to vanquish your enemies during life, you will see only their backs when you come to die. I am going to leave you, and I trust in the Lord that I am a vessel of mercy. You will find in the purse in the pocket of my black gown just enough money to pay for burying me. If it should ever rest with you to do a good turn for Thomas and Barbara, don't forget their kindness towards your mother. I would rather than anything that you had a talent for preaching, and were inclined that way. But it can't be helped. Try and be religiously useful in whatsoever circle you may move—you'll never repent it. If I am able to see you from the other world, I should like to find you a deacon."

At the time I never imagined these directions would be

thy last. When next I saw thee, Barbara Bartley had done all that death had left undone for thy face—closed thine eyes. Thy departure, according to Barbara, was as the "d'outing of a candle!" Clearly Death was not unkind to thee. He left a cheerful smile upon thy face, a smile as of a child in it's cradle dreaming. The more I looked at thee, the more did'st thou seem to smile, as if trying to tell me thou wert happy. Thy unwrinkled cheeks were white as snow, but across thy nose ran a streak of blue—the trail of thy spectacles as thy blood grew cold. By thy bedside three hearts beat rapidly and regretfully at the thought that never more would they hear thy voice; three consciences testified that thou had'st done all that in thee lay to purify them and place them upon the path of life. And though thy lips moved not, I fancied hearing thee saying :—

" I have fought a good fight, I have finished my course, I have kept the faith; henceforth there is laid up for me a crown of righteousness which the Lord, the righteous judge, shall give me at that day: and not to me only, but unto all them also that love his appearing."

Troublous was thy life; at many junctures wert thou really poor, but the great crowd that came to pay a last tribute of respect to thy memory showed that others besides myself saw something in thy character worth the emulation. Never was Will Bryan so often and so severely reproved as by thee. And yet his testimony concerning thee on the day of thy funeral was, that thou wert "a stunner of a woman." Thomas and Barbara Bartley have, by this time, grown old, but they have not yet ceased to speak of thee; and though Barbara still has but " a grip of toe letters, same as Thomas," she has not, of Sunday afternoons, given up the habit of putting on thy spectacles and turning over the leaves of thy old Bible, as if she sought to imitate thee.

CHAPTER XXVI.

DEGENERACY AND AN APPARITION.

Time is a rare old physician, excelling all his rivals in a two-fold qualification, indispensable to his profession—the power of healing and deadening. In the latter he has a helper, older and more experienced than he, by name the Devil. When I found myself from home, without a mother and worse than fatherless, I fancied there was not one earthly comfort left to me, and that none of the things of this world had any charm. I thought, also, that nothing would be easier than to follow my mother's advice to the letter. I felt not the slightest inclination for anything but that. My course lay clear before me: a thoughtful, studious and religious one. All my leisure hours were to be spent in reading good books, particularly the Bible. No resort was to have any attraction for me but the chapel—that old chapel wherein mother and Bob spent their happiest hours. Looking back, I was obliged to confess that I had been kept in closer bondage, when under mother's care, than any other boy in the neighbourhood. But, I felt now, that it was mother who was right, and so resolved to keep within the old bounds; for I fancied it gave me the greatest freedom, and wholly suited my tastes and desires. My one great ambition was to become of use to religion; and there revived in me my former boyish aspiration towards the ministry. I did not see many obstacles in my path towards that position. I should only be following the natural bent of my mind, and fulfilling the best wishes of my mother. Besides, my character was untarnished, and I was resolved to keep it so; there should be neither gap nor turning in my straight path. How my heart deceived me! I can imagine Time ruffling his forehead, and the experienced assistant, of whom I spoke, laughing in his sleeve at these good resolutions. Was it possible that my nature contained some foul dirt-heap of depravity which had never yet been stirred?

The "Corner Shop," at which I was an apprentice, was one of the oldest establishments of the kind in the town. Abel

Hughes, my master, was considered a careful, just and sharp-
eyed man. Our line included the general drapery, but we
principally dealt in cloth and flannels, always of the very best
stuff. They were quiet times, and we were rarely busy except
on fair days; and it is my opinion that Abel Hughes cared not
in the least because the fairs were not held oftener than four
times in the year. Ours was a good and steady trade, done
with old customers and their families who had dealt at the
same shop time out of mind. They were, for the most part,
country people, the majority of them being Methodists, for the
verse had not then gone out of fashion: "Do good unto all
men, especially unto them who are of the household of faith."
As I have said, Abel Hughes kept the very best material; and
he charged a reasonable profit on it. He would neither over-
praise his goods, nor bate a halfpenny of their price; and
should a customer not like what was offered him, he was
advised by all means to leave it alone. I never heard Abel take
oath that this stuff or the other was worth more than he asked
for it. Lies were not so common in business, in those days, as
to make it necessary a man should fore-swear himself. I do
not think Abel spent a penny in his life upon posters; the only
demand he made upon the printing press being for bill-heads.
The shop window was small, and the glass in panes about a
square foot each, plate glass not having then come into use.
All the window dressing wanted could easily be got through in
an hour, and it was only about once a fortnight it was done.
The shop was rather dark, even in broad day, and had an
atmosphere of moleskin, cotton-cord and velveteen so thick
that I fancied I could cut it into lengths with my scissors.
When a customer came in, the first thing Abel did was to hand
him a chair and begin a conversation with him. There the
man would sit for half an hour, sometimes for an hour, or even
longer. Generally he would buy an expensive parcel, ending
up, for the most part, by being asked into the house for a
"cup of tea," or a "bit of dinner." But little business was
done after sunset; and although gas was laid on, only one
jet was ever lit, just to show that the concern was kept going.
There was not much book-keeping work. One long, narrow
arrangement served as both day book and ledger; and, when a

customer paid his account, it was only necessary to let him see us cross it out in order to dispense with a receipt. There was nothing in the method of business to prevent the belief that Noah had used it before the Flood, if he ever kept shop. And yet Abel Hughes did well and saved money. What would have become of him had he kept shop in these days? In these days, when people beat about for customers in every possible direction, it does not matter what, when obtaining a customer and making money are, in some folk's sight, of as much importance as immortality, and immortality of no more importance than a yard of grey calico? Then the chain had not been broken about the neck of greed; traders stuck to their own particular business and lived amicably, without trying to undersell or cut each others' throats. They had no ambition to make a show, nor any overweening desire to cast their neighbours into the shade. If they attained a position free from care, got into comfortable circumstances, or had "a bit in an old stocking," they were satisfied. And there was nothing in the outward appearance of the people who had reached this happy stage to distinguish them from others who had not. That such and such a person was rich, was a topic for belief and not for proof. Seldom, also, was anyone seen making a parade of prosperity one day, and the next coming down with a crash, leaving his creditors to pull a long face at their own folly in trusting him. Still seldomer was anyone seen, after deceiving his neighbours and cheating them of their due—yea, deceiving and cheating, I say, not failing to live honestly, though they tried—still seldomer, I repeat, would these be seen afterwards holding their heads high in the town, filling public offices and appearing better circumstanced than ever before, or swaggering in the Big Seat or the pulpit. Such things are not so strange in these days, I am sorry to say.

But what I wanted to know was—what would have become of Abel Hughes had he kept shop in these days, supposing he remained uncorrupted by the times? Well, he would have had to go to the workhouse; and I believe it is there he would go rather than conform to the avarice, the deceit and the trickery of the age. I know he would not bounce, I know he would not lie; would not pretend to sell his goods for less than he himself had given for them; would not take a customer by the scruff and drag him into his shop; would not persuade any man to buy the thing he did not want; would not carry a countenance with a perpetual smirk—in a word, would not act the monkey. And so, in the very nature of things he would, Heaven knows, have had to die of want, or go into the workhouse, as I have said.

The Corner Shop had an assistant named Jones. I have noticed, by the way, that, without exception, every draper's shop has an assistant named Jones. I have a very vivid recollection of Jones, Abel Hughes's assistant. I fancy seeing him at this moment standing behind the counter, with the tip of his bright scissors showing above the edge of his waistcoat-pocket, and a swarm of pins stuck into the left lappel of his coat, like mountebank's children, making all sorts of tricks and endeavouring to show how far they can cross the centre of gravity without falling. A little, limp fellow was Jones, who made one think that Providence had intended him either for a tailor or an umbrella mender. He had a great shock of hair, all cut to a length and lying flat upon his pate, like a pound of candles. His head had evidently despoiled his cheeks, which were utterly bare; only, as if to indicate his sex, nature appeared to have gone out of her way to plant a meagre tuft upon his chin and permit some slight hirsute sprinkling of the upper lip, just like that of a stricken, grizzly old woman. Jones could on no account be said to wear a moustache, for his lip-hair was not worth the trouble of cutting, while a penny spent on a shave would be sheer waste of money. His blue-red, not over well-kept nose, was a standing libel upon its owner's sobriety. He had a fashion of holding his arms as if he found them in his way and could do much better without them. His feet were wide, flat and jointless and, in walking, turned out at an angle which made one think they wanted to go off in different directions. They struck the beholder as if they had once had a dreadful quarrel which they could never, despite all the coaxing of mediator Jones, make up. Summer and winter Jones seemed just the same—as if he were nearly frozen and nothing would suit him so well as to run to the fire to warm. I never knew him offended, no matter what was said to him. One thing he hated very heartily—a busy day. The night before a fair he could not sleep a wink. His favourite post was, out of everybody's sight, behind a pile of cloths, like a monument of winter, with feet turning outwards, like those of a round table, arms hanging like a doll's, eyes opening and shutting like a cat's on the hearth, thinking nothing, doing nothing. That was heaven for him. Jones was one of those creatures whom nature favours by refusing to denote their age, and who, as it were, are beyond the boundaries of a treatment extended alike to the horns of the cow and the teeth of the horse. A strange customer coming into the shop and seeing only his back, would take oath that Jones was an apprentice in his second year; if he saw but his profile, from behind a heap of cloth, he would have fancied him Abel Hughes's sister; if he saw his feet alone, he would conclude him to be an old man of eighty; if he got a full view of him he would be desperately puzzled whether to address him as " My son," or " Well, father." I said Jones always seemed the same; I withdraw the words. A close observer of him, as I was, could perceive that the weather affected him greatly. Small and attenuated though he was, the cold and wet shrunk him up like a piece of Welsh flannel, with the difference that, unlike the flannel, he did not thicken in the shrinking. I have no doubt that his intention in thus retreating into himself was to evade the fall of temperature, a task in which he was very successful. When the weather grew warmer Jones would take an occasional stroll, and afterwards begin to thaw. His mouth being always half open, the wind entered it and plumped out his flesh a little. All things act and re-act. The weather influenced Jones; Jones had an influence upon the weather. In winter, tho frozen look on Jones's face, his nose and hands blue with the cold, would make a customer's teeth chatter and give him the idea of adopting a warm top coat forthwith. It was a fact which Abel Hughes dared not deny that Jones could sell a larger number of over-coat pieces than anyone he ever saw. How was this to be accounted for? Why, because the fellow was a perfect refrigerator.

For all that, some people would ask why Abel Hughes kept a man like Jones in his shop. The reason was, I should imagine, that Abel was a merciful man, who knew Jones and his wife must have their daily bread somehow. Abel was also a just man, whose honour was above question; but the wages he paid Jones were very small—about a third of what assistants get in these days. And yet Jones, even Jones, had the impudence to marry a wife! For all I have heard the pair lived happily, and were wise enough not to add to the population. Abel Hughes had said that one Jones was enough in the world, and Jones believed him in this as in all things else. Jones's wife was a buxom, red-cheeked woman. When she walked out with her husband I will not say they looked like a cow with her calf, because that would be inelegant; but I will say this, that Jones looked by her side like a lion's provider, or, to be finer still, Jones stood, relatively to his wife, in point of size, as the cockle-boat does to the ship.

Why have I written so much about Jones? Because he was the means of stirring up and drawing forth my wickedness. We frequently hear parents advised not to let their children mix with mischief-making, irreverent companions. It is quite as important, to my mind, not let them associate with those who are too simple and unsuspecting. The temptation to wickedness is greater with these latter. If our first parents had not been quite so innocent, I question whether the Devil would have paid them so much attention. When we see the guilessness of childhood in a grown up man, the temptation to offer him the apple becomes exceedingly strong. I had not been many days in Abel Hughes's shop before seeing that I could put my fingers into Jones's eyes, and buy and sell him whenever I chose. From treading upon his corns, accidentally as it were, for the fun of hearing him squeak, down to persuading him to use a particular stuff for growing whiskers, my tricks upon Jones were endless, and such as would never have been thought of but for his simplicity. All this went on, of course, after time had worn away my regret, and the helper I have already mentioned had put a wet blanket upon my good resolutions. Jones could read, but I never saw a book in his hand, save at Sunday School. His head was as void of knowledge as a potato. He was credulous to a remarkable degree; nothing, almost, being too much for him to believe. Abel

Hughes's back turned, I would tell Jones the most fearful and wonderful things, the narrative being a mixture of what I had read and what I had invented. He swallowed every word. It did not strike me at the time that I was to blame for what I did, because had Jones been less gullible I should not have dreamt of stuffing him with fiction as if it were fact. Besides this, I thought that the minute and sedulous attention he paid to every word I said gave me a capital opportunity for "exercising my gift." I should be ashamed to relate all the tricks I played upon him, and it would serve no useful purpose even if I did. I will say this much further: Jones was the means of disturbing something within me—I do not know what name to give it, and it never entered my head at the time to call it sin. It was nothing anyone had ever taught me, and I know my mother would not have commended it. Something it was, I fancied, which had always lain within me, but which had not been awakened until now. I used sometimes to think it was a kind of talent; for I fancied hearing someone say, " Bravo, Rhys!" But it was not my conscience that said so; *that* said something else. Neither was it my mother's spirit, because, after I had gone to bed and shut my eyes, I fancied seeing her frown upon me. Had I been aware it was one of the enemies she had spoken of who thus commended me, would I have listened to him? Listen I did, anyhow; and I went from bad to worse. But to what purpose do I chronicle my evil deeds? I humbly trust they have been erased from the book of record.

I feel utterly unequal to the task of describing this period of my life. In a sense I was not master of myself. When I first went to Abel Hughes I was, owing to the trouble I had gone through, a serious boy, sad and with no disposition for play; considerations which earned me his confidence and good opinion at once. He fancied, I know, that it was not necessary to keep an eye on me. His sister, Miss Hughes, who kept house for him, was a kindly, religious old maid, who thought no harm of anybody, into whose heart my orphaned condition gave me speedy entrance. When, *tête à tête* with her, I told her of the hardships I had undergone, her eyes would fill with tears, and it was nothing unusual for her to get up, go to the cupboard, and bring me down an extra slice of pudding or some other delicacy. I saw the importance of making a fast friend of her, and completely succeeded. Abel Hughes, in the house, spoke no more than was necessary either for business or instruction. His sister was no exception to her sex. She was very fond of a chat, and I, on my part, endeavoured to appear as if I took a special pleasure in her small talk and trifling, all the while that something within me kept softly saying "fiddlesticks!" She liked to hear all I knew of everybody and everything. My store of knowledge was but scanty; but as often as it gave signs of exhaustion, I never hesitated seeking help from my imagination, which was lively enough always. I won Miss Hughes's favour, and that paid me well. If Abel fancied I had transgressed, Miss Hughes came forward to prove it was from ignorance I did so. If something showed itself in my character not quite in keeping with Abel's views, Miss Hughes would at once make it bright as burnished gold. Jones, also, was most useful in showing up my virtues. Miss Hughes had no patience even to speak of Jones, except as a means of proving my superiority over him. How did I feel? What did I think of myself? I felt myself a very different lad from what I was when mother was alive. I sometimes thought Miss Hughes did not know all about me. I could not help observing the difference between Miss Hughes and mother. I believe mother could see further through an oaken board than Miss Hughes could through her spectacles. Was I a bad boy? Who dared say so? True, Abel and his sister did not know one half of my history. Why should they? If mother knew all my affairs, even to my thoughts, Abel Hughes and his sister need not; a resolve at which someone said "Bravo!" But who? I did not know; but I felt, somehow, I was my own master, and that I could twist Miss Hughes round my fingers. I am surprised to think, and ashamed to remember, how free I made with her. I flattered her in the most shameless way. She asked me once how old I thought she was? (She did not know I had seen the date of her birth in the family Bible, kept in the cupboard and that, according to the entry, she was then in her sixtieth year.)

"Well," replied I, "though you look young, Miss Hughes, I shouldn't wonder if you were somewhere about forty."

She laughed and said I wasn't good at guessing.

I heard mother say Miss Hughes had never had an offer. Yet, for all that, I said to her, "I know, Miss Hughes, the reason why you never married."

" Well, let us hear it," said she.

" You didn't care to leave the master," I replied.

" That's a very fair guess," she rejoined, giving me two-pence, with orders to be sure not to tell Abel.

Was it I or Will Bryan who had changed?

" D'ye know what," said Will to me one day. " You are now like some other boy. I'll never call you 'Old Hundredth' any more. I nearly gave you up at one time. When you went to old Abe I thought your hair would begin to whiten before you were seventeen, and expected every Sunday to hear you cry 'Amen!' and 'Hallelujah!' in chapel, as your mother used to do. I don't wish to speak lightly of your mother, mind—far from it. 'Amen' and things like that suited her very well. but there was no reason why they should make an old man of you before you began to wear a hat. A thing of that sort isn't true to nature, you know. Just you watch the big cat and the little one; the big cat is quiet and sad-looking; the little cat frisks and tumbles and tries to catch her tail, just as if she wasn't in her senses. Or look at the mare and her colt; you'll see the old mare, when not at work, stand in the middle of the field without budging a step or moving, except a little of the head when the flies are about her ears. She looks as miserable as if she were thinking of her end in the tan-yard, and you might swear she was sleeping on her legs, almost. But watch the colt, how he prances around, nose in air, tail erect, and kicks at nothing. If somebody comes along the road, he'll run after him, 'tother side the hedge, with a 'Hehe! Hehe!' just as if he wanted to see all that was going on; for the world is new to the colt and the kitten, you know. It's the same, exactly, with old people and young. Though your mother used to badger me frightfully, I always thought as well of her as of anybody living—I'll take my oath of that. But to keep you, like she did, as if you were shut up in a clock-case, there was no sense or reason in that; it wasn't true to nature. She might as well have made you wear a night cap, or breeches and leggings and a beaver hat, and sent you every Saturday to William the barber to be shaved, as waste the whole week, like she used to do, starching and smoothing you up for the Sunday. Not true to nature, Rhys," he added in English; "at least that's Will Bryan's way of putting it."

I admit, with sorrow, that I was inclined to agree with Will, and that we thenceforth became faster friends than ever. His people became my people, his affairs mine. Will was no stranger to the Corner Shop. Abel Hughes's visits to Session or Monthly Meeting took him from home for a day or two, the rule being that as often as he was away Jones, as a protection from thieves (save the mark!) was to sleep on the premises. I found no difficulty, on such occasions, in prevailing upon Miss Hughes to let Will spend the night with me. Will could creep up Miss Hughes's sleeve with the greatest ease. He would delight her heart with good stories or good songs, both in English and Welsh. An invitation to the Corner Shop pleased Will always; he just "stuffed himself," as he expressed it, whenever Abel Hughes was from home. His great delight was to get a little fun out of "The Genius," as he used to call Jones. Mine was but a small, narrow bed, and I remember, on one occasion, Miss Hughes saying to my companion:

"Do you wish to sleep here to-night, William? I don't know how the three of you are to get into that bit of a bed."

"Splendid, Miss Hughes," replied Will. "Rhys one side, I the other and Jones in the middle, like a tongue sanguage."

"It's you should be in the middle, William, if you want to be like a tongue sanguage," Miss Hughes observed.

"One for you, Miss Hughes," returned Will. "But, according to your plan, there would be more tongue than bread, you know."

Miss Hughes marvelled why her brother Abel was not fonder of Will, whom she thought a clever, witty fellow. Abel never knew Will was in the habit of visiting the shop when he was from home. Once when Abel was at Session in Bala something occurred at his house which nearly brought Will and me into the hands of the law. I would not mention the matter only it has an important bearing upon my history. I shall narrate the foolish occurrence in a very few words. Will and I having wished Miss Hughes "good night" and retired to our room, Will, in a spirit of mischief, insisted upon placing Jones on his trial for the murder of a creature which I need not here name. Will acted as counsel for the prosecution and judge. I, who was the jury, found the prisoner guilty, and he was duly sentenced to be hanged. Jones enjoyed the joke immensely. In the top of the door was a large nail for hanging clothes on. To this Will tied a cord with a noose at the end. Jones, who was made to stand upon a foot-stool, placed the noose about his neck, with a laugh. Before we could look around, and by a pure accident, I believe, the stool overturned. For some seconds we thought Jones was only pretending to hang, just to keep up the fun. Fortunately, however, I noticed that the stool lay on its side and that Jones's feet were a couple of inches off the floor. I never was so frightened in my life. In less than no time I cut the cord and Jones came tumbling down, in a faint. Will, equally frightened, trembled like a leaf. We lifted Jones upon the bed, and I can never describe our joy on finding that he breathed. My conscience was ablaze at the idea that I had been within an inch of taking the life of one of the most harmless creatures in the world. When Jones came to himself he perceived my alarm and grief, looked at me compassionately, and said he forgave us both for everything. That, however, did not calm my conscience and my fear. As to Will, no sooner did he receive Jones's solemn promise not to mention the matter to any living soul than he jumped into bed where, five minutes later, was fast asleep.

For me there was no sleep. Jones would fall into an uneasy sort of slumber, lasting hours, and then wake with a start of terror. And so, many times. A hundred different thoughts crossed my mind, and I felt myself undergoing some important change of condition. The room was dark and the night seemed long. Shortly before dawn, so I took it to be, I suddenly lost sound of my bedfellows' breathing. Both lay as if dead. The silence was painfully oppressive. I saw the room becoming alight, but not with the light of dawn. It was swifter, and to my mind, if I may be permitted the expression, softer and more tender, like the approach of the

effulgent face of an angel. The light increased, more and
more; and yet it did not come through the window. It seemed
to be all within the room; every object in which had now
become visible. Still did the light increase, and so sweet was
it that my eyes became restful and enjoyed the sight. Was I
dreaming? I am not certain; only I believe I was awake—as
wide awake as I am at the present moment. The light reached
a climax of a kind whereof I cannot convey on paper any idea.
I never in my life saw anything I could fitly compare to it.
Before me in the midst of that brilliant but subdued glory
I saw my mother, sitting in a chair, not one belonging to the
room, but the old oak arm-chair she used to sit in at home. I
did not notice the kind of dress she wore, for I looked only at
her face, which, although it retained all its old peculiarities,
was lovelier a thousand times than I had ever known it. I
was not afraid, but I felt a guilty consciousness. Mother
looked neither angry nor happy. "Come hither," she commanded. I sprang out of bed and fell upon my knees before
her and, with my cheeks between my hands, rested my head
upon her knees, as I used to do when a child saying my
prayers before going to bed.

"My son," I heard her say; "I spoke to you of three
enemies, and of the armour. But, after all the trouble I took
with you, I fear you have no religion, and that you know
nothing of the great things."

She disappeared before I could say a word in reply. I
felt my forehead growing cold upon one of Abel Hughes's
chairs. Jumping to my feet I found the day dawning. Was
it a dream? I do not know. But, God be thanked, I never
forgot those words of my mother!

CHAPTER XXVII.

DAYS OF DARKNESS.

SHOULD some friend, more painstaking than the rest, have followed me to the end of the preceding chapter, he will, doubtless, laugh at me for a superstitious fellow. I cannot help that. I have touched but lightly upon the period when I left the straight path, when I lost those religious impressions and became careless about the knowledge and instruction I had received from one of the most pious of women. Was it because the remembrance of my conduct at the time was not so lively that I did so? No, but because my thoughts and actions were too vile and hideous for recital. Forget them, indeed! That is as difficult as to forgive them. God alone can do both the one and the other; but even He, I imagine, would find it infinitely more difficult to forget than to forgive, and had He not himself said He would forget, I might have thought the task impossible. Humbly and thankfully I endeavour to believe the word of the God of Truth; but the wrench it must give His omniscience to extend me His pardon is beyond my comprehension. If this be madness—Great Forgetter, forget Thou this also!

Was I a church member during the period referred to? I was, sure enough; and went up to the Lord's table regularly once a month. And, as far as I knew, none of the pious old brethren had any fear on my account; none of them spoke to me with especial reference to the state either of my soul or of my religious belief. The memory of my own case makes me shudder at the thought of the spiritual condition of hundreds of the young in our towns, religiously brought up, like myself, from childhood. In order to please the good old mother at home, or escape the reproof of a strict employer, they attend service pretty regularly; they partake of the sacrament, having reached the necessary age; but how much more do we know about them? They may go for weeks at a stretch without looking at the Bible; they may lead an utterly prayerless life; they may frequent forbidden places, filled with wantonness; they may feast on vicious and rotten thoughts; they may read

books which, were they printed in hell, by the light of the
never-dying flame, could not be more damning to their souls;
and what would we be the wiser? Do they not attend chapel?
They do, and we are thankful for that. They come within
sound of the eternal tidings of salvation to satisfy the mother,
and who knows but that God will be merciful unto them? Are
we sure, though, that the means of grace are not a burden to
them? What interest do they take in subjects Biblical? Do
they not consider them 'dry?' O, that we could be certain
they have lost one hour's sleep—only one—thinking of those
things which are to determine their everlasting welfare! Thou
shapely, handsome, tender girl—best of all workers for a
bazaar—O, that we might be certain thy heart doth flutter and
palpitate as fast over thy great matter as it did over the trash
in that penny dreadful we saw thee buy the other day! Is
there not some coldness, some distance that ought not to be
kept, between officers of the church and the young men and
maidens at least nominally under their charge, but of whom,
in very many cases, the only thing we know is that they come
to chapel? I am aware the difficulty lies in bridging that
distance without scaring their souls and driving them farther
away, without appearing meddlesome and without setting up
a kind of confessional. I know also, well enough, that the fact
that I myself have been guilty of the things referred to, all the
while that I kept my church membership, is no reason for
thinking others guilty in the same fashion. But who were my
companions in depravity, pray? I am bound to tell the truth:
church members, like myself. I am pleased to think their
numbers were small. Were I to print this history, I would
address a few simple questions to the consciences of our
church youths; as for example the following:—"John Jones
—or whatever your name is—leaving God out of the question,
would you wish your mother to know how many chapters of
the Bible you read from one Sunday to another? How often
do you pray, and what sort of prayer do you use? Have you
any objection to her knowing the places you frequent after
shutting shop or leaving the office? When with your companions, which do you think she would know you by—your
voice or your words? From what she heard you say, would she

take you to be her son? Would you care to tell your father on
what you spend your money, and where every penny comes
from? What would you take to let him see the book you locked
up in your box the other night ? If he knew as much of your
goings-on as you yourself do, what name would he give you?
Hypocrite? Does the opinion you have of yourself tally with
the opinion entertained by the "old people," your parents?
After committing acts of which you knew neither your parents
nor the church would have approved, have you not said to yourself, several times, "It will be all right when I go home, for I
shall get a deacon's ticket with the inscription :—

'To the Calvinistic Methodists.

Dear Brethren,—This is to inform you that the bearer, John
Jones, is a member of our church of Take-everything-for-
Granted. Grace be with you. Amen.' "

To the pure all things are pure ; and it may be that he who
has been guilty of much impurity is prone to believe that impurity is more common than it really is. Anyhow, I knew one
who regularly attended service because he dared not do otherwise, for fear of offending his employer. He did not absent himself as much as once from the Lord's Table, but had his master.
the deacon, known his real character, he would have had him
expelled the church sans ceremony. That one was myself.
My mind was depraved, my heart had become hardened and
cold, and my conversation—when the "brethren" were not by
to hear—unbecoming, to say the least. I was not unfamiliar
with the words of the Bible, but I used them lightly and in
jest, to create laughter and appear witty. I believe this was
the prime cause of my hardening of heart. I remember, at
this minute, a saying of my mother that a light use of Bible
words blunted the edge of their proper purpose. "Same as
that hatchet there, look you," she said ; "we have taken to
use it for breaking coal, hammering, and everything else,
almost, so that when we want to chop a bit of a stick there's
no getting it to catch." The saying proved true in my case.
Without boasting, I think I was, at that time, tolerably quick
of apprehension and not without the ability to put my
thoughts, decently and forcibly, into words. I do not know

whether it was this which created in me a liking for controversy; but I do know I was always ready for the work, on which account Will Bryan dubbed me, "Stir-the-Fire-Poker." I was invariably disposed to take the doubtful side of a question; my object being not to get at the truth but to beat my opponent, and to do so under disadvantages. As the habit grew upon me I got to think the fundamental difference between the true and the false, the evil and the good as of no consequence. With companions of no great ability or shrewdness I could give the false a more favourable colour than they could the true; and, like the fool I was, I began to admire myself and consider myself somebody. I went regularly to chapel, as I have said; but it was seldom I found a preacher to please me, because there were but few, so I fancied, who could say anything that was "new" to me; and I thought I could see holes in their reasoning and slips in their speech. By this time I had thrown up the practice of writing out the sermons, as one which was not worth the trouble. I liked Sunday School because it gave me an opportunity of showing off my talents. Heart alive! I have been thinking many times what a kindness it would have been had Evan the butcher, whom, on account of his size, Will Bryan used to call Daniel Lambert, taken me to the back of the chapel, given me a good thrashing with the stout ash stick he carried, and afterwards ducked me, head over ears, in the rain-tub. It would have done me, and many more like me, all the good in the world. I am describing my period of folly thus sparingly because I I should be ashamed for anyone to know what a lunatic I was. Although, from my up-bringing, fairly conversant with the truths, or rather with the facts of the Gospel, I was almost as ignorant of its spiritual blessings as a pagan.

Such was my condition when, as I have narrated in the previous chapter, I came near sending poor Jones to his account, and when I saw the apparition, if apparition it were. It is not of much importance what name I give the thing, whether dream or apparition; sure am I the occasion was a turning point of my life, and a blessed one, for which I have been a hundred times thankful. As I have already said, a swarm of thoughts crossed my mind that night. The words "My son, I fear you have no religion, and that you know nothing of the great things," pierced my heart like a red hot iron. I felt them to be true to the letter, and became frightfully wretched in consequence. Having accustomed myself to appear what I was not, I tried to do so once more, by looking cheerful and happy; but I clean failed. I lost my appetite, and Miss Hughes begged me to see a doctor. Many times did she say to me: "Rhys, I don't know what to think of you. You don't eat more than a bird, but I suppose I may just as well not ask you to take a little of that wormwood tea. What's the matter with you, say?" She did not understand my malady. I made a desperate effort to shake off the feeling by mixing with my old companions and entering into their amusements. But that was only adding fuel to the fire of my conscience; and so, on the excuse that I did not feel well, I left them, and thenceforth made it a practice of remaining within doors after shutting shop.

To escape Miss Hughes's chatter I pretended to be absorbed in reading; but it was little I knew what I read, for my mind wandered aimlessly about, returning ever to pore over my unhappiness. Everything presented itself to me in a new phase. Hitherto God, sin, and the other world had been mere names; but now they were living realities, of which the terror touched and penetrated every nerve of my soul, if I may be permitted to say so. Previously Communion was but a kind of club, of which I was a member; but now I began to regard the church as a spiritual congregation, a species of the elect, of whose nature and constitution, sustenance and support I knew practically nothing. Although my name was on her books, I felt there was a great, wide gulf between the church's life and character and mine. I meditated my condition for hours together. I tried deliberately to dissect it, and to put myself through a course of cross-examination: What is the matter with you? Are your wits getting into bad repair? What harm have you done that has not been done by others, and much worse? I would then remember, directly, that my mother had said these were the Devil's questions; and I derived no comfort from them in consequence. Looking back, I tried to coax my memory to dwell upon something favourable in my past; but conscience travelled ahead, and raised an army for my overthrow, so that

memory lost heart and let conscience have it all her own way.
I thought every instinct of my soul had conspired against me.
In secret I read a great deal of the Bible; but I felt it was of
others that the good book spoke; it was to others its promises
were. For me there was no light, although the quest was
my great aim in the reading. At all hours of the day and
night, especially when I was alone, came the unpleasant
consciousness of God's presence closing around me; only, when
I tried to pray to it, that Presence seemed to leave me and take
to flight. Never shall I forget one night in my bedroom, when
a Catholic sentiment seemed to take possession of me. I had
lain, musing sadly, until the candle had nearly burnt out,
when a dreary, oppressive feeling of loneliness stole over me.
God, I thought, had no compassion for me; He was angry with
me. My companions did not understand my disposition; or,
understanding, could not assist me. Angels, good or bad, took
no interest in me. I was alone, so I thought, in the great, wide
world; my soul had grown cold within me, and there was not
a single ray of warmth to cheer it. Suddenly I bethought me
of mother. She, who had loved me so well, could not have
forgotten me; and, O, madness! I fell upon my knees and
prayed to her. This was the straw I clutched at to save myself from drowning. Needless to say it brought no blessing. I
speedily saw my folly. I was not ignorant of the way of
salvation, because that had been made plain to me from my
youth; but I felt it was intended for others, and that I was
outside its scope. I considered my close familiarity with the
Gospel prevented me from seeing its inner spiritual meaning,
and that I was fated to remain in the outer court, a martyr
betwixt the world and the church. I endeavoured to form an
exalted notion of Christ, for his sympathy with fallen humanity, for his love and pity towards the sinner; but at the same
moment my heart would grow cold and my affection frozen,
while my mind placed an emphasis upon such sayings as "My
sheep hear my voice," &c.; and all my effort proved vain.

I remained in this state for weeks, during which, I recollect,
it was not the particular sins I had committed which troubled
me most, but a feeling of general, unmitigated depravity,
combined with a painful isolation from things spiritual and

supernatural. I did not give up the effort to pray, but my petitions were brief and pointless. I had played the hypocrite so often, and dissembled for so long in prayer that I dreaded being communicative. At one time, I remember, my supplications were somewhat as follow:—"Great Jesus, Son of God, I have dissembled much in Thy sight for many years, and I do not wonder Thou hast deserted me. Thou knowest, for Thou knowest all things, how bad I have been. Save Thou and I, none knows *all* my doings. If Thou wilt not forgive me, do not, I beg Thee, tell my history to mother or Bob, or anybody. Although I want to, Thou art aware I do not know Thee, and I fear Thou art offended with me for ever. Let me live a little while yet. Amen." On other occasions they ran thus: "Jesus Christ, lest thou be worse offended with me, I go upon my knees again to-night; but I have nothing more to say to Thee than I have said hundreds of times already, except that I have lost my health. But thou knowest all, so I need not tell Thee. Amen." Although I dared not go to bed without first falling upon my knees, it is within my recollection that I was sometimes possessed by a haughty, defiant spirit, similar, I should imagine, to that which characterised the fallen angels, when my prayers—if I may call them such—would partake of the character of the following:—"O, Saviour of sinners! what more can I do? I have called upon Thee hundreds of times, but Thou dost not hear. I have read, to-night, Thy Sermon on the Mount, and I find it condemns me utterly. But why did'st Thou say, 'Ask and it shall be given unto you; seek and ye shall find?' Have I not asked and sought? Were it not for fear of sinning further against Thee, I might almost think Thou wert not as good as Thy word. Thou knowest I am a bad boy. Who called Thee a friend of publicans and sinners? Were they not the same who called Thee 'a gluttonous man, and a wine-bibber?' I, too, am a great sinner; still Thou art no friend of mine. Dost Thou make any difference between sinners? Has Thou Thy favourites? What use is it my reading the Bible? It has nothing in it for me; and I find no pleasure in sinning. If Thou art resolved not to hearken unto me, let me alone to sin. Thou permittest that much even unto the devil. If I err, why dost Thou not open my understanding? If Thou puttest me in hell, I will eternally proclaim it to all that Thou did'st reject me, a youth of seventeen, notwithstanding Thy saying that ' Him that cometh to me I will in no wise cast out.' If I have sinned the unpardonable sin against the Holy Ghost, Thou knowest I did so in ignorance. My heart is like a stone, and I cannot change it. Much as I might like to love Thee, yet I cannot. But Thou knowest I hate the Devil and his angels with a perfect hatred; and though Thou placest me in their midst, I will never speak a word with one of them, never, never, even were he to put a red hot iron to my lips. O! have my wits gone astray? I hope so, because Thou pitiest the insane. Do with me as Thou seest best. Amen!"

Not a ray of light coming, from either reading or prayer, I, to some extent, gave over the work. I no longer read the Bible or prayed of mornings. I could not, though I tried, abstain from something which approached to prayer before going to bed. That, I felt, was too difficult. And unto this day I have a somewhat similar feeling. I find it easier to forget God in the morning than at night. I believe I am not alone in this, because I remember being, more than once, in irreligious company, not one of whom went to bed without first going upon his knees, although he never thought of doing so when he got out in the morning. The sense of dependence and responsibility is stronger in the night than in the morning. How foolish! We feel better able to take care of ourselves in the morning than we do just before going to sleep. Discontinuing the Bible I turned to works of humour. I failed, however, to get any fun out of them. To me the jokes were those of a clown made to a man who was on his death-bed. I fancy it must have been then I became convinced that it is only the true-hearted man, possessed of a considerable degree of piety, who can enjoy real humour, and that it is he alone who can fill his mouth with laughter without pouching his cheek with poison. Foolishly enough, I kept all my trouble to myself, and continued to look into myself instead of looking out. With one single exception I do not think that anybody had the slightest idea I was in such distress; and I should not have suspected him either, especially since I held but little communication with him, had I not, one day, received from him the English note following :—

DEAR RHYS,—I rather think you are in want of a *sachlian.* I can lend you one. The *lludw,*† of course, you can have anywhere you like. Glad to tell you that this chap is up to the knocker.—Yours truly,

WILL BRYAN.

I knew at once he had discovered the reason of my staying in at night and avoiding his company. I dreaded meeting him, for fear of his flouts. I envied him, because his parents, in the matter of religion, were lukewarm and unconcerned, while the pains taken with me and the thorough religious instruction I had received, made me think my responsibility infinitely greater than his. Will's note increased my unhappiness. Every day, almost, my master, Abel Hughes, took me to task for not being more attentive to the customers. He said I was getting worse, instead of better. That made me hate the shop. I despised Jones no longer; rather did I envy him, as having next to no soul. Little by little I sank into a state of indolence, dulness and melancholy. The Devil whispered me that religion was folly, the Bible a string of old wives' fables, and all my wretchedness but the result of indigestion. There immediately arose, however, the recollection of my mother's life, her probity, faith, rejoicing in the Holy Spirit, her resignation and fortitude under severest suffering, her boundless confidence and glorious triumph in the Valley of the Shadow of Death, from which the devil and all the infidels in the world could not move me. A great qualm of regret for her came over me. I knew I must be trying my master's patience greatly, and that the only good thing he could see about me was my staying in of nights. Sent on an errand, I would forget my business and be obliged to return to ask what it was. Behind the counter, I was confused and awkward, and often made mistakes in the price of things. My conduct made Abel tired and testy, but I knew Miss Hughes used her best influence in my behalf. One day Abel called me aside and said

---

* Sackcloth.   † Ashes.

he had been greatly disappointed in me. He at one time thought, he continued, I would turn out a good, active and capable lad; but he was sorry to find me getting worse and worse every day. "As a matter of fact," he added, "you're not worth your salt."

I felt he was speaking the truth, and so never opened my lips in contradiction. But his words had such an effect upon me that I determined to eat no more of the bread I did not deserve. What of self-respect there was left in me had been roused. My intention was to leave and trust to luck. At the moment, I did not care what became of me. Supper time arrived, but I would not sit at table. Abel had too much steel in his constitution to ask me twice; and Miss Hughes, having got to understand her brother and I had had words, enjoyed the meal but little, for she loved me greatly. I thought there was something dry and hard about Abel that night at the family devotions, and I could see that his sister paid no attention to them. For me it was a night to be remembered. I felt Abel Hughes's saying to be true that I was not worth my salt, and determined to clear my character before leaving, or else to reveal my condition. After prayers Abel, as usual, sat down in his arm chair and began to smoke. For a while he kept silent. Obstinate, firm and resolved, I eagerly watched my chance for a talk. After long waiting—all three, I fancy, feeling anything but nice in the interval—Abel in harsh, crabbed tones asked me whether I meant to go to bed that night. I replied I didn't until I had told him the reason of my awkwardness in the shop, and my bitterness and unhappiness of spirit. I told him, then, my trouble; but no sooner had I begun than I fell to weeping copiously. In all my difficulties, fears and despair, never a tear had coursed my cheeks since the day my mother was buried; but I had hardly opened my lips to tell my master my story before the dam broke down, and all words were drowned in a deluge of the heart.

The comfort there is in telling one's trouble! Seldom have I met with a kind-hearted woman who, seeing a strong youth in tears, did not chime in with him. Miss Hughes was kind-hearted. Those tears were a great blessing to me; not only as indications that my heart was not so hard as I had imagined, but also as a means of enabling me to gain sufficient self-composure to tell the whole story. I concealed nothing from Abel; no, not even the one thing I conceal here—something which had to do with him personally. I conceal it here in obedience to his express command. "Do not mention it to anybody else," he said; "because, if it gets to men's ears, although God forgave you, it might be brought up against you as long as you live." This he said to me on the morrow; but it is of the previous night I was speaking. I knew I had to deal with one who was every inch a man; a fact which enabled me the more confidently to relate all my feelings without reserve. I believed he would, after hearing my story, compassionate me, condone my failings, and direct me into the right path. I fully understood there were thick walls around his heart, but once I gained an entrance, I thought, I should not be easily cast out. He listened to me attentively; but I failed to see he sympathised with me. Indeed he looked on cheerfully, as if taking a delight in my misery. When I had finished, all he said was:

"Oh, very good! If that is the case, go on. You'll get better directly."

"Abel," said Miss Hughes; "is that all you have to say to him? You're hard-hearted."

"I don't want you, Marg'ret, to tell me anything about my heart. I know more about it than you are ever likely to find out, name of goodness," returned the blunt old Calvinist.

"But I'll tell you this much, at any rate," Miss Hughes retorted; "you ought to help the boy a little, and give him a word of advice."

"Do you know, Marg'ret, that He who began in us the good work will also finish it? It isn't well, look you, to raise one too speedily from the pit. And, another thing, if it is He who has opened the wound, He himself will find a salve for it, in His own good time."

"You should show the lad where the salve is to be got, or you may just as well not be deacon—that is my opinion," observed Miss Hughes.

"I warrant you he knows. He is not some half heathen come to Communion for the first time, like Thomas Bartley and others. You can't tell him anything he doesn't know already. When his complaint comes to a head he'll find the Doctor's address easy enough. The best thing for him to-night is to sup and go to bed," saying which the old man coolly refilled his pipe.

Although it was but cold comfort I got from Abel, I felt he had come to regard me in a different light. What with Miss Hughes's promptings and those of my own stomach, I was absolutely compelled to take a little supper, after which I went to bed. But not to sleep; only to reflect upon my situation. By this time the desire to leave had vanished; all my thoughts ending in a sigh for light upon my present condition and my future. How and whence the light came I mean to tell you in the next chapter.

CHAPTER XXVIII.

MASTER AND SERVANT.

A FULL, frank, unreserved confession of the truth, a scouring out of every dirty corner of the conscience, even though it were made before man, gives a kind of strength to the penitent. The unlocking of the heart's doors, and throwing them wide open, so that the pure fresh air may enter, brings health to the soul. The making another, as it were, a partaker of one's consciousness is to shift one end of the burden on to his shoulders. Why are we so anxious to hear that the condemned murderer has admitted his guilt? One reason is because we know it will make him stronger to face his dreadful doom; and there is also, possibly, a something else which we do not care to acknowledge, namely, a secret desire to share the load on his conscience. He who makes complete confession of his sin, though it were black as hell, partakes, in a measure, of the man's strength who tells the truth. He strikes the devil in the forehead, and lifts himself in the scale of being infinitely higher than the hypocrite. The father can use the rod with some degree of relish across that boy's back who is a sneak; but to beat the bad, mischievous lad, who openly confesses his guilt, excites a paternal rheumatism of the shoulder-blade which puts off the punishment—for ever. Why does God want to hear us confess our sins? Is it because He does not know them already? No, but because He wants to hear us tell the truth, even were that truth the ugly one of rebellion against Himself. There are natural sneaks, and there are spiritual; both equally abominable in the sight of God. Tell the truth though you be crucified for it, is His command. Truth in all its hard and hideous deformity is more acceptable unto Him than the simulating lie, hidden by groans and tears. To the hypocrite and the sanctimonious He will say: "If it is the darkness thou lovest, if it is thine own caves thou likest best to live in, I will take care thou art provided with a congenial dwelling place, where never gleam of light shall enter, save that of the inverted lamp of thy conscience."

Having, as it were, turned myself inside out to my master, although my condition was not more hopeful, nor my future one atom the clearer, I felt strengthened. It was as if I had repudiated the name hypocrite, and had summoned up sufficient courage to tell the naked truth about myself, so that, supposing I must go to perdition, I should not march thither under the banner of heaven. At eight o'clock the previous evening Abel Hughes and his sister knew next to nothing of the wickedness and sin of which I had been guilty. Descending the stairs on the morrow after a sleepless night, I reflected that the two knew almost as much of my personal history as I did myself; and yet I felt I could look them in the face more straightly and honestly than I had done for years. What gave me this confidence? For one thing, I was no longer the skulking cur I had been. For another, I believed both were truly religious, loved God, and on that account loved man, even though he happened to be in the gutter. Had I not been sure they were religious, would I have made them the full confession I did? I fancy not. Had I mistaken Abel Hughes's real character, into whose hands would he have committed me after I had admitted all my faults? Heaven knows. Abel Hughes! thy name is enshrined in my heart and memory! Thy rectitude and austerity were as severe as Sinai's own; but thy heart of hearts was saturated with the forgiving principle and appeasing blood of Calvary. I knew in whom I had trusted, though in fear. At breakfast I marvelled greatly at the courtesy and kindness displayed by Abel and his sister. I felt abashed and undeserving of such treatment. My feelings nearly overcame, my food nearly choked me. I could not help the notion that there was something God-like in the forgiveness and the courtesy of pious people. I fancied morning service had an unusual unction about it; of a truth I enjoyed Abel's prayer as I had not for long previously done. At the same time I felt unhappy and in disgrace, and I made up my mind to ask the master to have me expelled the church —which I believed he would do, whether I asked him or not.

Abel came into the shop shortly after me, and having cast his eye over an invoice, bade Jones check it, adding—"Jones, should someone inquire for me, say I'll be here directly; but don't come to fetch me, because I have a bit of business on hand. Rhys, you'd better come and help me."

He walked into the parlour and I followed him. He locked the door directly, and bade me be seated. He sat down opposite me. My heart beat like a newly caught bird's. I feared I had mistaken my master's real character after all, and had been foolish in confessing my every fault to him. And yet, I was not sorry I had done so, whatever the consequences might be. These and many other thoughts flashed through my mind in the course of a very few seconds. For a moment or two before breaking silence he looked me earnestly in the face, I making an effort honestly to return the gaze. Before he had said a word I fancied I saw beyond the seriousness of his countenance a back ground of mercy and forgiveness. I have thought, by the way, that some good, like most bad men, have two faces. Beneath the rough, frowning aspect you often find the tender, merciful one, or the man himself, just as you may discern under the hypocrite's smiles the Devil standing on his head. I fancied I saw the merciful man beneath the clouded brow of Abel Hughes, just before he began speaking thus:—

" Your mother, who is to-day, I am pretty sure, in heaven —she and I were great friends; and I promised her, before her death, I would take care of you and do my best for you. She had a high opinion of you—too high, I fear; but I warrant me she was judging you would turn out as you should have done, after all the care she took of you—all the religious instruction she gave you, and all her prayers on your behalf. When you were telling me your story last night, I felt very thankful that your mother was in her grave. I never remember meeting one who could possess her soul in patience under the bitterest trials like your mother; and, as you know, she had an abundance of them. But I firmly believe if she had lived to see your de-basement—and she surely would have seen it, because she was sharper sighted than I—it would be more than even she could have borne. It would have broken her heart. I recollect, at this minute, how she used to tell me, with brightening face, what a help she got in forgetting all her trouble with your father, all her poverty and hardship, from seeing you grow up in the way she liked; how you would learn chapters from the Bible unasked and could repeat parts of sermons while you were yet a mere child. When you were not within hearing, she would talk about you by the hour; and often did she ask me whether I thought you would ever make a preacher. Were she alive to-day she would a thousand times have preferred to hear that you had died of starvation by the road-side, than that you had fallen off to the extent you have done. But she was spared all this, and went to her grave believing her only son would not disgrace her teaching. Well, I must say I have been sadly deceived in you. I believe, however, you have made an honest confession. And, mark this—*I believe you.* If you thought I did not, you would be doing yourself a great wrong. I am pretty certain you have told me the truth. But have you told me the whole?"

" Yes, the whole, I think," replied I.

" Very well. Have you spoken to anyone besides my sister and myself?"

" Not a word to any living soul," was my answer.

" Better still. You have made a clean breast of it, and I do not see that any good can come of your telling anybody else.

These things might be cast in your teeth to the end of your
days; because it often happens that man is reproached for old
faults by his fellows, years after God has forgiven him. If I
had not myself known something, from experience, of the
depravity of heart of fallen humanity, possibly I might have
looked differently upon your confession. But I do know something of the struggle against temptation and being once and
again overcome, and I trust I know something also of coming
out of the fight victorious. Perhaps there may be those who'll
say my duty is to turn you out of doors, proclaim your faults to
the world and expel you from the church; and they might think
me merciful for not doing more. But I shall do neither the one
thing nor the other. Why should I? I am a great sinner myself. I reflected last night, after you had gone to bed, that if
we were each to make full and complete confession of our
faults, what strangers we should become to one another! I
thought, also, how small is the real difference between the best
and the worst of us. Tell me honestly, now—but, for that
matter, I know you will not do otherwise—have you declared
eternal war against the devil and the depravity of your own
heart? Are you resolved, with the help of God, either to
conquer or die in the strife ? "

"I have nothing to conceal," replid I. "I hate myself, but
I have no one in my own stead to dote upon. I hate my
actions and my evil habits of old, but I find no pleasure in any
other. The truth is, I have no love for myself or for anything
outside myself, which is the same, I fear, as to say I hate
everything."

"So," said Abel. "It would be vain for me to give you
those counsels which are given every day to all men—those
you have heard hundreds of times from the pulpit and in Communion, and which have, to a great extent, become meaningless by this time, both to those who give and those who are
given them. But did you ever before feel as you have felt for
the last few weeks? Try and call to mind, now."

"No, for certain," I replied.

"Good. Do you remember a time when you were tolerably
contented in spirit, when you enjoyed the service in chapel,

Q

and were able to go to bed at night undisturbed by fears and
the admonitions of conscience?"

"I do very well. Such was the case with me for many
years," I answered.

"Now," said Abel, "can you tell me what constituted your
happiness at that time? Was it your own purity; or was it
because you had never given yourself a thought? Was it
because you knew God, because you had caught a glimpse
of His divine majesty, His stainless sanctity, His hate of
every appearance of evil? Was it because you had felt His
infinite love in giving His Son to death for us, had rested your
soul upon Christ's atonement and sacrifice, and enjoyed the
peace which is in the Gospel in consequence? Was it that
which made you happy?"

"I do not know," replied I.

"Try and think. We will wait a minute or two, for you
may consider," said Abel.

"I fancy," I presently observed, "that my former happiness
consisted in an utter absence of a right knowledge of myself,
together with the fact that I had not realised a single great
truth concerning God and his ordinances. In other words,
now I come to think of it, I believe it was my ignorance of
myself and of God that made up my happiness."

"Just so," remarked Abel. "But one question more. You
recollect a time, do you not, before you had committed those
sins to which you referred last night? Good. When you began
committing them, I know it was the least heinous of them—if
it is right I should say so—you committed first, was it not?
Now in committing the first, how did you feel? Did you feel
as if you were travelling some new road, or as if you were
merely on an old one which had deteriorated? Did you feel
you had made a 'right about face,' as these volunteers say?"

"No, I think not," I replied. "I believe I was always in
the same road, only I found it becoming worse as I walked."

"I guessed as much," said Abel. "Now, taking your own
account, do you not see there is greater hope of your salvation
to-day than ever there was? Even during your best period
you never seem to have realised your condition as a sinner,
nor to have had any just comprehension of that God whom, in

scoming, you worshipped. Your ignorance was your castle of
bliss. You were on the way to destruction from your birth. But
now, here is God in His mercy raising a storm about you and
casting a tree athwart your path. You must return to the
cross-road and take an entirely new turning. And, observe—
this happens in the life of every man who is saved."

"How am I to do it? I fear God will not hearken unto
me," I said.

"Have you tried Him? Have you told Him the whole story
of the old way, and asked him to direct you into the new?"
asked Abel.

"I have asked Him hundreds of times for His guidance, but
I have never told Him all my history. To what purpose? God
knows it better than I do myself," replied I.

"It is there you are mistaken," returned Abel. "According
to your reasoning there would be no necessity for prayer at all,
because He knows the heart's deepest and most secret thoughts
and desires. But remember, He will not hear your prayer, or
mine either, while we keep back anything we know to be faulty
in us, and do not *tell* it to Him—not publicly, but in the
privacy of our own room, I mean. You may be certain that
the publican had gone over all the particulars before entering
the temple. I do not believe Christ would have answered the
prayer of the thief in such few words but that He was pinched
for time. There never was any good of doing things by halves.
Open out your heart before Him, and make a full and minute
confession of your faults. You need not fear you will bore
Him with tediousness to whom a thousand years are as one
day. Although the sins are an abomination unto Him, He is
not displeased to hear the sinner confess them, if in his heart
he be truly repentant, and show a sincere desire for forgiveness and a complete escape from their influence."

Abel paused a minute or so at this point, as if anxious to
ascertain whether his words had any effect upon me. I felt
profoundly all that had been said, but could find no other
words for reply than: "I thank you from my heart, master;
but my sins are great and manifold."

"They are," he rejoined, "greater and more numerous by
far than you have yet imagined; and so are mine. We both

—we all, for that matter - are in the same unlucky boat. You,
I know, have read more than the generality of boys hereabouts,
and so I don't mind telling you a bit of my experience, since it
is relating experiences we are. I never told this experience in
Communion, and if you live to my age, you too will have
experiences which you will never divulge either to the
church or your greatest friend, and will have feelings which
you cannot convey in words, even to yourself. When I was a
youth a little older than you are, the incarnation of the Son of
God appeared to me to be unreasonable, improbable and
beyond belief. I had not your religious rearing; but I received
a little day school, and was fond of reading and study. For all
that, I wallowed in the vilest sin. I used, occasionally, to go
and hear the Gospel, and took some sort of interest in the
preacher. Like Zacchæus of old I would climb to the top of a
tree for a good view of preacher and congregation; but,
contrary to him, Salvation did not come to my house. In
course of time there happened that great religious revival of
which your mother was ever and always talking, when I and
hundreds of others were convinced of our sins. In the frightful sight of my guilt then given me I perceived the reason for
the incarnation. And, if you have noticed, you have never
found one who, having been awakened to the enormity of his
sin, has doubted any longer the coming of Christ in the flesh.
It is those who have loose notions of sin who are the exceptions.
Call to mind the old religionists—those of the great revival,
your mother called them. Did you ever see their like for the
intensity of their love towards Jesus, a love that annihilated
every obstacle in its way? What was the reason for this?
They were people who had had a vision of sin such as is not
often got, I fear, in these days. But this is what I was saying:
If you have seen your condition in its true light—and I believe
that to some extent you have—do you not begin to perceive the
reason for the incarnation? Do you not see there is something
in your despair and in the depth of your wretchedness which
shows that His errand to the world has not been in vain?
Solomon, if you remember, in thinking of his insignificance
and misery, almost doubted whether God dwelt with man on
earth. But, for my part, I do not see there is anything in man

save his terrible wretchedness, which could have moved the
bowels of God's infinite compassion, nor any object grand and
deserving enough to call for His appearance in the flesh but
that. I am now an old man, and an old sinner, and am
prouder of the name than if I were an angel, because I feel I
am an item, an atom, in that great scheme whereby God was,
as it were, made to come out of Himself. It is here, my son,
that your salvation lies, if you are ever to find any. To me the
existence, the sin and the misery of man are inexplicable, save
in the glow of that accursed death upon the Cross. In the darkness prevailing from the sixth until the ninth hour alone do I see
what of light and hope it is possible for man in his condition to
find. It is the old story, you see, that I, too, have to tell; but
were it not for this same old story the country would not have
asylums enough to hold its madmen. And there is no other
story worth repeating, in your case—no other name under
heaven wherein it will pay you to confide. Have you ever
wondered at the silence of God? If you have not, you will,
assuredly, have some feeling of the kind, some day. When I
was a young man the thought of it used to oppress me greatly.
I often walked the night alone, especially if the heavens were
clear. The appearance of moon and stars made me melancholy.
How far, how old and how silent they were, methought! They
were fixed now in the firmament just as they were when my
father, grandfather and great-grandfather gazed up at them.
I marvelled to think how many generations of men, now in the
dust, had looked at them, as I did, in the same spot which they
had occupied in the time of the Druids, the time of Paul, the
time of Moses, Abraham, Noah and Adam. And yet how
silent, ever! How vast the experience they must have
gathered! And yet they never told me anything to calm my
restless mind! In vain did I ask what was beyond them; they
but twinkled, voicelessly, down upon me, creating within me
uneasiness and doubt and thoughts unspeakable even unto
myself. Many times did I look up, and for long, expecting
some extraordinary manifestation, but in vain. All went on
as usual. And did you and I go out to-night after dark we
should find everything just the same as when Isaac meditated
in the field. Well, thoughts like these made me gloomy.

There was something in the depth of my soul which 'asked a sign.' I recalled the story of the pillar of cloud by day and the pillar of fire by night, and fancied there was some sense in that; something which man could see and be certain about. I remembered, also, Joshua in the Valley of Gibeon commanding, in God's name, the sun to stand still, and it did so. There was something noble in that; something to bring peace to the uneasy mind of man. And then I would ask myself why had we been deprived of all such signs for centuries, why had ages been passed in most painful silence? I felt, somehow, as if God had gone from home, and left everything and every place empty and mute. At times I had such a strange, overwhelming desire to see God marching to the front from the distances to which He had retired, that I would have willingly been witness to another general Deluge, whatever my fate therein might be! What gave my mind unrest? I believe it was the original aspirations implanted in the soul after a knowledge of God's purpose and intent with regard to man and his future that had been seriously disturbed. But this is what I was leading up to: I never had a moment's peace and quiet for my mind until I got to believe, with all my heart, the great fact of the Lord's appearance in the flesh. Though I knew the story already, I had not believed it, believed it with an object, until I came to feel the depth of my depravity, and was made conscious of the elements of wretchedness, evergrowing and immeasurable, within my own being. Beyond the belief of Christ's coming in the flesh, there is but the silence of the grave for me, everywhere; there is no clear answer to one single question of my perturbed soul. But the life, teaching, death, atonement and resurrection of our Saviour defy the soul to put a question which cannot be satisfactorily answered.

"Now, my son, I will not ask you whether you know the story; I know you do, as well as I. But do you believe it, wholly, unhesitatingly and for ever? I do not expect from you a decisive answer. For my own part, I do not attach much weight to the instant belief which some people talk of. My own experience teaches me that man does not gain it except by hard study, deep and constant meditation, and prayer without ceasing. My great desire is to set you on the way to begin the work of seriously seeking the help of the Spirit to guide you aright. And if you but apply yourself assiduously, the day will surely come when you will be thankful for your present misery; when the eye of your mind will have been opened to see His love who remembered us in our low estate. Is there anything you would like to ask me?"

"I feel, sir," I replied, "that there are a great many things I would like to ask you; but I cannot give them form. I feel some great want, but I cannot give it words, and I am not sure I know its nature. I had thought there never was another who had felt as I did, but you have given much of the history of my own heart. I am conscious of a void which requires filling, and that that which would fill it is far removed from me. How am I to satisfy my want and find the peace which you have found?"

"Man's heart is by nature empty," replied Abel, "but once awakened, it constantly aspires. There is a danger, however—especially to him who has read and studied a little—there is a danger, I say, of his living upon the dreams of his heart, and taking those for religion. Guard yourself carefully against it. In many instances this makes the religion of the sceptic; because, as a rule, it is not amongst the illiterate, ignorant classes you will find a sceptic, but amongst the studious and well-read. How is this? Well, this is how I see it. Reading and study awaken the heart to its wants, cause it to question itself; and once the questioning begins, there is plenty of work to do. The sceptic keeps up the process of self-inquiry without getting an answer to one of his great questions. At first the questions are his great things; but in the end his great thing becomes his inability to answer. Little by little he satisfies himself with, sometimes boasts of, his want of knowledge. It being his own heart and understanding he appeals to, he is obliged to sum up his belief in the two words—*Don't know.* I make no pretence to being a philosopher, but I am certain I have a restless heart and soul that are asking questions ever. Well, if I couldn't reach higher ground and a better creed than that contained in the 'Don't know,' I should be the most wretched creature living. Better I were an elephant, or an ass, or a monkey, than a man. Were I certain, in my own mind, that the utmost I could attain to by investigation and study is 'Don't know,' I should take my hat off to every donkey I met, and call him Blessed! But, thank God! we have a revelation. To me two facts are plain. One is that man's heart, once awakened, keeps questioning ceaselessly; the other, that the experience of the cleverest men the world ever saw is that the heart's only answer to its own questions is, 'Don't know.' Now, if the Bible answers the profoundest and most abstruse questions of my heart—if it can explain my existence, my wretchedness and my future—if it can direct me to One able to allay the uneasiness of my soul—I shall believe that Book has emanated from God. If it were not so, why not show me its equal, nay its superior? I challenge any man, any nation, aye, the pick of all the nations under heaven, to produce anything like it that is not indebted to the Bible itself for both thought and matter.

"But where am I wandering to, pray? What I was talking of was the danger of your living on the dreams of your heart and fancying that to be religion. Some people linger within themselves in melancholy, sentimental study, their high places being groans and tears. That is not religion. Religion is something more practical than that. It is a constant going out of yourself, is religion. 'The kingdom of God within you,' that's religion, sure enough; but its 'goings forth,' like its Author, 'have been from of old, from everlasting.' You will get more good for your soul in one day from looking to Christ and endeavouring to do his commandments, than from a hundred years of looking into yourself. Do you know it is when you lose yourself in the desire to do the ordinary duties of life as a service to God that you become most religious? Behind the counter, serving a customer conscientiously and to the best of your ability, do you know you are pleasing God as well as when you are upon your knees in the privacy of your own apartment? Amidst all our stupidity, ignorance and darkness there appear some things of which we can be certain. You are sure in your mind that it is right to tell the truth; tell the truth, then, under every circumstance. You are sure that to live honestly is the proper thing; live, therefore, so honestly that conscience cannot raise a finger at you. Remember that whatever borders on shabbiness and meanness is detestable in

the sight of God ; and that the more of the gentleman there is
in your conduct all the higher in the world will you stand in His
esteem. Strive to keep your heart as pure as God's own. You
will discover directly—indeed I shall believe you have found it
out already—that you can do nothing as you ought to do it,
without His help and guidance. Every attempt of yours to
lead a Godly life will awaken and set in motion some conflict-
ing tendency of your nature, which will, I hope, bring you
to the only One who can help you to overcome them all. Try
and believe that God sympathises deeply with you in your
degradation, darkness and impotence; otherwise He would not
have sent His Son to die for you. But, believe also, that He
has no sympathy with you when you give in to your weaknesses. It is only when you are fighting energetically against
sin that His strength and sympathy will go forth unto you.
At the beginning of your religious career—and I believe you
are really beginning it only now—I would deeply impress upon
you that religion is not a matter of shilly-shally. You know
there are several in church with us, like William the Coal, who
frequently fall into evil, and afterwards are deeply affected by
the sermon, cry in Communion, and lay the blame on Satan for
their sins, as I have heard that that mischievous lad, Will
Bryan, taunts our friend with doing. They believe the feeling
under sermon and the crying in Communion are real religion.
I do not know what to think of them. I hope God has some
bye-law for their salvation. No, my son, it is not after the
fall, religion's bitterest tears are shed ; it is in the struggle, in
the fight, that the loud cry and the tears come. Perhaps I have
spoken too much. You have, as you know, sinned against
me; but I forgive you from the bottom of my heart, believing
you are sorry for your transgression. If I, encompassed by
weakness, can do this, how much more will He who is infinite
in pity blot out your untruth, if you are truly repentant?
Now, go back to your work, like a man, and remember, that
from this time forth I shall expect you to conduct the family
worship alternately with myself."

Abel unlocked the door and walked out, leaving me as if in a
dream, although not in so dark a dream as some I had been in
previously. I trembled at Abel's last words. Thenceforth,
however, I looked upon him not as a master, but as a father,

CHAPTER XXIX.

I GOT light and blessing from that conversation with Abel Hughes in the parlour. I saw it was possible that one could be religiously brought up from childhood, could take an interest in chapel matters, derive some enjoyment from the ordinances of the Gospel, aye, be of service thereto, and yet not have been aroused to the great questions of eternal life. Furthermore, I understood from Abel's words—and up to now I have had no reason to think him mistaken—that there was a particular juncture in the life of every believer, whether religiously brought up or not, when the spiritual light flashed upon his mind, causing him to see himself and all around him in an entirely new aspect. I understood also, and afterwards learned the fact by experience, that the more a man contemplates himself, and the deeper he penetrates the secrets of his own heart, the more sad and despairing does he become, the less likely to be of use either to himself or anybody else; and furthermore that the only medicine for one really awakened to his condition, one who has found that the depths of his soul contain but darkness and terror, is the fixing of his contemplations upon the glorious Person, spotless life and atoning death of our Lord and Saviour Jesus Christ. I recollect a remark of Abel's, made a long while after our talk in the parlour.

"Were you troubled with biliousness," he said, "is it by staying in your bedroom, looking at your tongue in the glass and wondering at its nasty fur coating, that you'd expect to get well? Not a bit of it. I know you'd have sense enough to take to your old walks again, and if that did not work a cure, you would call your companions together for a climb to the top of Moel Fammau, to get a view of the far-famed Vale of Clwyd. And I'll warrant you the fresh air of old Moel would shift every grain of bile from your stomach, and that you would not turn up your nose at your dinner on your return. It's the same thing exactly with religion. I have told you many times that you'll never do any good by looking too much into yourself.

Go out into the highways and fields of the Gospel. Muster your friends for a climb to the top of that hill on which the gentle Lamb suffered under nails of steel, and you shall find yourself healthier, purer and lighter spirited. Do you know what? There is a world of meaning in those words of old Dr. Johnson: 'Gentlemen, let's take a walk down Fleet Street.' Johnson had many memories full of a revivifying charm connected with Fleet Street; so, when wearied of himself or the company, he would get up and say, 'Gentlemen, let's take a walk down Fleet Street.' The old Doctor's words have been as good as a verse for me, hundreds of times. The Gospel has its Fleet Street for the believer, fascinating and full of bitter-sweet recollections. Scores of times, when tired of the shop, cloyed with grey calico a groat a yard, brown holland at ten-pence, and trifles like that, have I left everything and taken, with your mother or someone else, 'a walk down Fleet Street.' In going to chapel old Johnson's saying was as often as any in my mind, 'Gentlemen, let's take a walk down Fleet Street.'"

I endeavoured to act upon my master's advice, and succeeded to such a degree that I soon got to look something better than a roosting hen, with head under wing. I set to work to forget myself, to think more of Christ and his words, and to look at the bright side of the Gospel. I wondered I had not found out, before Abel told me, that herein lay the secret of my mother's happiness.

"Think of your mother," he said. "Do you know of any-one who met with so much trouble? And, for all that, did you ever see anyone enjoying so much real happiness? Where did her happiness come from? Was it from looking within? I don't believe it a bit. She had learned to look at One worth the looking on. It always struck me that the greater her trouble the greater her happiness. Her poverty only made her think of the riches that are in Christ, while the ill-treatment she received at the hands of your inhuman father but made her revel in the Saviour's gentleness and love. Don't be angry with me, but the truth is, when I used to hear that your mother was in trouble, I would laugh and say, 'Well, that's another feast for Mary Lewis.' Do you know what? You ought to be a brave lad, for you had a noble mother. I never saw one like her who could subsist so entirely upon the promises of her religion. In a manner of speaking, she had no business to die when she did. She was neither old nor diseased. 'Abel,' she said to me, when she went to live at Thomas Bartley's, 'there is no reason, is there, why one who has everything should live upon the parish? I'll never take a penny from the parish, that's the truth.' No more did she, as you know. I have thought a great deal about her. When she saw she would be obliged shortly to depend upon parish relief, it affected her as the husks did the prodigal son. I fancied hearing her say, 'Hold on, relieving officer! That kind of food is an insult to my family; I will arise and go to my Father.' I sometimes think that hers was a sort of insistence upon death, in order to prove the truth of the promise that the righteous shall not be forsaken. Thomas Bartley must have been of the same opinion, although Thomas, I know, did not understand the philosophy of the thing. I heard him say he 'craved like a cripple' for her not to die, but that die she would. I do not praise your mother for this. But there is something, you see, in religion of the best sort which makes one dreadfully independent of this world and its things. Try and get a religion like your mother's."

I have already said it was but little Abel spoke to me during the first years I was with him; no more than was absolutely necessary between master and servant. But after I had made a clean breast of it, his conduct entirely changed. His kindness and tenderness were boundless. On every opportunity he spoke freely and affably. After shutting shop he was constantly bringing some subject or other under my notice, and after examining me thereon, he would deliver his mind fully and lucidly. He would mention the books he had read, and point out their excellences and their defects. He spoke of the old preachers, described their appearance, dress and mode of delivery. He would repeat portions of their sermons in a manner which made me sometimes regret I had not been allowed to come into the world earlier. Abel appeared as if determined to break down every barrier, annihilate every distance between him and me. Since a lad I had entertained the greatest respect for him, and had regarded him as a model deacon; so that his condecension in thus noticing me, the trouble he took to teach me and to guide me in the paths of knowledge and religion, together with his frank and unostentatious generosity, made me love him, and feel wholly happy in his household. Miss Hughes rejoiced at my having been the means of making her brother so communicative and sociable; "instead of being," as she expressed it, "with his nose in his book, or his head in the chimney all day long." In a word, the old man had, in his latter days, found a son, and this gave him both the tongue and the heart of a father. Happiness smiled upon me once more. I took fresh delight, and a deeper and truer than ever, in the things of religion and the ordinances of the Gospel.

But I felt some uneasiness at the thought that I had not dealt decently by my old companion in mischief and iniquity, Will Bryan. I had never told him definitely why I shunned his company; and I had a notion that a thing of that sort was not gentlemanly, or what his friendship really deserved. I determined, therefore, to avail myself of the first opportunity I got to notify him that my mind had undergone a complete change, and that I wished to try, through the help of God, to become a good boy. From the bottom of my heart came the whisper, "Can I possibly win Will over to the same resolve?" I say it honestly, there was nothing on earth I would have desired better than to be able to persuade Will to leave his old ways; for I could not conceal from myself the fact that, although a church member of some sort, he was distinctly an ungodly youth. My soul clave unto him as Jonathan's did to David, and the idea of breaking my connection with him was a terribly painful one. He had a large heart and a generous, and I could not forget his fidelity and kindness to me in days gone by. As I stated at the beginning of this history, when we were lads there was a great difference of station between us. I was poor and needy, Will in the midst of plenty; although never, even by a look, did he show himself conscious of the difference. Scores of times did he keep the wolf from my door; and, knowing my proud spirit, did so with an unstudied delicacy which left my feelings unhurt. At

school I was weak and fragile; Will strong and hardy, the
strength being always at my service to save me from wrong.
Was it gentlemanly to forget all this? Was it right to break
off the acquaintance? I was certain that after what I had lately
gone through I could not hold communication with him without injury to my eternal welfare. Unable to bear the idea
that Will should think meanly of me, I resolved to reveal myself to him at the first opportunity. All the same, I feared the
encounter, because I knew him to be the stronger-minded.
Truth to tell, he was chock full of natural talent; a fact which
made me commiserate his absence from the right path. What,
I uneasily reflected, if he took to jeer me? Well, there was
nothing for it but to take the roasting quietly. I was anxious
that our meeting should appear wholly accidental. And so it
actually happened, for I came across him quite unexpectedly.
His face wore its usual cheerfulness, and I saw that my conduct
towards him had not made the slightest inroad upon his frank
good nature.

"Holloa! old millenium!" he cried, extending his hand.
"How be, these centuries? I was just beginning to think
you'd gone to heaven, only I knew you wouldn't leave without
saying good bye to your old chum. Honour bright, now;—is
it a fact that you've had a reformation, visitation, or whatever
they call it. Know what? I too am quite ready to go to
heaven or list a soldier—don't care which; I'm clean tired of
home. There's been a deuce of a row yonder this week, for
nothing at all, or nearly; and I'm not going to put up with
much more humbug."

"What was the bother about, Will?" I asked, taking up
step with him.

You know that old eight day clock in the kitchen?" he said.
"It had got to lose a bit lately—a fault by the way," he added
(in English, for whose accuracy or inaccuracy I do not hold
myself responsible), "not entirely unknown amongst other
orders of superior creatures. I always fancied," he went on,
in Welsh, "I could mend it if I only had the time; for, though
I had never tried my hand at clock cleaning, still, I ain't
stupid at such things, as you know. Well, the old people went
to Wrexham fair, with [relapsing into English again] strict in-

junctions that Will in the meantime should diligently apply
himself to weighing and wrapping sugar, which occupation the
said Will considered unworthy of his admitted abilities; and
t·e said Will, following his more congenial inclination, betook
himself to clock-cleaning, thinking that thereby he did not
waste valuable time by putting the time-keeper to rights. But
[in Welsh] it was a bigger job than I had bargained for, my
boy. In pulling the old arrangement to pieces, I had to make
notes of where each piece came from, and what it belonged to.
After cleaning the lot, and rubbing a little butter into every
wheel, screw and bar—there was no oil in the house—it had
got far into the afternoon, notwithstanding I had gone without
my dinner, so as not to lose a minute. It was high time now to
begin putting the pieces together if I wanted to finish before the
gaffer came home. So far—good. But when I went to set my old
Eight-Day to rights, and to consult my notes—you never saw
such a mess. Exactly like Parson Brown, I couldn't make
out what I had written. But I learnt this much—that a man
who takes to cleaning clocks, like the man who goes to preach,
should be able to do the job without notes. You can't imagine
the fix I was in. You must remember that I was labouring
under great disadvantages, all the tools I had being a knife and
a shoemaker's awl. I was sweating like a pig for fear old
Pilgrim's Progress should return from the fair before I got that
precious article together. However, I worked like a nigger,
and slapped up the affair some fashion. But when it was all
over, I found myself with a wheel to spare which I didn't
know in the blessed world what to do with; so I put it in my
pocket. Here it is."

Will showed the wheel.

"Surely to goodness, I put old Eight back in his place, and
wound him up; but first thing my nabs did was to strike, and
strike, and keep on striking until the weights got to the bottom,
and he could strike no longer. It struck thousands upon thousands did that blessed bell, and the sound of it got into my head
and made me quite stupid. It made such a row that I feared the
neighbours would think the Hall owner's daughter was going
to get married. After striking all it could, the next thing my
beautiful must do was to stand stock still. As long as I kept

shoving the pend'lum it went on pretty well, but directly I
stopped shoving he stopped going. To tell you the truth, I
laughed till I was ready to split. I could not have stopped if
someone was to kill me. So here endeth a true account of the
clock cleaning. But wait a bit. Presently, my boy, our
ancient pilgrims came home, and the first thing they did, of
course, was to go and look at the time. I had tried to guess it
as near as I could, and placed the hands where they should be,
so I thought. But the old woman spotted the clock to be on stop.
' What's the matter with this here clock, William ?' she asked.
' Has it stopped ?' said I. 'Looks like it, these two hours,'
she replied, jogging the pend'lum. I was nearly bursting with
laughter. ' What's-the-matter-with-the-old-thing ?' said the
dame fiercely, giving it a shake such as you've seen people give
a drunken man who has fallen asleep by the road side. In
order to get an excuse for laughing, I said, ' I rather fancy,
mother, he must have ruptured himself, like the Hall owner's
hunter, and that we must either open or shoot him.' But the
servant girl comes up at this point and lets on that I've been
engaged all day cleaning old Eight. You never heard such a
flustration ! Mother bust up; the guv'nor went mad. I half
believe the old man would like to have given me a licking, only
he knew he couldn't do it. This child subsided into his boots.
Next day they sent in great haste for Mr. Spruce, the watch-
maker, to set old Eight a-going. But I knew he couldn't, for I
had one of the wheels in my pocket. So did Will have revenge.
' I give it up,' said old Mainspring. But when this chap sees
the old folk's backs turned for six hours he's bound to work a
miracle on the old Eight Day. There! I've told you my
trouble. But, honour bright now, is it a fact that you've been
born again ?"

" Will," replied I, " don't you think it time we should both
turn over a new leaf ? I am not able to tell clearly whether I
have been born again or not; but I'll say this much—my mind
has undergone a wonderful change of late. I have got to look
upon everything in a different light, and I'm certain I can
never again find any enjoyment in the old ways. Hell, another
world, and the things of religion have been constantly in my
mind for months past, and I couldn't drive them out though I

tried. I wanted to tell you I had resolved to become a good boy, if I shall have help to do so. And there is nothing on earth I would like better than for you to take the same resolution. You have always been a great friend of mine, and if our mode of life differs so much that we are obliged to part, it will be a most painful thing to me. You know as well as I, and better, that it won't do to go on as we have done; it is sure to end badly. Do you not think of that, sometimes, Will?"

"Go on with your sermon. Say: 'we will observe, secondly,'" returned Will.

"No sermon at all, Will," said I. "Only a friendly conversation."

"Well, if it isn't a sermon, I've heard many worse," he remarked. "But to be serious. I had for some time seen that you had gone on that line, and I said so, didn't I? To tell the truth, I didn't much wonder at it, because religion comes natural to your family, barring your father—no offence, mind. If I'd been brought up like you, p'r'aps there'd be a touch of religion about me too; but you never saw less of that sort of thing anywhere than yonder, except the bit we get on Sunday. Though not quite a pattern of morality myself, still I think I know what religion is. If I hadn't been acquainted with your mother, old Abel, 'Old Waterworks,' and some half a dozen others, I should have thought, for certain, they were hypocrites, the whole bag of tricks."

"It isn't proper in you, Will, to speak lightly of your parents," I observed.

"I don't speak lightly of them," he rejoined. "It's of their religion I'm talking; and man and his religion are two different things entirely. As a man of business, clever at a bargain, as a money-maker, and one who takes care to find plenty of grub for a chap, the gaffer is A 1. But I'll take my oath he can't repeat two verses of Scripture correctly, any more than myself. He never looks at the Bible except for a couple of minutes before going to school on the Sunday. It is as good as new now—the Bible he had presented him on his marriage; not like your mother's, all to smithereens. I believe, though, that if his day-book and ledger caught fire to night, the old man

R

would be able to copy them out pretty correctly next morning.
It's a fact, Sir. Do you think I don't know what religion is?
He puts down four shillings a month for mother, four shillings
for himself, and a shilling for me, regularly, on Communion
book. But do you s'pose credit is given for that in the ledger
up above? It's all my eye, lad. I know how things should be
done, right enough, even if I don't do them myself. If the
gaffer fancies he can shut his conscience up in that way, I'm
wide awake enough to know we can't cheat the Almighty.
I'm as certain as anybody that it is necessary to *live* religiously three hundred and sixty five days in the year, and not fifty
two. Father and mother would make proper honorary
members of a church if there were any. But there are none,
I know, and so it'll be no go with them in the end."

"Your responsibility is so much the greater, Will; knowing
what you ought to do and not doing it," said I.

"Do you think you're telling me anything new?" he asked.
"I learnt all that when I was a kid. I am only speaking of
the kind of rearing I've had, and what I have seen at home.
'It is enough for the disciple that he be as his father.' There's
a verse of that sort, isn't there?"

"'As his master,'" said I.

"Quite so," quoth Will. "It's very odd I can never repeat
a verse without making some mistake, although I know
hundreds of comic songs, right off the reel. But, with reference
to religion, father and master, it's all the same; and perhaps it
may be father in the original, as they say. But to the point
at issue. I know what a professor should be, both on Sunday
and on Monday; but I've seen so much humbug, fudge and
hypocrisy carried on that it's made my heart quite hard, and
filled my pockets with wild oats, which I am bound to go and
sow, I fancy. Do you know what? I am quite ashamed to
stay in Communion. Everybody must be aware I'm not fit to
be there, and the Great King knows that my father, who
compels me to belong to it, is just as fit to be there as myself.
As a family, there is no more religion in us than in a milestone;
nor as much, for that does answer the purpose for which it was
made. You know I'm not a bad sort, by nature. I myself
have often wondered how I'm so good. I've sometimes thought

if I'd been son to some one like Abel Hughes, I should—well
how do you know what I'd have been ? But ' to be or not to be,
that is the question,' says Shakspeare; ' what is is, and there's
an end of it,' say I."

" You're in error, Will," I remarked. " You know you can
and ought to be something different to what you are. You
have brilliant talents, and it is a pity you should use them in the
service of the devil."

" You may just as well stop it there," said Wil. " You
can't tell me anything I don't know already. 'Twould be sheer
hypocrisy for me to say I'm turnip-headed. But, with religion, look you, brains without grace are good for nothing; and
grace, you know, is not a thing you can buy in a shop, like a
pound of sugar. It must either come straight from the head
office or not at all."

" Why don't you go to the ' head office' to fetch it, then ?"
I asked.

" I knew you'd say that," he replied; " but easier said than
done. Something keeps telling me—I will not say it's Satan,
because William the Coal has laid quite enough blame on him
already—something tells me I've not had my innings. Old
Abel, or someone, has bowled you out, and I'm very glad it is
so. But up to now I'm at the wicket; although, perhaps, I
shall be ' well caught' or ' spread-eagled' some day. I hope
so, because I shouldn't care to carry my bat out, you know. I
too would like to find religion, only it must be one of the right
sort. ' Beware of imitations' is a motto for every man. P'r'aps
you think Will is more hardened than he really is. Hold on a
bit! I'm not quite like Spanish iron yet. You never saw me
cry, did you ? But many a night, when I have failed to sleep,
and something within me kept telling me I was a wicked boy,
I've had a right good cry. But by the morning I hardened
again, and something would tell me I had let private apartments in my heart to some little devil who had become my
master. I never got the least help from father and mother
to turn him out. I much think it was to him your mother
used to allude; only she called him the ' old man.' The Bible
speaks, doesn't it, of some bad sorts of them who won't go out
without fasting and prayer ? Well, I can't for the life of me

pray—you can't possibly get them in the humour for that, over yonder—and I can't sham. Talk of fasting, why, I give my devil a dozen meals a day sometimes. I'll take oath he's as fat as mud by now. But to tell you the truth, I'd like to put him on one meal and starve him. I have studied a little of human nature, and I knew you felt shy of meeting me. You thought I meant to make fun of you. Far from it. I'm real glad you've been converted. You want to become a preacher, don't you? You needn't shake your head, it's a preacher you will be. I knew it since you were a kid. That's what your mother wanted you to be, and if she has asked it of the Almighty, He is bound to oblige her. P'r'aps you won't believe me, but I'll take oath I've often felt uncomfortable at the thought that I have done you harm. However, since you've had a turn, you'll make a better preacher than if you'd always kept on the straight line. You know no one can play whist unless he is able to tell how many cards of any particular suit are out. I never saw any of these milk and water fellows—those who have never done wrong—making much of a mark at preaching. They don't know the ins and outs, you see. They preach well, but nothing extra. Mark what I tell you: if you hear a man preaching extra good, and take the trouble to look up his history, you're bound to find he has been, some time or another, off the rails. Did Peter never go off the rails? Yes, and what is more his engine went to smash as well. But he made a stunning preacher afterwards. Boss of the lot, wasn't he? Well, if you're for becoming a preacher—you needn't shake your head, I tell you again, you're bound to be—I'll give you a word of advice. P'r'aps this'll be the last chance I shall have, because if there isn't a change of policy over yonder very shortly, this chap will be heard saying, 'Adieu! my native land, adieu!' You're cleverer than I am in Scripture, but p'r'aps I've noticed some things that you haven't, and I may be able to give you a bit of advice which you won't get in the Monthly Meeting. Well, remember to be true to nature. After you've begun preaching don't change your face and your voice and your coat, all within the fortnight. If you do I shall be bound to chaff you. It's God's work, I know, your change of heart; but if your throat and voice change, that'll be your work. And there's no necessity for it—they'll do very well as they

are. Don't try to be somebody else, or you'll be nobody at all.
D'ye know what? Some preachers are like ventriloquists. In
the house each remains himself, but directly he gets into the
pulpit, you might swear he was some other man, that other
man being the poorer of the two, because he is not true to
nature. Don't go droning your reasons to the congregation,
like one who isn't in his senses; for the fact that you are in the
pulpit doesn't give you a license to be sillier than you are anywhere else. If you were to carry on a sing-song argument with
a man in the street, or in the house, or before the magistrates,
they'd cart you off to the asylum, right away. To hear a
preacher tuning it, for all the world as if he were at a concert,
one minute, and the next breaking off, sharp, and talking like
anybody else, makes me think it's all a dodge, and turns my
heart to stone. When praying, don't open your eyes. I'll
never believe anyone to be religious who looks up to see what
o'clock it is, in the middle of prayer. I've seen men do that,
and it has spoiled the pudding for me. When you are a
preacher—as you are bound to be, so you needn't shake your
head—don't take on you to be holier than you really are, or
else you'll make the children all afraid of you. D'ye know
what? We had a preacher lodging at our house last Monthly
Meeting, of whom I was afraid in my heart. He was in good
health, and ate heartily, but kept on groaning at meals as if he
had an everlasting toothache. It was just as if he wore a coffin
plate upon his breast; I felt like being at a funeral, as long as
he stayed there. I'd have been bolder, I swear, with the
Apostle Paul, or Christ himself, had they visited us. It wasn't
true to nature, you know. If you want to give yourself airs
of that sort, just you keep them till you get back to the house
whose rent you pay. Be honourable, always. Don't forget to
give the girl at your lodgings sixpence, even if you haven't
another in your pocket; for she'll never believe a word of your
sermon if you don't. If you smoke—and all great preachers
smoke—remember it is your own tobacco you use, or there'll
be grumbling after you've gone. You know I'm fond of a bit
of nonsense; but, if you preach seriously, don't tell funny
stories after getting back to the house, or someone is sure to
think you a humbug. I like the preacher who is true to
nature, both in the pulpit and at home; but to hear one who

has *almost* made me cry in chapel, afterwards *quite* make me
laugh in the house, spoils the sermon for me. When preaching, don't beat too long about the bush; come to the point, hit
the nail upon the head and have done with it. Don't talk too
much about the law and things like that, for what do I and my
sort know about the law; come to the point—Jesus Christ. If
you can't make everyone in chapel listen to you, give it up as
a bad job and take to selling calico. If you go to college—
and I know you will—don't be like the rest of them. They tell
me the students are as much alike as postage stamps. Try and
be an exception to the rule. Don't let the deacons announce
you as 'a young man from Bala.' Preach till it be sufficient
to say, 'Rhys Lewis,' without mentioning where you come
from. When in college, whatever else you learn, be sure you
study nature, literature and English, for those will pay you
for their keep, some day. If you get on well—and you're
bound to—don't swallow the poker and forget old chums.
Don't wear specs to try and make people believe you've ruined
your sight by study, and to give yourself an excuse for
not remembering old friends; because everybody'll know it's
all fudge. If you are ordained, don't begin to wear a white
neckerchief on the very next Sunday. If you never wore one
it wouldn't matter, for I shan't believe Paul and his companions
did—they had no time to wait to get them starched. Never
break an appointment for the sake of better pay, or you'll
make far more infidels than Christians. Whatever you do,
don't become stingy, or christen yourself a saving man.
Honour bright! I hope I shall never hear that about you;
I'd rather hear of your going on the spree than that you had
become a miser. I've never known a miser change, but I've
seen scores of drunken men turning sober. It is stranger than
fiction to me, but if you went on the spree only once they'd
stop you from preaching; although if you were the biggest
miser in the country you'd be allowed to go on just the same.
Old fellow! don't you think this is pretty good advice, considering who I am? Monthly Meeting will tell you all you
want to know with respect to prayer and so on; but it hasn't
the courage to give you the counsels I have given. Give us
your paw and wire in, old boy!"

And Will left me before I could put in a word.

CHAPTER XXX.

THE POACHER.

I THOUGHT I knew my friend Will Bryan thoroughly. I had had every opportunity for so doing. He was so frank and open-hearted, that I fancied there was no difficulty in reading him. But from the conversation recorded in the preceding chapter, I saw there were strata in his character, of the existence of which I was not previously aware. I had always considered him the picture of health and vivacity, and as one whose talents shone although they had never been cultivated. He was no great reader; but of whatsoever he read he took in the meaning and spirit at a gulp. He was too listless to take pains, but then he did everything, apparently, without effort. All he saw and all he heard—sermons excepted—he took down, as it were, in shorthand upon his memory. He was a shrewd, keen observer of men and things. To use his own idiom, he was constantly "spotting" something or somebody, and it was but seldom he was far off the mark. On returning home together from places we had visited he would astonish me with the number of things he had "spotted," but which I had never noticed at all. I am not much surprised, now, that he used to call me, on such occasions, Bartimæus. I often envied his ability to see things as they were, and not as they seemed. I considered, always, that he had a natural faculty for detecting deceit and trickery, or as he called them "humbug" and "fudge." His shrewdness and his knack of setting things forth in their true colours—in few, but cutting words—had impressed me for years, and induced me to emulate him. But, for all that, I felt, as he himself admitted, that he had "done me harm;" for, many a time, when I fancied myself benefitting from a sermon or address, Will would destroy the good impression by pointing out some "humbug" in it of his own discovering. Although I could place greater reliance upon his honour, and presume farther upon his generosity than anyone else, still, I was convinced that he was an utter stranger to serious feeling, and wholly unconcerned about his spiritual condition. After I had resolved to reveal my intention

to reform, I expected, as already intimated, he would be
severely sarcastic at my expense. But I was dissappointed. It
surprised me to find him rejoice at my having "had a turn,"
as he phrased it, and that there was a longing in his own
heart for a similar awakening. He did not intend, he said, to
carry out his bat in the game he was playing. In the solitude
and silence of night had come a cry from the depths of his
consciousness: "Will, why art thou wicked?" But, as he said,
he got no help from his parents "to turn the evil spirit out."
Poor old Will! I have often thought if he had received a
religious rearing, if he had seen anything but worldliness and
worship of the golden calf at home, he might to-day be an
ornament not only to his neighbourhood but to his nation. In
the most reckless of us there is a kind of duality. Although
depravity may be uppermost, there is something at the bottom
of the heart which doffs its hat to goodness, to truth. I once
knew a drunken, wholly irreligious man who, on receiving a
letter from a son who had left home, giving an account of his
reception into full church membership, was so overcome with
emotion that he was obliged to beat a hasty retreat into
another room, out of sight of his family, in order to weep out
his joy. What a homage to religion! Whether on a throne
or off, it is virtue that is paramount, by common consent. Amid
all his frivolity and mischief, Will Bryan had his serious hours,
when Conscience insisted upon being heard, and his soul sighed
for help to cast forth the spirit of evil. I should never have
imagined that such thoughts found a place in his heart, if he
himself had not admitted to me that they had. The secret
history of his heart, told by one friend to another, often elicits
other history kept equally secret theretofore.

I do not know what made Will Bryan think I wished to become a preacher, because I am certain I never disclosed the
fact to him. When a lad, it is true, I delighted in the notion
of one day joining the ministry; but it was a secret which I
confided to not a living soul. For some years my mode of life
had been anything but favourable to such a notion, and the
boyish desire was entirely eliminated from my mind by the
time I had become of age and sense. When Will protested it
was a preacher I must be, nothing was farther from my

thoughts. I was in too much trouble about my condition and creed to think of anything else. And yet I must confess that Will's words: "You needn't shake your head; it is a preacher you will be," clung to me. He pronounced them with such emphasis and certainty that I felt constrained to ask myself was Will, like Saul, among the prophets? I scouted the notion; only no sooner did I do so than it would return. I recalled the strange and wonderful feeling that came over me on the night of Seth's death, after my attempt to pray by his bedside; how something had told me, on my way home, that I would some day be a preacher. But I could not help remembering, also, how wicked, how sinful, how flippant I had been, during the many years that had elapsed since mother died; and I fancied hearing unclean spirits at my elbow asking, amidst derisive laughter, "Who art thou, to think of preaching? Thou who hast broken every commandment a thousand times?" There were dozens of lads about my home who knew my old life. How they would smile in the sleeve did I dare to talk of such a thing; how they would recall my old tricks, whilst I preached! And how I would remember them on seeing my companions! What, me a preacher! Impossible! But then how came Will so confidently to predict it was a preacher I would be? He knew more about me than anybody else in the neighbourhood; aye, knew more of my faults. And yet he had said, "You are bound to be a preacher!" Impossible, said I to myself. I am certain neither of my salvation nor my faith. He who thinks of preaching should first of all be assured of his own salvation. It is not so with me. Once more did I discard the idea of becoming a preacher, it being out of the question, I thought, that such a thing could ever happen.

Weeks passed; and somehow, of late, I found myself no longer caring for light-coloured clothes—not because I thought of being a preacher, but because black clothes appeared more becoming. I had light clothes no worse than new in my box, but I would not wear, because I did not like them. I made up my mind that the next coat I got made for myself should be a little longer-bodied, although not so long as the preachers', not for anyone to think I was imitating them, than which nothing was farther from my mind. I took a special interest in books of divinity, and wondered a little why others of the like age did not relish them as I did. I remembered the time when I was much given to criticise the preachers, and to find faults in their sermons; but latterly I had got to wonder how really blameless they were, and how they managed to fulfil their duties so surpassingly well. Previously, I hated to find it becoming Abel's turn to take the " monthly " entertainment of the preacher; but now, I longed for its advent, and spent all the time at my disposal in the speakers' company. I can't, to this minute, help laughing at my simplicity. I regarded Abel's diary as a sacred book, so sacred that I dared not ask to see it, though I burned to know who was to preach with us in the coming months. And when Abel happened, forgetfully, to leave it on the mantle-piece, the temptation to look hurriedly through it was too strong to be withstood. After doing so, I felt as guilty, as, I should imagine, the Jew who, not being of the order of priesthood, had happened to examine the contents of the ark of the covenant! I am sorry to be obliged to admit that I have not been able to preserve the like feeling of respect towards the diary; because I subsequently discovered some things in it which could not always be depended on. Looking at it at the year's end, I found it contained quite as many " fairings "* as fairs, and that the moon had not changed so often as the " promises."

But to return. I loved to see a preacher coming to Abel Hughes's house; if he was a young one all the better—a student more especially. I could be more bold with these latter, and ask them an occasional question, such as, How old were they when they began to preach? Did they find the work very difficult? Was it of their own accord they had taken to it, or at the instigation of others? And so forth. Had I any thought of myself beginning to preach? Nothing was farther from my mind, so I fancied. If I secretly cherished any such intention, the memory of the disgrace attaching to my family, of which I knew not the minute it would be revived and brought painfully into prominence, was sufficient to blast, for ever, every

---

* An allusion to the Ministerial practice of exchanging indifferent engagements for better.— TRANSLATOR.

hope or desire of this kind there might be in me. Recollection of my feelings at that time puts me in mind of the incident I am now going to relate.

In the neighbourhood where I was brought up there was a strange character known as "Old Nic'las," or, more often "Old Nick;" a not inappropriate designation for, with my boyish notions of his namesake, I fancied Nic'las and he to possess a strong family likeness. The former was tall, had a stoop, was muscular and strong. Although at the time I speak of an old man, age had not softened or smoothed his natural roughness of aspect. His bristly hair obstinately refused to whiten, his repulsive countenance was too firm set to wrinkle. I believe he would have gone mad had he lost a tooth. In walking, he always held his head down and rested his hands on the small of his back, under his coat-tails. He looked no one in the face save from the corners of his cunning eyes. He was such a terror to the children, that when one of them cried or refused to come home on being called, the mother might be heard saying, "You wait a bit, my boy; here's old Nic'las coming," which was quite enough to stop the cry or to send the youngster running into the house for his life. Although mother never threatened Nic'las upon me, I feared him greatly, notwithstanding. I remember when we were a crowd of boys at play, directly we saw Nic'las coming, we scampered off to hide, and kept as still as mice out of the way until he had gone by. Will Bryan would not believe he was human. Will used to say he was a cross between a Gipsy and the Evil One. Nic'las held no sort of communication with his neighbours, for which, so far as I know, no one was the least bit sorry. A stranger to those parts, his life and circumstances were a complete mystery. Many, however, were the wild and fearful stories told about him, implicitly accepted by the credulous and the superstitious, no one being able to gainsay them. It was pretty generally believed that he was of high family and very rich. Mother was of opinion that he had sold himself to the Evil One, and was living upon the proceeds. I fear her views of the pecuniary resources of the Evil One were too broad; only, in face of such a charge, she would instantly answer that the love of money is the root of all evil, and that it was not un-

likely the Devil had an enormous old stocking stowed away
somewhere. Anyhow, it is certain that Nic'las was not poor,
for he lived in his own house, which he had bought for a pretty
good sum of money. This house, called Garth Ddu, stood in a
secluded nook, about half a mile from the town, and abutted
upon the domain of the Hall. Surrounding house and garden
was a high wall, built after Nic'las had become owner. What
was visible of the structure had an antiquated look about it,
the ivy mantling it up to the roof and making the windows
wholly useless. A stranger would have thought the place had
no occupant, and would have been confirmed in the notion by ·
the appearance of the patch of land attached to the house,
which had been neither grazed nor mown for years, and which
human being never trod save Nic'las, who might be seen
occasionally, head downwards, walking by the hedge-side, gun
under arm, as if searching, not for a bird but for a badger.
Since the day Nic'las got into possession, not a foot was known
to have entered that enclosure save its owner's, and that of a
disreputable old woman, named Magdalen Bennet, or as she
was commonly called Modlen of the Garth. Not even the tax
collector was ever allowed to go beyond the door in the wall.
Nic'las holding no intercourse with his neighbours, what of
business he had to do with the world was transacted by Modlen
alone. It was she who brought home his food, and the little
clothes he stood in need of; it was she who called for his weekly newspaper. Many were the attempts made to get from
Modlen some inkling of Nic'las's circumstances and mode of
life; but the only reply the old woman ever gave was, " it is a
question you are putting me." The utmost got out of her, even
by her best friends, with reference to the way in which he
spent his time was that he dug his garden and shot sparrows. All
conversation concerning her master being distasteful to Modlen,
and she being a good customer, the shopkeepers did not think
of pestering her with inquiries. And yet they could not help
wondering at the capacity of Nic'las's stomach, if he alone ate all
the food she bought for him. Moreover, when they thought of
the large amount of powder and shot sent him, they wondered
how a single sparrow had been left alive in all the country. It
was Modlen's story, probably, which gave rise to the belief that

Nic'las had a magnificent garden, well worth the seeing, and made many people grieve that so lovely a glade should waste its sweetness in almost the same manner as that desert flower of which the poet sings. The hermit life he led, and the halo of mystery surrounding his past had, at the time of which I write, become an old story, of which people no longer spoke or thought. It was pretty generally believed that there was something wrong in the head of the queer man of Garth Ddu. The common impression, combined with the fact that blows had been heard within the garden walls, efficiently protected Nic'las from the prying intrusion of his neighbours.

Will Bryan and myself held but little communication after the colloquy recorded in the previous chapter, and, to his credit be it said, this was to be attributed more to Will's resolve not to "do harm to me," than to any other cause. I had no longer any particular friend, with the exception of Abel Hughes; but, then, he was an old man. I spent my leisure time for the most part alone; and the more I read and studied, the more did the great questions of life weigh down my soul. No sooner did I find light thrown upon one mind-trouble, than I was in the midst of another, and I hardly ever got the better of my dejection save at short intervals. I often pined for a companion of my own age and disposition, to whom I could lay bare my heart; because, when I found myself in a difficulty or got fresh light on any subject, some spirit of speech came to me, and I longed for a hearer. I never was in robust health, and this disposition to stay within doors proved very injurious to me. When the weather was fine, Abel absolutely compelled me to go out for a walk. One night, towards the end of May, I remember well, after shutting shop, going, unasked, for a long stroll into the country. It was exceptionally clear and beautiful out of doors; so I took the zig-zag path by Alun's side, passing, as I went, a number of clerks amusing themselves angling. Having gone far enough, I fancied I could get back sooner by another route. I crossed a couple of fields and, as I now remember, trespassed in so doing, and came into the high road leading by the Hall, whose surroundings I enjoyed, and whose isolation I drank in with delight, spite the fact that, for reasons already recorded, I felt no respect for the owner. I thought, if I may be permitted to say so, there was at once a simplicity and a god-like majesty about those tall trees shadowing the road on either hand; and that saying about "the trees of the Lord" came into my mind with a new and mystic meaning. No wonder, thought I, Will Bryan should talk so much of "nature." I don't know whether anyone else feels similarly, but, ever since I can remember, a feeling of reverence comes over me when I find myself in a great umbrageous forest. Perhaps it is something I, as a Briton, have inherited from the Druids of old; or it is possible the feeling may be commoner than I have imagined. The inspired writers, for instance, speak with respect of the cedars of Lebanon. It may be some will smile at the idea; but I have thought that you meet with more of God in a wooded country than in a bare and exposed one. At any rate, on that night, in a silence broken only by the baying of a hound at the Hall and the sound of my own footsteps on the hard roadway, I felt a sort of watch and ward kept over me as I walked, contemplatively, between that avenue of giant trees, standing out like grenadiers of God. On reaching the spot where the wood was thickest and gloomiest, and wherefrom the twilight was almost completely excluded, I saw coming to meet me a big man, slowly stalking and with head bent to earth. When we had got a little nearer each other I perceived it was Old Nic'las. The sight fairly made my flesh creep. I had not come across him for some time, and there was something in his look that night which agreed so well with the depressing loneliness of the place, that I lost every grain of that feeling of security which had possessed me only a moment previously. The sentinel trees seemed no longer grenadiers, but grim mantles, offering cover for a ghastly murder.

With trembling hand I buttoned up my coat over a still more trembling heart, and walked rapidly on. "Good night, Mr. Nic'las," said I, in as bold a tone as I could command. Nic'las answered never a word, and did not even raise his head. After I had proceeded a few yards, I looked back and saw Nic'las going leisurely on his way. How foolish to be so frightened! Nic'las, poor old fellow, was an innocent creature enough. Leaving the main road, I struck the path leading by Garth Ddu, which

I reached in a few minutes. I could not help stopping to take
a look at the old house. How silly, thought I, of the people of
the neighbourhood to associate such fearful, baseless, fables
with its owner. In all my life I had never heard that Nic'las
had said a nasty word to anybody. He had an odd way of living,
it was useless to deny; but, so far as the facts went, no one
could say that Nic'las was not a harmless man, after all. If he
chose to make himself a mystery and a riddle to those around,
he had a perfect right to do so, for he never did anybody wrong.
There was, I thought, a charm about a secret, recluse life, and
Nic'las, doubtless, found a pleasure in it. At the same time,
I felt a great curiosity with respect to the house, especially
now that its owner was from home. I should like to see the
garden of which there was so much talk. The wall was not too
high for me to climb. I resolved to make the attempt, and had
just begun the task when I felt a strong grip laid upon my
collar, and myself shaken as a terrier shakes a rat. The hand
was old Nic'las's.

"A thief is it! A thief in the house of Nic'las of Garth
Ddu! Rather venturesome, eh?" he cried, giving me another
shake which almost shook my soul from my body.

"Who are you?" he went on. "What are you? Where
d'ye come from? Speak! Say your prayers! or by ——
I'll pull you into four quarters and a head!"

If he hadn't held me by the collar, as a cat holds a mouse in
her paw, I am certain I should have fallen from sheer fright.
I tried to speak, but mouth and tongue were dry as a cake, and
I couldn't get out a word. I believed, for certain, he was
going to murder me, but I could not have cried out had I been
given the world. A hundred thoughts flashed across my brain:
death by torture, another existence, my condition, mother,
Bob, Abel Hughes, with all their associations, and if ever I
prayed it was then. All this took only a quarter of a minute
to think of; I, the while, gazing terrified at the fiendish face
of old Nic'las, unable to utter a cry. Almost directly, he
slackened his hold of me, but without letting go, and I could
see by his looks that he was half satisfied with the scare he
had given me. In a somewhat milder tone he asked me, once
more: "Who are you, and what do you want?"

I don't know how it came about, but all of a sudden my tongue eased a bit, and I was enabled tremulously to answer:

"I'm no thief Mr. Nic'las. I'm 'preutice to Abel Hughes, and I only wanted to see your garden; in my deed to you."

"Wanted to see my garden, eh? Modlen's been palavering, I know, that the garden is worth seeing; yes, worth the seeing. If the old hag doesn't keep her tongue still, I'll shoot her, dead as a door nail, that I will. And every boy I catch climbing my garden wall, I'll flay him alive, and throw his flesh to the dog—that'll save me buying meat for him. You want to see the garden, do you? Well, you shall see it, for it's worth seeing. Ha, ha! Come inside."

With one hand Nic'las kept his grip of me, while with the other he drew from his pocket a latch key, with which he opened the door in the wall. He led me through and carefully closed the door behind him. He then released me and ordered me to follow him. What was my surprise when I beheld the famous garden! It was a perfect wilderness, and, from its appearance, the owner could not have put a spade into it for years. With the exception of the path, which went about it, it was fairly hidden with thorns and brambles. Some of the bushes were dead or decayed, while others appeared to have broken heart for want of nourishment. For all that, Nic'las took me round, pretending to point out different kinds of fruits, flowers and plants which the place contained, using their technical names, and descanting elaborately on each variety, just as if he had been a professional gardener. When it was all over he laughed a harsh, jeering laugh, and said: "The garden is worth seeing, is'nt it?"

His classical gibberish concerning thorns, briars and weeds, being ended, he began mumbling disjointedly, as a maniac would; his words, as far as I can recollect them, being somewhat as follow:—

"Who's Nic'las of Garth Ddu? Where does he come from? Whom does he belong to? How does he live? You'd like to know, wouldn't you? But you shan't. You think Nic'las a fool; he is a fool, too. Who was Nic'las's father? David Nic'las, Esquire, great man, wise man, merchant, miser, idiot. Didn't he smother his wife before, no, after, Nic'las, Garth Ddu was born? Who saw her die? How much did David Nic'las, Esquire, merchant, miser, idiot, pay the doctor not to tell? Where did David Niclas, Esquire, merchant, miser, idiot, send Nic'las, Garth Ddu, to be nursed? Did he pay a hundred, two hundred pounds for poisoning the child? When did David Nic'las, Esquire, merchant, miser, idiot, get to know Nic'las, Garth Ddu, had no brains? What did he offer the schoolmaster to kill him with Latin? Did he offer a hundred pounds? Did he offer two hundred? Did David Nic'las, Esquire, merchant, miser, idiot, try to kill Nic'las of Garth Ddu, twice? Did he try three times? Did David Nic'las, Esquire, merchant, miser, idiot, get a stroke once? Did he have a stroke twice? Did he have a stroke three times? When David Nic'las, Esquire, merchant, miser, idiot, got the last stroke, did Nic'las of Garth Ddu sit on his chest, and squeeze his throat? Did he do so once? Did he do it twice? Can't you answer me? Haven't you a tongue? Where did Nic'las, Garth Ddu, get his money from? How did he get money? Would he have had money had he not sat on David Nic'las, Esquire, merchant, miser, idiot's breast? How much did he get? Did he get two thousand? Did he get five thousand? Did he get ten thousand? Don't you hear? Won't you answer?"

"I must have time to consider, Mr. Nic'las," replied I.

"Consider!" he returned. "Never take time to consider, or your head'll go wrong and you won't be able to sleep for a week, for a fortnight, for three weeks. You'll have to walk all night, if you're going to consider. Never consider, or you'll get soft in the head. Can't you speak? Are you deaf and dumb? I had a cousin who was deaf and dumb. He was always considering, and he died in the Asylum. They wanted Nic'las, Garth Ddu, to go to the Asylum, so that they might get his money. What do they do in the Asylum? Nothing but consider. Do they consider a week? Do they consider a year? Won't you answer? Wait a bit; I'll make you."

Near by was an old thorn-grown summer-house, into which he dived, bringing out with him a double barrelled gun.

"Do you see this?" he said, recommencing his ravings. "What's it good for? Will it kill once? Will it kill twice?

s

Here, take hold of it and shoot me. One barrel at a time, mind. No, stay; I'll shoot you first in the head with one barrel, and you shoot me, after, in the breast with the other. Toss up who'll shoot first! Heads! Tails! Who's to shoot first? Let me consider; but I musn't consider or my head 'll go wrong. Why does Nic'las, Garth Ddu, keep so many cats? To drive the Devil away. Sometimes a spirit of murder comes over me, and I'm bound to kill somebody. Who'll I kill? If I killed Modlen, who'd fetch my things for me? What do I do? Kill a cat, and pull her all to ribbons; the evil spirit goes away then. But what if the cats won't come? What am I to do? Shoot the old tree there, see; this way."

Nic'las discharged both barrels into the trunk of the old tree. I was for some little time unable to make out whether the strange old creature was fool or knave; but while his rhodomontade was in progress, I became convinced he was a knave of the first order, or, as Will Bryan would say, a perfect humbug. It was patent that he was only making an artificial effort to impress me with the fact that he was insane. There was not a particle of insanity in his features; and I noticed that he constantly scanned my face to find out whether his vagaries frightened me. In a very few minutes I grew perfectly self-possessed, and no more afraid of him than if he were a sparrow. Immediately the report of the gun died away, I saw a short man coming from the house, and making towards us, presumably to find out the meaning of the shots. Obviously that man's appearance was as unexpected to Nic'las as it was to me. I and the new-comer recognised each other directly he came up.

"Holloa, Rhys!" he cried, extending a hand which I refused to take. "Nic'las," he went on; "d'ye know who this chap is?"

Nic'las shook his head.

"Our old pal's kid," said the new-comer.

Nic'las opened wide his eyes in astonishment and, obediently to a sign from his comrade, went into the house.

"Won't you shake hands, Rhys? How did you find your way here, tell me?" resumed the man, directly Nic'las was out of sight.

"Uncle," I replied—for he was none other than the man whom I hated most on earth ever since I had first seen him when I called him "the Irishman"—"Uncle," I said, "if I shook hands with you I should expect my hand to rot from that moment. I detest you with all my heart. Let me out of this accursed place."

"What's the matter with the boy? Why are you so cross? Why hate me?" he asked.

"Why?" rejoined I. "You know why, very well. It is you who've been the cause of all my mother's misery and mine. It was you who ruined my father. It was you who taught him to poach. It was with you he was when he did that deed which compelled him to quit the country. Why do I hate you indeed! Because it was you, of all people, who gave my mother most trouble, my father alone excepted. How often have you been to our house interfering with our comfort? How many times did my mother give you the last shilling she had in the world so as to get rid of you? And how much oftener would you have worried us if you hadn't been afraid of Bob?"

"Bob was a fool," he observed. "Didn't your father and I give him a chance of bolting on the night of his arrest? But he wouldn't, and so, like a ninny, he was taken to gaol."

"Don't you call Bob a fool," said I. "Bob would have been ashamed to take help from two such scoundrels as you and my father. Uncle, tell me the truth—if you haven't forgotten the way—where is my father? Is he hiding in this abominable hole? Tell the truth, for once in your lifetime!"

"He is not," was the answer. "Your parent is in a much warmer place."

"Where? Speak plainly, and tell us the truth. Where is he?" I asked again.

"How can I tell? I never was on the grounds where your father now is. All I know is that he has kicked the bucket; and it's a blessed shame you haven't a bit of crape about your hat; you a Methodist, too!"

To my discredit, be it said, my heart leaped with joy at the news.

" Do you really mean to say my father is dead?" I queried.
" Don't deceive me, now—tell the truth for once."

" Never was truer word spoken," he replied. " You know
your father was fond of drink. Well, both of us had been in
luck a bit. He got hold of too much brass for his own good;
made too free with the whiskey, and had a stroke. I told him
many times to take care; but it was no use talking. He turned
up his toes in Warwick. I happened, as it were, to be, at the
time, in Leamington—for the sake of my health, you know. I
took in Warwick on my journey, and there met your father,
whom I happened to know. I looked after him as long as he
lived—it was in some not over-respectable public house he had
put up—and emptied his pockets directly the last breath had
gone out of him. He didn't want to die, one mortal bit, knowing
well they are all teetotalers in the other world. But it was his
own fault entirely—I had warned him against the drink. The
Union paid for burying him, I being only, as it were, a friend
of his, you know."

" If you are telling the truth," I remarked, " this is the best
bit of news I ever heard. And if you had only died with him
I should have been perfectly happy."

He simply laughed, and said: " Well, when I die, you, as
my nearest relative, will come in for all my shooting grounds
—and they are very extensive; reaching from Warwick to
Roined, in Denbighshire. What do you think? Tom of
Nant's ghost looks after one end of the estate, and Shakspeare's after the other. They are the two head keepers.
according to your father. No wonder you want me to die, so
that you may be able to say you own your uncle James's estate."

" Give over fooling, and let me out of this horrible place,"
said I, walking towards the door in the wall.

" Wait a little; what's your hurry? How does that ——
old roundhead behave towards you? Have you any objection
to my visiting you on the sly, when I'm hard up? I see you're
a bit of a buck, so p'r'aps you'd like to find uncle James looking you up occasionally. Have you any such thing as half a
crown about you, that you can spare? Where did you get
that watch from? Now I think of it, what'll you give for the

pawn-ticket of your father's? You ought to have something to remember him by."

I must tell the truth, however ugly. Some strange, improper spirit, took possession of me—some strong desire to throttle the churl. But I had strength to resist the impulse—as was best for me, no doubt.

"Open the door," I said, "and let me get away."

"You haven't paid the gate," he observed.

Son of my mother, I gave him all the money I had about me, which was two shillings.

"Thank you. I shall see you again, when you are more flush," he remarked, taking a latch-key from his pocket and opening the door.

Directly I found my feet outside, I turned upon him, and looking him resolutely in the face, said, "Uncle, I have you under my thumb now. I've found out your retreat—the den you are hiding in—and if ever you show your face to me again, or I hear that you've been seen in the neighbourhood, or any of your work is being carried on here, remember, I shall reveal the whole to the police."

"What!" he cried. "Are you going to split on me? Do you want to slaver your own clothes?"

"As sure as you're a living man," I replied.

"Look here," he returned; "you'll never see me again. So do your worst, my proud chicken." And he tried to spit in my face as he slammed the door in my teeth.

I went joyfully home. The great burden which had weighed upon my mind had dropped to the ground. And yet I could not help asking myself, had my uncle told the truth? I knew he was better versed in telling lies.

CHAPTER XXXI.

DAVID DAVIS.

HAPPY is that man who can look back upon life and, with conscience testifying to his truthfulness, say that under every circumstance he has behaved exactly as he ought to have done, according to the light which was in him. Where does such a man exist, now-a-days? If we gave conscience fair play I am certain the greater number of us would say our conduct did not always come up to our standards of moral obligation. I fancy a few, even of those philosophers who have searched deeply into the subject and written copiously thereon, will be found to admit that they have not invariably acted in accordance with the clear and exalted notions they have formed of the fundamental canons of duty. One sometimes plumes himself on his own particular view of the right, and stiffens at the thought of his orthodoxy. But worldly circumstances are awkward old things, and what wonder is it if man does happen, now and then, to depart a little from his creed, or that he finds another system called opportunity—if that be the best word for expediency—more connatural to his desires when dealing with the affairs of life. It is one thing to possess orthodox views; another to comport ourselves at all times in accordance therewith. But, thank Heaven! there are yet in the world men who, every day, endeavour to act up to their conviction, let the consequences be what they may.

Inasmuch as I have vowed to tell the truth about myself in the present history, I must admit, against myself, that I have not, under every circumstance, acted in conformity with my own idea of what was right. After that sudden and unexpected encounter with my uncle, the first question which occurred to my mind was—What ought I to do? Conscience straightway answered: "The path of duty is clear. Go to the police at once and tell them what you have seen." But something whispered me he was no fool who put the words together, "Circumstances alter cases." There could be no harm, I thought, in taking time, and considering the business thoroughly, before finally determining what to do. Again,

something hinted, would it not be just as well to take counsel
of a wiser man than myself; would it not be better to
to tell Abel Hughes the whole, and act upon his advice? I did
not like the hint; and so resolved to take at least a few hours
to turn the matter over in my own mind before deciding upon
a course of action. I went home and retired early to rest, so
as to have leisure to reflect upon my discovery. The more I
thought of the occurrence, the more surely did the consideration
of expediency gain a footing Personal advantages, one by one,
insisted upon stating their claims, while duty—pure, clear, un-
selfish duty—was steadily pushed into the background. Who
was he whom, when first I saw him, I called "the Irishman?"
My uncle—full red-blooded brother to my own father. What
sort of a man was he? One of the most cunning, lazy,
degraded scamps that ever trod the earth of Cambria. So
despicable did he appear to mother and Bob that both tried to
keep me completely ignorant of his existence. On the night
Seth died—when I met the depraved wretch near the Hall
park, and learnt from him our relationship—Bob, finding
he could no longer keep it from me, told me his history. From
early youth, Bob said, work had been distasteful to the man.
While honest people were about their duties he was in bed;
and when they were at rest he would be prying up and down
the country. He never worked; and yet he managed to live, eat
and drink—the latter especially. Where did he get the money
from? It was he knew that; although his neighbours were not
without a guess. They believed the game on the Hall estate
was made to pay tithe towards uncle James's maintenance.
Though he knew what it was to lodge at the county expense,
more than once, his power of deceiving the police and game-
keepers and escaping their clutches for so many years was a
marvel to all who knew him. My father was a competent
workman; but he, too, was given to tipple, and to sit for hours
in the public house. Tippling begat idleness, and idleness begat
poverty, and poverty begat sons and daughters—harshness,
bitterness, bad temper, cruelty. With such a family, who
can tell the life my poor mother led before I saw the light of
day? The trying task it must have been to live religiously
with the nefarious scoundrel, my father! I have already
noted, briefly, some of the cruelties practised on my beloved

mother; and although I cannot help thinking of them in this place, their further description is altogether too painful a business to undertake.

My uncle James, so Bob told me, had not much trouble in enmeshing father in his evil habits. Before long the pair came to be looked upon as professional poachers who succeeded surprisingly in escaping the clutches of the law. This was attributed to my father's Herculean strength, which was said to be the terror of the police. Uncle James, as I have often intimated, was but a weakling; but he possessed a cunning, craft, and daring beyond my father. The havoc wrought by both on his property made the Hall owner dance with fury and frequently change his keepers. At last he found a couple of men who were not quite afraid of their own shadows. Both were Scotch. But they had not been on the estate a whole month before they were both wounded and laid up. For some days one of them was not expected to recover. From that time forth two old inhabitants—uncle James and my father— were lost sight of, and, although much sought after, never found. All this happened before I was born. Mother was "worse than widow" now, to use her own words; but Bob was wont to say that this was the luckiest thing that ever happened to her. I have already described, at length, the hardship she underwent before Bob became able to support the family; but that hardship was nothing in comparison to the grief of mind which my father's irreligion caused her, and the constant fear she was in lest he should come to visit us, or be caught. Her sorrow was renewed and deepened by the surreptitious visits of my uncle, which mother always took as a reminder that her husband could not be far off. These visits occurred, regularly and without exception, at awkward moments, and on dark nights, up to the time when Bob got big enough to put a stop to them—their object being always the appropriation of the whole of mother's money. After every visit mother would for days remain sad and silent. I rather think she never breathed a word about my uncle's visits to anyone save Thomas and Barbara Bartley; and I make no doubt but it was to protect her from all such undesirable occurrences that the two kind-hearted old neighbours persuaded her to end her days

with them at the Tump, for nothing else would ever have
induced her to break up her home. I had, for some years past,
been flattering myself that the neighbours had about forgotten
father and uncle, for none of them as much as mentioned their
names to me. I, however, had sense enough to discern that
it was their delicacy and a feeling of respect for the memory of
my religious mother which made them behave towards me as if
nothing of dishonour had happened in my family history. Not
a day passed over my head that I did not think how possible it
was for the whole of such history to be revived, and for me, in
consequence, to be obliged to hide my head in shame. As often
as the desire to become a preacher possessed me, the thought
that my father and uncle might, at any moment, be dragged
forth from their hiding places into the light of day, would
choke it back at once. But quite unexpectedly, as narrated,
here the news came of my father's death, occurring, if true, far
from home. Think how pitiful must be the family connections
of one who is made glad when he hears of the death of his
father! It is useless my attempting to conceal the fact: I
rejoiced greatly. I felt like one let out from some dark, dank
dungeon into liberty and fresh air. And yet my head was in a
muddle, and my conscience kept telling me that I was not
acting straight. On the one hand, I had discovered Nic'las to
be deceiving his neighbours and leading a life which was not so
retired as he pretended. To say the best of it, he gave shelter to at
least one character who was a fugitive from his country's laws.
It was now in my power to strip Garth Ddu of its false
seclusion. Ought I to do so? I asked myself, and conscience
answered, "You ought, without delay." Besides, there was
my uncle. I knew him to be one who did not deserve to be at
liberty. His crime—*the* crime—was by this time an old one;
but that did not lessen its enormity a bit. He was wanted of
the law that day as much as on the day he did the deed. There
would be no difficulty in convicting him, for the two half-
murdered gamekeepers were still alive and in the service of the
owner of the Hall. They would be able to identify him at once.
Although the act of which they had been guilty was eighteen
years old, I had only to whisper some half a dozen words in
the Hall owner's ear to fan his vengeance into a flame on the

instant, and neither trouble nor expense would have been spared to secure my uncle's arrest. The culprit was my father's brother, no doubt, but he did not, on that account, deserve any mercy at my hands; it being to him that I had to attribute the greater part of my early troubles. He had ruined my father's character and shortened my mother's life. My sense of justice distinctly told me it was my duty to disclose his whereabouts to the police; and something within me—probably revenge—kept saying, " What a splendid opportunity of repaying the old fox for all the worry he has been to me and my family ! "

That was one side of the question; but it had another. The man best pleased by my turning informer would be the owner of the Hall; and I did not care to add one jot or tittle to his happiness. It was he who had sentenced my brother Bob to two months' imprisonment without even the semblance of evidence of wrong doing; he who taunted him with my father in public court. I had not then, if I have now, forgiven his meanness and injustice. Since the day Bob was wrongfully taken to prison, I had cherished a deep hatred of the police, however foolish it might have been; my sympathies, spite myself, always resting with the prisoner. Will Bryan, too, had, years previously, created a prejudice in my mind against them by his nickname of " the pettifogging Bobbies," and I, therefore, did not care to furnish forth a sweet morsel for the officers. Besides, I reflected that in my native place— as in almost every other—there existed a good deal of follow-feeling with the poacher who was not regarded in the same light as other law-breakers; and if some few would be found to admire my unselfishness in giving up my uncle to the authorities, the greater number would be sure to look upon me as a traitor, and one who, as my uncle said, had " beslavered his own clothing." Moreover, were I to make public my discovery, that which I had always feared would descend upon me in one downpour. Although father had died—supposing uncle spoke truly—the memory of his crimes would be brought up afresh to form a topic of conversation in the smithy, the Cross Foxes, the Crown, and on every hearth. Old neighbours, in answer to the questions of those who did not know the circumstances, would be compelled to say it was of that youth's father, who was with Abel Hughes, the people talked. The chapel children, with whom I had lately laboured pretty assiduously, would wonder that the man upon his trial was my uncle, and that the dead man, as bad as he, was my father. A thing of that kind would not be pleasant to contemplate. I reflected, further, that if I were to notify the police of my uncle's retreat, it was ten to one they would not be able to catch him, the probability being that by this time James Lewis was far enough away, and that old Nic'las would say my story was a lie from beginning to end. In that case I would only be reviving unpleasant tales to no particular purpose, save that of making many people believe I was poking fun at the police. But what most affected my determination were my mother's words: "If ever you meet with your father, try and forget his sins; and, if you can do any good to him, do it." I believe the spirit of that injunction applied equally to my uncle; and furthermore, that had mother been similarly circumstanced, she would not have delivered her brother-in-law into the hands of the authorities. She was a good woman, and why could I not be good, also, while keeping this secret to myself? I resolved to remain silent, feeling pretty sure, at the time, there was no danger of my uncle's showing his face to me again. Whether the resolution was wise or unwise will hereafter appear, if I succeed in completing this autobiography.

It is no difficult matter to keep a secret when the keeper happens to be the man whom its divulgence would most injure. Keeping it for another's sake—there's the rub. Even the Devil does not tempt us to disclose a thing to our own shame, or that of our family. That is his reserve fund for drawing upon in the future. The man who refuses to lend his tongue to the relation of his neighbour's faults and scandals when the relation would do no good, apprises the world that he will, some day, be a citizen of that country wherein there is no "fault-upbraiding," and where angels will not object to consider him one of themselves. A few days after the occurrence noted, I began to compliment myself upon my prudence; only, I must admit, I did not possess that feeling of unalloyed happiness which a man enjoys after he has done the right, although the doing was against his own interest. It was akin to the feeling which the worldling enjoys after he has driven a good bargain. God, however, knows that I had in me the desire to do what was just, although I had not the moral courage to do it at the expense of bringing myself into misery and disgrace, and the undoing of the programme I had drawn up in my own mind. Well would it have been were this the only time I gave in to expediency. I have heard, and I am not sure I myself have not more than once remarked, that the performance of a single act to which conscience does not say Amen, prepares man for the commission of other acts of the like nature. Is this true under every circumstance? Not so was it with me on this occasion. My work of taking self-interest and self-happiness into consideration to the neglect of clear duty, roused the whole of my moral nature to greater activity and a determination to fulfil that which I considered myself bound to do. But this possibly was, after all, merely an effort to atone for my sin. I was strongly inclined to believe my uncle's story concering my father's death, and felt lighter-spirited, and freer to do what I could in the cause of religion. I had an excellent master, and was at liberty to attend every service held in the chapel—a liberty I was not backward in using. Poor old Jones was never over-desirous of going to chapel; being nowhere so happy as in the shop. Like a well-trained sheep dog, he knew one thing, and one only. He knew how to measure cloths, fold them and put them in their places. Had Abel Hughes said to him, pointing to the pile, "Jones, lie down there!" he would have obeyed and looked happy without, I quite believe, ever moving from the spot again, until ordered or whistled to by Abel. This made it easier for me to attend services and meetings. I fancy Abel thought it no use sending Jones to chapel; it was just like trying to make the negro white with soap and water.

What changes had taken place in chapel since last it came under notice in the present history! Noting changes always makes me mournful, and compels me to think how short the life of man is and how speedily we shall all have given up our posts to other people. To the reflective, I think there is no place like the chapel for bringing home this lesson. When one

has been away for a few years only, how he is struck with the
change that has taken place in the congregation! How many
strange faces he sees in looking about him, and how many of
the old ones does he fail to come across! He wonders how
some of his old acquaintances' heads have whitened, and others
have become bald, so quickly; forgetting, possibly, that his own
head has been following the fashion. It was in the period, if
I remember rightly, when I was between nine years of age and
twelve, that I last mentioned the chapel and its affairs in the
present history. Comparing the two periods, how different
seems the look upon it when I was eighteen years old! Every
face was new in the Children's Meeting. John Joseph, our
old leader, was in Australia; Abel Hughes, from old age, and
because he could not put up with all the bother of the Sol-fa,
had given over attending. Who were the leaders now? Will
Bryan called me "boss of the kids." Alexander Phillips *(Eos
Prydain)*, looked after the singing. The literary society,
christened by my old companion, "the Society of the Flat
Hairs," which had done great good to many in its time, had
long been dead. Sol-fa killed it—unintentionally, of course.
It had become almost impossible to get the boys to learn grammar, write essays, or take part in doctrinal controversy; such
things were too dry for them. They found the Sol-fa Society
more diverting. This one had several advantages over the old
Literary Society. It was so much nicer to sound "Doh" all
together than to conjugate a verb, each by himself; and then
sight-singing was of greater advantage in this world, if not
actually also in the world to come, than a proper understanding of the subject of justification by faith. Besides, the Sol-fa
Society had been established on wider, sounder and more liberal principles than the Society of the Flat Hairs. It embraced the
young folk, the middle aged, and the old, male and female. As
the Society generally had its unquestionable advantages, so
had the particular phase of it last named; because, under certain circumstances, by the change of a single letter, a singing
meeting could be converted into another one of an entirely different kind, and yet such an one as would give satisfaction to both
sexes. Thus, if a meeting had been spent in the *mode* "lah,"
it was the easiest thing in the world to terminate it in some

other mode. The blessings attending the Society were very many
and obvious. Under the old Literary and Theological Society's
dispensation, the young men grew shy, timorous, and as bash-
ful as if they knew nothing at all. But once brought under the
influence of the Sol-fa Society, they were taught to hold their
heads up like men, and show the world they knew "what's
what." It was only then they really found they were men,
and must act as such, and let the vulgar rich know that they
were not to have all the gloves and the rings to themselves.
The formation of this Society marked an important epoch in the
history of the neighbourhood. Speedily the habit which the
young people had of carrying their Bible to chapel began to disappear, the Tune Book taking its place. True, here and there
an old woman, who knew no better, would grow wild from seeing this book usurping the post of its predecessor, but it was
useless kicking against the progress of the age. Like every
other reform, this one met with great opposition from old fash-
ioned folk. My master, Abel Hughes, though ordinarily a sensible man enough, was always a bit Toryish when new things were
introduced. I have, sometimes, seen him refuse to convert Sunday night Communion into Singing Meeting, and also making a
determined stand against rehearsing choral pieces on the Sabbath in view of a forthcoming National Eisteddfod. I heard
him, with my own ears, declare that singing was of no more
importance than preaching, and that the Tune Book did not
deserve greater attention than the Bible. He positively
refused to ask the preacher to "cut it short," so that more
time might be allowed the singing. For all "Eos Prydain's"
wild glare at him, Abel would not give over slurring and singing with might and main such words as—

> "He, led unto Calvary hill,
> Was willingly nailed to the Cross."

Had Abel lived a little longer he would, doubtless, have
learned better things. Seeing the marvellous effects wrought
by the Sol-fa Society, I threw in my lot with it very heartily.
I remained a member for quite a month; during which period I
learned not only that I had a most unpromising voice, but that
I had neither the patience nor the brains to become proficient

in the mysteries of the science. To tell the honest truth, I was rather taken a-back at the outset to find that a little boy of eight, whom I had great difficulty in learning to spell in Sunday School, was. of all the Society's members, the best sight-singer. I saw there was a danger of my losing influence over him in class on the Sabbath, and so " made myself scarce," as Will Bryan phrased it. I am sorry to this day that I did not apply myself to master the Sol-fa ; for it is evident to one who pays the slighest attention to the signs of the times that a knowledge of this must become indispensable very shortly. The rising generation will, doubtless, find at a Sessional Ordination Meeting the catechism of the Confession of Faith giving way to the black board and an examination in Sol-fa; while to obtain the "voice" of our churches, the preacher will never think of passing as fit and proper according to New Testament standards unless he is also able to explain minutely the difference between the major key and the minor. Sorry am I that I neglected the opportunities which were once within my reach ; and by this time I am too old to learn.

But, there, I see I am too much given to passing remarks, and that there is a danger, should these lines be read, of my being thought sarcastic. The chapel had witnessed many other changes, not the least of which was the absence of divers old brethren, for whom I had entertained a great respect when a boy. Edward Peters, whom I have already mentioned, the crabbed old man, careful keeper of the books, had been for some time confined to the house. Never did he go to bed of Sabbath nights, however, without first ascertaining the amount of the collections. Lest I should forget it, let me here say that one of his last words before dying was, "Remember, the quarter's pew rents are due next Monday night." He was a cocoa nut : hard in the shell, but with the milk of true religion at heart. Hugh Bellis, lachrymose under sermon—Will Bryan's " Old Waterworks "—had left " the children of weeping and groans," and entered, with sails full set, into that joy of which he could not speak while on earth save with sweetest tears. Of the old deacons none remained but Abel Hughes, and of him my whole heart said, " O king, live for ever !" David Davis, who came to us from another church a deacon already, was acknowledged as such on joining us. I must refer to him again. Thomas Bowen, the preacher, the children's great friend, of whom, did time permit, I should like to say a good deal, he too had gone, so everybody who knew him believed, to that same country to which Hugh Bellis had voyaged previously. John Lloyd, perpetual fault-finder, named the "Old Scraper" by Will Bryan, was still in our midst. Will had, for some time, changed the name into "Chapel nuisance inspector." Thomas and Barbara Bartley remained faithful, their religion ever brightening. They had come to be considered the two originals in Communion. To them Abel Hughes, when he found the conversation flagging, would turn round suddenly and say, "Thomas Bartley, what is your opinion upon the point? And it was rarely indeed that we did not get something to liven us up. Thomas did not make, but relate an experience, always; oftenest diverting, and all the more so that, as Will Bryan said, it was "true to nature." I must give a few examples of this before finishing my history. I have alluded several times to William the Coal, given to drink and lay the blame on Satan. William was now too old to "follow the harvest," and so was tolerably religious. I remember Abel Hughes, speaking of William, saying that poverty was indispensable to the godliness of some people. Although an ardent Calvinist, Abel held most liberal views in some matters. I heard him say that he hoped when death came to William the Coal, it would find him poor; "because," said he, "William always keeps very pious on an empty pocket." I mention these characters, and these alone, because I have had occasion to refer to them previously.

Our deacons at the time were three—Abel Hughes, Alexander Phillips *(Eos Prydain)*, and David Davis. Never were three more unlike. Abel, as I have described, was a studious old man, of deep convictions, who had read much both of Welsh and English; one, to whose opinion at the Monthly Meeting, our preachers paid a deal of deference—a man of undoubted piety. He was slow, but sure, like fate. "Eos Prydain" was young and unmarried, expert and assiduous with the singing, gay-spirited, and a favourite with the younger folk. He gave his best years to the exclusive study of music, and succeeded

in making himself a master of the art. Seldom have I seen his
equal for arranging and carrying out a concert. His fidelity
to the musical portion of the service was, so the old people said,
"a pattern." His life was almost flawless; his only fault, if
fault it were, being a tendency now and then to turn the leaves
of the tune book during the sermon, and to warp his mouth
into a circle as if he were whistling from the chest. David
Davis was a middle aged man, uni-lingual, brought up in the
country, religious, sensible, earnest, a man of one book, of
whom the proverb rightly told you to beware. His main objects in life were his religion and his farm. He knew no more
about politics than Abel (not Hughes, but son of Adam). He
had two masters— God and his landlord. To the latter he paid
a deserving respect; to the former he gave his whole heart.
Both found in him a faithful servant, honest and upright. He
would have had more money in the bank if he had not given
so much time and thought to making himself a purse which
neither moth nor rust could corrupt. He grieved more over a
backsliding member of the church than for the sheep which had
strayed from his farm. On the loss of three of his bullocks by
the plague, he thanked God he had others left alive as good as
they; but on the death of a pious church sister, David Davis
stayed in mourning for weeks. The potato disease was not a
pleasant matter for him, but the depressed state of religion
pained him much more. He was heartily thankful for an
abundant harvest, but a hundred times more so for a revival of
religion. Occasionally, and only when he thought of it, he
consulted the weather-glass; but not a day passed that he did
not consult the Bible to ascertain the state of the weather
awaiting his soul, whether storm or fair were in store. The
world and its hurry-scurry affected him almost as little as they
do the man on board ship in mid-ocean. Like that man, too,
David Davis had a compass, and knew tolerably well the port
for which he was steering. He was a man of serious feeling.
I never heard him laugh, but his face wore an unconscious
smile which showed the quiet mind—a smile which is the
Devil's particular dislike. You sometimes meet a man about
whose religion there is a fluffy effeminacy, which makes you
think he would be less religious were he more enlightened,

T

David Davis was not one of that sort. He made the Bible the chief study of his life, and the Bible itself was his chief exposition of the Bible. In reading a portion of the life of Christ by one evangelist, it appeared to me that every word the other had written thereon was present to David's mind, and could be quoted from memory. I admired him greatly, and wondered that a man who did not understand English had mastered his Bible so thoroughly. It may be, after all, that I formed so high an opinion of David Davis because he made so much of me, whom he took with him to hold prayer meetings in private houses, and because it was he who first induced me to "say a word." I was eighteen years old, the secretary of the Sunday School, which I had begun with prayer many times; although I had never "said" anything in public. With David Davis, I had often held prayer meetings about the houses, but had never "said" anything. In coming away from one such meeting, David Davis caught hold of my arm, and said, "Rhys, the next prayer meeting will be held at Thomas Bartley's house, and I would like you to say something on a chapter. You will, will you not? The friends will be glad to hear you. 'Let us not be weary in well doing, for in due season we shall reap if we faint not.' You have a week to prepare, and you will do so, will you not?" His words gave me a kind of electric shock. I fancy I said something about my diffidence, but I did not say "I will not." Perhaps it would have been better had I said "I won't," or "I had rather not," as I shall show in the succeeding chapter.

CHAPTER XXXII.

THE MULTITUDE OF COUNSELLORS.

In the earlier recollections of most of us some old house or the other is sure of being bosomed. In my case the memory hovers lovingly about the Tump—Thomas Bartley's old house —with its cosy kitchen, its ancient black furniture, its great settle, pewter plates and wide hobs, on which I have hundreds of times sat. Everything connected with that kitchen is present to my mind at this moment, even to the chunks of bacon, the ropes of onions, and the wormwood, lapped in an old newspaper, dependent from the ceiling. Hanging by a leather lace upon the wall was an old parish constable's staff, painted blue and red probably before the modern "Bobby" was born. I remember Will Bryan, while looking at it, say, as if to himself, "I wonder how many a poor fellow was knocked over by that very weapon." From the time I used to walk in mother's hand to the Tump—when my chief delight was to hold the light to Thomas Bartley's pipe—down to the time her spirit winged its way thence to another world, my reminiscences crowd in upon me. It can be said with certainty that the humblest cot which has been a nursery for heaven is surrounded by a sanctity wholly absent from the palace whose rich apartments have known nothing but pomp and revelry. Seth's simple soul —as far as my knowledge goes—was the first to pass to glory from the Tump; but I am certain it was not the last. When a member of the family leaves home, a knowledge of the kind of country he is going to becomes precious. If the new sphere is found to be an eminently good one, the chances are that the fact will create a desire for emigration in the whole family. It would have been difficult to persuade Jacob to go to Egypt had not his son Joseph been there to receive him. Thomas and Barbara Bartley, as mother used to say, were readier to listen to the talk about another world after Seth had gone thither to live. They looked upon the prayer meeting held in their house as one for a discussion of the affairs of that far-off colony. As I have intimated, I had, for some time, been accustomed to take part in such gatherings, to the great satisfaction of Thomas Bartley, who declared that I could read "like a parson." It was, no doubt, a matter of surprise to Thomas, who had only "a grip of the letters," that any young man should be able to read at all.

The reflection was by no means unpleasant, that it was in Thomas Bartley's house the prayer meeting was to be held at which I was expected to expound a chapter, on the invitation of David Davis. All the week long hardly anything else found a place in my thoughts. I was in a bit of a fix as to which portion of the Scriptures I should take as a text. At one time

I fancied one of the parables would be very suitable; but after thinking a little over the one selected, I saw I could say hardly anything in respect thereof; so I concluded it would be more proper to attempt an exposition of one of the miracles, and deduce some lessons therefrom. No sooner had I settled down to work in this direction than some difficulty arose, which made me think I had made another mistake. It would be easier, I then reflected, to deal with a single verse than with a whole chapter; only that would make me look as if I wanted to become a preacher all at once, and it was not meet I should think of anything of the kind. Had David Davis picked out a particular portion of the Bible, so that I might prepare myself a little, I believed I could have done something with it. It was then I first felt that which I have often felt since, namely, how easy, how smooth and effortless it seems to talk sense upon a verse or chapter, when we listen to another doing it, and how difficult it becomes when we set to work to prepare something similar ourselves. After a discourse with nothing particular about it, you may hear one here and there, among the untalented, say "Why, I could have preached a better sermon than that myself." Try it, my good man, and you will very soon see you can't, nor as good; otherwise, why should you find yourself in such a sweat over a scrap of a letter to your aunt, and why are you ashamed of it all when done? Do you know, also, good man, that that which reads the most simply and naturally, or which descends the preacher's lips the easiest, is that which has oftenest cost the most trouble? But this is what I was saying: I spent some days changing my texts, and failing to fix upon any portion of the Bible I felt I could say something about, however simple I had considered the task before I began. Pressed by time to make a choice, I at last settled down seriously, read all the commentaries within reach, wrote out every word I meant to "say," committed the whole to memory, and on going over it, made particular note of the time it took to deliver, lest I should be too long or too short, so that by the night of meeting 1 felt myself pretty well prepared for the work, and pretty confident of making a good impression upon those friends who happened to be present. I considered the occasion a most important one for me as affording an opening for my ministerial career. I pictured in my mind a great many things as the result of "saying a little on a chapter" in the house of Thomas Bartley. I may just as well tell the honest truth—I thought that inasmuch as no one but David Davis and myself knew of what was going to take place, I should take several people by surprise. I fancied them talking together on the way home from the meeting, one saying, "Didn't the boy discourse well upon the chapter to-night? He's got the making of a preacher in him, sure to you. I was quite astonished." To which the other would reply: "I didn't much wonder; there was always something serious about him." These and many other vain things did I imagine. Excepting David Davis, I thought I need be afraid of none who frequented prayer meetings in private houses; and David was always so kind to me that I need not fear him. I therefore did not feel at all nervous. It was but rarely Will Bryan came to prayer meetings, if he happened, to use his own expression, to be "better employed" elsewhere, and I did not, consequently, expect to see him there. And even if he should be there, what difference would that make to me?

Wednesday night came, and I went to the meeting full—well, full of something. I was a little late, so as to be more like a preacher, perhaps. One of the brethren was busy reading, and the room was rather full. I sat down near the doorway. When I raised my head, Thomas Bartley motioned me to come nearer. I signalled back that I did very well where I was. My gesture made me out to be nobody, though I thought myself somebody that night. I felt a kind of pleasure in this mock humility. Thomas continuing to beckon, I, in order not to attract notice, obeyed. When I got into a position which gave me the benefit of the candle-light, whom should I see in a corner but Will Bryan! When my gaze met his, he gave me a wink, as only he could—from about a tenth of the width of his eye, but full of meaning. A great lump got into my breast on the instant. I believed it was the Evil One who had sent Will to that meeting, for he had not been to one, before, for many months. For the first time, I felt timid. The brother prayed, but I did not listen. I tried to compose myself as best I could, and to collect my scattered thoughts; but spite of everything the lump in my breast increased and came nearer and nearer to my throat. I wasn't the least bit afraid of Will, so I fancied, and yet I would rather than anything if he had not been there. David Davis called another of the brethren on to continue the service. We were singing a stanza when my legs began to tremble at a terrible rate, and it was not of the slightest use my trying to reason with them, or asking them to stop. To my comfort, I suddenly remembered I had not pre-arranged with David Davis that he should, on calling me forward, ask me to "say a word," lest I should appear to do so on my own initiative. I imagined David would not think of the thing now; in which case I resolved to do nothing beyond pray. The reflection steadied my legs, and lessened the lump in my breast a little. The second brother finished praying; upon which David Davis said: "Rhys Lewis, come forward, my son, to continue the service and discourse a little upon a chapter." My hopes were instantly scattered. I went up, bent on doing the best I could. In singing the next verse I was compelled either to look at Will Bryan or close my eyes. I understood his glance as well as if it spoke to me, and what it said was: "Didn't I tell you that you were bound to be a preacher?" I read the chapter I meant to expound; and hardly did I know my own voice, for its hoarseness. When I began to "discourse a little," every thought and every word I had prepared took flight, and I never saw them afterwards, from that day to this. I found the room beginning to darken, and the people growing bodily less and getting farther away than they were when I "went up," while the candle, like my breath, seemed on the point of going out. The next thing I remember was hearing David Davis praying loudly and rousingly. I felt eaten up by shame. The castle I had built had gone to smash, my poor heart lying buried beneath the ruins. I knew myself to be an object of pity throughout the house—a situation galling to the ambitious spirit. One thought alone remained to comfort me; except David Davis, nobody knew but that my discourse was wholly unpremeditated, and even he did not know I had taken the trouble I did in the preparation. As soon as the meeting was over I slunk away, silently and hurriedly, without looking at a soul. It was impossible, however, I could escape my old companion. Will had cornered me before I could get through the court-yard gate.

"I think I can translate your feelings fairly well to-night, old fellow," was his greeting. "I'm sorry from the heart for you, I'll take my oath. You weren't quite equal to the occasion and, we may as well say fair, you had a break down. But don't break your heart—never say die. It was all your own fault. You shouldn't have attempted an impromptu exposition; it isn't many of the dons who can do that, on the spur of the moment. If David Davis had any sense he would have given you a day or two to prepare. It's enough to daunt the best man breathing to call upon him there and then to expound a chapter. If you'd only had a couple of hours' notice you'd have managed to say something decent, I'll swear. As it was, there was nothing else to expect but that you should make a fool of yourself. When I heard David Davis call you forward I took it for granted there was some understanding between you; but I saw directly there was none, and I rather wondered at your tackling the business, you knowing nothing about it till that very minute. It was an awful pity. I wish I knew all the Scripture you do. I think you are not short of common sense; but you're deficient in one thing—and that is cheek. What's the Welsh word for cheek, do you know? Cheek, mind you, is not the same thing as brazen-facedness, although they're very nearly related. Cheek, in my opnion, is one of the fine arts, and is a thing that every man ought to cultivate, to a certain extent. I don't know whether I can make my meaning clear to you. How shall I say? Let's see now; cheek is not so vulgar as impudence; it is of a higher order of things. The mule is impudent; that is, he isn't shy; but then you can't say the mule is cheeky. The bantam cock is cheeky, but nobody thinks him impudent. Cheek means self-confidence, even when there is nothing to be confident about. I should like to make this matter quite plain for you, but I'm just the same now as you were at the meeting —labouring under great disadvantages through non-preparation. I don't say cheek is good in itself, but it's a means to an end. It isn't so bad as humbug, and not so girlish as affectation. Many a good man has lived and died without the world's knowing anything about him, all because he wanted cheek;

while many an one has got to the top of the tree with nothing
but cheek to be thankful for. Cheek takes it for granted that
you don't know anybody better than yourself, until you get
sufficient evidence. If you see a man of a retiring disposition,
you may take your oath he won't get on in this world. He'll
do very well in the next, I've no doubt, because the Almighty,
doesn't He, puts some value on humility, knowing it to be a
very rare article. But, this being the world we are in, and not
the other, I hold cheek to be a thing to be cultivated—to a
certain extent. You must remember that ninety-nine out of
every hundred men are duffers; and that in the majority of
cases cheek'll stand instead of talent and knowledge. I don't
mean to say, mind, that you have no talent—honour bright.
Take a man with talent but no cheek, and a man with cheek
but no talent, and I'd give three to one on the latter. Look at
those two travellers who call yonder. There's Mr. Davies,
long-headed, quiet, dresses the same, always, and understands
the grocery trade to a T. He never tells lies, and will take a
straight answer from father that he has no order to give.
There's Mr. Hardcastle, again, with no more in his head than
in a mouse's, but who has a new suit of clothes every three
months, all pockets, cuffs, collars and rings, every bit of him,
who won't take ' No ' for an answer, and whom it is impossible
to insult. He has learned some score or so of set phrases, half
of them lies, before leaving home, all of which he reels off
each time in exactly the same way. He is sure to get an order,
simply because he is cheeky and father's a duffer. D'ye know
what? When the gaffer's away from home I give Mr. Davies
a thundering good order, out of pity for him and because he's
true to nature. As to Mr. Hardcastle, I could spit on that
white waistcoat of his. After all, however, Mr. Hardcastle is
the man for this world, the majority of shopkeepers being
duffers. But that's the point: if you want to get on, you must
cultivate cheek. Your talent and your knowledge will be
worth nothing without. The Bible gives examples of this, if
I remember rightly. I don't mind telling you I'm not much
of an authority on the Bible, and so, if I am wrong, you'll
correct me. Now isn't it admitted by the learned that John
was a cleverer man than Peter? But who was master? Who

was to the front in all things? Just fancy Peter's cheek in
stepping forward to preach at the very next Monthly Meeting,
after that dirty trick of his, everybody knowing what he
had done! That's the coolest bit of impudence I ever heard of,
I'll take my oath. If John had done anything half so shabby,
he'd have been too much ashamed to open his mouth again; and
think of the loss that would have been! There's the woman of
Samaria again, who came and asked Christ to cure her son, [I
knew it was the woman of Canaan and her daughter Will
had in view], she wouldn't be put off, and, having plenty
of cheek, she got what she wanted. D'ye know what?
I've thought that woman would have made a first rate commer-
cial—she would never have left a shop without an order.
Speaking in this impromptu fashion, I fear I can't make it clear
enough what I mean by cheek. You must know you won't
get along at all if you're nervous; and for nervousness cheek
is a perfect cure. To cultivate cheek observe the following
rules:—Never blush. I have noticed when you happen to say
something silly, or make a mistake, you redden up to the
ears, like a girl. Never blush; it isn't manly. If ever you
blunder, look as if you had just said or done the best thing in
the world, and nine out of every ten people will not know you
have blundered at all. Cheek means keeping cool. At public
meetings never sit by the door; take care to be always in front;
and when you stand up do so on tip toe, because you're none
too tall, more than myself. Make it a point to let everybody
know you're present. Speak as often as you get the chance—
oftener if you can; and, so as to be prepared, take care to have
some twenty or so of set phrases in stock which, with varia-
tions, will do for any subject; for fear you should have nothing new to say. Anyhow, be sure you speak. D'ye know
what? I've seen, before to-day, a dull man get upon his legs,
say a good thing by sheer accident, and be set down by the
duffers as a man of genius, on the spot. Before and after every
public meeting, don't forget to shake hands warmly with the
reporters, keeping up your dignity at the same time. You'll
never lose by it. I've heard of some who report themselves;
but don't you do that—it isn't true to nature. I know very well
what you're thinking of. This is merely the way of the world

you'll say; but you'll see by and bye there's more of this sort
of thing about religion than you've dreamt of. You're
bound to find two things tell against you: in the first place
your voice is not strong, and in the next, to my way of thinking, you're never likely to grow stout; it isn't in your family
to fatten. You're sure to find leanness a disadvantage. Fancy
a thin man saying something in a squeaky voice—a sort of
falsetto as these musicians call it—and another great stout
man, a reg'lar thorough bass, saying exactly the same thing in
double F——, which has the most effect on the duffers? I tell
you that double F chap'll be written down a great man, and
the falsetto chap a snob. By the duffers mind; not by the
wide-awakes. But I see I'm not sticking to my text, which is
cheek. You know as well as I do, it is here the English beat
us Welsh people hollow. You'll never hear an Englishman
say he can't do this, that, and the other thing. To hear him
talk, there's nothing on earth he can't do, and the duffers believe him. You'll now and then find a John Jones, who's a
real good sort, if he only knew it, touching his hat, and appearing to take pleasure in looking on at a John Bull eating his bread
and cheese. What's the grand secret? Cheek. Do you catch
the point? The man who's without cheek looks worse, while
the cheeky man looks better than he really is. Don't think me
inconsistent. I repeat it, I hate a humbug, and like a man
who's true to nature. But there's a danger of the man who has
no cheek looking less than he is. *Nottabinny:* mind you have
cheek, but mind also you have something else besides. Cheek
comes in wonderful handy, and passes current with a great
many people. But if you've nothing better, you're bound to
be found out by the wide-awakes. At least, that's the opinion
of yours truly. Remember Lord Brougham's saying—'What
is the first secret of eloquence? Preparation. What is the
second? Preparation. What is the third? Preparation.'
Never attempt to speak in public without preparation, until
you've acquired cheek and learned a lot of set phrases which
will do for any occasion—with a slight variation, as I've said.
I'm not quite square with the guv'nor or I'd ask you over to
supper to-night. Under the circumstances, therefore, I know I
can't rise to the demands of ordinary etiquette. Cheer up,
old boy, and don't look down in the mouth. So long!"

Little did Will know, as was best for me, I had had a week's notice to prepare, and that his words, instead of comforting, drove me further into the furnace. I was glad to get away from him and go home, little thinking that another furnace awaited me. My supper was on the table, and Abel sat smoking in his arm-chair—both as if expecting me. Miss Hughes had retired to rest, not being, as Will Bryan would say, up to the mark. I felt thankful, while eating, that Abel knew nothing of my break-down, and uncomfortable, also, at the thought that he would be sure to get to know; and that before long, too. Presently he began questioning me about the prayer meeting—who was at it, what sort of meeting we had, who had taken part in it, and so on. I answered sparingly. From the half sarcastic smile upon his face, I guessed that some one had gone before me, and given him the ill news.

"How did you get along with your discourse upon the chapter?" he at length said.

"Some one has told you," I replied, and, before I could say another word my feelings utterly overcame me and I burst into a good cry.

"What's the matter with you?" asked Abel, when I had come a little to myself. "All I know is that David Davis invited you last week to prepare something for to-night's meeting. What has happened? Why're you so distressed?"

I gave him the particulars of my disastrous failure. "Never mind," he said, when he had heard me out. "It may be a blessing to you as long as you live. I remember two lines of a doggerel English song:

> ' There's many a dark and cloudy morning
> That turns out a sun-shiny day.'

Tell me, do you think of preaching?"

"I have thought of it," I mournfully replied; "but I'll never think of it again."

"Don't be absurd," returned Abel. "You never saw a good carter who had not at some time or other upset his trolly, perhaps hurt himself and the horse into the bargain. You and I got an occasional tumble before we learned to walk. You

would never have know how to swim had you lost heart when
your head first went under water. The first step in a useful
life is often a false step, and the greatest success has often
begun in failure. I had guessed for some time that you had
set your mind on being a preacher; which was the reason I
gave you liberty to attend every service and meeting. And if
I had not believed you, to some extent, adapted to the work, I
would have spoken to you long before now. If you have set
your mind on the ministry, let nothing hinder or dishearten
you. It is not possible you could have thought on a better or
more honourable calling. Were I permitted to begin life afresh,
I think I should pray, night and day, that I might be inclined
and made fit to become a preacher. To my mind, there is no
circle of life like the preacher's, in which a man may be of
so much real use. The very name has had a great charm for
me ever since I can remember. It may be my weakness—but
I prefer the name preacher to that of 'parson,' or 'minister,'
or 'pastor.' To me the name preacher conveys the idea of a
pulpit, of association meetings—powerful influences which subdued Wales; and there is a sacredness about it of which the
other names give no notion. Don't misunderstand me as to
this. 'Minister' and 'Pastor' have their attractions; while
the name 'Parson' has a meaning into which a good deal of
prejudice enters. It is of the association of ideas attached to
the word preacher I'm talking. When Wales loses the meaning of the name 'preacher' in that of 'clergyman,' woe unto
her! I am not without fear that there is a move in such a
direction in these days, and that it is traceable in small things,
as for instance in our chapel announcements. When I was
young, the deacon used to proclaim, 'We expect Mr. 'Lias to
preach here next Sabbath;' but now you'll oftenest hear: 'The
Reverend Peter Smart will minister here next Sunday.' Don't
misunderstand me, I say again. What I fear is that the reverence will be for the Reverend and not for Peter Smart. Thank
God! there is no earthly title that can express the love and
veneration of the Welshman's heart towards the true preacher.
It borders almost on worship, and long may it continue so, as
long as it is not sinful, say I. But the tribute is one which
should be earned in the pulpit. You know there is no more

ardent an advocate than myself for giving a preacher the very
best education. If all were of my way of thinking, nobody
should be admitted to preach, in these enlightened days, who had
not first undergone a course of college training, unless there was
something marked, indeed, about his natural talent and disposition. But, spite all education, if the man is not a preacher,
his M.A. is of no more use than that girl's education was who
had been to a boarding school and came home having learned
to say 'Ma' instead of Mother. The respect, the love, the
half-worship which, as I have said, the Cymro has at heart for
the preacher have been won naturally and deservedly. The
other day I saw, in the newspaper, some self-opinionated creature reproaching Wales with her respect for preachers, ignorant, poor man, that he could pay the old country no higher
compliment. I often fear lest our churches should permit anyone to preach who may offer himself, and that the respect paid
the preacher should thereby become unsettled and ultimately
lost. As I just now said, it would not be possible for you to
think of a higher and more honourable calling than a preacher's. The mere name is a sufficient introduction for its owner
to the best people in the world, and a guarantee of pure and
spotless character, or at any rate ought to be. I have oftened
puzzled myself to think what sort of consciousness may be the
preacher's. It must be a glorified one. His duties are such as
should accustom him to the highest form of happiness attainable
here on earth, and they afford, also, the best preparation against
the terrors of death and the spiritualization of the world to
come. In this world he gets of the best that man has, and a
great deal more; and, upon his entrance to the world eternal, he
will be welcomed by the King Himself as a good and faithful
servant. To my mind, the most successful merchant is but a
beggar in rags beside the true preacher, who is at once man's
chiefest friend and God's next door neighbour, if I do not
blaspheme by saying so. Where are the names of our rich
carousers in castles, sixty years since? Rotting, like their own
bones and their dogs'. But the names of their contemporaries,
who proclaimed the glad tidings, live on in the hearts even of
those who never heard them!

"That is one way of looking at the preacher. But there is

another. I do not want to frighten or discourage, only to sober you. Man's character is determined by his motives; and possibly there is nothing man—thoughtful man more especially—feels so deficient in as the power of understanding his real motives. Every young man who thinks of preaching should fear and tremble. If not actuated by the purest motives, it were better he went and hung himself. I have had the deepest sympathy with some men I have known who purposed, prepared for, and began preaching, but who were frightened into silence by the awful responsibility of the work. The man who has an eye to the pulpit, as a means of feeding his ambition, of helping him to a post of honour, or of satisfying some craving of the heart to which he cannot give a name—that man shall have nought but God's frown. He will one day find himself lower than the devils and a subject of mockery for thieves and murderers. One of the English poets gives a dreadful description of that man's condition. It begins thus:

> ' Among the accursed who sought a hiding place
> In vain from fierceness of Jehovah's rage,
> And from the hot displeasure of the Lamb—
> Most wretched and contemptible—most vile—
> Stood the false priest, and in his conscience felt,
> The fellest gnaw of the undying worm!'

I have thought Paul must have experienced a sort of electric shock when he said, 'Lest that by any means when I have preached to others I myself should be a castaway.' But, as I have said, I've no wish to frighten you into putting your intention to preach on one side; rather would I be of help to you to proceed, if your motives are just. Perhaps it will be of advantage to you to inquire a little further into the history of the first preachers—the apostles. They were not perfect in their views and intentions any more than ourselves. But one thing characterised them which ought to characterise every preacher; their love for, and fidelity to their Master was genuine—there was to be no doubt on that point. 'To whom shall we go?' said Peter; not to whom shall *I* go? He spoke for them all, on that head—'Thou hast the words of

eternal life ; ' without Thee we shall be without words, we
shall have nothing to say.' I don't know whether Peter was
conscious at the time that their business would be all 'say'
directly ; only I shall continue to believe he felt at the time
that there was nobody worth saying anything about but Christ.
You take care you are right on that head. If it be some itch
of selfishness which impels you to preach, the interest of that
will soon burn itself out, and you'll find yourself left a cold
lump living under the Churches' act of toleration, a burden to
yourself and everybody else, fulfilling engagements in places
where they would rather have you than no preacher, or put up
with a prayer meeting, and where they must pass the Sabbath
somehow. But if you are moved by fire from Heaven, that fire
will never go out ; and you will find sinners huddling about
you for warmth for their shivering souls, and basking in the
heat on your hearthstone. I know of no more pitiful being
than the preacher who lives on the sufferance of his fellow men,
scorned of God for his worldliness and earthliness. Talking of
worldliness : make up your mind at the outset, if you wish to
become a preacher, to give yourself wholly up to the work.
Never think of keeping shop at the same time. As preacher,
the stock you must look after is too large to give you time to
look after another stock of an entirely different kind. All I
can do for you, I will. Although I am not poor, you know I
am not rich ; but perhaps I may be able to do something for
you in the way of money ; for money you must have. I am
astonished, very often, at the little our rich folk do towards the
support of our young preachers, who, as a rule, are badly off.
I have often thought how difficult it must be for a student,
although he may have a large and a warm heart—how difficult
it must be for him to get along with an empty pocket, and how
useful he would frequently find a ten pound note from one of
the wealthy. When the poor student is given a trifle, the fact
must needs be proclaimed throughout the length and breadth
of the country by the Monthly Meeting, and he is branded as a
beggar by his friends forthwith. Anything of that kind is
simply scandalous. No wonder that here and there a really
deserving youth—and it is the most deserving who always do
so—should bear his hardship in silence rather than see his

name blazoned abroad by the papers as the recipient of five pounds. I hope and believe that you do not expect to find preaching a paying business, in a worldly sense. If you do, you'll be disappointed. There are a thousand better ways of making money. You often hear that preachers are avaricious. The charge is a shameful libel, to my mind; and is made, almost without exception, by those who are money-grubbers themselves. Most of the preachers I have known, who depend on preaching for their livelihood, lead a hand to mouth existence. True, there is a special Providence watching over the most deserving amongst them, who are permitted, by God, to find favour in the hearts of rich young women. Watch and pray against idleness and self. You know—I don't—whether self had anything to do with your failure at to-night's meeting; and whether it was the winning honour or the bestowing found first place in your heart."

Strange! Abel understood me internally almost as well as I did myself.

CHAPTER XXXIII.

MORE OF WILL BRYAN.

WILL Bryan's worldly-wise observations and Abel Hughes's serious and encouraging counsels drove me, I shall believe, to the place I ought to have oftener been in daily. My resolution, at the time, was to relinquish, for ever, the idea of preaching; and I prayed much to be rid of the desire; although I feared in my heart I should be heard. I felt as if I were two different personages—one anxious to preach, and the other doing his best to prevent and dishearten him. I believed it was the latter was right; and yet my sympathy lay with the former, who I constantly hoped would win the day. In course of time, I might possibly have overcome the one inclination, had David Davis given me rest; but rest I should not have. I was pretty certain that I had not the slightest hankering after my old habits of evil. I felt that my chief enemy was self. Abel Hughes having first cautioned me against it, I found this enemy with a finger in everything I did. I was on the point of determining never to do anything publicly in the cause of religion until I had, by concentrating all my attention upon myself, introspectively, destroyed self, and then ——. When I announced my intention to David Davis, he came near laughing; but, as if suddenly remembering he was a stranger to the habit, he substituted a broad grin, and said:—

"Excellent intention; but the most selfish one you could have devised. You won't be a bit the better, twenty years to come, from that plan. How are you to get at self by doing nothing? It is by the performance of your duties alone that you can lay hold of self, and bring his neck to the block. If you go wasting precious time in the search for him, he is sure to slink into hiding somewhere. It is not by retreating within yourself you can kill self—he must be crucified without the camp. And do not wonder if you find self alive even when you get to be my age. I have heard of people, down in England, who deal in what they call legerdemain. With their left hand they can lay hold of themselves by the hair, while with the right they will take up a sword and cut their own head off—that is to say, to all appearance—and next minute another head comes in its place. When the story was first told me I reflected that that was just what I had been doing with self. Some days I fancied I had his head fairly on the block, and had cut it 'snug off,' as Evan Harries of Merthyr used to say. But on the morrow, self would be as much alive as ever. Talk of doing nothing until you have killed self! Why, you'll never work a stroke if you wait till then. Self won't take to be killed by any child's play. I have, however, thought it possible to scotch him, and the best way to do that is to forget him, neglect him, and devote yourself, body and soul, to God's service, by doing good. And one must *learn* to do good, as Isaiah says. That is not a thing you can do in a day, to your own satisfaction, to say nothing of God's. The first thing the Gospel does is to apprentice a man to well-doing. And I'll tell you what — it is 'prentices we always shall remain in this old world; we shall never be masters of the

U

business, nor freed from our apprenticeship till we cross over
to the next. Besides, life is so short, look you, that we must
apply ourselves at once to learn, lest we appear awkward, and
as those who are not out of their time, when we get amongst
the tradesmen. I, too, often doubt my motives—who does
not?—but, when I can't rise to higher ground, what I do is to
try my hand at a little good, just to spite the devil, and show
him that, who and whatever I may be, I want none of his acquaintance."

With much other discourse did he counsel me; and I
think I was benefitted thereby. Whilst taking part in a public
meeting the reflection that I did not do so on my own initiative,
nor without inducement from brethren of proved judgment
and piety allayed my fears not a little; it seemed to place a
share of the responsibility upon their shoulders. To my no
small consolation I had no further "breakdown," to quote Will
Bryan, like the one in Thomas Bartley's house, although it
went hard enough upon me many times. The little facility of
speech I acquired at prayer meeting became a source of great
comfort to me, and I would often catch myself humming
a tune on coming away. There was nothing sinful, I
thought, in a silent rejoicing of spirit when David Davis
or someone else gave me a word of encouragement or of
praise. I remembered noticing, repeatedly, those preachers in
Abel Hughes's house, who, if they had had a brilliant meeting,
almost invariably enjoyed their supper, and *vice versâ;* the
reason possibly being a consciousness that they had earned
the meal, and again *vice versâ.* By degrees I came to
understand that I was pretty generally regarded as a "candidate;" a fact which, when I realised it, had at first the effect
upon my mind of a bridle which everybody was entitled to
seize. If I happened to stay out late, I felt that the first man
I met had a right to say: 'What do you want out, this time of
night?' When laughing, I asked myself, on the instant, did I
think I had laughed too loudly?' If I chanced to speak to a
young woman—which I must plead guilty to having done,
occasionally—I felt as if some one was always watching me,
and measuring with a two-foot rule my face and smile. In
short, I thought I had lost all personal liberty. I had no

longer the right enjoyed by others of shaking my head and refusing to step up, when called upon, to officiate at a prayer meeting. I dared not say "I would rather not," whatsoever duty the Sunday School superintendent ordered me to do. In a word, I lost the sense of self-ownership, and felt transformed into a piece of public property. Small and great, dwarf and giant, considered it their bounden duty to ply me with advice, which they varied endlessly, and which they, doubtless, gave with the very best intentions. Such was the interest, apparently, taken in me, and such the multitude of counsellors, that I at last expected everybody I met to be ready with a piece of his mind. And it was not often the expectation was disappointed. Some said that if I meant to begin preaching, I should take it easy, and go slowly; others that I should hurry and lose no time about it. Some advised me to set to work reading, late and early, and not waste my time going about; others thought I should read less and go more out into the open air, if I wished to live long and become of use. Here and there an one would exhort me to get myself well posted in literature, politics, general knowledge, and every new book I could lay hold of, all this being indispensable to the present-day preacher; while others advised me to let all such things alone, and to give my whole time to a study of the Scriptures, adding that the young preachers' great fault was a want of acquaintance with the Bible, and the giving of too much time to other books. "Whatever you do," said one to me, "don't go to college to be spoiled, like the rest of them." "Of course," said another, "you'll be bound to go to college, or you'll never be worth anything. Even if you learnt nothing there, people would think more of you for having been." "Be sure you're free and easy with everybody," said one of the brethren; "I hate a stuck-up preacher." "I hope, if they permit you to preach, you will remember to keep a watch upon yourself; be reserved and don't give people room to talk," said an ancient sister to me.

One night, after mentioning to W. B. the different kinds of good advice I had received, that personage said: "Use your common sense, man, if you have any common sense about you; and if you havn't, why, give up the idea of preaching at once.

I don't mind telling you, you'll be obliged, directly, to mind
your p's and q's, and look after your centre of gravity. But
then, you needn't behave as if you were shut up in a clock-case.
There's no use your showing like a rooster stepping through
the snow. A thing of that sort isn't true to nature; and I'll
never believe grace goes against nature—that is, sinless nature.
I should think there must be a verse on the subject somewhere,
only I can't remember it just now. 'Trust in God and keep
your powder dry,' old Cromwell used to say, and he was no
duffer. If you try to act upon everybody's advice you'll have
to work overtime every day, and it'll be *Hic jacet*, and 'Alas
poor Yorick' with you directly. I always tell the duffers to go
to Jericho; only it won't pay you to do that. You must be
civil to all, try and spot the wide-awakes, and take their
tips."

I thought there was a good deal of sense in Will's opinion,
delivered though it was in a style peculiarly his own. I remained a long while a "candidate" before my case was formally laid before the church; chiefly because that was my desire. I was but young, and I was anxious for a fair proof of
myself and to furnish proof to others, so that there should be
no mistake on either side for which we should afterwards be
sorry. I had another object in view, to wit, the escape from the
necessity of preaching a trial sermon in Communion. I knew
it to be the general rule with candidates for the ministry to
give a sermon in Communion, to show what they were able to
do. I considered this method of testing a young man's capacity and fitness the most unnatural and unfair that could be
devised, and was certain in my own mind I could not undergo
it. I often pictured myself in the condition of one who
attempts to preach to a congregation composed exclusively of
critics; preaching not to edification, but to show how much
ability I possessed. I knew I could not act; and I would
rather remain another year in my present condition than be
put to such a proof. There were plenty of opportunities—there
are plenty of opportunities still—for a young man to show the
church and neighbourhood whether he is adapted for the
ministry without placing him in any such unfair and disad-
vantageous a position as this one. Another reason for my

delay was a real desire to ascertain, with certainty, the purity
of my motives, and my consecration to the work. I remembered hearing Abel Hughes speak of some, who having been
plagued with the " preaching fit," were subsequently completely cured of their complaint. I feared lest it was a "fit" I had
on, and argued with myself, that if this were so, it would soon
pass over. I had, also, a not very easily definable feeling, from
which I am not even yet wholly free, namely, a deep desire for
a visible and decisive proof of the particular truths which perplexed me—a proof, likely enough, it was impossible I could
get, or, possible, would have made vain my faith. How to
account for it I do not know. but I often find in myself a yearning after the impossible. Months passed by, but the "fit"
did not. Every opportunity I found of speaking to preachers
whom I could make free with I availed myself of, in order to
draw from them all the knowledge obtainable of their experience and state of feeling when in my situation. It was but
very little, however, they were able to tell me of the ordeal
their minds had gone through that I myself had not experienced
already. And yet, I persistently believed they had met with
something I had not, if they could only describe it. I whetted
my imagination in the conjuring up of terrors probably.
in store for me were I self-deceived. In fancy I put myself in
such a fiery situation, that not even hell, I think, would have
been ashamed of it as its own creation. The utmost I could say—
and I could say that—was that as far as I knew, I was moved
by no false intentions. I thought it quite possible I might be
making a mistake and be displaying a want of judgment in
thinking of the ministry; but I was certain I had no unworthy
object that I was aware of. I will not attempt to deny that I
was constantly conjecturing what would people think of me;
and I often asked myself the question which the Greatest asked of others—' Whom do men say that I am?' As one who
had set his mind on preaching, and who did a little in that way
without a license, I was conscious of not appearing to many in
as favourable a light as I could. I knew several who held that
he who revealed a desire to preach should have a soul of fire, a
large experience, and an ardour which gave an air of attraction
to everything he said. It was useless to expect this of me. The

recollection of my youth disqualified me from giving advice. I
also called to mind a remark of Abel Hughes': "I never like
to hear a young man over much at counselling and talking to a
mixed congregation, as if he were an experienced elder. It is
wholly unnatural, in my opinion; and I question whether any
good is done by it. I prefer seeing a young man preacher half
drowning to seeing him paddling by the bank. To hear a
youth of twenty imitating an old man grates as harshly on me
as if I were to hear an old man of eighty squabbling over a
game of marbles. And yet you'll see things quite as incon-
gruous as that sometimes; it is a sign of weakness in either
case."

I knew very well my addresses at meetings in the houses and
small chapels of the neighbourhood were dry and didactic —
more so than they should have been, owing to the fetters I had
forged for myself. On occasions when I was fairly filled with
zeal, I made every effort to cool down, lest I should appear self-
assertive, and that which I was not. A deep impression was
made upon my mind once by seeing a young preacher go about
confabulating with the friends. Coming to old Betty Kenrick,
he said: "Well, old sister, do you think you know Jesus
Christ by this time?" To which Betty answered: "I hope I
do, and have done, long before your father was born, young
sprig." I do not commend Betty for answering, in that way,
a young man who was a stranger to her; but the incident was,
for all that, not without its moral. I rather fancy that particular young man's clothes did not fit him quite so tightly at the
end of Communion as at the beginning. I felt some degree of
pleasure in assisting the friends in small country chapels when
they were without a preacher; but when David Davis told me,
one day, he wished to bring my case formally before the church
as a candidate for the ministry, I was filled with despondency
and dismay. In one sense I would have preferred backing out;
only, at the same time, I could not bear the notion. It was
evident I could not always continue in my present condition.
If I permitted my cause to be brought forward, I felt I should
be aiming high, placing myself in a different position to the
rest of the church, and taking upon me a responsibility which
I dreaded. Frequently I fancied a voice saying: 'What

hast thou to do to declare my statutes?' I sighed for clear vision, but it would not come; and I asked myself what reason had I to give for seeking to preach when I could not definitely prove my calling?

On the other hand, as I have said, I could not bear the notion of relinquishing my incentives to the work and suppressing my most pleasing sensations. I did not understand myself—a fact which I thought strange. How did others understand me? Was it possible that other people could form a clearer estimate of me than I could of myself? I resolved that events should take their course. In a few days my cause was brought before the church. I do not purpose giving a minute description of the occurrence. A great many questions were asked me which I replied to just as I thought and felt, without attempting to place myself in a different light from the real one, or to affect more than I could in truth perform. I was told to withdraw while the brethren were canvassing my merits. Whilst waiting for the verdict I feared my answers must have made some people think I was not over clear in the head. I hardly expected my application would be favourably entertained; and I almost wished it would not be. Presently I was called in, and notified that it had been agreed to refer my case to the Monthly Meeting with a request that some of the brethren be deputed to inquire into the matter and take the voice of the church thereon. Well was it for me that there was no need of a word in reply; for, had there been, I could not have spoken it. I found myself in a turmoil of thought, some part of which I would try to reproduce had not something happened which remains livelier in the memory—something I can never forget—and which is all the easier to relate because it has reference to another.

It is possible I may have spoken too much of Will Bryan. I shall not make much further mention of him. As I have said, more than once, the acquaintance between us deeply influenced my life. His personality had impressed me greatly, from childhood up. Although some sort of a church member, I knew, and others knew as well, that he was not by condition of mind and natural inclination what he ought to be. I feared his heart was sadly indifferent to religion, and at one time

determined to sever my connection with him, for good; only I
found that to be a more difficult task than I had imagined.
His magnanimous spirit, his open heart, his shrewdness, and
especially his sharp, ready tongue, renewed my admiration for
him every time we spoke, and made me forget, for the moment,
his failings, numerous though they were. Although he made
no profession of the fact, I could not help perceiving his fond-
ness for me; and I was certain no one living felt a greater
interest in my welfare than he. I had noticed of late, with
grief, that Will halted more than ever in his attendance at
chapel; what was true of him being true also of his parents.
But this, notwithstanding, my old companion was at Communion when my cause was brought on; and glad was I to see
him there, chiefly, I will admit, because I knew I should get
from him a detailed account of every word that transpired after
I was sent out. Naturally enough, I had a curiosity to learn
what was said of me in my absence, and I knew Will could
supply me with the whole. I have endeavoured to transmit to
paper all I have considered worth recording of Will's utterances, as nearly as I could, both in form and substance, to the
way in which they left his lips. That I shall try to do once
more. When we left Communion I think it was I who, for
once, was waiting for Will, and not Will for me.

"Just the thing," said he. "I wanted a chat with you."

"I knew, Will, you would tell me all that took place," I
returned. "How did things come off after I was turned out?"

"A *verbatim et literatim* report would do you no good in the
world," he observed. "The only thing that tickled my fancy
a bit was Old Scraper insisting that you should be asked to
preach before Communion, so that they might see the sort of
stuff there was in you, and Abel answering him that the plan
would work admirably had you happened to be newly come
from America, and no one knew anything about you. I can
think of nothing else worth the mention, except that that
old thorough bred, Thomas Bartley, when the hands went up on
your side, raised both his own—just like Whitefield in the
picture—as an apology, I thought, for the unavoidable absence
of Barbara Bartley, owing to a severe attack of rheumatism.
But let that be. You have to-night reached a point I have

a long while looked forward to. All you now want is to go
on. My conscience to-night is a little easier than it has been
for some time. I know very well it was I who threw you off
the metals. I dreamt the night we came near hanging Jones
that your mother had come from the next world to rebuke me.
She frowned upon me, and I shall never forget that look of
her's. I was never happy afterwards, although I tried to appear
differently, until I had found you on the rails once more. You
and I to-night are at a junction I had all along known we'd be
safe to come to. We have travelled a good way together, but
I have known from the first we were not bound for the
same destination; and here's the junction, you see. I speak a
trifle figuratively, but you know very well what I mean, I dare
say. The fact of the matter is, we must now bid good-bye, as
the song says, to those

'Dear happy hours that can return no more.'

I am for making myself scarce, and you may never see me
again—a thought which brings a lump to my throat, I'll take
oath. Have you heard anything about us over yonder?"

"Heard what, Will? I don't understand you," I replied.

"It is all U P over there," rejoined Will. "Everybody'll
know it before the week is out, and I can't stand that. Didn't
I tell you father was a duffer? I remember the time I used to
think he was coining money, and was a clever man at a
bargain. But when I got to know what was what, and how
things stood, my verdict was—duffer. I've seen this, for some
time; but there was no use talking of a change of policy—it was
in the old rut father would walk. Like a certain other creature
we wot of—more noted for the length of his ears than for the
sweetness of his voice—he'd insist on crossing a clover field and
make straight for the hedge to browse on thistles, dock-leaves,
coltsfoot, and rubbish like that. What is the consequence?
Why others have gobbled up the clover, and there's nothing left,
even on the hedge—not as much as a Robin Redbreast's cast off
nest, or a finch's. And what's the outlook? Liquidation by
arrangement and starvation! And I am going to cut my hook,
in consequence. Where to? I don't know. What am I going
to do? There's the rub! I shall come of age next week

(D.V.), and I shall be just as well off then as I was twenty-one years back to date. You know I've not had much more schooling than you have had, and yet I sometimes fancy I'm not a perfect greenhorn. When I got to be wise enough to see my loss, I made it a point of keeping a close watch of human nature, or as the Wesleys say, the nature human. It's about the best thing one who has not had much schooling can do. But I made one great mistake—I didn't study my bread and cheese. What can I say I am? I'm neither gentleman nor tailor. I have not been enough behind the counter to learn to serve—I was never much inclined that way, my delight, as you know, being to drive a horse. I did not care whether it was a load of bread or a load of young girls, as long as I had a horse to drive; and I can handle the ribbons with any man, whoever he may be. But next week, Hugh Bryan, provision dealer, won't have a horse to drive. And there's such a difference between driving your own horse and driving somebody else's! Do you imagine I'd ever become a gentleman's servant? Never; if I had to break stones first. That's the meanest job I know of. My stomach would never stand taking pay for keeping hand to hat everlastingly, and for lending my legs to show off my master's cashmere. Well, what am I to do? How am I to earn my bread and cheese? The question is span new to me, and I don't know how to answer it. I needn't tell you how I was brought up—in want of nothing save grace and good advice. I never remember the day I didn't have a jolly dinner. But how'll it be next week? D'ye know — I was never really down in the mouth before.

"Will," said I; "you've nearly taken my breath away. How have things got to this?"

"It's too long a story," he replied. "I don't want to be hard on the gaffer—I'm sorry from my heart for him, I swear. But it was all his own fault. If he had only stuck to his own business, things would have been all right. You know the old man was always grasping. Well, after he had made a bit of money, some one persuaded him to speculate. I begged him, a year ago, to drop it; but no good. Fifty pounds a month, my little man! How was it possible he could stand it? Had he taught me how to get a living I should not have minded so

much. It's a queer idea, but I've often thought, of late that
if I had happened to be my own father I'd have brought
myself up much better. People may possibly think me selfish
for skedaddling, but I can't stand the disgrace. And there is
Suze, poor girl! I couldn't look her in the face. It's lucky
there's been nothing definite between us. I must be going.
Something urges me."

"You've given me a shock, Will;" said I. "Many a time
have your help and sympathy been very precious to me. But
I never remember the occasion, before to-night, when you
wanted sympathy yourself. Will you take one piece of advice
from me?"

"What is that, old fellow?"

"Whenever you go, and wherever you go to, will you take
care to get a ticket of membership? And, after you are settled
in your new home, will you enquire for the chapel and send on
your ticket to the deacons? I may as well tell you the honest
truth, Will, I have a fear you'll go wrong."

"I had hoped," he replied, "that you wouldn't have
mentioned this; but since you've done so, I, too, must say
something which has been on my mind this long time. It
would take me a day to tell you all. For me to ask for a ticket
would be only humbug. I have dissembled a great deal too
much already. You fancy, I dare say, you know my history
pretty well; but you know nothing. I can't conceal the fact
from myself that there isn't the least spark of religion about
me. Do you remember your mother saying there was an "old
man" in my heart, and I making fun of her? The old
woman was perfectly right. What she meant, as you know,
was depravity; only she had a rather odd name for it. I don't
know how to tell you the story of my mind, and I would much
rather not try. I feel, somehow, as if I were gospel-proof; and
I've not been able now, for some time, to remember a single
verse that doesn't tell against me. Lots of them come to mind,
now and then. To tell you the truth, I have not read the
Bible since I don't know when—because, as often as I did so,
those verses which were against me were the ones I always
spotted. I'm but young, and yet I feel as if I'd stolen a
march on the Gospel; or I ought perhaps to say, as if I had

been left behind. Have I killed anybody? No danger. Have I wronged anybody? I don't know that I have. Have I got drunk? Never. But a chap needn't do any of those things to be left behind. What have I done? Lots of little things: learned comic songs instead of learning the Bible and the "Preceptor;" gone to the billiard table oftener than to the Lord's; poked fun at everybody and everything, and parodied the hymns of Williams of Pantycelyn. In the chapel, when a preacher came near bowling me out, I would stick to my bat; and by this time all the sermons are 'wides.' I feared anybody should see a tear in my eye; and, when one would be just on the point of coming, I would call myself to account and order it back. Not a tear has wanted to come now for some time. The fault, perhaps, may not be all mine. I was'nt brought up as you were. Father would make me go to chapel on the Sunday; but there would be no more talk of chapel, or of religion either, afterwards; only hemming and hawing and rowing, every day. Father did with me as you've seen Ned the blacksmith do with the iron. On the Sunday, in driving me to chapel, he'd put my conscience in the fire, and on the Monday he'd dip it into the water-trough; with the result that it has become as hard as a horse-shoe."

"Will, ——" I began.

"Don't interrupt," he commanded. "I know what you're going to say—repentance, a fresh start, and so forth. I know all those things. I do not want to know now, but to feel. A man can't repent in the same way that he signs the pledge. There must be a change of heart, as "The Mother's Gift" says. The Bible speaks of someone who hadn't the chance of repenting—that is one of the verses against me, and there are lots of them. The worst of it is, I do not, somehow, feel as if I wanted to repent. I feel a sort of weight beneath me urging me along, as if I was being carried by a crowd of people, and couldn't help myself, although I knew all the time I was going to the wrong place. Your mother, fair play for her, gave me many a piece of advice; and I remember once you were almost offended with me for calling her 'Old Ten Commandments.' But what I meant by that was that she was always telling me what I ought to do. And so she was. Don't do

this thing, do that, was what she always had for me. I knew
at the time the old woman was quite right and resolved to do
as she told me, after I had had my fling. But I took too much
fling, and I can't return. I'm past feeling, I fear—nothing in
the world affects me. I am only a youngster, but I feel old in
insolence and obduracy. Only fancy! So young! I feel
almost as Wolsey did—'Had I served my God,' &c.—you know
the words. I'm out of heart and tired of myself; but yet I'm
not repentant. I feel remorse, but no repentance—if I understand what repentance is."

"Will *bach*," I remonstrated; "you forget that God is —— "

"O, don't talk!" he broke in. "You can't tell me anything
new. I know what you're about to say—that God is merciful;
that I should pray to Him, and so on. But I have tried to do it,
on the sly, and felt every time I was only sponging. Do you
know what my belief is? That I have offended God for ever
by those parodies of old Pantycelyn's hymns, for I'll take my
oath the Almighty and old Pant are great chums, and He'll
never forgive me for what I've done. But let's drop it. Good
night."

He pressed my hand and hurried off before I could say a
word. I determined, nevertheless, to see him on the morrow,
with a view of giving another direction to his mind. Early
next morning, however, a lad in Hugh Bryan's service brought
me a note, addressed "Rev. Rhys Lewis," which, on opening,
I found to read:

"Dear old fellow.—

Exit W. B. As the old song says,—
It may be for years,
And it may be for ever.

Keep along the path on which you have started, and profit
by the example of

Yours truly.

P.S.—I have snatched the honour of first addressing you as
Revd., trusting that you will always well sustain the title.—
W. B."

CHAPTER XXXIV.

THOMAS BARTLEY ON A COLLEGIATE EDUCATION.

WHAT is the indispensable requisite of friendship? All similarity of pursuit. Birds of a feather flock together. Does the
fact that two people are friends always presuppose that they
are of like dispositions if not ideas? Not always, I imagine.
When neither ideas nor inclinations are alike in the friends,
in what does their friendship consist? Mutual admiration
cannot account for it, for there may be admiration without
friendship, and friendship without admiration. I have known
one friend laugh at another who could not bear anybody else
to do so. Does friendship consist of some prerogative enjoyed,
as lord-paramount, by the heart independently of any instinct
of the soul? I do not know. I know this—that Will Bryan
and myself were similar neither in dispositions nor ideas; and
yet when he made his "exit," as he called it. my heart gave a
turn, and I shed internal tears. Until then I did not know we
were so close knit. I felt the effects of the unwinding for
months. Will's departure left a great void in my heart, as I
fear it will leave in this history, where he does not come
under notice again for some time. His prophecy with respect
to his father was fulfilled within the week; but I have nothing
to do with that event. I got not a word from my old friend
after he left, which I took to be a bad sign, for I remembered
hearing him one day remark that, if he happened to leave home,
none of his companions should hear from him unless he had
good news to send, or something to relate equal in interest to
the capture of a wild elephant or a fight with a tiger.

Man tires of much talk about himself; and I do not think
anyone would undertake to write an autobiography except on
consideration that others whom he came in contact with would
figure largely in the work. Of greatest interest to me has that
been which I have learned from observing other people's excellences and defects. In the life of the ordinary young preacher there is a good deal of sameness; his history this week will

be his history the next, and few are the circumstances of which
a description would be specially interesting to anybody but himself. And yet, as I said in the first chapter of this history, the
occurrences of a commonplace life are so commonplace that
no one has thought it worth his while to reduce them to writing. There are thousands of verses and popular sayings which
accurately reflect the feelings and experiences of the common
people. They are neither poetical nor "inspired," and no one
knows their authors. Some one *composed* even the expressions
" Good Morning " and " Good Night." But who? There is
nothing "inspired" in these and the like, their only distinction
being the universality of sentiment they convey. And yet they
are immortal! We, the common people, use the same words
and phrases every day in a thousand different places and circumstances, without tiring of them or dreaming of accusing each
other of being trite. If the weather happen to be genial, how
many thousand tongues are there ready to say it is "fine,"
and do say so as if it were the most original remark ever made?
The same man will say it is "fine" twenty times in the day,
the last time with as much emphasis as the first. I almost believe it is the commonest things that possess the most real
and lasting interest. The hale man never tires of the loaf
which is on the table three or four times a day, while there is
reason to think a "club feast," even once a week, would sur-
feit him.

Although nothing particular, as the saying is, happened for
some time in my history after that which I have noted in the
previous chapter that could not be said to have happened in the
life of nearly every young preacher, and although I am now
skipping a whole year of my life, I cannot see that a minute
account of the period would be uninteresting, if I could only
summon up courage to describe every day events, and provided
the description were "true to nature," as W. B. expressed it.
Talking of courage, you must have courage to call a spade a
spade. The misfortune is that everybody should be conscious
everybody else knows—or ought to know—the spade's name,
and it is, therefore, never mentioned. Has not every young
Calvinistic Methodist preacher lost some hours' sleep in fear
and trembling at the thought of the night on which the two

emissaries of the Monthly Meeting are to come over to pump
and cross-question him? And was he never disappointed after
the event? Were not his examiners much less formidable than
he had in his mind portrayed them, and their questions much
easier to answer than he had feared? How did he feel after
preaching his first sermon? Was it not as if he had drained
himself dry, and would never be equal to another. Did he not
find that the sermon in delivery was a very different thing from
what it was on paper? Did he not discover here and there a
hole and hiatus in it of the existence of which he was not
aware before he came to deliver it? In preaching, has he not
been painfully conscious that his sermon became thinner towards the end, and concluded raggedly and abruptly? Many
a Sabbath night, in his bedroom, has he not felt small and humi-
liated at the notion of how much more he had thought of those
who would admire than of those who would believe him? Has
he not fallen in his own estimation when his congregation
was but the night and God? Has he not, hundreds of times,
despaired of reaching that most enviable stage at which he can
exclude every selfish consideration and sink himself in one all-
absorbing desire to serve God and benefit his fellow-men? Did
he not at one time feel over-much delicacy in permitting certain matter-of-fact things—the tithe for instance—to have a
place in his calculations? And did he not find himself one day
familiarised with the taking of such things into account? Has
he not been often astonished to think how much he is like other
people who have not professed as he has? What idea had he
of the Monthly Meeting before becoming personally acquainted
therewith? Did he find that ancient institution the hallowed
one he had expected? He knew, of course, that everybody
present was either preacher or deacon; but did he not form
some foolish notion that they were almost as the angels? More
closely acquainted with them, has he not marvelled how like
they were to other folk, and especially himself? Has he not come
to regard the occasion as on one which he made the discovery
that they actually ate and drank like other people—to say the
least? That some could laugh quite heartily? That others
could converse in whispers while one of the brethren was at
prayer at commencement or conclusion of service? Aye, has

he not seen some who lost their tempers? He had been in the habit of thinking highly, had he not, of —— as wondrously spiritual and devotional? Did he think quite so highly of him on finding that he stayed in the chapel-house for a smoke until the brother finished the prayer which commences meeting? Returning from service, was he not on better terms with himself; did he not console himself with the reflection, "We were all made from the same clay; we all of us have our weaknesses?" What is his experience in respect of the members of the Monthly Meeting? Has he not found that the ablest and holiest were his best and truest friends, and those who did most in his behalf? Were they not the little ones in Christ who were least faithful to, and most discouraged, him? When he preached to the county ministers, were not they he feared most those who were most considerate and cheering; and those whom he feared least the most patronising and contemptuous? In going about to preach, Sunday after Sunday, has he not been more than once dismayed to find himself so cooled down as to be able to do the work mechanically? Was he not disappointed to find that preaching did not kill his own sin? Has the sacred calling never placed new temptations in his path and roused some natural tendencies which had till then lain dormant? Has he not often feared that his preaching produced effects which were more beneficial to other people than to himself? Has he not frequently observed that he was not so sanctified and spotless as he knew some people took him to be? And has he not thanked God a hundred times that his hearers did not know his state of mind and heart as well as he himself did? Having ascertained that some had thought too highly of him, has he taken the pains to undeceive them? Having found that others held the same opinion of him that he did of himself, has he not been angry with them? Has he not regarded those whom he knew to think well of him as men of penetration and ability; and those who have thought differently as wanting in judgment? After a flat and unprofitable Sabbath, has he never determined to preach no more? And after a happy one, has he not rejoiced that he did not give his resolution effect? Despite the painful sense of selfishness and depravity which has occasioned

X

him so much anguish, do not the hints he sometimes gets that
he has been of good afford him a pleasure he can neither
value nor describe? Has he not been able, on occasion, to
say: "Thou hast put gladness in my heart, more than in the
time that their corn and their wine increased." These are but
ordinary factors in every young preacher's experience, and a
chapter could be written on each of them; but who has ever
done so? They are of such common occurrence, as already
stated, that nobody has thought them worth the setting down
in writing. I had intended once to describe them in detail, but
I see from the size of this autobiography that I, too, like my
predecessors, will be obliged to leave the work to someone else.

I had preached almost regularly every Sunday for about
eighteen months, had been received a member of the Monthly
Meeting and had passed the examination for admission into
college. I was perfectly well aware that I did not "shine,"
as the saying is; but my conscience was easy that I had done
my best. Although my poor old mother, in her day, considered
she had done well by giving me "a whole twelvemonth's"
schooling, I felt I had to fight almost every step with greater
vigour, diligence and assiduity, on account of my not having
received in early youth much more instruction than the cane of
Soldier Robin was able to impart. And yet I was encouraged
to go on by the kindness of friends, particularly of my master,
Abel Hughes. So backward did I find myself that I dreaded
mixing among young men of good education, and I am certain
I should not have dreamt of going to college if Abel had not
kept that constantly as a goal before my mind, and urged me
forward. I came out of the examination about the middle of
the class, and after that it was useless to think of turning back.
I had but little money by me, having spent nearly all my
earnings on books and clothes. I depended for the necessary
college supply on the promise made me by Abel Hughes, and
trusted wholly that my master would, silently and unostenta-
tiously, help me. He was my bosom friend, and had repeatedly
renewed his promise to me in confidential converse. I knew
he had not mentioned his good intentions towards me even to
his own sister. When he did a kindness, his delicacy and his
respect for the feelings of the receiver were so great that I often

fancied he would like to have been able to conceal his charity
even from himself. I noticed, many times, that in handing
an alm to a beggar he would talk of something else, as if
endeavouring to divert his own attention and the recipient's
from what he was doing with his hand. I remember well one
night in August, about a fortnight before the time I meant to
go to College, I was preparing for the journey, and feeling a
little fidgetty, never having been more than two nights
together from home in all my life. I had just shut shop, and
my master Abel was sitting on the sofa near the parlour
window. He seemed fatigued, sad, and languid. He at once
began to talk of my going to college. Seeing me put my hat
on, he asked me where I was bound for, and I replied I had
promised to call on Thomas Bartley.

"Will you be long?" he asked.

"I don't think I shall be," was my response, with the
addition: "What is it, sir? Would you like me to stay in?"

"Not on any account," he rejoined. "But I do not feel like
myself at all to-night, somehow."

"I'll stay," I observed. "I can go to the Tump to-morrow
night."

Abel, however, insisted I should not. "There isn't much
the matter with me," he went on. "I'll be better directly, and
I expect Marg'ret in every minute. Thomas Bartley, doubtless, will be waiting you."

As I was going through the doorway he called after me.
"Wait a minute; one never knows what may happen," he
said, opening a cupboard close by, taking out his cashbox, unlocking it, and drawing from it one or two bank notes, which
he suddenly replaced, with the observation: "What is the
matter with me? Am I getting childish, or what? Isn't there a
fortnight yet? Away you go; never mind me, and make haste
back."

On the road to the Tump I could not help thinking there was
something strange in Abel's demeanour that night, and I
resolved to return soon, in consequence. But once under the
Bartley roof-tree it was no easy matter to come away quickly.
To do so without taking supper was, I immediately saw,
altogether out of the question; for hardly had I sat down

before Thomas threw a threatening glance at the ham on the
ceiling. His best welcome always was a ham-and-egg tea, and
a prince's need not have been better. Amongst many others I
remember the following observations of Thomas Bartley, made
in the course of that visit.

"Mighty nourishin' food, look you, ham and eggs is, if you
have the right quality. I wouldn't give a fig for a cart load of this
American stuff. How can you tell what they fatten their pigs
on, poor critters? I don't know how these town's folk venter
to eat eggs. D'ye know what I heard my cousin Ned say he'd
seen with his own eyes once in quite a 'spectable house in
Liverpool? This is his story: at breakfast time the maid
would bring in about a dozen boiled eggs, and place 'em on the
table. And there would the family go breakin' one after
another and smellin' 'em, and the girl carryin' 'em back as fast
as she could, until at last, p'r'aps, they might find two or three
out of the dozen fit to eat. But the odd thing was, they
thought nothing about it—they did the same every day. Well,
ooft to their hearts, say I. Barbara, let's have them eggs
on the middle shelf, between the plates there, right opposite
you; yes, that's them. Those was laid to-day—they're the
game hens'. So you've made up your mind to go to Bala,
then? D'ye know what? We'll be very sorry to miss you,
won't we Barbara?"

Barbara nodded.

"Yes; to be shwar. I've never been to Bala nor anywhere
else up north; and I don't know nobody there, either, 'cept the
two men as comes here fair days, sellin' stockings about the
streets; and decent men enough they are. I'd like awful to go
to Bala, for once in my life, if it was only to see the lake
the man walked over after it was frozen. It was a fearful time,
that. When he found out what he had done he died on the
spot. I heard James Pulford recite a poem to 'Bala once,
composed by Robin Ddu. I don't remember it, though.
'Bala went, and Bala'll go'—something like that it began—
you'll hear it, I dare say, when you get there. I rec'lect father
sayin' of a thing which was quite safe that it was right as Bala
clock. Jest you take notice of it when you get there. D'ye
know what? if we hear of a cheap excursion Babara and I

wouldn't mind one awl-tip comin' to look you up. You wish
we would, eh? I know very well you'd like to see us. Pitch
into it, lad; I don't see you eat much; you've a hundred
welcomes, as you know. Are there many at Bala larnin' to
preach? What is it you say? They don't larn to preach
there? O! well, indeed, say so; 'cause I've hard some of
'em who came down here, and I found nothing extra about
'em—to my taste. I'd rather hear William Hughes of Abercwmnant nor the best of 'em. But then, I ain't much of a
judge. Well, what in the blessed world do they larn there if
they don't larn to preach?"

"Languages, Thomas Bartley," I replied.

"Haha! what languages? tell us."

"Latin and Greek," said I.

"Hoho! I see it now! Fear they'll have to go missionaries
and so that they might be able to preach to the Blacks, ain't
it? Proper, indeed. *You* don't want to go out to the Blacks,
do you? I thought not. Can you tell me what's the reason
so few of 'em goes to India to preach to the Blacks after they've
larnt the languages in college? They tell me there's scores of
Blacks there as never hard a word about Jesus. That's an
awful pity. They may's well not larn the languages if they
don't preach in 'em. I might's well not go 'prentice to a shoemaker if I didn't think of makin' shoes afterwards. You
haven't finished, surely? Take another cup of tea, man.
Well, it's your own fault. But it's of the languages I was
talking—what did you call 'em? To be shwar, Latin and
Greek—the language of the Blacks, isn't it?"

"No, Thomas; Latin and Greek are not the language of the
Blacks," I answered.

"Whose language, then?" he asked.

"Oh, the languages of old people who've been dead for
centuries," responded I.

"Dead men's languages! What in the blessed world do you
want to larn the languages of dead folk for? Is it makin'
fun of me you are, say, like your brother Bob used to?"

"I am telling you the honest truth, Thomas," I replied.
"The languages are learnt for their own sakes and for the
treasures they contain."

"Well, if I never took another hop a-hoeing, this is the queerest thing I've hard of! I had always thought a language was somethin' to be spoken. Tell me, which is the Black's language? They must, surely, larn that, or they can't go missionaries."

"The language of the Blacks is not taught in college, Thomas Bartley. The missionaries must go to the Blacks themselves to learn that," said I.

"Well, if ever I hard such a thing with my ears before! Larnin' the languages of people who are dead and not larnin' the languages of people who are alive! But since we've begun talkin' of the thing, what else do they larn, tell me?" he went on.

"They learn mathematics," I returned.

"Matthew Mattiss! and what may that be?"

"How to measure and weigh and make all sorts of calculations, and things of that sort," said I.

"A handy thing enough," remarked Thomas. "That's the reason, I s'pose, why so many preachers turn farmers and shopkeepers. Do they larn anything else there?"

"English language and history," I replied.

"Proper," observed Thomas. "If a man doesn't know a bit of English in these days he's bound to be left behind. And history is an interestin' thing enough. One of the best I ever heard at it was James Pulford the tailor. When I used to go to public houses I doated on that man. There's nothin' better I like in a sermon than a bit of history. When Barbara and I've forgotten everythin' else, we'll have a pretty fair grip of the story the preacher's told. But, for all that, I don't find those college boys any great shakes at tellin' a story. William Hughes, of Abercwmnant, beats 'em flyin'. D'ye know what? William, last time he was here, told a story of a little girl a dyin' which I shan't forget's long as there's breath in me. If I was to drop dead on the spot I couldn't help cryin' while he was tellin' it. I'm glad in my heart they larn history in college; only some of'm are dreadful long a larnin.' There was a lad of a preacher here lately who had been three years in college so they said; but I couldn't for the life of me make head nor tail of him. He spoke of some 'mechanism,' 'unity,' or something which I couldn't make top nor bottom of. But, tell me—I almost forgot, and I knew I had somethin' to ask you—what sort of livin' do they get there? Pretty good, I should think."

"They don't provide for any one, Thomas. Each must provide for himself," replied I.

"But how in the world do the boys get along? Are they 'lowed so much a week to live on?" he asked.

"Oh, no," said I. "Every one has to find his own food, drink, lodging and washing. They're permitted to go about preaching, and on the little they get for that they live."

"Never 'll I go to Caerwys fair again, if that college isn't the rummest place I've hard talk of!" observed Thomas. "The boys, you say, don't larn to preach there; they don't larn the language of the Blacks, only the language of some old people's bin dead for cent'ries; they don't get any pay, everybody livin' on his own hook, starve or not; and the only thing worth talkin' of they *do* larn is History and that other thing—what did you call it? Matthew ——? to be shwar, Matthew Mattis. What in the wide world do you want to go there for, say? Do they larn anythin' about Jesus Christ there? I didn't hear you mention it."

"Doubtless they do, Thomas," replied I; "but the place is almost as strange to me as it is to you."

"Most the pity. If 1 were you I'd go a month on trial and take my food with me. D'ye know what? It's just this minute struck me that every one I've seen comin' here from college preachin' looked half starved; and it's not a bit of wonder after what you've told me 'bout the way they manage there. The longer he lives, the more a man hears, the more he perceives. I always thought the college an uncommon nice place, though I used to wonder why all the boys, poor things, looked so pale and dispirited. I fancied they were only a bit nervous, like a witness in the box, and that if I was to see 'em on the Monday mornin' I'd find 'em all right, p'r'aps. But they must have bin gettin' better livin' there at one time, 'cause I remember, when a lad, happ'nin' to go to chapel; and who should be preachin' but John Jones, of Llanllyfni—it was in college he was at that time, I should fancy—and his two cheeks was like the rose. Tell us: if you didn't happen to have a call to preach for a month or two after goin' to college, what'd become of you?"

"Well," I replied, "I must trust to Providence."

"I never saw good in that story," rejoined Thomas. "God helps those as helps themselves. There was a man livin' in this neighbourhood a while since—before your time—and he was a bit of a believer too—the most careless man about his own affairs I ever saw, and he was always talkin' of trust in Providence. But do yow know where he died? In Holywell workhouse, poor fellow! In a manner of speakin', I almost wish you hadn't told me the kind of place that college is; 'cause after you've gone there, Barbara and I'll be always thinkin' whether you get enough to eat or not. I see you leavin' a good place and venterin' into the upper country where they lives hard—as the stockin'ers used to tell me. For my part I don't see the game is worth the candle. I wouldn't ha' cared so much if they only larnt to preach there. But you know what'st best for yourself, and it isn't my business to interfere. If your mother was alive, though, I doubt if she'd 'low you to go. What does Abel say? Is he for your goin'?"

"Oh yes," I replied. "Abel is anxious I should."

"Well, I'll give in to him. He's a reg'lar caution, Abel is. I never knew him make a mistake," observed Thomas.

"Mentioning Abel, Thomas Bartley," I returned, "makes me think it is time for me to go. Abel is not over well tonight, and I promised to be back soon."

"Sorry to hear it," Thomas said. "Hope it's nothin' serious. I don't know what'd become of us in that chapel if somethin' was to happen to the old sarja majar. We should be all higgledy-piggledy. D'ye know what? When your mother was alive it was as good's a sermon to hear those two talk. They never spoke of 'mechanism' and things of that sort, only of Jesus Christ, and heaven; and I a-takin' of it all in, like a sow in the barley. I would'nt a tired of them the whole night long, and I hated to see Abel get up to go, for I felt as if I hadn't had half enough. Do you know what I used to do? I hope it was no sin, but whenever I saw Abel comin' I turned back the clock-hand half an hour. 'Twouldn't have done for your mother to catch me, she was so guzzact in things of that sort, you know. Well, I won't keep you, since Abel's out of sorts. Remember us both to him. Good night! Stay! here you are, as long's you're determined to go to college, take a piece of this flitch of bacon and welcome. We shall have quite enough left. Well, well; it's your own fault if you don't. You know you're a hundred times welcome. Good night."

I was glad to get away, to enjoy a roar, as Will Bryan used to say. If Will had been there, I thought, what a splendid account he would have given of my chat with the "old thoroughbred Thomas Bartley," as he called him! A hundred reminiscences came to mind, as I hurried along homewards, of the way in which Bob was able to smooth the wrinkles in mother's serious, care-worn face, after a visit paid to Thomas Bartley's house to "draw him out." Bob could mimic the old shoemaker to the life; and I know him making mother angry with herself, because she had been compelled to laugh in her own despite. It may be that there are moments in the life of every man when he seems demented. Had I been photographed that night, swiftly striding past the Hall Park, my face would have presented a strange look, as I laughed and cried, alternately. Thinking the matter over, now, I am surprised to find that Thomas Bartley had so much to do with the principal events of my life. But little did I imagine at the moment of my return from the Tump I should ever have to recall that night save as a means of amusement for my companions.

I had left the Corner Shop barely an hour and a half, and was within a few yards of it on my return, when I met Jones, who had been searching for me, everywhere save at the Tump. He told me Abel was dreadfully ill. What else he may have said I never knew, for the next minute I was in my dear old master's room. I shall never forgive myself for leaving him that night. I found him reclining on the sofa where I had left him when I went out. Sitting on a chair by his side was Doctor Bennett, or, as we called him, the works' doctor, behind whom, at the head of the sofa, was Miss Hughes making desperate efforts to hide her heart-beats. The scene is vividly present to my mind ; how can I forget it ? With her left arm, which seemed tenderness itself embodied, Miss Hughes supported the patriarchal head of the only man she had ever loved with all her heart, while her right hand held a glass containing some kind of cordial which her brother refused to, or rather could not, take. I think there were two other women in the room, but I do not remember who they were. Until then, I would not have believed it possible a man could undergo such a change in so short a time without being externally assailed. The "fine old fellow," as Will Bryan called him, had sunk, one helpless inert mass, his glory all departed, like some mighty tower whose foundations had been struck by lightning. The face, beaming with reason, intelligence and amiability but two hours since, was now like that of an imbecile in his cups. The tongue, which never once spoke aught that was not sensible and instructive, had now forgotten its office, and there came nothing from the lips of its owner save some inarticulate sound like the stridulous notes of the deaf-mute. His right arm excepted, my master's body was completely paralysed. I had been in the room some minutes before he took any notice of me. When he saw me he was visibly agitated, and began to cry like a child. Pointing to me, and then to the cupboard, he tried hard to speak. I knew well enough what he meant, but took upon me not to understand him. Again and again did he endeavour to make his wishes clear. The doctor asked me if I could tell what he wanted, and I said—well, I said that which was not true, namely, that I did not know. It was manifest to all in the room that Abel wished to say something to me. I knew perfectly well what it was. But, supposing I had told the doctor and Miss Hughes it was my master's wish that I should be given some of those bank notes from the cash box, would they not have contradicted me? I was certain, however—as certain as that I am writing the words at this moment—that that was his one and only wish. I believed he still retained his intellectual faculties unimpaired, but that the media through which, for five and seventy years, they had made themselves known, had refused obedience any longer. Time and again he tried to talk to me and, failing, broke into tears. The doctor told me I had better leave the room, since it was clear my presence disturbed the sufferer. But I respectfully declined. I had left him, once, when I ought not, and I was not going to do so again. It was hard, indeed, on me. My heart bled with pity for the best, tenderest, godliest man I had ever known. It was in my power to set his mind at rest by revealing his desire; and it was most important to me personally that I should do so, for my future, to a great extent, depended upon it. But I dared not do this without throwing suspicion upon my motives. Silently and earnestly I prayed that my master might have strength to speak; but every minute, as it were, bore him farther away, and diminished our hope of his ever again being able to commune with us. With much trouble we got him to bed, where every possible means were used to restore him, but without avail. As I said, he had not wholly lost the use of his right arm. I sat by the bedside, my hand in his. He lay for hours, as if in happy sleep, only, when I tried to withdraw my hand, he turned uneasily. The doctor, saying he might remain in that state for days, went away, promising to return in the morning. Miss Hughes, who was persuaded to retire to rest, seeing she could do nothing for her brother, had procured an experienced nurse to stay up with me to watch the sick man. The weather was warm, the place still, and presently the "experienced nurse" fell fast asleep. Dr. Bennett had not the slightest hope of my dear old master's recovery; neither, any longer, had I, although I earnestly prayed God—not with any selfish purpose —that his tongue might be loosened, were it only for a minute. Was I heard? If I said yes, who would believe me? I had been watching an hour, for two hours, and the "experienced nurse" sleeping for exactly the same space of time. The breathings of my beloved old benefactor were so light and soft, that I feared he had passed. I gently let go his hand. He awoke, peacefully as a child in its cot, looked at me, and said—well, I never repeated those few words to any living soul; because I thought Doctor Bennett might pronounce the thing impossible, or that I had been dreaming; while others might say I had a selfish motive in telling the story; and others that the whole was but animal magnetism. It matters not in the least, by this time. I know this much—I made no use of his words

to gain my own ends; but I treasure them up in my heart as a
remembrance of how true he was to me in his last moments.
A minute later his spirit had crossed the great gulf. And in
the whole annals of Death, I believe there never entered its
dark portal a more just, more faithful, or more perfect man,
but One.

CHAPTER XXXV.

TROUBLOUS.

IN the storm which felled the grand old oak, whose roots
spread wide and deep, the encompassing earth was rent, and
other oaks, for a distance round, were rendered less secure.
Those nearest the prostrate one felt most the shock of its down-
fall; some of them being so deeply barked that summer breezes,
rain, and dew, and heat could never heal their scars. The
death of Abel Hughes deprived the town of one who had
carried conviction to the hearts of loafing " corner men," and
even worse characters, that he was a good man. The tradesmen
lost from their midst an example of one who could deal with
the world without lying, and at the same time earn a livelihood honestly and without stint. Let us hope he was not the
last of those old-fashioned people ! But it was to the chapel and
the cause that the loss was greatest. The inhabitants could not
think of Methodism without Abel. Rightly had witling Seth
called the chapel Abel's chapel, and, when he fell, the members
felt as if their sanctuary had lost its inward life. There were
not a dozen belonging to the church who could remember the
Big Seat without Abel in it. The majority had recited their
verses to him in the Children's Communion, and been received
by him into full membership. The affairs, temporal and
spiritual, of nearly every family connected with the church
were known to Abel; and there was hardly a Methodist house
in the town that he had not been in, by someone's bedside with
counsel and with prayer. Old men and women on the parish,
like others higher stationed, could pour their woes in Abel's

ear, confident that their secrets would never be divulged. For
many years he had acted as pastor to the church, with this
distinct advantage, that he could tell the truth in public and in
private, fearless of dismissal or visible falling off in the collections. The truth will stand; but how many of us are ready
to stand by the truth without trying to trim it after our own
particular fashion? "And they knew that they were naked."
Possessed of truths which we are certain should be spoken, are
we not apt to dress them up in our own aprons? On the other
hand, men are met with, boastful of their honesty, their fond-
ness for telling the truth and plain speaking; but who display
an impertinence and a rudeness which make the sensible regard
their bluntness of speech as the outcome of ignorance and bad
manners. Truth is a knife, in the estimation of people like
these, and "the truth that kills" is their only truth. Some
churches, even unto this day, keep their religious butcher and
executioner. The former's chief delight is in cutting up his
co-religionist into four quarters and a head, and exhibiting him
upon his stall; the latter likes to hang him at once, and have
done with it. Speaking metaphorically, Abel could wield a
knife, but not the butcher's. He used it, not to take away life,
but to spare it. Once he believed there was danger, he never
dilly-dallied. He brought home to the patient's mind the unspeakable value of his soul's health, and that to save it he must
undergo the severest operation. And, as a rule, those who had
been longest under his hands were his warmest, fastest friends.
I think it was the common experience of those who were bred
in the church that, as children, they considered Abel Hughes
too sharp, precise and severe; but that, as they gathered age
and sense, their estimate of him softened. In their childhood
he seemed a sort of sour green crab, which set their teeth on
edge; grown up, they came to regard him as a great, round
apple—yellow, ripe and sweet in the mouth. It was not often,
as Thomas Bartley said, that Abel made a mistake. Many a
time have I seen several church members ardent and determined concerning this thing and that, but directly they got to
know Abel differed from them, they began to doubt—not Abel,
but themselves. Often, in Communion, have I known John
Lloyd rise to his feet and dilate hotly upon some complaint or

other. You might think from his speech that religion had died
out of the land, and that certain persons in the church, whom
he did not name, had been guilty of every form of wickedness
conceivable. Abel would thereupon get up and, with some
dozen soothing words, would clear the air and still the ferment.
He would then walk straight up to old Betty Kenrick or
Thomas Bartley to ask an experience; and two minutes later
everybody had forgotten all about John Lloyd and his lecture.
Will Bryan detested John Lloyd, and nothing pleased him
better than to see Abel give his enemy a "sitting on," as he
used to call it. "Did ye spot how Abel put out Old Scraper's
bonfire by spitting on it?" Will would sometimes ask me in
Communion. "That was the smartest bit of work I've seen,
for I can't tell how long, I'll take my oath." Abel had an awl
of his own which never failed to flatten out a blustering, pre-
tentious wind-bag. He never spoke of it afterwards, but I often
thought that a feat of this kind afforded him a little secret
pleasure; for, in his corner by the fire at home, a smile of
satisfaction would spread across his face, as if he were enjoying
a good thing all to himself. He was strict, as I have said. He
could not tolerate a harum-scarum religionist; but whatever a man's shortcomings and defects might be, he always
sympathised with him deeply. I have mentioned, in a previous
chapter, that I never saw his like at reading the human heart.
He had studied his own for an age, and I heard him say, several
times, it was the most deceitful of all things. He was able, on
that account, to understand and guide the young man fighting
against temptation and doubt. He could feel for the toiling and
the troubled, make allowance for the raw and inexperienced,
who had any good in them, and participate in the spiritual joy
and sorrow of the old and tried. But idleness, carelessness,
hypocrisy and cant he found unbearable, always. I had
better advantages than anyone else, almost, for knowing him
thoroughly. To me he never once appeared to pride himself
upon his own virtues; but when he saw those virtues shine,
even in a less degree, in others, his face fairly beamed with
pleasure. He had set himself so high a standard of conduct
that his failings were kept continually in view; and he regarded
with envy some people who, to my mind, did not deserve com-

parison with himself. His sincerity and force of character gave
him an authority in the church which no one either dared or
desired to question.

I must acknowledge it was not these reflections which filled
my mind when Abel died ; but others much less disinterested.
I saw that I had lost my most precious friend, at a time
when my future, humanly speaking, was almost entirely
dependent upon him. I am ashamed to think how selfish I
was. For the moment, I feared all my prospects blighted. I
remember well feeling astonished and hurt to find no one
sympathising with me. Everybody talked of the loss it would
be to the cause, and all the sympathy ran towards Miss
Hughes. " Poor Miss Hughes ! " " What'll Miss Hughes do
now ? " " Miss Hughes, poor thing, will be left alone in the
world, now she has lost her brother." " Who will Miss
Hughes get to look after the business ? There's that boy,
there, going to college ; it would be much fitter for him to stay
at home to help Miss Hughes, if he has any feeling in him."
" Surely, Rhys Lewis won't think of leaving Miss Hughes in
her present trouble. He ought to be ashamed of himself if he
does." That was how people talked. All thought of Miss
Hughes and, as far as I was aware, no one thought of Rhys
Lewis. Why? Because no one knew it was Abel's chief
desire that I should go to college. He had never told a living
soul, save me, that I should not want a single penny as
long as I was away and that I was always to consider the
Corner Shop my home. I realised my loss in all its bitterness,
and felt myself unfriended and alone. I knew I was selfish,
but I could not help it. I saw all my plans upset, and thought
that nothing remained for me but to abandon my intention of
going to college and settle down to business once more. Simultaneously there came to mind Abel's injunction not to think of
keeping shop and preaching; and I thought I should be bound
to give up the preaching also. My heart sank within me. I
had not an atom of taste, nay, I had a positive dislike, for
business. This was not my fault, I fancied. It was Abel
Hughes who had led me into it; had created in me a hatred
of trade, and disposed my mind to other things. For a
considerable time before his death he allowed me the widest

liberty. I was asked to do but next to nothing in the shop, if he saw I was diligent with my books and was not idling. But now, I feared all the trouble he had taken with me had been in vain, and that all my own efforts had gone with the wind. The more I thought of all this the more I commiserated myself, the less ready was I to become reconciled to my fate. As described in a previous chapter, Miss Hughes had been remarkably kind towards me, even during my mischievous period, and my indebtedness to her was great. She was a simple, innocent old soul, who resembled her brother in nothing save in kindness and fidelity. She took no interest in the questions Abel and I used to discuss, and I wondered many times to think how little she comprehended those matters of which the knowledge had made her brother noted. To her there was no difference between preacher and preacher; they were all good, and she had as much respect for the least of them as for the greatest. She read a chapter of the Bible in her bedroom every night without fail; and then went peacefully to sleep. I do not know that she ever read anything else except on the Sabbath, when she took up *Y Drysorfa,** opening it at random and nodding over it, directly. She knew next to nothing about the business and, I feared, but little about her brother's circumstances, either. But for all that, she was a good woman, who filled the sphere of life she was called into excellently well. She kept the house clean and beautiful, and her hospitality to all whom Abel brought beneath his roof was cordial and sincere. Abel's sudden death was a heavy blow to her, and one which, apparently, excited not only my own but others' deepest sympathy, for "many came to comfort her concerning her brother." In view of the number of our visitors—well-intentioned people, no doubt—I think I did wisely in calling in a sensible woman to look after Miss Hughes, and prevent her from being killed with kindness. One of the things which affords me the greatest consolation at the present moment is, that I myself carried out the funeral arrangements to the satisfaction of all, without consulting anybody save David Davis.

---

* "The Treasury"—a connexional publication of the Welsh Calvinistic Methodists.—Translator.

No; not so, either. I marvel when I think of the state of
dreamy absent-mindedness I was in at the time. In everything I did, I felt my dear old master at my side, and I seemed
to be doing it all according to his command. On the sad day
we buried him, and when I was conscious of, rather than
saw, the crowd of people that came together, I remember
wondering into how small a gap they put poor Abel, and how
large the one, which never could be filled, that he had left
behind. When David Davis and I were returning from the
churchyard, I fancied hearing my old master addressing us
with a "Thank you, Rhys; thank you, David. Ye did well."
To which we replied, "We have only done that which it was
our duty to do by thee."

David Davis accompanied me back to the house, and we both
went into the kitchen, there being "of women some" with
Miss Hughes in the parlour. If these lines are ever read, I
dare say I shall be deemed foolish for noting such trifles. I
had hoped David would sit in Abel's old arm chair; but instead
of doing so he took the chair he usually sat on when Abel was
alive. The old chair was empty, and beside it, on the wide
hob, lay the pipe, exactly in the spot it was left four days ago.
Neither David nor I spoke a word, but I knew we both
appeared as if constantly expecting Abel to come in. How
difficult it is to realise the departure, nevermore to return, of
one who has for years been a part of your life! After talking
over one thing and another, David presently asked me what I
intended to do? Did I consider it wise, under the circumstances, to go to college? I said I was not prepared to answer.

"No one would blame you, now, as things have happened,"
he went on, "if you did not go to Bala—Abel taken suddenly
away, Miss Hughes left all alone, and knowing nothing
about the business. Indeed, everybody would think the more
of you if you were not to go. What if you were to wait
another year, to see how things turn out?"

He spoke feelingly and persuasively; but his words stabbed
me to the heart. What, thought I, David Davis exhort me
not to go to college! I was hurt, and said to him, a little
excitedly, "David Davis, if I don't go to college now I never
shall. If I find, after taking time to consider the matter, that

Y

it is my duty to stay here, I shall bid an eternal good-bye to preaching; if otherwise, nothing will prevent my going. But to-night I do not clearly see what my duty is, and I do not choose to discuss the subject."

"Pray for light, then," returned David, rising to go. But before he left I took him to the parlour to Miss Hughes, whose friends, with the exception of the "sensible woman," had by this time gone. I had held but little converse with her since her brother's death. In her affliction she left everything to me. When I attempted to consult with her, "You know best," was the only answer I got. Naturally enough, she began to cry immediately on our entrance, and for some time was not able to say a word. I followed her example, for, of a truth, although selfish, I was not hard-hearted.

"David Davis," she presently observed, "hasn't Rhys done well? I always did like him—he knows that himself. When he came here first he was very wicked, and Abel was so strict. I used to take his part, as he knows. You won't leave me to go to that old college, will you, Rhys?"

David answered for me, for which I was very thankful: "You'll talk of that another time, Miss Hughes," and after adding a few consolatory words, he went away.

I felt very wretched that night. For some hours I sat by the fire in a reverie. The old clock had stopped, and no one had thought of setting it going again. I feared Providence clearly meant me not to go to college, and consequently not to preach. Abel Hughes had told me, more than once, that no young man, in these enlightened days, should think of the ministry without first spending some years at college; and I fancied, then, it was almost impossible Abel could err in judgment. I reflected that if I stayed with Miss Hughes the whole care of the business would devolve upon me; Jones being merely a kind of useful fixture. All my time must be devoted to the shop, so that reading and sermon-making would be utterly out of the question. On the other hand, if I went to college, how was I to get the means of subsistence? I could not hope to win prizes. Those would be taken by the well-to-do, properly-supported young men who had received a good education in early life. I had heard that some of the boys were able to live

on very little at Bala, and I thought I should like to show myself able to live on less than any of them. With the exception
of a few shillings lying loose in my pocket, all the money I
owned was in my purse. How much had I? Taking my
purse out, I emptied it into my hand and placed it upon the
table. I counted my money carefully: six pounds in gold, ten
and sixpence in silver, I remember well. I was gazing at the
coin as it rested in the palm of my right hand, when I heard
Miss Hughes and her companion coming along the passage to
bid me " good-night" before going to bed. I hurriedly thrust
my wealth into my pocket and brushed the purse aside, lest
they should discover how earthly my contemplations were. A
few minutes later, the house was perfectly quiet, and I again
fell to racking my brains with reference to my situation, and
vexing myself by thinking how completely my circumstances
and plans for the future had changed in less than a week. I
did not know how long I remained in this state. I was sure it
must be late at night, because the stir in the streets had
ceased, and nothing was to be heard save someone passing
slowly around the corner of the house. I thought it was the
policeman. The same step sounded three or four times over. I
knew I could not sleep if I went to bed; I had got to feel so
uneasy and sick at heart. Fancying a mouthful of fresh air
would do me good, I slipped out quietly, carefully locking the
door behind me. It was a lovely moonlit night, with a nice
light breeze blowing, although it was not cold. The details of
the occasion are still vividly present in my memory. Deep
silence reigned in the streets, as if all their dwellers were dead.
I turned down one street and up another, just as if I had a
particular destination in view, which, however, was not the case.
In the second street I saw a light in the upstairs window of a
little cottage, where, I remembered, there lay a young girl
who was very ill. Yes, I reflected, it is worse with her
than with me, and there are those about her who cannot
give sleep to their eyes for sorrow and the " multitude
of thoughts within them." Going on a little, I heard a
sound in the distance, and paused to listen. It was the rumble
of a barrow upon the pavement, from which I understood that
" Ready Ned " was on night duty. It was at night Ned

always worked, at night that his work must be done. For
more reasons than one I took another direction, proceeding
along which I remember a white cat gliding, spirit-like, across
my path. Hurrying on, I saw, just before reaching the top of
the high street, a slightly built little man wearing a soft hat,
slouched somewhat low over the eyes; a tired, hard-up tramp,
most likely. I bade him good night, but he made no reply. I
thought no worse of him for that, it being possible, I fancied,
he may be fatigued, empty-stomached, angered at a cold-
hearted world, too wearied or careless to reply, and saying to
himself, " What's your ' good-night' worth if you don't give
me anything ? "

Presently, I had left the town behind me, without seeing one
other creature save William the Coal's mule grazing the hedge.
I knew it was he before coming up, from the clink of his fetter.
I remembered that " Duke" was of a wandering disposition,
and that William was obliged to chain him by the leg in order to
keep him within the bounds of his own parish. " Duke " was
busily browsing, and occasionally shaking his head, with the
greatest gravity, as if discussing something with himself in a
negative sense, for at that time of night it was impossible he
could be plagued by the gnats. When he heard me approach,
" Duke" stopped eating, arrested his jaw in the midst of a bite
and began wondering, apparently, why William had come to
fetch him thus early, for his ears went up like a double note of
admiration. Seeing his mistake, " Duke" went on with his
grazing and argument. I went on, too, my mind rambling
over all sorts of subjects, but always reverting to myself. I was
conscious of a deep and earnest desire for knowledge and for
being of service to both God and man. And yet everything
seemed to be driving me back behind the counter, doomed for
life to sell cloths, flannels and calico ! I tried to cheer myself
and look at things in a different light. What mattered it if my
life were spent in the shop? There was no scarcity of young
men, better qualified than I, for the ministry and more ad-
vantageously placed in preparation for the work. I looked up
into the infinite, star-studded, sky overhead. What difference
would it make, I asked myself, if eternal darkness settled down
upon that tiny solitary speck in the far-off distance? No one

would miss it. And yet that star shone with a lovely lustre, and, doubtless, served some useful purpose or other. Yes, there are clouds in the firmament of blue. How beautiful the luminous moon, in her radiance! Ah! there comes a cloud across her face, which hides her wholly. How like, now, she is to me! But, see, the cloud passes—one part of her placid countenance is already in sight—aye, the cloud has cleared away again, and gentle Luna beams brighter than before. Can the cloud pass from me, also? Everything is possible unto Him.

Such were the thoughts of my heart when I fancied hearing footsteps behind me. I looked back, but saw no one. Turning suddenly upon my heel, I made for home. I had not gone many yards when I saw a man get up from the hedge side, and walk to meet me. It was the tramp I had passed on the road; only he did not now seem to halt in the slightest, neither did his hat-cantle cover his eyes as before. I believed he had some evil intention towards me, and at once thought of running away. But how could I tell what arms he had? It would be wisest to face him boldly, and make the best of a bad matter. When we met I recognised him instantly.

"You must'nt think me too proud to speak just now, because I refused to answer you," he observed. "O, no, I'm never above owning my relations; but I take care not to lower myself by talking to all sorts. And how ——"

"Uncle," I broke in, "do you remember what I said to you the last time I saw you?"

"'Good-night!'" he replied.

"You know that is not the occasion I'm referring to," I rejoined. "Do you recollect what I told you in the garden of Nic'las of Garth Ddu?"

"Well, wait a bit; my memory is not so bad, as a rule. What was it, though? O! I remember now—that you'd give me a sovereign next time you saw me. How a man does forget things, to be sure."

"You know better," I retorted. "You know that what I told you was—if ever you showed your face in this neighbourhood again, I would give you into the hands of the police; and I'll do so, too."

"Bosh!" he returned, contemptuously. "Look here—when

you want a good shot, never take a double-barrelled gun.
That's the disadvantage of a revolver. It's good for nothing except at short range. Am I not your uncle, your
father's brother? To whom would the disgrace be if you gave
me up to the police? To James Lewis or Rhys Lewis? What
does James Lewis care about disgrace? I know a certain proud
chap, though, who wouldn't like it at all—eh? But there, I
don't wan't to quarrel with you. It isn't respectable for
relations to fall out. Let byegones be byegones. So, old
Abel has gone to his account, has he? The old screw—he'll
have a lot to answer for, like myself."

"Here, uncle," said I, "I'd rather you killed me than spoke
disrespectfully of my good old master."

"Well, well," he continued; "I don't want to hurt your
feelings. It was a capital thing for you that Abel took himself
off. You'll be boss, now; for what does the old gal and that
born idiot, Jones, know about the business? If you don't
make your fortune now, the fault will be yours. I hope you
won't deal shabby by me. I'm the only relation left you in
the world, and I've been real unlucky of late. Haven't had a
haul I don't know when, and it was a narrow shave I wasn't
nabbed last week. I had to fight like ——."

"I can't bear to listen to your ungodly talk, and I must
leave you, uncle," said I.

"I don't wan't you to take apartments for me," he went on;
"because that wouldn't pay either of us. But I'm in want of
cash, and cash I must have or starve. P'r'aps you haven't
much about you to-night; but I can come over to see you,
now and then, since you're to be boss, and are a late bird, like
myself."

"As long as I am there you'll never set foot inside the
house," I declared. "And besides, I'm as poor as yourself."

"That's your own fault," he remarked. "If you hadn't
swallowed so much of the flummery ladled out to you by your
mother you need never have been poor. Trust me, if I had
had your chance."

I must tell the honest truth: at his mention of my mother,
I felt I could throttle him with pleasure, and had to punish
myself very considerably in order to prevent myself from flying

at his throat. So severe was the internal struggle with my
worse nature that I was, for a minute, unable to speak. On
regaining self-possession—God forgive me my mad words—I
said to him :—

" You scoundrel! Say another disrespectful word about my
mother and I'll pull you limb from limb. My mother taught
me to lead an honest life."

Uncle retreated two or three yards, looked at me in astonishment, and fumbled for something in his pockets. I was not a
bit afraid, and was quite prepared to fall a sacrifice to his wrath
in defence of the repuation of, to my mind, the best mother in
the world. After a minute's silence he said, with perfect
composure:

"I'm glad to see a bit of the family pluck in you. I'd
always considered you a bit of a chicken; but I think a
hundred times better of you, now. If I said anything wrong
about your mother, I apologise. She was a good sort, in her
way, and she did me an occasional kindness. But why do you
everlastingly want to quarrel with me? Let's be chums. That's
where your father beat you—he was as cool as a turnip, always.
I'm sorry if I've offended you. But you know what I'm after.
I'm stone broke; I haven't a brown to buy a bit of grub with,
and I know you wouldn't like to see me getting into trouble."

"I don't want to have anything to do with you," said I.
" Tell me which way you wish to go, and I'll take some other.
I shan't walk a step with you."

" Agreed," he said. " But give me what you have about
you, first. It isn't much, I dare say."

Impulsively, I turned out my pocket into his hand, thinking
I had only a few shillings loose among the coppers. Thanking me, he went away, and I returned home. The encounter
fully determined me in the course I should take. It was no
longer possible I could stay at home to be plagued by this
horrid wretch. I felt he had got the upper hand of me, that
he knew my weakness, and that I dared not denounce him to
the authorities without bringing disgrace upon myself. Obviously he was not aware that I preached, and by going to
college he would lose scent of me, for he dared not make
inquiries. I believed it was Providence that had brought me

face to face with the vagabond that night, and was inviting me
to throw myself into its arms. I resolved to do so, and go to
college, come what may. Although I could not help my
family connections, I felt thankful at the thought that, associated with the rest of the scholars, none of them would know my
history. And possibly, I argued, even some of them may have
a history which they would not like everybody else to know.
Having made up my mind, I felt happy and in my element.
Indeed my bliss was such that I could enjoy the altered look
on "Duke" as I went by. My old friend had eaten to satiety,
and was nodding where he stood, one leg resting limply, and
his head bent low and still, as if he had long since carried the
point in discussion. "Duke," I fancied, had, like myself, his
story, if he could only tell it, and could preface others—a more
interesting one than mine, it may be. I walked rapidly on, and
let myself into the house as softly as I could. When I lit the gas,
one of the first things I saw was my purse upon the edge of the
table. I took it up; it was empty! Alas! I had given every
farthing I possessed to the "Irishman," as I used to call him
when a lad. I grasped the situation with grief. Having made
up my mind to go to college, here was I, without as much as a
penny to pay my fare thither. Stupified and sorrowful, I stood
on the middle of the kitchen floor, where Abel Hughes had
many a time exhorted me to put my trust in God. Verily, He
was trying me sore. I sat down, laid my head between my
hands upon the table, and cried my eyes out, nearly.

<hr />

CHAPTER XXXVI.

A WELL-KNOWN CHARACTER.

I LOOK upon the night I have attempted to describe in the last
chapter as one of the great nights of my little life. Friendless
and lonely, I felt as if all things had conspired to deprive me
of the object on which I had set my heart. I feared I was out
of favour with God, and that all my convictions and dealings
with religion were but hypocrisy and pretence. Without
flattery, I knew that as a preacher I was tolerably acceptable

of men; but why, I asked, does God, in his Providence, seem
to be placing every obstacle in my way? I could say, honestly
and unhesitatingly, I was no money-lover, and that my heart's
affections were fixed solely on preaching and fitting myself for
the work. Still, I felt I could do nothing without money, and
there I was, by my own folly, left "as poor as a church
mouse." I thought so little of money that I had not yet
learned to take care of it. As I have already said, I believed I
was deeply desirous to be of use in my day and time; but by
now I hadn't a penny to assist me in the work. My mind re-
verted, with discontent, I fear, to the scores of people I knew
who were rolling in riches, but who had never dreamt of
serving anybody but themselves; and Will Bryan's words
came forcibly to memory—"Old pockets! They are but
intelligent pigs. It must be, look you, that the Great King
does not place much value on money, or He wouldn't have
given so much of it to the dunderheads;" and he would add,
"Sir, says Mr. Fox, they are sour."

The question suddenly occurred to me had I been too much
accustomed to rely upon Abel Hughes, and had Providence, by
stripping me of all external help, invited me to throw myself,
as I did, into its arms? It seemed presumption to think of
going to college with nothing about me save a sufficiency of
clothes and a few books. I remembered the man Thomas
Bartley spoke of who, trusting to Providence, had died in
Holywell workhouse. Anyhow, I resolved to do my best with
the work I had begun, and tried to believe that God would
speedily give me light upon my circumstances. Very early
next morning I notified Miss Hughes of my determination to
go to college. She was astounded. She had never believed,
she said, I could be so cruel towards her. I tried to reason
with her; but to no purpose. It was through her heart she
saw everything, and not through her head. She offered me a
good salary if I stayed on with her; but I refused. After
much talk, she generously said she would give me a share of the
business. That offer, also, I rejected. She then fell back upon
the most effective argument a woman has at command—she
began to cry. She taunted me with all the kindness she had
shown me—pointed out how poor I was when I came to the

Corner Shop—the comfortable home I had found there—what a mercy it was I had been brought under instruction by Abel—and what a figure I would have cut but for that. She said I was unfeeling, unkind, hard-hearted, ungrateful, selfish. Many other epithets did she use. She declared I cared for nobody but myself, and that it would not matter to me if I saw her " going on the parish." The fact that she knew nothing of the business, she said, kindled no spark of sympathy in me. For all she could tell, she added, she might be without a home before three months were over.

I listened to her in silence, feeling, at the same time, that I was guilty on every count of her indictment. My fears were confirmed that she did not know anything of her brother's affairs. I asked her to calm herself and wait till the morrow, when I believed I should be able to give her good advice. She answered, tartly, that if she could do without my services she could do without my advice, as well. I said not a word in rejoinder, for which, I must now admit, I repent. I went to the shop, and, with Jones's assistance, worked hard all that day and through the night. Miss Hughes did not know, nor do I think she cared, what we were about, nor did she speak a word with either of us. I ought to have said that, immediately after Abel's death, she handed all his keys to me, perfectly heedless of what she was about, and ready to die with her brother. Once I began the task I never rested until I had made an inventory of the whole stock. Abel, with but few exceptions, giving his customers no credit, it was no difficult matter to speedily set the shop books to rights. At the end of twenty-four hours I had a pretty clear notion of the property my master had left behind him. As I was jotting down the very last item Jones perched himself on his stool, placed his head—which, for some time, had been swimming—upon the counter, and slept like a top. Under other circumstances I should have thought it very bold of me, but taking into account Miss Hughes's helplessness, and conscious, moreover, that my dead master was not frowning on me, I hesitated not in ransacking every cupboard, chest, and drawer that the place contained. I remember well, on opening one drawer in an oaken cupboard, wherein Abel kept his private papers, I remember, I say, the devil coming out of it, and he and I engaging in a very hard fight. In this drawer was a bundle of bank notes, and, said the devil to me: "Do you hear Jones snoring? Do you remember Abel's intention to endow you with a number of these? You know no memorandum of them has been kept, and, even if there had been it would be a very easy matter to destroy it. If you were to take two, or three, or four of them, it wouldn't be more than Abel would have given you, were he alive. It is exactly the same thing for you to take, as for Abel to have given them. It will be no theft at all, because, in a sense, you own some of them already. The probability is you won't have as much as a 'thank you' from Miss Hughes for all your trouble. Well, if you're not prepared to take two or three, take one—just one; you are certain Abel Hughes would have given you more. Remember you haven't a single shilling in your possession, and that it is impossible you can get along without money, so that whatever may be the sum taken *you* are sure to make good use of it."

With many other promptings did the Enemy attempt my overthrow; but, thank God! I remembered the armour wherewith my mother had clad me. Never in my life was it of such use as now. Sheathed in it, I made the Devil flee. After completing my self-imposed task, I went to talk to Miss Hughes with an easy conscience and with hands on which there was no hair—considerations of greater value than millions of money. My reception was cool and unconcerned, but I cared not for that. I addressed her, as far as I can recollect, in these words:

" Miss Hughes, it was unnecessary you should have reminded me of all your kindness towards me, because I never forgot it, for one day. I know you think me hard-hearted for leaving you and going to college. But I fancy you believe me honest, or else you wouldn't have trusted so much under my hands, neither would I have done what I did. I have reason to believe that you know nothing of the situation you have been left in by the death of my master. It is surprising to me that so sagacious a man should have kept this knowledge from you, and more surprising still that he never made a will. Without asking your permission, I have entered upon a tolerably minute inquiry into his circumstances, and I find that, after paying all his creditors my master died possessed of property which—including stock, money on the books, in the bank and in the house—amounts to about fifteen hundred pounds. This will be sufficient to support you comfortably, assuming you live to old age; and my advice is—you can reject it if you like—that you sell the stock and business. I think I know a friend who would willingly take everything off your hands. But as for my staying here to look after the business—that is out of the question. I am determined to go to college; and I am certain that if you could only consult my old master, he would tell you that I am doing right."

My words acted like magic on her; her sourness melted like snow on a slate in the sunshine, only much more quickly. She looked incredulous one moment, satisfied and tender, as her wont, the next; for she and I had been great friends always.

"I spoke nasty things to you, Rhys," she observed. "I did not know what I was saying. You'll forgive me, won't you? I always did like you; you know that yourself. You have more sense than I. Poor Abel used to say, when you were a boy, that you could twist me round your fingers. You know best, and I'll do as you tell me. If I got anyone here in your place, he would only rob me; what do you think? I have known, this long while, you wanted to go to Bala; so I won't try to stop you. You'll get there everything you want, and you'll be just in your element. Must you go next week? Can't you make it a fortnight? What'll you have for dinner? Shall I stew some kidneys for you?" &c., &c.

"Simple woman!" something whispered to me. "Ask her for that which you are bound to have—money." "I will not," said I. "No; independence is worth something, and I shall not ask her for a penny piece, although I'm sure she would not deny me, were I to do so." It was quite clear she knew no more about the college than did Thomas Bartley, and that she regarded it as next door to heaven, where they neither wived, nor ate, nor drank. Poor old thing! If she enquired she would have found that the students were guilty of one and the other of all these things, to a greater degree or less. Thomas Bartley and Miss Hughes were not the only ones, it seemed, who fancied Bala a place flowing with milk and honey, and that once a young man

got there he was all right. For anything I know, not a single
member of the church to which I belonged had the slightest
objection to my going to college. Monthly Meeting had
unanimously desired me to go. But, Thomas Bartley excepted,
no one living asked me what my prospects were of supporting
myself there, although they must have known I had not, at
the time, lost as much as one of my teeth. I do not mention
this in any carping spirit. The only man, so I imagined, who
realised the importance of the enterprise which a poor youth
embarked upon whon he went to college, was Abel Hughes;
and he, by this time, was in his grave. For all that, I resolved
to challenge Providence. Was the challenge accepted? We
shall see. I considered it my duty to do all I could for Miss
Hughes before leaving her. To cut the story short, I succeeded,
with the help of a man experienced in such affairs, in making
arrangements for the transfer of the business to the friend who
was anxious to get it. I reckoned Miss Hughes, after all had
been settled, would be worth about fourteen hundred pounds,
or about a hundred less than my original estimate. In view of
the present contingency, I had arranged with the buyer to
consider little Jones as part of the fixtures; a transaction
which eased a good deal the load my mind had laboured under
ever since the night when Will Bryan and I came so near to
hanging the miserable creature.

In the midst of hunting up my effects and packing my books
into an old tea chest, I several times stood stock-still and
dumb, while something said *to* me: "What a fool you are to
throw up a good place, refuse a capital salary, and lose the
chance of one day becoming a prosperous trader. You must
be mad!" But then, something else, *within* me, said: "What
does it matter? The 'old pockets' may have all the business
and money, for my part, if I can, in any way, get to college,
and pick up some sort of a living there." I believed my
intention was simple and straightforward, and, further, that
Providence would not allow me to starve. I knew if I told my
best friends of my poverty, they would have cordially helped
me; but I could not stoop to that. It was a Friday night, and
I was to leave for College on the following Monday. I had
no engagement to preach on the Sunday, having refused

to enter into one, lest I might be obliged to go to college in the
meantime—for which I was now sorry. I remembered Will
Bryan's observation about my being "poor and proud." But
I could not help it. I had inherited this stupid independence
from my mother, and I prayed earnestly for help to keep it,
because it had become very precious in my sight. On the
Friday night, Providence appeared fully bent upon humbling me
to the dust and compelling me to do what I had never done
before, namely, to ask the loan of a sovereign which I had no
prospect of paying back. Of whom should I borrow? There
was only one man on earth I had the temerity to apply to, and
that was Thomas Bartley. As far as he was concerned, I felt as
if the sovereign were in my hand before I had asked for it; and
he was so ingenuous, methought, that I could, with some confidence, preserve my dignity in the borrowing. Thomas was
evidently the man. But I resolved not to ask even Thomas
until the last hour, lest I should be forestalling Providence;
for I strove hard to believe that it would take care of me.

These thoughts were hovering about my mind when Miss
Hughes knocked at the door of my room and came in, saying,
" Rhys, William Williams, the deacon at Blaenycwm, wants to
see you." I was down in the kitchen before you could have
counted ten, although I had counted a hundred things in the
interval. William was a noble old fellow, whose errand was
to get me to preach at Cwm on the Sunday, the Rev. ———
" having broken his appointment, without giving any reason
for so doing." My back went up on the instant. I never remember, save that time, rejoicing to find a man break an
engagement. But, the sly dog I was! I advanced several
weighty reasons why I could not come to Cwm, the chief being
that I was going to college on the following morning. But
William urged that that was the very reason why I should
accept the invitation, adding that he would take care I was
sent home on the Sunday night. After much persuasion I
gave the promise required. I had, it will be seen, learned early
how to bluff in negotiating an engagement, but, thank goodness! I speedily learned to give over the habit. I now felt
Providence was beginning to smile upon me. I was in
excellent spirits on the Sabbath, at night especially, while

being conveyed home with half a sovereign in my pocket. I believed, nevertheless, it would be prudent for me to borrow the sovereign of Thomas Bartley, so that I might have "something to fall back on." Thomas and Barbara promised to come to the station on Monday morning to bid me good-bye. While at breakfast the thought struck me, what if Thomas hadn't a sovereign in his pocket? On consideration, it was not likely that Thomas carried any gold about him, well off though I knew him to be. It was clear I must visit the Tump to make sure of my loan. I accordingly hurried through with breakfast, there being only a couple of hours to spare before the train started.

"Why do you eat so fast?" Miss Hughes asked.

"The time is short," I replied.

"You remember, Rhys," she said, "that I shall expect you to spend your Christmas holidays with me, if you're not too proud. I will keep your bed for you, for by that time I shall have gone to live to 'the Cottage.'"

I thanked her, and began to fancy Providence was now setting to work in earnest.

"Were there any wages due to you from Abel?" she queried.

"None," I responded. "I got my money in advance, a month ago, up to last Saturday."

"Here," she rejoined; "I know you'll find everything you want in college; but p'r'aps you won't get much pocket money. Here's five pounds for you, if you'll accept 'em."

I came near shouting Hallelujah! The tears sprang into my eyes, and in order to hide them, I coughed at a terrible rate, as if a bread-crumb had gone down the wrong way. I thanked Miss Hughes heartily for a kindness which she, I knew, rejoiced to find I had not refused. There was no necessity now for going to the Tump and asking the loan of a sovereign. I was thoroughly set up, and as merry as a lark, in consequence. I parted with Miss Hughes on the most excellent terms. And, to tell the truth, I did that which I had not done for many years—since, in fact, my wicked days, when I wanted a shilling—I gave her wrinkled cheek a kiss; and, amidst the tears and sobs of the kindly, simple old soul, who bade me be sure to write her, I too, as Will Bryan said, made my exit.

I felt very happy on the morning I first left home, for two reasons. To begin with, it seemed as if Providence were clearly showing its approval of my resolution to go to college; and secondly, I had strong grounds for believing that I had a warm place in the affections of numerous friends who came to wish me farewell. Not the least amongst these were David Davis and Thomas and Barbara Bartley. Whenever the Bartleys went away by train they took care to be at the station at least an hour before the appointed time. Although I had come that morning quite fifteen minutes earlier than was necessary, Thomas protested that I was within an ace of losing the train. Barbara sat upon a hamper on the platform, punctuating, with a nod of the head, every paragraph of her husband, who spoke unceasingly; I trying to take in every word he said, thinking it would afford matter of amusement for my fellow-lodger at Bala, whoever he might be. When the train came in, I shook hands with the friends and with Barbara, who was too tired to get up from the hamper, I thought. As soon, however, as I was seated in the carriage, she jumped up to her feet, and Thomas, taking hold of the hamper, swung it on to the seat beside me, saying, softly, in my ear: "It's for you, that is. Take care of it, and remember, directly we hear of a cheap trip to Bala, Barbara'n I are bound to come and see how you are." And before I could say a word, Thomas was powdering his way out of the station, with Barbara leaning upon his arm.

I was overwhelmed; and yet the act was Thomas Bartley's all over. I felt certain the hamper contained valuable treasure to the young man of hearty appetite. But I showed no curiosity to know its contents (as I might have done by trying its weight or putting my nose to the cover for a sniff), there being another young man—my sole fellow-traveller—in the same compartment, whom I did not want to see that I was not perfectly cognisant of the nature of my prize. We were whisked along towards Corwen. Presently I began taking stock of my fellow-traveller. I do not know whether other people have felt the same—perhaps they have, foolish though the feeling be —but in travelling by train, let the number of those in the same compartment be what it may, the impression will cross my mind, after I have been in their company for a short time, that I have seen them somewhere previously, and ought to know them. Of course, this is only a delusion, and I do not know how to account for it. Do we, I wonder, segregate faces—classify them—and, on coming into the presence of strangers and looking at them a while, do we, unawares, single them out as belonging to one section or the other? And do we, after much staring, fancy we ought to know the unit, the individual, by the class to which he belongs? I cannot tell. I felt sure I ought to know my fellow-traveller, although common sense told me I had never seen him before. I guessed him to be three or four years older than myself. He was white-skinned, jet black-haired and eyebrowed, wore homespun clothes, and, I believed, hailed from Carnarvonshire. He had a book in his hand, which, however, he did not read, for he looked sadly out of window—not on the landscape I was certain—but at something else unknown to me; possibly his home, his family, or uncertain future. For some time he seemed wrapped in the profoundest study. I burned with a desire to speak to him. I was sure, in my own mind, of the sort of voice he had, and entertained no doubt whatever but that he was a Welshman. Presently I remarked, in English, that the weather was delightful. He answered, in the same language, but with a decidedly Welsh accent. He evinced no desire to enter into a conversation, for which I was sorry, because I liked his face very much and, however idle might be the notion, felt that my fellow passenger's spirit and mine had consorted before ever we saw each other in the flesh. Speedily I, like himself, became absorbed in my own thoughts. We both got out at Corwen, which at that time was the farthest place we could go to by train. I had secured my precious hamper, and was looking after my box and tea-chest, which were in the van, and had my name on them, when someone tapped me lightly on the shoulder and said, "Mr. Lewis, is that your hamper, Sir?"

"Yes," replied I; "what about it?"

"Oh, nothing," he returned, "only I wanted to take care of it for you. What's up? Is there a strike? There's only two of you come to-day, and I'd made sure of having a good

z

load. That's the way with you students; you always do things drib-drab, instead of clubbing together and making one job of it. Have you anything else besides these two boxes and the hamper?"

At first I could not make him out. He was a burly, cheerful, bold-looking man, and yet his boldness became him. It would be difficult to guess whether he was butcher, farmer, or horse-dealer. However, I soon discovered that he wished to convey me and my things to Bala. I asked him how came he to know it was to Bala I was bound?

"Man alive," he returned, "even if I hadn't read the address on your box I should have known you, directly. I could pick a student, and any sort of a Methodist preacher, out of a thousand. I am so used to them, Sir. D'ye know, I spotted the other one and clapped him into the coach before you could look about you?"

"Here's a wonderful man for you," said I to myself. "I never knew till now that I was like a student; and how can I be, since I never was at Bala?"

All the same, I was not sorry that this man, whoever he was, should have taken me for a student. I followed him as a dog does his master. I saw at once that my angel was very well known. From the greetings he got I found his name to be E——. I noticed that, here and there, one who was pretty free with him would address him by the name of the stuff which they often make pudding with. I did not know, at the time, whether this was his proper or a nick name. When he had led me to his conveyance, I was surprised at perceiving that "the other one," Mr. E——, had spoken of was my serious fellow-traveller by train. So, this "other one" was going to college, like myself! What a pity I did not know it sooner! How had Mr. E—— found it out directly he saw him, while I had been in his company for some time and the fact had never once crossed my mind? I consoled myself with the reflection that "the other one" was as dense as I was. While Mr. E—— was putting my luggage into his coach, I cast my eye upon the horses, my first impression of them being that there was no danger of their running away and leaving us behind. I was in a bit of a fix as to whether they were frames of new horses which had not acquired flesh and become

perfected, or whether they were old horses on the eve of vanishing. Although not much acquainted with horse flesh, I
fancied, after looking them well over, that the sharply defined
points of these brutes proclaimed them to belong to the vanishing class. A minute inspection of them resolved itself into
this: "New horses," I thought, "would not be wise enough to
take advantage of a respite to indulge in a nap; therefore
these must be old." I noticed that one of them smiled in his
sleep, as if dreaming of the time when they fed him on oats,
while the other started up, now and again, in terror, as if he had
just become aware that the tanner was taking aim at him
with a gun. It suddenly struck me that, as I had heard the
students did, they, too, perhaps, "lived on very little." My
fellow-passenger was already seated in the coach, lost in contemplation once more. Mr. E—— was not very ready to
start with so small a cargo. After much fussing, inquiring,
searching and haggling, he succeeded at last in luging a
couple of old women on board. As an apology for the delay,
he said to me, when I was taking my place beside him on the
dickey—"We must have a bit of ballast, you know, Mr.
Lewis, or we shan't be safe." It was one of the most marvellous things I ever saw. The crack of Mr. E——'s whip, accompanied by a guttural sound, not unlike a curse, had the
effect upon those horses, literally, of the cry above the dry
bones! The poor creatures were instantly all life, their dread
of the driver being such that they would rather have dropped
stone dead on the roadside than disobey him.

"They are excellent things to go, Mr. E——," I remarked.

"That just depends on who is driving them, Sir," he returned. "The students complain shockingly that it is impossible to make them move. See here;" and once more Mr.
E—— uttered that fearful guttural sound and used the
whip unsparingly. The horses strained themselves to the
utmost, panting in the back with fright, as I have seen animals do at the unexpected burst of a thunderclap.

"It is I, Sir," added Mr. E——, "who lets out horses to
the students for Sunday appointments. And if they were only
to do as I tell them, the creatures would go the pace fast

enough. But they are too quiet by half; these students are.
Do you know what? Every horse I've got can tell a student
from another man. They know students are preachers, and
take liberties with them in consequence. There's no use in
being too particular, Sir; if you want horses to go you must
———— them. *Fnogodariochiwaliaid!*[*] D'ye see how they step
out, now? Where are you going to preach next Sunday? I
should think you'll want a horse. You come to me on Friday
night. What! no engagement? You're sure to get one, next
Sunday, 'cause half the students won't have come back, and
there'll be lots of letters wanting preachers, you shall see. I
know all about these things, Sir. Have you been to Bala
before? Where are you going to lodge?"

It would be impossible for me to describe, accurately and in
detail, the information and guidance I got from Mr. E————, in
the course of the drive from Corwen to Bala—all of burning
interest, and all eagerly drunk in. He gave me the history of
the family I was going to lodge with, from top to toe. Without my asking him but few questions, he outlined for me, in
his own peculiar fashion, the principal characters of the town.
Before I had reached my journey's end I knew who lived at
Rhiwlas, at the Big Bull, the Little Bull, the White Lion,
Plâs Coch, and Post Office; the names of the chapel deacons,
the doctors of divinity and medicine, and of many others. But
what he loved to dwell upon was the students. He knew them
all personally, the counties they came from, and with whom they
lodged. He said of one that " he was a cure;" of another that
" he had nothing at all in him;" and of a third, that he
was " a bit of a swell," &c. He told me several stories
about them, with every one of which his own horses had something to do. I considered Mr. E———— a very entertaining
character, and I am certain I never in my life learned so much
in so short a time. I liked him for taking such interest in the
students. I failed to discover whether he was a religionist or
not, and I thought it would be impertinent to ask. His in-
timate acquaintance with the chapel people and cause, and his

---

[*] Our Jehu's guttural objurgation to his cattle. The wary English
reader will, doubtless, make no more attempt to pronounce than I did to
translate the word.—TRANSLATOR.

knowledge of the collegians, made me think he was; but when he addressed the horses, parenthetically as it were, with his "Ynogodariochiwaliaid," I feared he was not. Little did I suspect at the time I should have so much to do with Mr. E—— during my stay at Bala. There quickens in my memory at this moment many an interesting occurrence connected with him which would afford a fat pasture of amusement for the students' rack, and the noting of which would have been a special pleasure to me. But inasmuch as it is not a memoir of Mr. E—— that I am engaged on, I must leave that to an abler hand. Is it possible that in a world so full of sighs, and with so much harmless but effective material for driving away melancholy, nobody acquainted therewith will take in hand the setting forth in due order the character of one who differed so much from his fellows, and who, in his own way, was so eminently serviceable to Methodism?

Such was the attention I paid to our driver that I clean forgot my fellow-traveller. Not so Mr. E——, who, before we reached Tryweryn bridge, looked over his shoulder, and said, "Mr. Williams, where'r you going to lodge?" And, upon receiving a reply, "How lucky! you're both going to the same house. We'll set these petticoats [alluding to the women], down on the bridge." The occurrence was much more "lucky," in my sight, because I felt a great interest in my taciturn fellow-student. A few minutes later he and I were sitting in a small and sombre parlour, with the housewife—a joyous, kindly, little Welshwoman—preparing tea for us, and telling us that we were the only students in Bala on that day. "But," said she, "they'll all be here, I think, in a week, or a fortnight at the latest."

When two men meet, of similar mind and purpose, knowing they are likely to live together for some years, but the scantiest ceremony is necessary to bring about a mutual understanding and confidence. Needless to say, Mr. Williams and myself got to know much of each other within the half hour, and that we had become old friends before the students mustered in anything like force. Mr. Williams hailed from Carnarvonshire, and was, as his face proclaimed him to be, an honest, serious, straightforward young fellow. It is not for me to say how he felt; but as for me, I counted myself happy and fortunate in, for the first time, being brought into contact with one who understood me, one who trod the same path, was possessed of the like aim, and combatted the same difficulties, one with whom I could converse without reserve and without fear of his making a laughing-stock of me. Although older by some years than myself, I felt sure that I was the better Englishman, and knew more of the way of the world, for which I was indebted to Will Bryan and the place I was brought up in. After a little talk, however, I found he was the better divine, and I knew, before I heard him, that he was the better preacher also. So he was, and so he is to-day, an infinitely better preacher than I. They are rare hands at preaching, these Carnarvon boys. It is my opinion that the more English the place he is reared in, the worse preacher a man makes, and *vice versâ.* Williams came up exactly to that which I had dreamt my fellow-lodger would be. I cannot help acknowledging my great indebtedness to him. One occurrence comes fresh to mind, and I cannot refrain from laughter in recalling it. I think I have already stated that Abel Hughes always took care I dressed well. The day I went to Bala I had on a good suit of black clothes. While freely conversing with me, I saw that Williams was making careful note of my attire, and speaking as if he were thinking of something else. I guessed correctly what was transpiring in the ante-room of his mind. After taking a stroll to view the town and lake, and as we were recommencing our conversation by the—, I had almost said fire, only I remembered that Bala folk do not believe in fire as early in the year as we did in ——shire—Williams said,—

"Mr. Lewis (he had not yet begun to call me Rhys, nor I to call him Jack), I am afraid we are a little unsuitably yoked. It's best I should tell you the truth at once: I am but a poor lad. Mother, a widow, is dependent on me, and what troubles me mostly to-night is, did I do right by leaving her? It is plain to me that you are of a respectable, well-to-do family ——"

Before he could say another word I had exploded with laughter.

"Mr. Williams," I remarked, "I'm a bit of a bard. And

do you know my *nom de plume ?* ' Job on the Dunghill.'
You've seen the name, many times, of course. I am the very
party, sir; " whereupon I gave him a compendium of my family
history (excluding my father and "the Irishman" from the
relationship), and of my resources, actual and probable.
Strange to relate, Williams became perfectly happy on hearing of my poverty! In order to convince him I was telling the truth, I narrated the story of the hamper which
he had helped me to carry into the house. In further con-
firmation, did not he and I fetch the hamper into the parlour,
and overhaul its contents ? And did we not, that night, get
additional proof of what was in it, and so on, day by day, until
we saw the bottom ?

And, lest I should forget to mention it again, let me here
say, that the twain whose hearts' were gladdened by the good
things of that hamper, never, during their stay in college, saw
the day that they had not a meal they could go to. They both,
I shall believe, placed their trust in the loving care of the
Master, and were not disappointed.

CHAPTER XXXVII.

THOMAS BARTLEY VISITS BALA.

BEFORE starting from home I had, foolishly enough, I am
aware, formed a most extraordinary notion of college life, and
one which I hardly know how to describe. Cognisant of the
fact that the students were almost without exception preachers,
I pictured them in my mind as a set of staid, serious and
melancholy young men, gathered together from different parts
of Wales, whose aggregation weighted and deepened each other's
individual gloom. I fancied what was called the term to be a four
months' funeral, at which forty youthful invitees, more or less,
all in mourning, were engaged listening to the Principal, or
one of his assistants, reading the Burial Service above the dead
languages, the resultant blessing being derivable I knew not
whence or how. So ran my notion; and not so either, it was

much more vague. But O, how disappointed I was! I speedily found that the students could laugh and make merry like other lads; that they could enjoy a bit of harmless fun and unbend themselves without bruising their conscience. Indeed, I have thought, many times, that had Will Bryan been present, he would have said there was no "humbug" about them, and that they were "true to nature." I quickly learned that melancholy and piety were not the same thing, that there was a vast difference between sanctimony and sincerity, and that the most natural, free and careless youths— in the best¦ sense of those words—were the most guileless and true. I know two birds who wear coats of the same colour as the preacher's—the crow and the blackbird. One croaks and the other sings, but I am not, even yet, convinced that it is the crow which gives the Creator the greater glory, its more numerous, more commonly occurring progeny notwithstanding. But I often could not help asking myself, what if David Davis were to hear and see us, students? Would he not say we were much too blithe-spirited, and that he had a doubt whether we had been called to preach the gospel? Had he been present, however, he would not have been allowed to see anything which did not come up to his ideal of the sedate. But would he have seen the boys? No; only the special aspect they chose, for the time being, to wear. What was the inference I drew? This: that never was student seen save by student. Is it not a general fact that to be able to feel free, natural and unstrained, you must be conscious that the company is all of the same class and temperament. The presence of a David Davis causes man to draw the veil over a portion of himself, if not to do something worse, namely attempt to show that which he does not possess. Metaphorically speaking, has not every man, and every section of society, a David Davis, who compels the assumption of a special aspect? And have not the lower animals their David Davis? I find the sheep and the lambs frisking on the slope of the hill and revelling in enjoyment, after their manner and kind; but behold a David Davis, in the shape of a harmless little dog, approaching, and the play is instantly at an end. On a lovely morn in spring, the birds in the bush by the wayside warble sweetly, and the passing traveller pauses

to drink in their melody; but the warblers have seen him, and
their song has ceased. Ever David Davis. In the month of
June the attendants at the great smoky town's Sunday School
get a trip into the country. There are old and young in their
midst. After consuming their delicacies upon the grass, twenty
or more of the young people will be seen silently stealing away
to a spot apart to amuse themselves. Presently, in the course of
a stroll, some pious and revered old man comes in their way.
They know him well, think highly of him, and hope, some day,
to be as he is now; but his appearance spoils their sport.
David Davis! Is there not some freemasonry, or whatever it
may be called, running through all circles of society down
to the individual himself? Man is not wholly like himself
except when by himself. Under every other circumstance he
simply lays himself out to meet the eye and the notions of some
David Davis. Does it follow, therefore, that man never saw
other man than himself, and that he himself never saw himself
save when by himself? And does it follow that the oftener he
is by himself the better? Not the last, at any rate, I trust.

    •   •   •   •   •   •   •

How different soever Bala and the students were from what
I had imagined before seeing them, I am confident they were
still more so to my old friend Thomas Bartley when he paid me
a visit, which he did, if I remember rightly, after I had been
about two months at college. As a sort of fillip to my spirits,
and lest I should forget it, perhaps this is the place where I can
best give a brief account of that visit.

It was a Monday morning. I was returning from Trawsfynydd, where I had been to preach on the Sabbath. I had
stayed rather long at Rhyd-y-Fen drinking tea and eating
oaten bread, expecting a couple of friends by car who had been
preaching, one at Llan, Festiniog, and the other at Lampeter-
on-Gwynfryn. It was between one and two o'clock in the
afternoon when I reached Bala. On entering my lodgings, I
could hardly believe my own eyes! There sat Thomas Bartley
in my chair, the room filled with tobacco smoke, and Williams
sitting opposite him, his face all smiles, from ear to ear.
Thomas presented a comical appearance even to me, his old

acquaintance; and the more so because I had not seen him for
some time turning out in a blue dress coat. But I knew that
what most tickled Williams's fancy was my friend of the
Tump's shirt collar, which was simply prodigious. Had Thomas
blackened his face with burnt cork he would have made a perfect Christy Minstrel. It was only on special occasions that he
wore these great collars, when, I remember, my brother Bob
used to say that "Thomas Bartley had gone for coke again,"
the reference being to the habit the carters had of putting
crates to their trollies when hauling that particular material.
I feel convinced that this collar had its history, if I could only
get at it. It was famous! When Thomas wore it, as on the
day of his "club feast," one felt, somehow, it was the collar
that went to dinner, and that Thomas merely went to keep it
company. But though the collar was the chief thing, and its
owner only secondary, in comparison, still, the former served
as a sort of forerunner, for the collar would be seen for some
time before Thomas. I think I have already stated that
Thomas was high in the crown, and that his nose was long and
sharp, his chin receding deep into the neck, the configuration
of head and face reminding a student of a problem in Euclid.
But, as I have observed, I am almost certain that to Williams
the most striking feature about that get-up was the outrage-
ous collar which I noticed he was examining keenly. Indeed,
even I, who had seen it many times previously, could not help
admiring it, and admiring Thomas also, as I saw him nestling
within those ramparts as a man of easy circumstances may
be seen sunk within an easy arm chair. But I am digressing.
I marvelled, I say, to find Thomas Bartley in my room.

"Well, boy," he exclaimed, as if he had not seen me for ever
so long; "how be, these hundreds and thousands of years?"

"Right well, Thomas," I replied. "Who in the world
would have thought of seeing you in Bala?"

"To be shwar. Six o'clock this morning, look you, as I
was in the middle of feedin' the pig, the fit took me in the head
to come and see you. But I never thought Bala was so far.
D'ye know what? it's a goodish step from there here. I'd
always thought there was a train the whole way; but, when I
got to inquire, Corwen was the last station. Howsumever,

you never saw how lucky I was. At Corwen Mr. Williams
here knew me. I never thought he'd sin me before; but it
sims he had, in the station yonder, when you were goin' away.
I got a lift from a lot of students, and we had a real pleasant
chat, didn't we Mr. Williams? Wonderful tidy boys they
were too; but you are like each other, 'markable so. Where've
you bin so long, say? Mr. Williams told me you'd be here
some time since. Where were you at it yesterday?"

"Trawsfynydd, Thomas," said I.

"Trawsfynydd? Well, wait you, now; isn't it one from
there M—— Ll—— is? I thought so, too. He's a rare un,
M—— Ll—— is. I always said, if I happened to get into
trouble, it's M—— Ll—— I'd have for couns'ller. Did ye hear
of that time he was at Ruthin, Mr. Williams, a long while ago,
now? No? I'll tell you, then. It's as true as the Paternoster. Well, to you, there was a man there—'twas the time
of the 'Sizes—who was tried for stealin' bacon—bacon, mind.
They'd 'ployed Macintyre to prosecute, and he, poor chap, had
'ployed M—— Ll—— to defend him. Well, to you, Macintyre
was layin' and pitchin it on wonderful, and the man's case got
to look shockin' black. But, by'm bye, here comes M-——'s
turn; and he goes at it! He called a butcher forward, and
asked him what he meant by bacon? 'A pig's sides, salted
and dried,' says he. 'To be shwar,' says M——. Then he
calls the shopkeeper on and, says he, 'was the meat as you
say this man stole, was it dried and salted?' 'It wasn't,' says
the shopkeeper. 'False ditemant,' says M——; and he won
the case, straight off. He's a rare un, is M——. Tell me, is
there any of his fam'ly livin' at Trawsfynydd now? There is?
If I had time I'd go and see 'm, if I's never to move. D'ye
know what, boys? It's awful close here; open a bit of that
window, Rhys. It's no wonder in the world you both look so
pale; there isn't a breath of air here. You might's well live
in a bambox as in a snip of a room like this, with the door
shut and nothing in the blessed world in it but a table, chairs
and books. You're bound to lose health. If I was put in a
place like this for two days together I'd die, on the spot.
There! That's somethin' like; we'll have a puff of wind in a
minute. And how does it get on, Rhys? D'ye like your place?
Is there plenty of provijuns here?"

"It's got on very well up to now, Thomas," I returned. "How are they all with you? How is Barbara, and why didn't she come along?"

"Well, Barbara's only so, so; sure to you. She's troubled shockin' with the rheumatis and pains in the legs. I'd a hard scuffle to come here to-day, and she'll be very glad to see me back agen, I can tell you. She wished to be remembered to you, kindly. D'ye know what? I haven't bin from home, before, for five and twenty years."

"What do you think of Bala, Thomas?" I asked.

"I haven't seen much of it yet," replied Thomas. "But, from what I've seen, it looks, to my mind, very much like a town built in the middle of a field. Why on the blessed earth don't they cut those trees, there? Ain't the crows troublesome, sometimes? Never saw a row of big trees, like the Hall's, in the middle of the street before. I should fancy you've no Local Board here."

"Bala people think very much of their trees, Thomas Bartley, and place a very high value on them," observed Williams.

"Now I think of it, 'deed, Mr. Williams, I shouldn't wonder but what they're handy enough on fair days for tyin' cattle to. But they struck me as odd when I first saw 'em. Here you, Rhys, are you goin' to take me a bit about to see the town, say? I haven't much time, you know, and the house'll be on wires till I come back. Have you got time?"

"I think I have," I answered. "I'll show you as much as I can. I take it for granted, Thomas, you've had something to eat."

"Yes, name of goodness. I had dinner with Mr. Williams here, suffishant for any man; and I did oncommon hearty, I can tell you."

"Good," observed I. "After I've had a wash I'll show you around."

"A wash! What d'ye want to wash for? You're like a pin in paper; there isn't a speck on you. Are you gettin' a bit stuck up here, say?"

Williams laughed, and I ran away to perform my ablutions.

In a minute Williams followed me to my room, threw himself on the bed, and rolled about, laughing until his sides were sore.

"Rhys," said he, "this is about the most original character I've ever met with. The boys had a sovereign's worth of fun out of him between Corwen and Bala, and they charged me to be sure to tell you to keep him here as long as you can. Couldn't we smuggle him into the class, eh? It would be a perfect treat."

"That would not be quite the thing," I returned. "It is a bit of a nuisance to have to show him around. If the creature had left that collar of his at home, I wouldn't have minded so much. All the town will be staring at us."

"Rubbish!" rejoined Williams. "He'd be nothing at all without the collar. That collar is worth a hundred pounds. Shall I come with you? If you say yes, mathematics may go to Jericho for the afternoon."

"Shall you, indeed!" I exclaimed. "I was on the point of offering you five shillings to come and share the shame with me."

Descending to the parlour, we found Thomas on his feet, re-loading his pipe. Seeing us ready to start, he said, "Is Mr. Williams coming along? Well, clean shoe! Wait a bit, Rhys; I haven't seen you take anythin' to your mouth since I'm here. Have you had nothing to eat?"

"Yes, Thomas. I had a feed at Rhyd-y-Fen."

"Rhyd-y-Fen—where's that? Is it far?"

"Rhyd-y-Fen is a public house half way between Bala and Festiniog," I replied.

"What! What!" cried Thomas. "Do they, in the north country, 'low you preachers to go to pubs? There's no harm in the thing, in my opinion, and I always used to say Abel Hughes was too strict in such matters. But let's be off, boys;" and Thomas lit his pipe.

"Perhaps it would be as well for you not to smoke going through the town," I remarked.

"Where's the harm?" asked mine ancient. "Are you so stuck up as all that in Bala?"

"There's no harm in the thing, that I know of, Thomas," I replied; "only respectable people don't do it here."

"'Deed! And I had heard you were awful smokers here! But, whatever, as that man from the South said, let's go and look what we can see. I want you to show me three things — Bala Green, that your mother ever and always used to talk about; the lake and the clock. I heard my father, hundreds of times, say of a safe thing that it was as right as Bala clock."

"We'll go and see the lake first, Thomas," said I, for I was anxious to pass quickly through the town in the direction of Llanycil, so as to escape notice. But that was a bigger job than I had thought. Thomas insisted on stopping to look at everything. Standing in the middle of the road, his hands under his coat-tails and his hat tilted back upon his nape, he shouted, " Rhys, wait a bit! Let's take breath, boy! Well, these trees do look funny, stuck in the street, if I was never to move! Here's a slap-up pub; what's it's name, Rhys?"

" The White Lion," I said softly, and as a hint to Thomas to pitch his remarks in the same key.

" Oh, White Lion," he rejoined at the top of his voice.

People stopped to stare at us. Shopkeepers came to their doors, children crowded round us, and I felt certain, in my own mind, that from Thomas's great collar and strange appearance, they all expected to see him form a ring and turning somersaults in front of the hotel. I did not know what to do, for shame. I felt angry with Williams who enjoyed as much the fix I was in as he did the doings of Thomas Bartley, to whose side he stuck close. Moving on, I heard Thomas cry out "What's the matter with you, children? What are you gapin' at? Did you never see a man before? These are the strangest lot I ever set eyes on. I hard a deal of talk about ' little Bala children.' D'ye know what? If you don't get away, I'll put my stick across your backs; that I will! Rhys, what's your hurry? Is it all one street this town is, Mr. Williams? I don't see anythin' particular about it. The shops are nothin' to speak of, and the whole place looks quiet enough. I'd always thought Bala was a town full of chapels, churches, clocks and schools. D'ye know what, Mr. Williams, here's another awful nice public. What's the name of this?"

" The Big Bull," responded Williams.

Page 367.

"Rather a queer name, isn't it, Mr. Williams? Do you at Bala talk like they do at Bulkeley, tell us? Little bit of Welsh and a little bit of English, mixed. Holloa, Squire! Got him at last, you see. Can you give me a light?"

This "Squire" was Mr. Rice Edwards, who stood on the pavement in front of his house smoking. Thomas Bartley crossed over to him, Williams followed, and I went slowly on. After going a few steps I looked back and saw a strange sight. Mr. Edwards and Mr. Bartley looked like a couple of pigeons pairing. The peaks of the great collar and Mr. Edwards's eyes were in dangerous proximity, while the bowl of Thomas's pipe was held on that of Edwards's. The latter was blowing, his cheeks puffed out as if he were playing a bugle, whilst the former was drawing, his cheeks panting in a way which clearly showed he had lost his jaw teeth. I perceived that the great object in view was to light Thomas Bartley's pipe, and I perceived also that Williams was holding his sides in enjoyment of the spectacle. My advice to Thomas not to smoke in the streets had been given in vain. I heard him first whistle and then shout to me: "Take time, man; the end of the world hasn't come yet." I was in a hurry to get out of the town, where everybody was leering at us, and grew terribly savage with Williams for wilfully prolonging the hob-nobbing between Mr. Edwards and Thomas Bartley, which latter, after he had lit his pipe, seemed perfectly at ease. I walked rapidly ahead, like one distracted. Presently, I heard Thomas, at some distance behind, talking away in the old loud tone.

"Baptist chapel, did you say, Mr. Williams? Ho! Not much of a place, is it? Don't suppose they thrive very well, here? To be shwar. I don't, myself, like their way of doin' things, at all. Only think, now, of dippin' some one like my Barbara yonder, troubled with rheumatis and pain in the legs; wouldn't it be enough for her life? Yes, name of goodness. I've hard— I don't know if it's true—but I hard that in a case of that sort they warms the water; only that, to my mind, looks too much like killin' a pig. I much rather the Methodis' way; though 'twas in Church I was christened, in the year—let me see, now—I forget, but it's down in father's Bible—all our names is. Rhys, do you want to cut us, say?"

For all my old friend's extraordinary appearance and the notice it attracted, I would not have cared so much if he had not continued to talk in a shout. I was heartily glad when, at length, we got clear of the town. No sooner, however, was I rid of one trouble than I found myself in another. When we were some hundred yards or so outside the town Williams gave me a dig in the ribs with his elbow, and motioned me to look ahead. I saw, coming to meet us, one of our teachers, who had been taking his customary stroll. "Out of the frying pan into the fire," I muttered, after which I began thinking how we could pass without more than a lift of the hat, when Thomas said :—

"Here, you boys; who's this man comin' to meet us? Isn't he the master?"

"Yes sure," replied Williams readily enough.

"I thought so, too," rejoined Thomas. "And a proper man he is, sure enough. They tell me he's very clever, and knows a heap of languages. I should think he does—a man can tell that by his looks. I've heard he's the best man of the lot when it comes to a push. I never heard him preach but twice, and I liked him oncommon. I understood every word of his sermon, 'cause he gave a man time to consider—not like John Hughes, Llangollen, poundin' away without hop or stop, and leavin' you behind, you didn't know where. I never saw anythin' so lucky! I must have a talk with him, so that I might have somethin' to tell Barbara when I get home."

"His time is short, Thomas," I observed, "so perhaps we had better pass him with only a 'good afternoon.'"

"No danger," said Williams. "You may be sure, Thomas Bartley, he'll be glad to speak to you, since you're a stranger to Bala. And if you were to ask to be allowed to visit the college, I'm certain he'd give you permission, in which case you'd have much more to relate after going home."

"To be shwar," cried Thomas.

I felt mad enough to choke Williams, which he perfectly well knew. I saw it was no use trying to persuade Thomas to forego his intention, since Williams was determined to egg him on. I fairly dripped with sweat, Williams with amusement. Even had Thomas Bartley not been in the com-

pany of a couple of students, I knew his appearance would attract the attention of our respected teacher, whose face, long before we came up to him, gave indications of that sense of humour which the truly great-minded almost invariably possess. Without giving me a chance to introduce him, my old friend strode forward, hat in hand. and said :—

" How're you this long time, sir ? I havent seen you since the *Secession* over yonder; and that's years ago now; though you look just the same as ever, sir."

" Mr. Thomas Bartley, sir; one of our members who has come to see Bala," said I.

" Very good," returned our Teacher. " I am pleased to see you, Mr. Bartley. I hope you're pleased with Bala."

" You can't think how little I've seen of it yet, sir; only one street. But I should fancy, from what I've come across, it is a fairish place."

" How is the cause getting on with you, these days, Mr. Bartley? You had a great loss in the death of Mr. Abel Hughes."

" Capital, sir, capital ! For some time after Abel died it was all higgledypiggledy with us, but by now it's come purty straight, everythin' considered. When're you comin' over our way to preach agen, sir? I'd like, awful, to hear you, 'cause I understand every word you say. And I wish very much you'd teach these young people to preach a little more plain—they're too deep for me and my sort. D'ye know what, sir? There was one of 'em there lately and I couldn't make sward or thatch of him. He spoke of ' mechanism ' or ' unity,' or somethin'—I don't remember the word, for certain—and Barbara 'n I could make neither horse-hair nor hobgoblin of what he said. I protested before David Davis I'd tell you sir, the very first time I saw you."

" Well, indeed, Mr. Bartley, I have talked a deal to them on the subject. What we want is for some one, like yourself and others, with influence, to give them a word of advice, and give it often. It would do them a lot of good."

" To be shwar, sir," observed Thomas. " I thought of askin' you, sir, would it be anythin' out of your way to let me see the college when you are all at it ?"

2 A

"Well, perhaps Mr. Lewis will bring you to class at five o'clock, Mr. Bartley."

"Thank you very much, sir; and good afternoon now, whatever," said Thomas.

Hardly had we separated before Thomas turned upon his heel and shouted:

"Mr. ——; beg your pardon, sir; but have you such a thing as a match about you? To be shẁar. I don't know how in the world I came to leave home without one.

I heard no more, and was afraid to turn my head. I was fairly boiling over with vexation, and ready to sink into the earth, Williams being equally ready to split his sides when Thomas, on rejoining him, said: "No, he hadn't one. He doesn't carry any, or I should have one and welcome, he said. But I'm bound to get a light somewhere, before long. Is there a house handy? D'ye know what? He's a very decent man, is that master of yours. I rather 'n a crown he gived me leave to come to college to see you at it. I shall have so much more to tell Barbara when I go home."

My debt to Thomas Bartley was a heavy one, but I would have been quite willing to give every farthing I possessed to see him turning homewards at that moment. After that permission to visit class, I did not know what humiliation was in store for me. It would have appeared inhospitable had I told him that if he came to the college he would not get home that night. In my native place I could have enjoyed the fun very well; but in Bala it made me wretched, for I felt as if he were my father. Although I strove to look cheerful, Thomas as declared I was very much down in the mouth, and was sure I felt annoyed about something. Williams, on the other hand, was at the zenith of bliss, Thomas and he being whip and top together, the whole time. He undertook with alacrity the duty of showing Thomas "the lions," and I knew he was delighted with the matter of fact way Thomas regarded them all. When we got into a good position for a full view of the lovely sheet of water for which Bala is famous, the most poetic sentiments which fell from Thomas were: "D'ye know what, Mr. Williams? This here lake wouldn't make a bad sea, at a pinch. I should think there must be a deal of fish in it. What fly do you use? Cock-a-bundy? I never in my life saw a finer place for rarin' ducks."

He refused to visit Llanycil churchyard because, said he, all churchyards were alike. They only made him think of Seth; and besides, he wanted to return to Bala to see the clock. Williams went to the trouble of explaining to him that it was in the imagination alone the famous clock had its existence; at any rate, he and I had failed to find it.

"Ho!" remarked Thomas. "A bit of a skit, p'r'aps; same as people say that the best thing for mendin' bruises is snails' feet oil."

I strove hard to delay our return, with a view to prevent my old neighbour and protector from visiting the class; but Williams was one too many for me. He took care to land us back at our lodgings by half past four, when, so I afterwards understood, he had ordered tea to be ready. Viewing the preparations which Williams had bespoken, I saw that he had only done what I ought to have done, namely, given Thomas Bartley a welcome. I felt ashamed at my remissness, of which I was glad Thomas was not aware. I saw there was a danger of his thinking our "provijuns,' as he called them, better than they really were, and that he would bruit the fact abroad, for there was really no stop to his tongue. Hardly had the thought crossed my mind before Thomas said: "D'ye know what, boys? You live like fightin' cocks. But there, you'll never do anythin' better, for unless a man gets purty good feedin' he may as well shove his cards into the thatch." Thomas little suspected it was a "club feast" we were having that day.

The meal was over in a few minutes, and Williams insisted upon going to class at once, his object, I knew, being to give the boys an inkling of Thomas Bartley's personality before the Teacher came. But I beat him this time.

"Thomas wants a smoke, first," I observed.

"To be shwar," said Thomas, "if there's time."

Williams, however, saw that we were in class at five o'clock to the minute. It was the class for Greek Testament study. Although we freshmen understood no Greek, we got, nevertheless, all the advantages of exposition in a language we did understand. Nearly the whole body of students, therefore,

attended.   The gathering that evening was a fairly numerous
one.   We were greeted on our entrance with deafening cheers,
and I saw at once that Thomas Bartley's fellow-travellers, between Corwen and Bala, had been " up to their games again,"
as Williams would say.   I had an unpleasant consciousness
that it was not for Thomas personally the cheers were intended, but for his mighty collar.

Thomas gracefully bowed his acknowledgments, thereby
eliciting another cheer, and then sat down, between Williams
and myself.   Williams almost immediately got to his feet, and
said, " Mr. Thomas Bartley, gentlemen, a friend of Mr. Rhys
Lewis's ——," but before he could say another word, the
Teacher came in ; and lo, a great silence fell over all.

" D'ye know ? " murmured Thomas in my ear.   " There's a
wonderful lot of you, and you *are* so much alike ; all 'cept that
man with the crooked nose.   What is he ?   A pupil teacher ? "

Thomas nodded to the Teacher as if he were an old chum.
The nod was courteously responded to, and the Teacher turned
his face away.   I noticed the back of his neck flushed crimson,
as if suddenly sunburnt.   The work of the class was proceeded
with for about twenty minutes.   For the first five, Thomas
looked on curiously and critically, like a man who adjudicates
in a musical competition ; for the next five, he seemed a bit
patronising ; during the third, he gave signs of considerable
uneasiness, and said to me, softly : " Will you be much longer ? "   After that he subsided into his great collar, whence I
feared every moment he would snore.   The boys all the time
kept throwing furtive glances at Thomas, Williams and myself, and making faces which spoke volumes.   I much feared,
I repeat, that Thomas would begin to snore, and possibly it
was the like fear that made the Teacher, at the expiration of
twenty minutes, address us in English to the effect following :—

" Perhaps we had better leave off there.   You see that Mr.
Lewis, with my permission, has brought a friend with him to
the class this evening.   This is an unusual thing, and must not
be looked upon as establishing a precedent.   But I thought
that Mr. Lewis's friend might give you, as preachers, a word
of advice.   Words of wisdom are not to be despised, from what-

ever quarter they come. I was observing, Mr. Bartley," he went on, in Welsh—Thomas awaking and getting up from his collar, as who should say, "yes, that's my name"—"I was telling these young men that you might have a word of advice for them. Will you say something, Mr. Bartley? The young men of to-day need a great deal of talking to."

" You never saw a poorer hand at sayin' a thing," responded Thomas. " But I don't care to be odd and disobedient. I've hard much talk about Bala, sir; and when Rhys, here, came to you — his mother and I were great friends; it was she brought me to religion, and I knew nothin' till she began expoundin' to me, and she was a wonderful ooman. I told her, many times, if she'd happened to belong to the Ranters, she'd make a champion preacher (cheers). Wait a bit now; what was I goin' to say? O, yes! When Rhys came to you, I determined I'd run up and see Bala, some day; so this mornin', as I was givin' the pig his food (cheers), says I to myself, now for it. From Corwen to Bala I had a ride with some of the young preachers here, and I *was* surprised, sir. I always used to toink the students was poor things, with their heads in their feathers, half broken hearted and half starvin' theirselves. But I never saw decenter boys. They weren't a bit like preachers, they were so powerful funny. D'ye know, sir, Mr. Williams here (placing his hand on that personage's shoulder) can act you to the life. If I'd only shut my eyes I wouldn't have known but 'twas your very own self."

At this point there were thunders of applause, participated in by all save Williams, who reddend to the roots of his hair. I was not sorry to see him thus put into the pot, for, in the course of that afternoon, he had enjoyed himself more than once at my expense. For a second or two Thomas looked as it he could not make out the meaning of the plaudits; as if he did not know whether it was a good hit or a big mistake he had made. After slightly hesitating, he added—" It's as true as the Paternoster, sir." This brought on another burst of applause which confirmed Thomas in the notion that he had said something transcendently fine; so, he went on:

" But I must tell them to their faces, sir: I don't see they are so clever as all that at preachin'. I confess I'm a bit dull

—I was old comin' to religion—and I'll 'low it's but few of 'em
I've heard preach, and p'r'aps those weren't the best. When
you preach, sir, I understands you, champion; but to tell the
truth, honest, I couldn't make horse-hair nor hobgoblin of the
students yonder; and Barbara couldn't do anythin' in the
blessed earth with 'em. They don't talk enough about Jesus
Christ, sir, and heaven. A man like myself has a purty fair
grip of that. There was one of 'em over there who spoke
more'n enough of 'mechanism,' or some'at like that, but I
knew no more than a mountain hurdle what he meant. Rhys
told me you didn't teach 'em to preach, sir; which is an awful
pity. I know you're wiser nor me, but if I was you, sir, I'd
make 'em preach before you—one every week—and when he
had done, I'd show him where he had failed, and if he didn't do
as you told him, I'd give him the sack. It's by preachin'
Welsh the boys expect to get their livin', and it's no good larnin'
the languages of people who've been dead hundreds of years if
they can't preach in a language which everybody as is now
alive understands. That's my opinion, sir, but p'r'aps I'm
wrong; 'cause all I have is a grip of the letters. I'm surprised
it's in an empty house you keep school, and I'm glad, now I've
seen you, that I gave half a sovrin to the sickly little man who
came about collectin' for a new school. That was one of the
noblest men I ever saw with my eyes, sir. He told me it was
from Bala we got all our crowin' cocks, and I never hear the
young ones in our court-yard without thinkin' of his words.
If you've noticed, sir, it's a queer enough clamour young cocks
make, for four months or so, if there isn't an old un there to
set 'em a pattern. But, whether or no, they come little by
little to tune it lovely. I takes a bit of interest in fowls, sir—as
Rhys knows — and, to me, the most disagreeable thing on
earth is those chicks which you can't tell whether they're
cocks or hens. If they don't show purty quick what they are,
I chop their heads off. Well, I'm glad from my heart to see
you all so comfortable, and I hope you'll forgive me for takin'
up so much of your time."

Thomas resumed his seat amidst loud and long-continued
applause.

"What's the meanin' of these cheers, Mr. Williams?" I
heard him ask. "Did I speak middlin' tidy?"

"Capital!" replied Williams.

"Well, Mr. Bartley," observed the Teacher, "I much hope the young men will attend to the pointed observations, and act upon the valuable advice you have given them. When next the students preach with you, take careful note whether any improvement has taken place. If they do not show clearly whether they are hens or cocks, let us know, Mr. Bartley, so that we may cut their heads off."

Amidst tumultuous applause the Teacher shook hands with Thomas Bartley and went away. Directly he had left the room one of the students got up and locked the door.

"What's goin' to happen, now?" Thomas asked.

"I don't know," I replied. Neither did I, but I could see there was something up.

"Friends," promptly said D. H., of Aberdaron—the same of whom Thomas had asked whether he was a pupil teacher—"it appears that the talk of 'mechanism,' referred to by Mr. Bartley, is not the only fault of which we, as students, have been guilty; although there is a close connection between 'mechanism' and that which I wish to bring before you. It would seem that our brother ——— of Flintshire, in returning from an appointment this morning, by unpardonable negligence and want of skill has occasioned and caused a valuable horse of Mr. Rice Edwards' to have a fall, which broke its knees, whereby great loss has been entailed upon the said Mr. Rice Edwards, and dreadful pain upon the said horse. It is not meet we should look lightly upon an act of this kind. Let us enquire into the case. According to the rules now in force with us, we must place our brother upon his trial. I will act as judge; Mr. V. P. will be prosecutor, and, so that the accused may have every fair play, Mr. Rhys Lewis, who comes from the same county, shall defend him. I nominate and appoint Mr. Thomas Bartley as foreman of the jury, and Mr. John Jones as interpreter."

"Tell us, is it in earnest or in jest he is speakin'?" Thomas inquired.

"In jest," replied I.

"Ho! a bit of a skit, eh?" he rejoined cheerfully.

In much less time than it takes me to write, the trial was in full swing. I do not wish to attempt a particular description, although I could furnish one. The accused looked *like* an accused—dejected. D. H., the judge, sat in the teacher's chair on top of the table, with a white handkerchief bound about his head for a wig. To all appearance Thomas Bartley fully realised the dignity of his office of foreman, and lost never a word of the pleadings. V. P., gifted and eloquent, made an incomparable prosecutor. He called several witnesses to character, on the horse's behalf, who testified to its being a trustworthy animal, altogether unlikely to go upon its knees, except from the inexcusable negligence of the rider. I failed completely to shake their evidence with regard to the animal's general health and soundness of limb. With the students, and them alone, I shook off the restraint I had been in during the afternoon, and threw myself heart and soul into the defence of my co-countryman. But all to no purpose; it was a bad case, and every witness was in favour of the horse. The trial lasted an hour and a half, much amusement being derived from the witnesses' refusal to speak English, and so compelling Mr. John Jones, whose command of Saxon was the poorest of the lot, to interpret. I made the best speech I could in my client's behalf, conscious all the time that I hadn't a leg to stand on, and that my only hope lay in the sympathies of Thomas Bartley as foreman of the jury. My arguments were pulverised by the judge when he came to sum up. I fancy it must have been the weakness of my defence which caused his lordship to go out of his way to give the accused a chance of adding something on his own account to that which I had already urged, before the jury retired to consider their verdict.

In a silence like the grave's, the defendant was heard saying: "A bad indictment, my lord. It was a mare I had, not a horse."

The scene which ensued is still vividly present to my mind. Completely overcome with laughter, some of the boys lay stretched on the benches, while others rolled about the floor. Thomas Bartley stood on one of the forms waving his hat and shouting with all his might as if he were at an election. The meeting broke up in convulsions. On the way to our lodgings,

I had the greatest difficulty in preventing Thomas from crying out and attracting the notice of the inhabitants. Every now and then he would pause and remark, "As good as M—— Ll—— of Ruthin, spite of chin and teeth; of chin and teeth, if I was never to move. D'ye know what? That's the jolliest gatherin' I ever was at; but as for the first part of it, it was the flattest affair I ever saw with my eyes. I couldn't make out what in the blessed earth was going on. Where's Mr. Williams sneaked off to, eh? Don't you see him awful like your brother Bob? What have you on foot for to-morrow night? I'd like wonderful well to be with you a week, only I must sail home, or Barbara 'll be in a fit."

When I explained to Thomas it was impossible he could return till next day, he trembled to think of Barbara spending a whole night by herself. But he had to submit to the inevitable; which he did with the repeated observation that he was sorry he had not brought Barbara along "just as she was." When Williams made his appearance, with three of the other students, he was consoled not a little. I saw that my fellow lodger was determined to make the most of Thomas Bartley. There were six of us packed into a small room at supper that night. The meal was the great thing with Thomas Bartley; Thomas Bartley the great thing with the guests. If I had not gone to too great lengths already, I would give a summary of the conversation. The boys enjoyed themselves hugely; but the sigh he every now and then gave vent to, clearly showed Thomas's thoughts to be with Barbara at the Tump. His stay with us over night caused a considerable change in the sleeping arrangements. At cock-crow next morning, I heard Thomas walking to and fro and shouting "Get up, you folk. It's quite middle day." And we got never a minute's peace till we had obeyed. Thomas had to meet the first train at Corwen; so, when the clock struck six, he, Williams and myself, were crossing Tryweryn bridge in Mr. Rice Edwards's carriage. Before bidding each other farewell, Thomas took me aside and said, "how's the pocket stand, my son?"

"I've not been hard up, as yet, Thomas," I replied.

"Here you are," said he; "take the loan of this for ever;" and he forced a sovereign into my hand. Blessings on him!

It was not the only sovereign I had from him whilst at Bala. After a pressing invitation to Williams to come and spend a week at the Tump, Thomas went home to relate the history of Bala and the college. And such a history! After that visit, Thomas, of course, knew all about the students. I could tell from his question, "What have you on foot to-morrow night?" that he thought the scene he "saw with his own eyes" on that Monday evening in college, was a specimen of what took place there daily. Little did he know that a "trial" of the kind I have described, happened only once in two or three years, and that what he had termed "the most miserable thing on the face of the earth" was our regular employment. The long hours and hard labour, the fear and vexation of spirit, of which every student knows something, never crossed his innocent soul.

Thomas Bartley, more the pity, is not the only one who entertains an erroneous impression of a collegiate life. I have gathered, from observations heard in divers parts of the country, that some people who should know better, cherish opinions quite as foolish in kind, if not in degree.

CHAPTER XXXVIII.

A FORTUNATE ENCOUNTER.

* * * * * *

As far as learning was concerned, I believe I was as "disinterested" as almost any one who ever attended college. During the four years I was at Bala, I allowed the other boys to take all the prizes. Not being particularly talented, and the "start" I got in Soldier Robin's school being none of the best, I speedily found it was no easy task to compete with young fellows who had been well educated previously. Besides, preaching was a necessity, for my stay at college depended upon it. If I ceased preaching, I must also cease eating; and, at the time, I could not see my way clear to do either the one thing or the other. The Sabbath journeys were oftenest long ones, as to Trawsfynydd, Festiniog, Tanygrisiau, Maentwrog, Rhydymain, Corris, Aberllyfni, Machynlleth, &c. It was only once I ever preached at Llanfor, for which Edward Rowland reproached me many times (peace to the memory of the good old Christian!) the chief reason being that I could not travel thither, and also because I did not like to see a dozen students coming to Llanfor to meeting instead of attending Sunday School at Bala. Each one of them had his own tape measure. The fun they got on one occasion when a friend of mine, preaching at Llanfor, spoke of Adam in his "uncircumcised condition!" He never heard the last of it, as long as he remained at Bala. What did I know but that I might make a similarly foolish slip, which next morning would be posted up on every partition of the college. But I must not speak of the old college's partitions—*Mirabile Visu!* I said that the journeys were long. The distance took up the whole of Saturday morning to think about, and the journey itself the whole of the afternoon to accomplish; the return occupied the whole of Monday morning, and the pulling myself together after that shaking from a ride on one of Mr. R. E's "old sixteens" the whole of Monday afternoon. That made two days of my week, without mentioning the Sabbath, on which the other boys who were not *bound* to preach were at work with their books. These things, combined with a lack of natural talent, prevented me from distinguishing myself in the examinations. On the other hand, the trouble my brother Bob took to instruct me, my own exertions and my resolve to attend the classes as regularly as possible, kept me from the bottom of the form. I had the consolation of not being an extreme man; at no time was I at either top or bottom, but somewhere about the centre. And I flatter myself that I continue so, and that I still endeavour to walk the middle path in judgment. But it is to this I have for some time been gravitating: although I did not make my "mark" in college, I am certain that a mark was made on me which can never be erased. I got the greatest good from my stay there, learned hundreds and thousands of things I did not know before, and of which I cannot now estimate the value. A new world was opened to my mind, and although I was not as others were, able to penetrate far into its mid-most

regions, still, it was a discovery to know it existed. It was
something to be able to see with my own eyes the leaf upon
the water. It is worth a lad's while to go to college, if it were
only to let him know how much there is to know, to rub the
rust and shake the dust off which he had gathered at home. I
am not saying much when I mention that there was not in the
church I was brought up in one lad, Will Bryan excepted, who
was stronger than myself in natural insight; and it would be
sheer hypocrisy for me to say that the fact did not cause me to
form a distinctive notion concerning myself. But after going to
college I was not long in finding out that I was nothing and
nobody, and that among my fellow students many a man
might be found who could put me into his waistcoat pocket.
My hide would have been as hard as the hippopotamus's not to
have received any benefit by rubbing against those who excelled me in every way. If a young man can spend three or
four years in college and come home again, without great gain
to himself, the fault is his own entirely, and he does not deserve to be fed. My experience of the period is that it was the
most blessed and happy of my life; and I look back upon it
with the sweetest regret. Many were the friendship's knots I
tied there which neither time nor distance can undo. With
but little effort my memory can vividly recall before my
mind's eye, at the present moment, the faces of all my
companions. Where are they now? One or two of them
were taken home before the end of their college term;
and one or two others followed without being permitted to
"do" but little. The majority, however, remain scattered
up and down the world. Several, appointed pastors of flocks,
are already useful—famous, some of them—in the ministry,
while others shift for themselves as best they can, preaching here and there on the Sabbath, and doing nothing
in particular during the week. Speaking of this matter, I remember that, as the time drew near when we must leave
college, the question most of us asked each other was: What
are you going to do? It was an important question, to some
of us especially. We had given up our old occupations, which
by now we were unfitted to resume. It was not all of us who
had comfortable homes to return to, or wealthy relations on

whom we could depend; and divers of us, as the time approached, found ourselves in a serious fix. Notably was this the case with me. During my four years of college life Miss Hughes was wondrous kind in asking me to spend vacation time at her house. But I foresaw that the circumstances would be different after I had finished my course, or rather after I had left college. Even if she were willing to receive me again into her home, I considered it would be shameless presumption to take advantage of the fact. I could not bear the notion of playing the part of gentleman-idler during the week, and going about to preach upon the Sunday. Williams, my fellow-lodger, was precisely in the same predicament, and many were the serious "confabs" between us as to what we were going to do. At times he would treat the question jocularly.

"What wonder is it, tell us," he said to me one night, "that Methodist preachers should cast about them for some old gal with plenty of tin? Look at us two: we shall be leaving Bala within the month, and what are we to do for a livelihood? I swear no one shall say of me that I did nothing through the week besides wearing a frock coat. I see you have a much better chance than I. Four years in college has so spoiled my hands that I needn't think of re-commencing my old occupation, but as for you, you can put an advertisement in the *Liverpool Mercury* :—

WANTED—By a young man who has spent four years at college, who knows a little Latin and Greek, and a lot of Divinity, a situation as draper's assistant. Can preach well. Salary no object, provided he gets his Saturdays to go to, and his Mondays to return from his *teithia*.[*]

"As for me, I see nothing left me to do but to try for a situation on the railway as ticket collector, unless I 'go out to the Blacks,' as your old friend Thomas Bartley says. What if you were to try and creep up the sleeve of the Bishop of St. Asaph, and I were to do the same with the Bishop of Bangor, eh? It

---

[*] Sabbath journeying.—TRANSLATOR.

would be no great feat for a couple of laths like you and I to
creep up a Bishop's sleeve, for they tell me it's dreadfully
wide. If we succeeded, I wonder are we scholars enough,
without having to begin this business all over again at Lam-
peter? Scholar or not, we'll preach better than half of them.
What do you say? Have you any other plan?"

Williams possessed a good deal of sly humour; and I could
not help laughing at his picture of our future, despite the importance of the subject and my sadness of heart. As the time
approached for us to leave college, the question came home to
us both with greater seriousness daily—" If we are obliged to
return to our old occupations, to what earthly purpose have we
spent four years in this place?" We were both anxious for a
sphere of work where each would feel in his element, and to
which we believed—whether rightly or wrongly—that we were,
to some extent, adapted. But although, to tell the honest
truth, we were both intently on the watch, there was neither
sound nor sign, from any quarter, of a call to the care of a
church. We had devoted ourselves to, and humbly thought ourselves set apart for, the work in which our hearts and souls
were centred; and the thought of going back to our old occupations was depressing. But, as far as I could see, nothing
else awaited us; for we were resolved not to lounge about after
leaving college. Williams was more hopeful than I; as easily
he could be, because I knew he was conscious of the fact that
he was an excellent preacher; the best, indeed, the college at
that time contained, to my mind. The " friends of the place "
must have been of the same opinion, too; for Williams
preached twice in Bala itself during his four years' stay there
—a sure sign for good and an unfailing promise of a bright
future.

But, after all, the word is a true one that " the last shall be
first." Some weeks before I left Bala I received two important
letters—that is, important to me. Williams was an early riser,
I a late sleeper. In passing, is not the ability to rise early a
talent? I am certain it is. My brother Bob was bound to go
early to work every day; but he never turned out of bed without being called a dozen times by mother. He could, however,
stay up at night as long as you liked. I am just the same.

But Williams had a talent for rising early. One morning, some weeks before leaving college, as I have said, I came downstairs about eight o'clock, to find that Williams had gone out for a stroll. On the table were two letters awaiting me. I recognised the writings on both—one as that of Miss Hughes, and the other as "Eos Prydain's." I gave precedence, always, to Miss Hughes's letter. Opening this one, I found that it enclosed another in a hand wholly strange to me. It was in English, and as follows:—

OLD BAILEY, B——,
May 1st, 18——.

SIR,—There died this morning in our gaol, a man named John Freeman. Six weeks ago, having been found guilty of poaching, he was sentenced to three months' imprisonment, with hard labour. He was never strong from the outset, and shortly after coming here he took cold and rapidly became worse. A few days before his death, he expressed a desire to speak to me privately. I had fancied from the first that he was "an old bird;" and he at length admitted to me that his real name was James Lewis. He requested me—and I promised—to apprise you of his death, whenever that took place. What he specially wished me to make known to you was that *everything he had told you was not true.* He did not know your address, but he believed you would get the letter some time, directed as I have directed it. I have now fulfilled my promise to the deceased. He will be buried to-morrow. We should have buried him to-day, only we were short of coffins, and I did not think he was going to die so soon.

Yours truly,
J. F. BREECE, *Governor.*

Rhys Lewis, Esq.

I read and re-read the letter, in stupefaction. My uncle James, as I have many times said in the course of this history, had been the moving cause of the most of my troubles, and I detested him heartily. And yet, on reading of his disgraceful end, and of his words to the governor, a pang shot through me such as I will not attempt to describe. I held the letter in my hand, and looked, amazed, through the window into Tegid Street—for how long I do not exactly know—my mind reverting to my earliest impressions of my uncle, when I knew him as "the Irishman." De Quincey somewhere speaks of a man who fell overboard into the sea. He remained under water only a very few seconds, but, when picked up and he became conscious, he averred that all the events and all the sins of his life came vividly to his mind during those few seconds. I, for my part, believe I was no more than half an hour staring out of window, but in that time there passed before my mind the chief events of my life in the order of their occurrence. I knew Mrs. ———— had been in the room laying the breakfast, and had said something to me, but I could not tell what; and I remember it was Williams who broke my reverie by shouting from behind me : " Well, you Seventh Sleeper, have you got up at last? What had news to-day? You seem as miserable as if you were at the grave of your grandmother ! " I tried to rouse myself and look cheerful. After beginning upon the breakfast I recollected Eos's letter. It ran thus :—

————, *May* 1*st*, 18————

DEAR BROTHER, — We understand your term at Bala is nearly at an end. It is needless for us to tell you, who know the history and the circumstances of Bethel Church as well as we do, that the cause suffers for want of some one to take care of it, especially since the death of your old master, Abel Hughes. We have long felt that our children and young people do not receive that care and attention which they ought to receive. We have for some time been talking of getting a pastor ; and, last week, we two brought the question before the church and took the liberty of mentioning your name as of one whose college course was nearly at an end and who, having been bred in the church, knew us well. The hint received a very general approval. Of course, we did not take a vote, not having yet got permission from the Monthly Meeting ; but we thought it wise to inform you that it is our intention to apply for the same—indeed you may look upon it as settled that we shall—lest you thoughtlessly promised to go elsewhere. We believe you need not fear that anyone here will think the less of you because of your youth. We expect to see you over in a few weeks, when we shall discuss the matter further. Until then, wishing you every success, and with kind regards,—Yours on behalf of the church,

DAVID DAVIS,
ALEXANDER PHILLIPS, } DEACONS.
(Eos Prydain),

I tossed the letter across the table to Williams, whose joy on reading it I shall never forget. I am certain he could not have manifested greater delight if some one had left him an estate. The call to the pastorate of the church I was brought up in was as unexpected an event as could have happened. I took it as a great compliment to myself, and, but for the other letter to which I have referred, would have regarded this one as a subject of rejoicing also. But, bracketed with that letter, it was very sad news for me, and brought on an attack of my old enemy—lowness of spirits. I sent word at once to my old friends, David Davis and "Eos Prydain," thanking them for their kind letter and adding that I should be returning home in a few weeks' time. After doing so, I said to my companion:

" Williams, don't mention this to the boys or anybody else; because on no consideration can I accept the call."

" Don't talk nonsense," he returned. " I'll mention it to all I come across. What's the matter with you? Are you off your head? Not accept what you were most wishing for! I used to think you couldn't bounce."

When he and I were playful, we "thee'd and "thou'd " each other; but always when we spoke seriously it was " you " and " yourself." That morning Williams was joyous, I sad.

" You know the story of the skeleton in the cupboard," I observed. " I, too, have a tale which I cannot unfold, even to you. Possibly I shall tell it some day, but not now. I am dispirited and sad; and I know you would like to share my burden with me, but it can't be to-day. The fact is, I must go away for two or three days, and that without delay."

" My dear fellow," said Williams, feelingly, for he had a very tender heart; " you are telling me nothing new. I have known for some time there was a concealed bitterness about

2 B

your life of which I had no right to seek the explanation. Can I be of any service to you ?"

" You can—do not say a word about this call of mine, for I cannot accept it. Also, if you please, go to R. E. and ask him to send a conveyance after me, along the Corwen road. I am bound to leave at once. Perhaps I shall explain all this to you some day."

Taking nothing with me but my top coat, and the little money I possessed, I left; Williams, without another word, going off to order the carriage. It was a long journey, which would occupy nearly the whole day; but I was determined to go, being tired of wearing a mask and living in fear. I was speedily caught up by R. E., who drove me to Corwen in good time to lose the train. After a long wait, I welcomed the loneliness of the railway carriage, wherein I could give the rein to my thoughts without being obliged to speak to anybody. Hundreds and thousands of things passed through my mind. I read Mr. Breece's letter over and over. Sometimes I thought it a forgery; my uncle being villain enough for that. But what purpose such a forgery could answer I was not able to see.

If the letter stated a fact, I persuaded myself I understood the meaning of the sentence, "everything he had told you was not true." The words opened up a possibility which turned my heart to ice, in view of which I saw that I could not accept the call to the pastorate of Bethel. To me it was surprising that a church, of which half the members were cognisant of the history of my family, should have given such a call. But, in the course of two and twenty years, people will forget a good deal. During that period many things were made known to me, to my sorrow, of which the chapel folk were utterly ignorant. I could not help my family connections; but were the sins of the fathers to be visited upon the children in my case ? I feared they were. Was Providence leading me to settle down in my old home in order to set my teeth on edge for the sour fruit whereof my predecessors had eaten? How could I think of accepting the call ? And yet, what reason could I give for refusing? I had no other place to go to, although I longed for an excuse to go far enough away—to Australia or somewhere. Again, I had neither part nor lot in the making of my

unhappiness. I sometimes thought I was magnifying the terrors
of the outlook and fearing that which would never come to pass.
At any rate, I vowed that day to get whatever of light there was
obtainable upon the thing which bestrode me like an ever-present
nightmare; and this I hoped to accomplish before giving
slumber to my eyelids. My intention was to pay a visit to
Mr. J. F. Breece, be he whom he might. If the letter were
not a decoy, it might turn out that my uncle had told the
writer a great deal more than had been communicated to me.
I saw that my journey would not be altogether in vain, which-
ever way it happened; and my anxiety had by now been
worked up to such a pitch that I could not hold out much
longer. If my fears were realised, then my future would be
clouded over once more, and I could not accept the call to the
pastorate of Bethel church. Not only so, but I dreaded that,
before I could be happy, I must leave the land of my birth.
But, I reflected again, why must I do this? I had endeavoured to keep a conscience for God, and, if the worst came to the
worst, no reasonable man could blame me for it. But, said I,
everybody would be pitying me and sympathising with me,
which would be every bit as bad. What! was it pride of heart
that made me tremble at that which was possible and probable?
Had I not enough religion and moral courage to bear any disgrace with which, as originator, I had personally nothing to
do? And yet, something would persist in reminding me that
blood was thicker than water.

I had never previously been to B———, and knew nothing
about the place save from hearsay, a fact which had no
tendency to lighten my spirit. The day, also, was dull and
heavy, and the rain descended in one continuous drizzle. Besides this, fate seemed to be against me, for I lost the train, a
second time, at Chester where I had to wait two hours before
I got another. I now saw it would be late when I reached
B———, and feared I would not be able to see Mr. Breece.
Sick enough at heart, I arrived at the big, bustling town. It
was nearly ten o'clock when I sprang upon the platform. I
awoke from my dreams on seeing the multitude of lighted
lamps and the crowd of passengers darting hither and thither
through the station. Was it too late to wait on Mr. Breece? Well,

I should be none the worse for trying. I rapidly made my way to the cab-stand, but before reaching it I was met by a sprightly young fellow who accosted me with the words, "Cab, sir ?"

I nodded in the affirmative.

"Old Bailey," said I, taking my seat; to which he replied, "Old Bailey? Know it well, sir. Better be outside than inside that place, as the worm said to the blackbird when he was about to be swallowed," saying which he banged the door and away we went.

The rattle of carriages along the streets was simply deafening to one who had newly left the quiet of Bala. Looking out, I was astonished at the interminable stream of humanity going and coming on either side of us. A glance at one side alone, for a few minutes, took in hundreds of faces which I saw for the first time and the last, every one of whom, methought, had his story and his trouble, as strange to me as mine were to him. Though the lamps and the other lights were numerous, they served but to show up the dirty fog which filled the streets. I fancied that what of smoke had ascended from the chimneys during the day had now come back to keep company with the drizzle, of which there was a ceaseless downpour. I perceived that the principal business establishments were shut, thus bringing into prominence the small tobacco-selling shops, the public houses, and the gin-shops, which seemed busier and livelier than they could have been at mid-day. I do not think I passed a single "vault" or gin-shop without seeing someone going in or coming out. Out of one reeled a soldier, in a red coat, and, close behind him a woman, bonnetless, but with a shawl about her head, pinned under the chin. Passing another place, I saw a man, of whom it was difficult to tell whether he were old or young; but he was lame, and so very ragged that I believed he had not a whole pocket about him, and that bound to keep his money in his fist until he had deposited it upon the counter. At one public house, a man leaned his back against the door-post, his chin resting on his waistcoat, and his eyes looking as if they were engaged counting the buttons of his breeches; and by another a fribble in a frock coat—buttoned up to the throat and hiding a multitude of sins—sniffing the per-

fume near the doorway, in default of any better enjoyment.
The hideous faces I saw that night in the light of those taverns!
Had their owners, fifty years back, been shut up to half
starve in dark cells, from which they had only recently been
able to escape, some through the chimney and others through
the key hole? How proud I felt of the Welsh, red-cheeked,
healthy, honest!

This was what was running through my mind when I noticed
that the lights became fewer. I looked out, and there was
nothing to be seen but great warehouses, silent and dark.
Hardly a soul walked the streets now, and nothing was to be
heard save the rumble of my conveyance and someone
whistling. The whistler seemed to be following me. I put my
head out to listen, and found it was my driver. I recognised
the tune; it was our old "Caersalem," which, until then, I did
not know was in vogue with the English. I held my head out,
feeling as if I were in a Welsh chapel and fancying that I heard
the words: "Thanks be to Him, For rememb'ring the earth's
dust."

I settled it in my own mind that cabby was in the habit
of attending chapel. We soon got into a gloomy quarter of the
town. I began to think it was very foolish of me to expect to
see Mr. Breece at a time like that. Directly, I saw a great,
high, thick wall which, by the light of our lamps, looked black
with age. A minute after, my cab drew up before a wide gate-
way, of which the entire surface was almost covered with nail-
heads. Beside it hung an unusually large lamp, from a bracket
fixed in the strong wall.

"Here we are, safe and sound," said the driver, opening the
door for me. He stood with his back to the light, which shone
in my face, and was about to put out his hand for his fare when
he started back and, with a surprised look at me, said,—

"Holloa, old hundredth! Are you yourself, say?"

My heart gave a jump, and I came near hugging the fellow,
who was none other than the friend of my youth, Will Bryan!
Before I could exchange a dozen words with him, however, a
small door, set in the big one of the Old Bailey prison, opened,
and out stepped a tall, round-shouldered man, behind whom
the door was closed with a bang. He was bound to pass us,

which he did without looking at us, and keeping his eyes upon the ground. He could not, however, escape the lamplight. When he was out of hearing Will Bryan said:—

"I'm blowed if that chap isn't old Nic'las!"

"You are right, Will," I returned. "Nic'las it is, sure enough. For my sake, follow him and find out where he goes to, even if it took you two hours, and come back here. You shall know the reason again. I, for my part, will try and discharge my errand, but whether I succeed or not I shall remain here until you return."

"At your service as detective in chief," cried Will, in his old form of speech, as, jumping upon his cab, he drove off.

I gazed after him for some seconds, but he was quickly out of sight. Turning upon my heel, I rang lustily at the bell of the gaol. But I see it will take another chapter to relate the adventures of that strange night of my history.

CHAPTER XXXIX.

WILL BRYAN IN HIS CASTLE.

I RANG the Old Bailey bell vigorously, as I have said. I felt agitated and sad, and the unexpected appearances of Will Bryan and old Nic'las did not lessen, in the slightest, the multitude of my thoughts. Promptly, in response to the summons. I heard someone walk up at a brisk pace, the jingle of his keys denoting his important, though unenviable, office. A minute later the door was opened, and the light of a lamp, carried by the opener, blazed across my face, almost blinding me.

"Who was I?" "What did I want?"

"Was the governor in?"

"He was."

"Could I see him?"

"I could, if my business was important."

"O, certainly."

"Good. Come in!"

I was led into a small, square room, in which there were but
a table and two chairs, and there left by my guide, who
pulled-to the self-locking door behind him. I waited, in fear
and trembling, the call to the governor's presence; although it
was with that very object I had come all the way. Mr.
Prichard, the keeper of Flint prison, was the only gaoler I had
ever seen, and I remembered that he had a look before which
even the innocent trembled in their shoes. The fuming
authority his face showed! How his sharp, wild eye pierced
one through, scraping up his very back bone! I never heard
of anybody committed to Flint gaol whom Mr. Prichard's look
did not terrify, old Ned James excepted. When Ned was sent
up for the second time, Mr. Prichard shouted in his ear,
" Well, Ned! Ned!! Ned!!! Have you come here again, then ?"
" I never was in a place in my life which I couldn't go to
afterwards," replied Ned, with perfect self-possession. If Mr.
Prichard, the keeper of Flint prison, thought I, carried such
terror in his looks, how much more so the keeper of the Old
Bailey ? The door opened, and, with trembling limbs, I was
ushered into the presence of Mr. Breece. But the trembling
was needless. Mr. Breece did not resemble Mr. Prichard in
the slightest. He was a little, delicate, harmless looking man.
Mrs. Breece was in the room at the time, knitting. She was a
large, stout lady, of pleasing appearance, to whom her lord
seemed to be a sort of appendage. On my entrance the gaoler
rose, gave me a look of welcome over his gold spectacle-rim,
and bade me take a chair.

" Mr. Lewis, I understand ? " said he.

" Yes, sir," I replied. " I hope you'll pardon me for disturbing you at this hour."

" Don't mention it! Don't mention it!" he rejoined.
" When there's business on hand, I never look at the time."

After some general conversation, in the course of which I
noticed he had a habit of repeating his words, Mr. Breece remarked, " Excuse me, Mr. Lewis, but are you in the ministry ?"

" I am sir," said I.

" I guessed as much," quoth he; " so you'll take a glass of
wine with me. Mother ! if you please, hand us the ——"

" Don't trouble," I interposed. " I do not take any. My

errand is short and simple, and I will not intrude upon you for
more than a couple of minutes. This morning I received a
letter from you informing me of the death of a man named
James Lewis, a prisoner in this place. My visit is to be
attributed more to curiosity than to anything else."

"Oh!" ejaculated Mr. Breece, whose face changed on the
instant. Casting a keen and searching glance at me, he added, " Yes, yes, I wrote you and thought no more of the matter
—more—of—the—matter. He was your father, it seems, eh ?"

"No;" replied I, feeling glad at being able to say so.
" But he was some sort of a relative, of whom, I can assure
you, I was not by any means proud. My business is to know,
if you will be good enough to tell me, whether he said anything to you beyond what was contained in your letter. I have
my reasons for asking this which it would be of no use or interest that you should be made acquainted with."

" I understand you, I understand you," returned Mr. Breece,
resuming his former affability. " No; no, to the best of my
recollection, he told me no more than I wrote you. Have you
many relations, Mr. Lewis ?"

" As far as I am aware, he was the last," I answered.

" Ah!" exclaimed Mr. Breece, in surprise.

" Of course, you buried him to-day, as stated in your letter,"
I observed.

" No," he replied. " No. Wait; did you say, Mr. Lewis,
that he was the only relative you possessed ?"

" On my oath," I replied, for I saw that he doubted me.
" As far as I am aware, he was the last of my family."

" That is strange," said Mr. Breece ; " if, indeed, it is strange
too ; for we are constantly being deceived—constantly. I suppose I must take your word, as a clergyman ; but, this morning, just as I had given orders to place the body in the coffin,
there came a visitor here who represented himself to be a
brother of the deceased ; [I felt uncomfortable at the words]
although I must admit he was not a bit like him ; indeed, he
seemed a strange character, and was obviously a man of
means. He begged to be allowed to provide a suitable coffin
for his unfortunate brother, and put down a five pound note on
the table in payment—on the table, sir. Could I refuse him,

you think? Sir, I always say that, when death sets to work,
the law must give way—give way, sir. Will I punish a dead
man? Never sir; never! That would look like fighting
against Almighty God, sir. I at once ordered a good coffin to
be made for the dead; and it *is* a good coffin. Indeed, in a
manner of speaking, it is a pity to put anything so expensive
in the earth. He who paid for it loved his brother dearly. If
you had only been here ten minutes earlier you would have
seen that strange man—a character, sir, quite a character."

I rose to go, saying "I am very much obliged to you, Mr.
Breece for your kindness, and I again apologise for troubling
you at such a time of night."

"Don't mention it, don't mention it," returned the Govern-
or. "Things of this sort will happen, sometimes. Here you
are! Would you like to see the coffin? I'm sure you'll be
pleased with it."

"If you'll be good enough, sir," I replied.

Mr. Breece touched a bell at his elbow, and in a minute the
man whom I had previously seen made his appearance.

"Gloom," said Mr. Breece, "has coffin No. 72 been screwed
down?"

"That is what we are just doing, sir," was the answer.

"Take this gentleman to see it. Good night. Don't mention
it, sir; don't mention it. You're very welcome."

I was led across a wide court-yard, then through a door-way
opening on to a long corridor, through another door and
another, both self-locking; then down a flight of stone steps,
and along another corridor, there being something in the atmosphere, the strong doors and damp walls which made me think
that all in that place had been dead for generations—my guide,
Mr. Breece and his wife excepted—so dark and dismal were
the surroundings. At length we came to the mortuary
chamber where, so I then supposed, never a whiff of fresh air
had entered, and where the living were compelled to be as the
dead—without breathing. The ceiling of the room was low,
the walls were bare and dank as if snail-beslimed for centuries,
and the odour of death hung thick all about. When I first
went in, I thought it was the subterranean character of the
place which made me fancy rats were gnawing at my boots and

crawling between my legs until my guide, with a curse, made a kick at one. I was then certain it was no fancy, but that he, too, was being pestered by the same vermin. I had had but little to eat that day, and felt weak and faint. But I tried to bear up, for I had not come all that way for nothing. At the farthest end of the long and narrow room was a board whereon lay the "nice coffin," beside which stood a man in his shirt sleeves, with a paper cap on his head, who on hearing me and my guide approach turned to look at us, holding a screw-driver poised in his hand, his face wearing an expression like that of a man caught robbing a grave. He took the trouble to explain to me the excellent points of the coffin! What cared I about that? My great object was to see the body which was within. I had to give the joiner a shilling to un-screw. However mad the notion, I feared my uncle James had only simulated death, and that this was but a deep-laid plan of his to escape from prison. To tell the truth, I seriously expected, while the joiner was taking out the last screw and removing the lid, to see my uncle sitting up and laughing. But it did not happen so; and, blame me who will, I felt greatly relieved. There he lay, in the same old clothes, and as dead as a doornail. He, who had ruined my father, brought my mother and myself the greater part of our troubles, spent every farthing of the money I had saved to go to college, and who found no evil too great to commit, was now powerless and still, vanquished at last by the Great Van-quisher! So as to make sure, I felt his hands and his forehead. They were cold as the encompassing walls. Previous to that night I had seen but two dead faces—Seth's and my mother's. The change there was here! The Devil had set his mark on this one, to whom the pangs of death had been horrible. Me-thought the difference between the pleasant, cheerful look upon the face of Seth in his coffin, and that upon the one before me was as wide as heaven is from hell asunder! He was my uncle, brother to my father; but I fear that but few worse men were ever placed between four boards. Looking at him, I felt a certain degree of awe; and yet, I thought, everything about contributed to make a fit end for a character so degraded and sinful. Although my clothes were sticking to me with a cold perspiration, I felt a sort of chuckle at the knowledge that he would torment me no more. Whatever might be the other troubles in store, one half of the Ephialtic burden had been lifted from off me. I hurried away from the scene. On finding myself without the walls of the Old Bailey, I took a long, deep breath and, as if unconsciously, murmured, "O blessed liberty !"

In that part of the town the streets were quiet and still, and I saw no living creature during the whole of the time I was walking back and fore, like a soldier doing sentry duty, waiting Will Bryan. I walked and walked, my mind running upon Bala, where I longed to be. Little did Williams, whom I fancied snug in bed, know where I was at that moment, or the thoughts that were hovering around my heart. Had he known, he would not have slept a wink. It had ceased raining now for some time, and the moon shone forth. I was glad to see her. I knew her, and believed she knew me, ever since I was a child, and when I used to think we, Welsh people, owned her. Will was such a long while in coming that, at times, I feared something had happened to him, and that he would never come at all. Occasionally I felt ready to faint with hunger ; but I would speedily forget all that, and my musings would traverse a considerable portion of my life. Looking back I saw God's hand bringing me safe through many a distress. What purpose had He in leading me hither ? My thoughts were tangled, but was the dawn about to break ? Will was a long time coming ; but I remembered mother used to say that every wait was a long one. I fancied, in the distance, hearing the rumble of approaching wheels, and set to listening intently. Were they Will's ? No, for they went another way. A church clock near by struck twelve. Presently I fancied hearing footsteps on the pavement beyond, and bent my ear to catch the sound. Yes, some one was approaching. He walked swiftly along, and whistled as he went. To prevent suspicion I walked to meet him, intending to return after he had passed. When within forty yards or so of him the man broke out into song—part of a duet entitled, if I remember rightly, "All's Well," in which the questions and answers occur : "Who goes there ?" "A friend." "The word ?" "Good Night," &c. The singer was Will, whose well-known voice brought my spirit healing.

"Well, old soot-in-the-soup, are you tired of waiting?" he asked. "You must excuse me for not coming by cab; the nag was dead tired, and we haven't far to walk to my crib. Now let us have a little of your 'stranger than fiction.' I know by your jib you're in a row. Where in the wide world have you come from? D'ye know what? I have been thinking about you thousands of times and asking what if Providence were to tumble us across each other, some day? But, weary pilgrim, tell thy tale!"

"First of all, Will," said I, "did you find out where old Nic'las went to?"

"Yes, and got a tanner for doing so," replied Will. "It was only after leaving you it struck me how difficult it would be to dog a chap in a cab, so I drove up straight to my nabs, and said, 'step in, sir;' as if I meant to give him a lift for nothing, you know. The old boy rose to the bait. 'Sixty-five Gregg Street," said he, and when I put him down, he gave me sixpence. We shan't be two minutes passing the house. I'll show it you. But what's the row? What's the meaning of all this? Spout!"

It was no uneasy or roundabout task to explain to Will my object in coming to B———, he knowing more of my and my family's history than anybody else. I gave him a brief account of what had happened to me after he made his "exit," to all of which he listened with deep interest. I knew I could reckon upon his confidence and help. Indeed, but for so Providential a meeting, the one-half of my errand to the town would have been left unfulfilled. We walked, arm in arm, without my looking where we were going to, although I was conscious of being led through various streets, and of having turned to the right and the left many times. I had just finished relating what I had seen in the Old Bailey, when Will pulled up and said softly, "Here it is." I looked about me, and saw we were in a narrow, quiet street. The houses were high and, judging from the number of windows, contained a great many occupants. There were shutters upon the lower windows. Will whispered me again: "Here's the house—65, Gregg Street. It was to this old Nick went. We had better ask if supper's ready? A strange feeling came over me, which I cannot describe. It was made up of fear, odd thoughts and curiosity. The residents appeared to have retired to rest; but Will directed my attention, with his finger, to a streak of light above the shutters of No. 65, and walked as stealthily as a cat towards the window, I following. We heard talking inside. Will placing his right hand on my shoulder and his left foot on the low window-sill, stretched himself to his full height, and tried to peep above the edge of the shutters. Failing to do so, he descended, and invited me, I being about an inch the taller, to have a try. I went up, and was able to survey the room. But my heart beat so fast that I almost lost the use of my eyes. However, I managed to make out that there was a bed at the farther end, with someone sitting upon it; but I could not see his face, because Nic'las, whose form I well knew, was standing between me and him, pouring from a bottle, which he held in his right hand, something into a glass, which he held in his left. I was getting anxious for a view of the face of the man on the bed, when my attention was attracted by a sharp click at my side, like the creak of a key in a lock. I looked, and behold a tall, powerful policeman handing me neatly down from the window-sill. Before I knew that my feet had touched the ground, my wrist was in one loop of a pair of handcuffs, of which the other was about Will's. It took the officer about half a dozen seconds to do the business, which he went through without saying a word. Keeping hold of my coat collar, he made a careful search for the number of the house. I was on the point of dropping from fright. Will quickly regained his self-possession, and was the first to break silence.

"Officer," he said, "I must give you credit. You are a smart fellow." Looking thoughtfully, alternately at the handcuffs and myself, he added: "Just as it should be. We've always been attached, even from childhood;" whereupon he began to argue with the officer, who, however, refused to have anything to say to him, the only word we could get out of our captor being the single one, "March!" which we did. The officer walked close at our heels without saying anything, save "right" or "left," when we came to the corner of a street.

"This is the worst day's work I've ever seen with my eyes, I'll take oath," observed Will. "We've made a regular hash of

things, and there is no use, you know, arguing with a Bluecoat. I must speak a little grammatically, or he'll understand
us. The question is, how shall we get out of this? Set your
mind to work on some good scheme now. Why do you tremble
so? An innocent man has no cause to tremble. You know
us to be as harmless as William the Coal's mule. By the bye,
is old William alive? Does he still keep laying the blame on
Satan? We, too, I fear, must lay the blame on the old fellow
for this job. How shall we manage it, say? Bluecoat, you
know, will swear lots of things, to-morrow morning. Speak,
for you may just as well not be down hearted."

"There is nothing to be done except to tell the truth and
take the consequences," said I. "But, let me get free from the
clutches of this man when I may, I must go back to that house
again."

"They'll never believe the truth," remarked Will. "Were
we to tell the truth, namely, that we only wanted to see who
was with old Nic'las in the house there, d'ye think they'd believe us? Not likely! There are many ways of telling the
truth. It is necessary to speak figuratively sometimes, you
know. If Bluecoat doesn't put in a lot of lies, I don't see how
they can do anything to us. But we may possibly get fourteen
days; which will be a lasting shame in the case of a couple of
innocent lads. I never knew anything so awkward. After I
had thought of having a pleasant night, going over old times!
If I was sure Blue coat wasn't an exception, I'd try and bribe
him; but there's no knowing, he's so quiet. If we had pretended to be drunk it would only be five shillings and the costs.
Have you no plan? Say something; you needn't give up the
ghost. I try not to use an English word lest Bluecoat should
understand me. I never remember talking such pure Welsh
—I am surprised at myself. Let's have an understanding as
to what we shall say, for fear we'll make a mess of our story.
How would it be for us to say we were after the servants? There
are sure to be servants in a house like that. What if they asked us their names, and we were to answer—Ann and Margaret?
Then, supposing we were asked the kind of hair they have, and
we said black? But what if their names turned out to be
Maud and Cecilia, and their hair red? How should we look

then? No, that story won't wash. Tell us your scheme?
D'ye know what? I never thought you had so little pluck.
You needn't go into your boots, man—you won't be a bit the
better. At the same time, I'm terribly sorry for you. I don't
care a fig about myself, because some chum or other of mine is
sure to look after the nag. But the idea of a Methodist preacher
in quod! D'ye know what? I nearly dropped into poetry;
only " nag" and " quod" don't rhyme very well, do they? I
hope to goodness they won't get to hear of this job in the—in
the academy. Bluecoat doesn't understand that word, I'll
take oath. It would be a deuce of a thing if they got to know
about it in Bala. You would lose your Diary on the instant.
But it'll be no use for you to-morrow to say your name is
R. L., you know. You must be a Welshman with an alias.
What if you were to say your name was Melltathraneoros-
ilanerchrugog? They wouldn't know any better. I am bound
to take another name, I being a bard, a sample of whose work
you've seen in " nag" and " quod." Have you nothing in the
world to say?"

Will remained silent for some minutes. I spoke but a very
few words. Indeed, I was too much afflicted in spirit to keep
up a conversation. I wondered how Will could take matters
so easily. I was on the point of telling him my trouble, and
my fears lest the affair should become known at college and
my home, when Will began again:

" I clean fail to see a way out of this scrape. Appearances are
against us. The fate of both, on Bluecoat's oath (that rhymes,
doesn't it?) depends entirely. It has just struck me whether
Providence has resolved to give every one of your family the
blessing of going to prison for a while. Some of them you
know, were quite at home there; then there was your brother
—one of the best lads breathing—he too had a spell. And now,
here's you. Are you down in Elian's Well, say? Wait you,
weren't Paul and Silas in durance vile once? I slip into English unawares. Well, we are as harmless as they were. And
how did they get out of the bother? Was it not by singing and
prayer? Well, if you'll only pray I'll sing until the place re-
sounds. I'll take oath!"

While Will was uttering those last words, we were both

astonished by a loud laugh from the officer, who, addressing us in Welsh, said: "Boys, what was your business at that house?"

"Holloa! John Jones from the land of my fathers! Where's your latch-key, to open these cuffs? *Oes y byd i'r iaith Gymraeg!* * Yes, that's it. *Cymry rhydd Cymry fydd!* * cried Will delightedly, as the officer was freeing us, which he promptly did. While he was taking the handcuffs from our wrists, Will heaped up words of commendation upon his head, amongst the most honourable of them being "trump," "old brick," "A 1," &c., twisting together pleasantry, gratitude, a full and satisfactory explanation of our conduct, all on one string, without pausing to take breath, and winding up with an offer to stand the constable the price of a dinner.

"No!" replied the officer. "'Bluecoat' is 'an exception.' He won't take to be rewarded. Go home now, like good children."

"You are true to nature and an honour to your country. You ought to be made an inspector at once," declared Will.

After some further conversation with our captor we left, on good terms and in good spirits.

"D'ye know what?" said Will. "I'll never again say Bobbies are humbugs without exception. There are good sorts in their midst, also. I think, sometimes, it is worth a man's while to get into a scrape, for the pleasure of getting out of it again. Only once was I ever in the grip of one of those chaps before—about a year ago. I knew a girl in this town— there was nothing definite between us, you know, only we were extra good friends—and one night I went to send her home. I accompanied her to the house and remained there some time— longer than I thought. I warrant you it was eleven o'clock, when, all of a sudden, I heard the mistress coming down from the sitting room; and the girl, instead of being straightforward and saying who I was, shoved me into a pantry, or some such place, where it was frightfully close. Well to you, I heard the missis ordering the girl to bed, and afterwards locking the

---

* Well-known Welsh sayings, meaning "The world's age to the Cymric tongue," and "Free Welsh the Welsh shall be," respectively.—TRANS-LATOR.

front door and the back; but I never thought she would take
the keys with her. After that I heard both going up the
stairs; but I believed the girl would return to let me out.
Nearly smothered, I opened the pantry door, or whatever it
was. The fire was as dark as the black cow's belly, and I
didn't know what in the world to do. I waited a while, and
presently I heard the girl softly stealing down in her stocking
feet. Never was I more glad to see candle light. I was in a
hurry to get out, because I knew it wasn't right to stay in
anybody's house on the sly. I was real sorry for the girl,
when she told me her mistress had the keys and that it was
impossible for me to leave. But I was *bound* to get out, if I
had to break a hole in the wall; because it wouldn't be true to
nature, or honourable, to stay in the house all night. Said I
to the girl, "What would be easier than to go through the
front parlour window?" "Well, yes indeed," she replied,
being Welsh. So she put the candle on the table, and away
we went to the parlour. I remember very well that the moon
was shining on the window. There was a flower stand near by,
and in my haste I upset one of the pots and smashed it. Fairplay for the girl, she said, "The cat'll get the blame for that."
The lower part of the window, I should think, had not been
opened for I don't know how long, and after I had raised it
some ten inches or so, it wouldn't budge a peg. There was nothing to be done but to squeeze myself through. When I was
about half-way out, there I stuck, as tight as a wedge, and I
thought once it was there I should remain. But I got help.
In a couple of minutes I felt someone tugging at me, and the
buttons of my vest being all torn away. It was the bobby—
the point to which I was steering, only I've been rather long
with my story. When the girl saw me in the policeman's
hands, she burst out crying at a fine rate, which was the first
time I knew she was fond of me. 'Don't cry Gwen *fach*,' said
I to her—her name was Gwen—'I'll come and see you, directly
I get out of gaol,' which made her ten times worse. I never saw
her again. But this is the point: that bobby knew very well
I had done nothing wrong, and yet he wanted five
shillings for letting me go. After a good deal of argument I
brought him down to half a crown. Their screw is such a

2 c

small one, you know, they must get a job of this sort sometimes to make up for it. Are you tired? Or are you not so
swift of foot as you used to be? You drag in the under-
standings in a most remarkable way. Have you a touch of
rheumatism, tell me? We haven't far to go, now."

"The less the better," I responded. "I'm dreadfully tired.
But do you know, Will? It is 65, Gregg Street I have for
ever in my mind. How can I gain admission into that house?"

I then told my friend what I had witnessed before the officer
handcuffed us, adding: "I am bound, before leaving this town,
to get further light on what I have seen. It is evident Nic'las
does not stay there. He had his hat on, as if he were about to
start out. You understand my anxiety."

After much consultation between us, Will presently said:—

"I have it! Do you remember me bidding you not be in
too great a hurry to put on a white tie? Circumstances alter
cases; you must begin to wear one to-morrow. There are
people here who call themselves town missionaries—men who
are always going about looking up, not their friends, but someone who is sick or ungodly, to try and do good. Somehow or
other they get at all those who are ill, as if they knew the scent
of them. I have only been four days ill since I'm here. One
of these people came to see me three times during that period,
and told me a lot of good things—if I had only done them.
There are two things I don't like about them: one is, they
expect a man to believe right off, without giving him time to
consider; and the other, they puff the Gospel too much, to my
mind. They are not like the old _Corph_, which thinks the
Gospel too good to need puffing, and that those who want it
will come to chapel to ask for it. No, these town missionaries
are like the patent medicine men, who advertise every day, and
leave a paper in every house, giving an account of a lot of
people who've been cured. What puzzles me about them is
that they are never in the glums, like your mother, old Abel,
and others in the chapel at home, whom I knew to be extra
pious. No danger! The town missionaries are always jolly,
as if they had never sinned! I'll take oath they are good people,
because they don't want anything with a body except to do him
good. Still, I can't swallow it how they're always so happy.

And they expect everybody else to be the same. I sometimes think that if the angel Gabriel had sinned as much as I have, though he got forgiveness, he'd be down in the dumps, occasionally, even in heaven itself. But these town missionaries never are; and the common people and the poor respect them and let them into their houses to give them advice. D'ye see the plan? You can speak English properly, and there's nothing to prevent your going to 65, Gregg Street and killing two birds with the one stone. But here's my crib. Don't expect to find a smart place, for I haven't begun to keep a butler, yet."

Will took a key from his pocket and let us both into his lodgings. When he had shut the door we were in perfect darkness. Will struck a match. On a little table behind us, I saw a candlestick. Will on lighting the candle said,

" I am the last in to-night, or you'd see a lot of candles here. This house is for all the world—you follow me upstairs, and don't make more noise than you can help, for everybody is asleep—for all the world like a dove cot. There are eight of us staying here, every one with a room to himself, and not one of us knowing yet in which room the landlady, her daughter and the servant live. But they are here somewhere. Here is my room. The best thing I can say about my billet is that it's clean. Make yourself at home while I get the grub ready. Here's a place for you to wash; for you shan't eat in my house without washing, after handling that son of a gun's corpse."

I was astonished. In size the room was only about four yards square, and yet it contained a bed, a cupboard, two chairs, a round table, and several other necessaries besides. On the table was a clean white cloth, with a cup and saucer, two plates and two knives and forks. By the fire side were a kettle and a coffee pot.

"I see," remarked Will, pulling off his coat for a wash, "that you are taking stock. Which would you rather? Tea or coffee?"

"Well, Will bach!" I exclaimed. "And you have come to this!"

I could hardly help laughing.

"Come to what?" asked Will. "To one room? I maintain it's true to nature. Every creature God made, except man, lives in one room, after leaving the open air; and it's the merest humbug to have a lot of rooms. Besides, how can even man live in more than one room at a time? The thing is a physical impossibility. You mustn't think 'tis hard up I am; as I shall show you directly. Say the word: tea or coffee?"

"Tea," I replied.

"Same here," said Will unlocking the cupboard, taking out the indispensables and deftly preparing the meal.

"You needn't have a better woman than this landlady of mine," he observed. "Sometimes I don't see her for a whole week together. When I want anything, I write the order on that slate, put the money on the mantlepiece, and, by the time I get back, all will be snug on the table. When I first came here I never used to lock the cupboard, and I must admit my landlady, at that time, would take the loan of some of my things, now and again. I'll tell you how I caught her. I found that the tea got low rather quickly, so what did I do but catch a live gnat and clap it into the canister. When I next went to open it the gnat was gone. That was a proof positive. But the fault was mine; the woman was perfectly honest if I only locked the cupboard."

All this Will spoke on his knees, before the fire, toasting ham upon a fork. In a few minutes the meal was ready. After a little reflection Will said, "I see there is a drawback—I have only one cup and saucer; but, for this occasion you take the cup and I'll take the saucer."

So we did, and from that day to this I never remember enjoying a meal more heartily. Subsequently, at my request, Will related his history. Although I believe I could repeat it almost word for word, I shall only attempt a chronicle of the principal facts, doing so as near as can be in his own words, which were as follow:—

CHAPTER XL.

THE AUTOBIOGRAPHY OF WILL BRYAN.

"You know," Will began, "what made me leave home. I can tell you in two words—high stomach. I who had been in the habit of holding my head so proudly, who used to drive like fury through the streets, who had acted the gallant with the girls there! No, I couldn't bear the disgrace of my father's liquidation. I had a little money put by, but not enough to emigrate on; so I made for this big town, thinking I'd hit upon a job in three or four hours. But, after coming here and seeing all the people, I felt lonely and disheartened. I was afraid to ask for a job because I hadn't learnt to do anything except drive. I knocked about until I had finished my money and then—you'd never believe the difference there is between a high stomach and an empty one. For some days before my money gave out, I had been mooning around the stables picking up stray bits of information, because I saw it was to that it must come. You know I wasn't quite in rags, and perhaps there was a little too much swagger in me; so, at first, the cabbies used to touch their hats to me, as if I was somebody; which, to tell the truth, I was sorry to see. It went to my heart to be obliged to sell the watch-guard mother gave me when I was eighteen. But what was I to do? I kept on going to the stables, and I fancy the cabbies must have thought me some gentleman's son who had quarrelled with his father—they were so awfully respectful to me. They had spotted I was hard up, and they used to quarrel as to who should stand me a glass; thinking, I should imagine, it would be nothing to see me, some day, after I had squared it with my father, throwing them a five pound note. That was all right; for why should I tell them my history? I pawned my overcoat. By this time I had made chums with the owner of stables, horses and all. He would shake hands with me and, on the quiet, try to pump me as to my antecedents. But Will was too deep for him; and continued to be a great mystery. One day—I think it must have been the day I took my watch to my uncle's—I

asked the gaffer for a job as a cabby. He laughed until he
nearly made himself ill, thinking it was only a hobby of mine.
But I stuck to him. In a couple of days one of the men was
laid up with inflammation of the lungs, after being out over
night. I applied for his place until he got well and, in fun,
was given it. As I was crossing the court-yard on the dickey
there were roars of laughter, the master laughing loudest.
But Will was also laughing—in his sleeve—and hoping, I fear,
that the poor man would be long ill, because I was really hard
up. They soon saw that the young swell, as they called me,
could handle a horse with the best of them. I was wonderfully lucky that day, and the next, and during the week. So I
settled for a wage, master laughing at the way in which he fed
my hobby, he thought.

      •   •   •   •   •

" Mixing with the cabbies, I am sorry to tell you, I got to
live as they did, and to indulge in the ' everlasting two
penn'orth.' I was not seasoned, as they were, you know; so,
one day, having taken too much, I pitched on my head off the
dickey. They carried me to bed here, and there I lay for four
days, when the town missionary came to see me and give me a
word of advice. He understood by my speech that I had not
been brought up in China, and took a wonderful interest in me.
He reasoned with me and reckoned on that slate how much a
cabby paid every year for painting his nose red and blue, and
damning his soul into the bargain. It was a goodish sum. I
resolved, before getting out of bed, that no more two penn'orths
should go down Will's red lane again; and none ever went.
When you remember the kind of fellow I once was you'll
wonder at what I am now going to say. After becoming ' teetot,'
I got to be a regular miser. Once I began to save and acquired a liking for it, I was afraid to spend a penny. The last
thing I used to do every night before going to bed was to
reckon up my money. In a few weeks' time I was the owner
of some pounds, which I kept under my head at night and
carried inside my vest by day, for fear they would be prigged.
I wouldn't put them in the bank for a reason you shall presently know. I lived on bread and butter and tea; and preferred

putting sixpence in my purse to getting something appetising
for supper. One morning in the stables I was a bit behind
with the horse. Two other cabbies were standing over me,
waiting me to finish. My vest being unbuttoned, out fell my
purse, and some fifteen sovereigns or so rolled about the ground.
Both men nearly fainted at the sight; both were there and then
confirmed in the notion that I was a gentleman's son who was
worth his thousands; and both wondered at my strange hobby.
They talked of nothing else to their chums that day; and the
next, the gaffer challenged me as to my previous history. He
knew I hadn't robbed him, because I brought in more money
than any man in his stables. I kept them all in the dark and
bought a swell suit, all pockets; punishing myself a bit to
make up the money I had paid for it, although I needn't have
done so, because customers picked me out, on account of my
being respectably dressed, and gave me, occasionally, an extra
fee. Having more money than I could safely carry about with
me, I bought a lever lock for the box there, and fixed it on
myself, lest anyone should spot me. It cost me four and
six, and I gave eightpence for a gimlet, screws and a
screw driver. After coming home at night, I would find
enjoyment in counting my money over and over. And then I
used to vex myself by calculating how much more I should be
worth if I hadn't bought so many two penn'orths. Sometimes
I would be astonished and doubt whether I were myself; my
conscience telling me I was a humbug, and that I wasn't
true to nature. The way I'd shut her up was to call to mind a
lot of pious old Methodists who, I knew well, were not as I
was; and I'd recollect how they used to groan at parting with
a shilling. By this time I could sympathise with those I remembered coming to father's shop to buy. How I used to
notice the way their shoulders rose with every groan! And yet
my conscience insisted upon saying I was no better now than
in my drinking days. But I soon taught her to say other
things. I had an idea, all the while, of going on my own
hook; because I never liked the notion of being a servant.
You know my delight was always a horse, and if I know anything at all, it is about a horse I do know it. That was the
reason Mr. Edwards of Caerwys and I were always such

chums. Very shortly—tell me if you are tired of the story—
very shortly, I came to know every horse in the town, and
their points, good and bad. One chap here had an animal
which was a real good sort, one with bone in him, you know.
But the fellow was starving him. He was always three sheets
in the wind, and thinking he was buying feed for the animal,
when he was calling for two penn'orth. D'ye know what?
My heart used to bleed for that poor creature, and many times
did I give him my own horse's nose-bag out of pity. And
Bob—the horse's name was Bob, the same name as your brother
—knew me as well as you do; and perhaps you won't believe
me, but I have seen him, when I would be driving to meet him,
stand stock still on the street, out of respect for me, or as if he
were expecting something, I don't exactly know which. However, Bob got worse every day, until at last he could hardly
come up to the scratch. He was quiet and spiritless that so,
had someone fired a gun within an inch of his ear, he would
never have winced. One day, in the cabstand, he took to
shivering at a fearful rate. A lot of people got about him, all
expecting, every minute, to see him drop. I pulled him out of
the cab, but he wouldn't move a peg. Everybody said 'twould
be best to settle him. But before they did so I offered to buy
him for a sovereign, as he was; and I got him. I remembered
one of Mr. Edwards's recipes, threw my rug over the horse,
and ran into a chemist's shop across the street, much fearing
the poor thing would die before I came back. I knew it was
starving the horse was, for he gaped just like a man who is
hungry. By the time I returned, Bob had got past noticing
anybody, and I thought it was all up with him. The chaps
kept asking me what would I take for his skin. I said nothing; but as he was in the midst of a gape, I poured some of
the physic down his throat. I then asked the chaps to help
me to rub his legs. They took hold of him, one in each leg, to
get up the circulation, just for fun, they thought. Well, I'll
take my oath that before ten minutes were over Bob began to
revive, and look about to see what we were doing. There were
hundreds of people gathered round and laughing. One of
the fellows at his forelegs — an Irishman, and wonderfully witty—presently yelled out that he had been bitten,

whereupon there were roars of laughter. You will hardly
believe me, but in half an hour Bob was eating a nice warm
mash, as well as ever I saw him in my life, and the crowd
shouting 'Hooray!' The man who had sold him to me
always looked like a calf, but he now looked black as my hat.
He wanted to cry off the bargain, but the crowd protested.
They called me a smart fellow; knowing nothing, of course, of
Mr. Edwards of Caerwys. Well, I hired a stall and tended the
horse. I fed him and slaved, and Bob got better every day—
for he wasn't old you know—until at last he got to kick and
bite everybody about him, but me; with me he behaved like a
Christian. Between everything I reckon he had cost me a
matter of five pounds or so, when I gave my master a week's
notice. I bought a second-hand cab cheap, and, when I turned
out on my own hook, Bob had filled up his coat, and was shining
at such a rate that the chaps swore I had been using Day and
Martin's blacking on him. To a certain extent, I became
famous, and got as much work as I liked. The man of whom
I had bought Bob was for going on the spree every time he saw
me; but I couldn't help that. The more money I got, the
more I wanted, and I thought of nothing else—I never looked
at book or paper. I made a good deal by pretending to be a
bit of a vet. Are you tired of my story?"

"Yes, and have been for some time, Will," I replied. "If
you've nothing better to say, give it up. You are not a bit
like yourself."

"Have patience a minute," said Will. "Is it at the beginning or the end you put the best things into a sermon? If at
the beginning you are not worthy of the craft. Well, to you,
one night, after rather a good day's work, and when I' believe
I ate a quarter of a pound of sausage for supper, I reckoned
my money, and found myself worth forty-eight pounds, exclusive of the concern, which made me feel happy and independent, somehow. It was the sausage did the job, I
believe. Unconsciously I began humming a tune. And what
do you think it was? The old 'Black Flower;' and I do
not much fancy anyone ever got a blessing from singing
that particular ditty besides myself. Well, I began looking

it over to see whether I remembered it, and when I came to
the words,

> 'How fares my father, mother dear,
> How is the 'state succeeding?'

I clean broke down, an awful regret came over me and I
cried till I was tired. I fell to thinking of the old things, my
mother especially, and what a selfish young devil I was to be
scraping up money, I did not know what for; until I at last
got to feel, I should imagine, something very much like
religion. I had not written the old folk since I had left home,
and I didn't know whether they had anything to eat, or
whether they were alive or dead. This is not true to nature
said I, and I had another spell of crying. I at once set to, and
wrote the gaffer, asking him if he was alive, how was he
getting on, and what was the amount he had failed for? I put
the letter into the post that night for fear I should change my
mind before the morning. After dropping it in, I felt as if I
were no longer cabby, but Will Bryan, and I can't tell you the
pleasure I got when I found my old self coming back. I had
not changed by the morning, and was on fire for an answer to
my letter, which I got by return, written by the old woman;
my father, she said, being too cut up. But I knew that was
only a dodge of hers, for fear my father would say something
nasty which would drive me fifty miles further away. Old
Hugh was not so tender hearted as all that. The mother
craved like a cripple that I should return home, and said how
glad she was to hear from her prodigal son. That was a
mistake; for there's no analogy between the prodigal son and
myself. That chap's father was a wealthy gentleman, who gave
him half the estate. After spending thousands of pounds, he
had to go feeding pigs, and come home again in rags. My
father went to smash, and I never had the chance of spending
five pounds of his. Neither did I lower myself by pig-feeding;
and I'll never go home in rags, I swear. There's no analogy
at all, I repeat. Four hundred pounds it was the old boy had
failed for. The creditors accepted five shillings in the pound
which he had paid. He was now getting along very well and
had given over speculating,so mother said. But surely, you must

know all this. And just fancy the old woman's cuteness: 'Suze, is still single' she said. The gaffer would never have thought of such tactics. Though I knew it was my mother's cunning which made her mention Suze, the arrow went home, and I'd have at that moment given all I was worth for a glimpse of the girl. But, for all my regret and the feeling of my old self's return, I beat it down, and declared I would never go home until my father had paid every farthing of his debt; for I could never think of returning unless I were able to hold my head erect. I wrote back to say I was in a good place— they do not know yet I am a cabby, and don't you split—and I made a bargain with them that I would come home after they had wiped off the whole debt, which I would help them to do. And that is what has been going on now for some time. We have cleared away about two hundred pounds, including the composition. Here's a receipt for ten pounds I got from the gaffer this morning—read it."

Will handed me the letter, on looking at which I observed, "Walter Bateson is the name I find here, Will."

"Certainly," said Will. "That's why I fear to put my money in the bank. I did not like anyone in this place to know my name, lest they should think me an Irishman; and for other reasons besides."

"This is not worthy of you, Will," was my response.

"What harm is there in the thing?" asked Will. "Look at them in Wales. Nobody of note there goes by his own name. There is greater reason why I should call myself Walter Bateson than that some John Jones should call himself *Llew Twllylwl!* 'What's in a name? A rose'—you know the rest. And the initials, 'yours truly, W. B.', still stand good. But the old people don't like it at all; and, to tell the truth, when I felt my former self return, I had a mind to throw my new name over, if I had only known how."

"I heard, when I was at home," said I, "that your father was paying his debts and speedily regaining his old position; but little did I know you were helping him. It is very creditable in you. You are doing well; but you would be doing better by going home to assist your parents in the business. I

am very pleased to meet you, Will; but permit me to say, you
have greatly changed. To hear you talk of money and ——."

"Hold on!" interrupted Will. "I know that myself. I
know I have lost my talent, and that I can no longer say anything worth the hearing. But you must remember that I am
coming back—I haven't reached myself, as yet; but I'm coming. I don't want to come too fast; but, when I reach the real
W. B., I'll go home and put the break on."

"Will," I remarked, "you say nothing about religion or
chapel. Do you never go to chapel or church?"

"There's no use telling lies—you'd never think how little I
have done in that way. You know I don't like the church. I
went once to the Dissenters' chapel here—Congregationalists
they call themselves—and sat near the door. The minister is
a Welshman, named Price, whom they are always advertising.
Well, out of curiosity I went to hear him. And what do you
think his text was? Morgan of Dyffryn's old one—about the
little foxes. I don't remember the verse, but it's somewhere
in the Old Testament. I, however, remember a lot of the
sermon because it had tickled me, above a bit. 'Just let's
see,' said I to myself; 'can you, I wonder, discourse as well as
old Morgan could on that particular verse?' I sat me down to
listen. In ten minutes I spotted it was translating Mr. Morgan's
sermon my nabs was, and so I bolted; for I consider the man
who prigs a sermon is no better than he who prigs a sovereign,
nor as good, because he gets paid for it, while the other fellow
gets three months. I went to no place at all for a good long
while after that. By accident, however, I turned one Sunday
night into the Wesleyan chapel here. I liked the minister praying first class—if he had only got quiet. But, I never came
across such a thing! A lot of the congregation got passing remarks so loudly upon his prayer that I couldn't make out
how he wasn't bewildered. He preached about Peter, after that
person had slipped and made a mess of it. I was rather well
up in the history, and was getting interested. But if Peter
only heard him, he wouldn't have thanked him I'm sure, for he
ran the saint down at a shocking rate. I didn't like the man's
doctrine, either. He said it was possible for a man to get religion and lose it after, for every thing depended on the man
himself. If such is the case, good bye to Will Bryan. I

reasoned, then, that if the man bungled about a thing in which
I was well up, how could I tell he was right in the thing
which I knew nothing about? I never went there again.
About a fortnight ago I found out that the old *Corph* had a
Welsh chapel here, and I went to it. It is not like the chapel
at home. It is a lot of swells is in the big seat. Looking
around I saw an Abel Hughes here and there among the congregation; but 'twas all swells in the big seat. It was a young
chap who preached, and by his cut I took him to be a Bala
postage stamp—no offence mind. Have you never wondered
that a new sect has not arisen to take up the good points of all
the denominations? Something of this sort, now: let them
adopt the style of the Church of England; the smartness of
the Congregationalists, the go-aheadedness of the Wesleyans,
and the doctrine of the old *Corph.* I don't know much about
the Dippers, but I should think they must have their good
points. Each sect excels the other in something. I like the
style of the English Church; they are more devotional, don't
look about them, or talk to each other during service; only I
think they must be awfully ignorant. Well, there's the Congregationalists; just see how smart and witty they are. They
are extraordinarily clever, only there's too much of the trail of
politics and the eisteddfod over them all. Nearly every one of
them makes an *englyn*,* and sports a *nom de plume*, only I
should not be the one to say anything about that. There are
the Wesleys again; see how ardent, how warm and how jolly
they are. Only I think they must be fearfully clannish. They
all pray in the same fashion, too; and are too forward at it—
as if they were talking to the man next door. Well, there are
we, the old *Corph.* I say 'we' because I consider myself a
sort of honorary member still. I always think the old *Corph*
is the John Bull of Wales. The Dissenters, you know, won't
admit this; but no matter. The old *Corph* reminds me of a
stout, unwieldy chap, very difficult to move. There is no use
trying to tickle him, he is too thick-skinned. He must have
his own time; but, when he does move, he moves like an

---

* Epigram.—Translator.

elephant, and no matter how much you hitch on to him he'll pull it to anywhere and back again. Do you twig it is figuratively I'm speaking? You know Duke, William the Coal's mule? I can't tell how he is, now, but time was when there was no stronger mule in the country. He wouldn't move a peg, however, unless he liked to himself, and nothing had any effect upon him except old William's goad. In the summer other mules had a bunch of hazel stuck in their heads to keep the flies away. But what did Duke care about flies? Nothing affected him but the goad, and if ever they make a post mortem examination of him they'll find his skin like a pepper box, I'll take my oath. I have seen Duke, though, whenhe was in the humour, draw twelve hundred weight of coal to the top of the bank, like a shot. I look upon the old *Corph* as much the same. Perhaps you'll tell me I'm showing a want of taste, and perpetrating an anticlimax; but you must remember I never was in college. What I mean is—the old *Corph* is too slow; it has enough power, but no go. It is too serious also; too much like a funeral. Now wouldn't it be possible to start a fresh denomination which would take up the good points of all the rest? What do *you* think?"

"I think, Will that you are 'coming back,' and that you have not yet lost your old pertness. But with reference to starting a new sect, don't you think it would be better if we tried, first of all, to combine the virtues you have been speaking of in our own persons? What would you say to beginning a new life? Do you never yearn for what you do not possess, or, possessing, do not wish to put it from you, like the 'two penn'orths' and the avarice. You do well by paying your father's debt; but what about your own? That must be paid, some day, you know. In other words, what do you think of the dread future which is awaiting you and I? What, by this time, do you think of religion?"

"I expected you to talk of that sort of thing," Will observed, sadly. "If you hadn't done so, I should have thought you were not fit to be a preacher. I believe your words are not cant, and that it is my good you are seeking. I, however, do not know how to answer your question. I would tell a lie did I say religion is not on my programme; but, up to now, it is

in the second part. I remember the time when it stood very
low down in that part, next to 'God Save the Queen.' I made
the very same remark to the town missionary, whose words I
shall always remember, 'How would it be,' he asked, 'if you
had to leave in the interval? You came very near going before
the end of the first part when you fell on your head off the
dickey?' Not so bad, was it? Well, to you, I have thought,
for some time, that religion has got higher up in the progamme
since; and now and then I seem to long for her turn to come.
Although still a young chap, I am just about tired of the comic
songs of my life, if you understand me. I'm nearly always
jolly, but I never was happy. No matter how jolly I am, I
know, all the while, there is something which stinks in the
corruption of my heart."

"I am glad you find the odour annoying, and that your soul
yearns after purification and true happiness. I must say——"

"Here," he interrupted. "I don't want a sermon. I have
heard thousands of those things. What I want is sound, com-
monsense advice. Never going to chapel, I have no chum,
and that is not true to nature. As to the chaps I mix with,
every day, they have nothing in their heads, and they don't
think of anything besides beer. Though I never found real
religion—because I do not think it possible a man can get the
real thing and lose it afterwards—I sometimes think I got a
sort of innoculation in the old chapel at home, such as has
prevented me from having any very bad attack of small pox
since. I had a slight touch when I came here first; but it
did'nt mark me deeply—at least, I hope so. Do you make me
out?"

"Of course," replied I. "We both were brought up
religiously from childhood; and, despite it all, we strayed from
the right road and wandered long. But I always hoped, Will,
you had not lost your good impressions—the 'innoculation' as
you call it."

"But your innoculation 'took' better than mine. I must
have a fresh one before I shall be safe," observed Will.

"Go to the Doctor, then," said I. "Inquire for the surgery.
By this time you have 'spotted' the Welsh chapel. I do not
wish to imply that other denominations are not as good as ours;
but our up-bringing, possibly our prejudices, prevent our

receiving as much blessing from them as we may expect from the old *Corph.* What is there to prevent your going to chapel regularly? You'll find friends there, very soon, for you have such a knack of introducing yourself. And who knows but that you will hit upon the Friend who will continue?"

"It is there I'd like to be, every Sunday," returned Will. "But, if I went, the minister and the deacons would spot me, inquire my name, and where I live. I should be obliged to say William Bryan, and give the number of the house; or remain a humbug. Well, the minister would come here and ask, 'Is Mr. William Bryan within?' To which the landlady would answer, 'There's no one of the name living here.' And how should I look? If I gave an alias in chapel, it would seem as if I was trying to cheat the Almighty; and that I will never do. I could get over the difficulty by changing my lodgings, if Walter Bateson had not been registered for the cab; and I do not know whether they permit initials. But I see every day I feel myself coming back that I shall have to drop the 'alter' and 'ateson,' and substitute 'illiam' and 'ryan' before reaching myself. If I do not find some decent way of getting out of it, I'll throw off my Inverness, show a bold front, and take my seat in chapel; you mark my word. But here you are, if you wish to be in trim for visiting the sick to-morrow, you must go to your kennel; for it is now a quarter to three."

There was but a step between us and the bed; and I was glad the journey was so short. I slept profoundly; and I remember, even now, that in the morning I was for some minutes, between sleeping and waking, that I could not make out whether I was handling bacon, or smelling someone shaking me. When I got fully awake, I found the facts were reversed. Will, who was at my head, had great trouble in rousing me; and a smell of bacon and coffee filled the room. Rubbing my eyes, I felt as if I had been in a dream, although the room and everything in it answered exactly to what I had seen, except that there were two cups and saucers on the table instead of one. Will and I spent some hours talking over what had occurred, before beginning the work of the day.

"Now for the choker" said Will; "if you are bound to go to that house. But, if I were you, I'd chuck up the idea; for, how much better will you be after going? I'll inquire for the choker in two minutes, and, while you are decking yourself I'll fetch Bob; because I mean to give to-day to the Queen."

Will used to govern me as a lad. I felt myself in his hands once more, and under some sort of compulsion to wear a white neckerchief, and to carry out his other instructions. I was ready to submit to any plan, almost, in order to attain my object that morning, because I felt under vow to the one I loved most, and, if I lost this opportunity, I knew I should never forgive myself for it. I found that Will had borrowed a trap, so that, as he expressed it, he "shouldn't be hailed." Much as I had heard about Bob on the previous night, I was too deeply engrossed with the outcome of my adventure to take any very great notice of the animal when I got the advantage of seeing him by daylight. But I re-collect remarking that he was in good condition and that Will said he was called "Lazarus" by the "chaps." Our plan was for Will to drive me to Gregg Street and leave me there to do my errand; then, at the end of half an hour, he was to fetch me to spend the day with him in any fashion I thought fit. But the way of man is not in himself. When we got within a hundred yards or so of the place at which we were taken prisoners the night before, Will pulled up his reins and said, in an excited tone, "I'll take my oath! Here's the very bobby who nabbed us last night, and he is motioning to us!" Such was the fact. Within the minute, the officer was at our side ordering us to stop. Will, like myself, was visibly agitated.

"Rhys Lewis," said the man in blue; "come down."

I obeyed, and, although I tried to appear bold, I felt myself tremble, and knew I was becoming pale in the face.

Will jumped down the same instant, observing, "I'll follow you wherever it is, even if the concern was to go to Bryn Eglwys;" and he threw the reins on Bob's back.

2 D

The officer smiled and said "don't be alarmed. Do you know me, Rhys Lewis?

I shook my head.

"Bryan, do you know me?" he asked.

"To be sure," replied Will. "Wasn't it you who lent me a pair of cuffs last night?"

"Will," said the officer, "don't you remember getting the loan of a cane from me, more than once?"

After looking at him for a second or two Will exclaimed, "Well, may I never become a wooden bedstead if this isn't Sergeant Williams! No wonder you turned out such a trump last night! And how are you, old A 1? Can't you get leave of absence for to-day?"

"Perhaps I can, Mr. Bateson," replied the officer.

Will, looking a bit sheepish, observed "True to nature, sergeant. The Welshman must have an alias—a bardic name, you know."

"I didn't know, before, that cabbies were noted as bards," said the Sergeant.

"Hush!" returned Will. "Least said soonest mended. I I feel just as if I were at home. Here am I myself, Rhys Lewis and Sergeant Williams, and it only wants William the Coal, Duke, and that old thoroughbred Thomas Bartley to make us complete."

At first, Sergeant Williams's appearance gave me the greatest uneasiness, for my reminiscences of him were none of the most agreeable. But my fears were soon scattered. After a brief conversation, Will sprang into his trap and drove off. The Sergeant came with me to 65, Gregg Street, and knocked at the door, which was opened by a sturdy, masculine-looking woman. I saw at once that she and the Sergeant knew each other. Having told her my business, he left me. I was led by the woman to the room I had tried to see into on the previous night, and after she had announced "The Minister," she too left me, shutting the door behind herself. Ever since awaking that morning, my heart had kept beating at a rapid rate. I felt that I had an unpleasant task to perform, and one which I could not shirk, even were the heavens to fall. Before me I saw him whom I had partly seen the night before, and similarly placed—sitting up in bed. Pulling myself together, as best

I could, I gave him greeting, in English, almost directly on my
entrance to the room, although a legion of thoughts had
swarmed through my mind before I spoke and before he could
answer. This was the first time I had seen the man's face;
but I carried in my breast a load of his history—a history
which was anything but comforting.

When I asked him how he felt, he answered in the single
word—"Bad."

Asked whether he entertained any hope of recovery, he sorrow-
fully shook his head.

I questioned him concerning his thoughts and previsions,
but could only get a shake of the head in reply.

I tried to lead his mind to God and His mercy to the chiefest
of sinners, and to as many as I could remember of the promises
of the Bible. But his only response was a head-shake, denoting profoundest misery and deepest despair.

After fairly exhausting myself in these directions, I, too, became silent. In thought I felt myself carried far back to a
bedroom in the house of Thomas Bartley, where I heard my
mother—up to the throat in death—enjoining me, again and
again: "If ever you meet him, and who knows but you will,
try and remember he is your father; try and forget his sins,
and, if you can do him any good, do it!" Then would my mind
revert to the night on which Seth died, when I met my uncle
near the Hall Park; to the words with which he enlightened
me as to the history of my family, and to the things which my
brother Bob had, on the same night, softly and in the darkness
of our room, told me concerning my father—his descent of the
downward path, his extravagance and his cruelties towards
mother. I remembered how I was obliged to stuff the bed-
sheets into my mouth lest I should cry out while Bob was telling me of mother, compelled to stay away from chapel because
of blackened eyes, after a beating from my father. I remembered wondering how she could pray for him who had just
struck her, and while her blood was yet undried upon her
apron from the blow. O, how I hated the wretch then! How
glad did I feel that I had never seen his face! But now I was
at his side, I heard the words—not as an echo of the past, but
as if they were being spoken for the first time by the same

sweet lips: "If ever you meet him, and who knows but you
will, try and remember he is your father; try and forget his
sins, and, if you can do him any good, do it!" Yes, I was
gazing upon him, my father! Hardly could I realise the fact.
He, the once strong man lay before me a helpless heap; and
there was no need of the aroma of whiskey which filled the
room to assist me to a correct conclusion as to the means by
which he had been brought to this pitiful state. My uncle and
he had run their course almost neck and neck.

Should I reveal myself to him? Would that be wise? Would
it serve any good purpose? Obviously, his life was near its
close; and I had done all in my power to make him understand the seriousness of the situation. I had tried to set before him the graciousness of the Gospel, and how it bade the
greatest sinner hope, to the last. I had reminded him of those
who had been called at the eleventh hour, and of the thief on
the Cross; but nothing I could say touched his feeling or
kindled any sort of interest in him. I asked if I should pray
with him; and he resolutely refused. What more could I do
for him? I never saw a man with so wretched a look; and I
trust I never shall again. He seemed as one who had taken leave
of all comfort and hope, and was fast sinking into darkness,
strange and unfathomable. My allusions to the promises
of Scripture only made him take one more plunge into the
depths. The verses I quoted, instead of consoling terrified
him, as old acquaintances whom he dreaded to meet; and I
noticed that, with what of strength remained to him, he tried to
move farther away from me towards the wall. He sometimes
seemed agitated, as if his heart were taking fire, for he would
clutch at the bed clothes tightly. At other times he became
quieter, as if he had started on a long journey down into himself and had forgotten that I was in the room. But he would
presently return, and, after looking wildly about him and seeing I was still there, would move uneasily towards the wall. I
felt my presence was a burden to him, and that he was in a
hurry for me to leave; because he held out his hand more than
once towards the whiskey bottle on the little table by his side,
withdrawing it again when he found I was looking at him.

By this time he took but little notice of anything I said and,

fearing I could do him no good, I got up to go. But the words again recurred to me, "If ever you meet him," &c., as if they had come from another world. Would I have done my best by him if I did not speak to him in Welsh, and tell him who I was? Would it not be something for him to know that my mother had forgiven him his inhuman conduct towards her, even were that the only forgiveness he ever tasted? I determined to reveal myself, and tried to pray that it would affect him for good.

"Robert Lewis," I said to him, in Welsh; "do you know who is speaking to you?"

He started at the question and stared hard at me, as he had not done before. He fixed his eyes on me—marvellously bright eyes, like two lamps lighting up his way to the darkness of despair, to be speedily quenched after his passing. I divined that his mind was wandering back in search of some reminiscence of me; unsuccessfully, of course.

"I am your son, Rhys Lewis," I went on. "Father, you will be glad to hear that my mother forgave you everything before she died."

I repented a thousand times that the words ever escaped my lips. They were brief, but they pained him more than all I had said. If I had thrown a bucket of fire over him the effect could not have been more fearful. He writhed and twisted in the most indescribable torment. In a shriek of fury, and with a force of which I had not deemed him capable, he ordered me out of his sight.

"Go away! Go away!" he screamed, recoiling from me as if I were an adder, and pressing himself close against the wall, which he would have gone through, if he only could.

Alarmed by his howlings, the woman of the house rushed into the room and looked at me like a lioness. What, she asked me, furiously, had I done to the sick man? I feared she would have planted her nails in my face and, altogether too overcome to give her any explanation, I fled from the spot for very life. Recalling that sight, the words of the unclean spirits

came often to my mind: "art thou come hither to torment us
before the time?" and the words of Ellis Wynn o Glasynys—

> Second sight I'd not have had,
>   For world a myriad:
> Though they were pangs I suffered not.

The visit lasted only twenty minutes or so, but it forms the
blackest spot in all my history. I admit I did not feel the anguish
which would have been natural to a son who saw his father
in such a condition, because I had never had any regard for
the man. Horror is the fittest word to describe the sensation
at my heart. The sight made me wretched, and the only
comfort I could extract from it was that I had carried out, to
the best of my ability, the last wishes of my mother.

The Sergeant and Will Bryan were expecting me at the
appointed spot. I told them the result of my visit, and got a
rebuke from Will for not having "chucked up the idea," as he
had advised. By this time I was in a hurry to return to Bala,
the examination taking place in the following week, which
would be the final one for me. I guessed the Sergeant had
something to say to me, and guessed correctly.

"Rhys," said he in an aside, "have you anything to conceal
from Bryan?"

"Nothing," I replied.

"Good," he rejoined, adding aloud, "Well boys, where
shall we go to?"

"I am for returning to Bala at once," I remarked.

"You don't go from here to-day if I had to chain you by the
leg, as William the Coal does with Duke," declared Will.

But neither the Sergeant nor Will could prevail upon me
to stay. Will told me there was no train for an hour and a
half, and I took his word. He conducted the Sergeant and
myself to an hotel where we could get something to eat or, as
he expressed it, "a last blow out on account of yours truly."
I made but a very poor meal, being anxious to catch every
word which fell from Sergeant Williams, of which I here
present a summary.

"It is many years, Lewis," said the Sergeant, "since I last saw you. That was on the night I came to your house to take your brother Bob into custody. I shall never forget that night as long as I live. I knew Bob to be innocent, and yet I was bound to arrest him. Bob and I were great friends, and I knew your mother very well. You remember, because I saw you running from the house, the two men who set upon us as we were leaving the court-yard. You know who they were. I made the other policeman promise to say nothing about the affair. Their object, as you know, was to give Bob a chance of escape, if he had only taken it. Next day, I met the owner of the Hall, as he was going to Church, and told him I was certain that Bob, John Powell and Morris Hughes were innocent, and that it was a mistake to have them locked up. He got into a bad way, swore at me, and called me a fool for interfering. I told him to hasten to Church to pray. From that very minute, I knew my doom was sealed. The old knave never rested until he had me removed. You remember the slaughter of his pheasants on the night Bob was sent to the county gaol? It was the colliers who were blamed; but was it they who did it? No fear. I know very well there were in the country two men of far greater daring than all the colliers put together. Bob knew it, too, and so did your mother, poor thing! After what had happened, I was not the man to go and tell the owner of the Hall who it was. If I had seen all his preserves on fire, and knew I could put out the flames by spitting on them, I wouldn't have done so; for his treatment of me was worse than a dog's. After Bob was sent to prison I had a very bad time of it. Nearly everybody hated me, although I couldn't help what had happened. Before that bother, I had a great many friends about, but they all cooled towards me, and towards every policeman in the place. I wasn't at all sorry to leave. I have lived here ever since, and am now middling comfortable. About three years ago, quite accidentally, I lighted on your father. He got into a dreadful funk on seeing me, for he remembered I knew he had been guilty of something worse than poaching. But he needn't have feared, and I told him so. A very fine policeman, ain't I? But I felt I was under an obligation to your mother and to Bob,

and I had no inclination to rake up old stories. After that, I
met him many times ; and, before he became an utter slave to
drink, I used to visit him at his lodgings for a chat and a
bit of news of the old home, which he and your uncle often
visited, raiding the squire's game. They didn't conceal the
fact from me, and I wouldn't have cared had they stolen every
pheasant in the place, for I owed the old —— a grudge. I
never liked your uncle, but I could get along very well with
your father; the reason, perhaps, being that we both had such
a deadly enmity toward the squire. Your uncle never cared
who owned the game, as long as he could get hold of it; but
your father took a special pleasure in saying above his prey:
' Here's the Hall owner's birds! They've cost him ten shillings
a head!' Your father and uncle feathered the estate system-
atically throughout the years, and if you were to put me on my
oath, I could not swear that some of the pheasants have not
been on my table, for I was a friend of your father's. Fine
policeman, ain't I ? In the eating of those pheasants, my old
vengeance was better than any sauce. I used to wonder why
the two escaped capture for so long, until I got the explanation.
You remember Nic'las of Garth Ddu ? It was he who managed
their expeditions, and found the pair a hiding place. Your
father would tell me Nic'las was an old dealer in game, who
knew half the poachers in the kingdom, and had done business
with most of them. He had made a lot of money that way, and
your father and uncle had been regular customers of his before
he retired. It was your father who persuaded him to buy
Garth Ddu, which was a city of refuge for him and your uncle
ever after. The two kept up a constant correspondence with
old Nic'las. As you yourself are aware, no one over yonder
looked on old Nic'las as quite a yard ' square;' but your
father told me, many times, that if ever anybody was thirty-
seven inches to the yard, Nic'las was the man. It was he who
was their scout, and he took pleasure in the work. He walked
the old paths, through the Hall Park and Berth Goch, at
every hour of the night, without being suspected by anybody,
but feared, rather, as a lunatic. He knew the exact spot
which the keepers were watching, every night through the year.
All that happened in the town was carried to him by the old

woman, Modlen. How your father used to laugh while telling me of the jolly nights they spent at Garth Ddu after a big catch! But it is all over now! You probably know Nic'las has left Garth Ddu. O, yes; he has sold the place these three months. He's living here now, looking the same as when I first saw him. It is he who supports your father. When your father dies, no one knows where Nic'las'll be next day. You must remember what I have told you is strictly confidential."

By now I had finished my business at B——. I had got more light on what had been dark to me previously than I expected, and was in a hurry to return. The Sergeant and Will came with me to the railway station, the latter, with perfect frankness, saying: "If I had known you were going to leave us on such short notice, you'd have had no drag through the sheets last night, for I haven't told you the thousandth part of what I want to. It is just like a preacher shutting up directly he has got into the swing. A thing of this sort is not true to nature. By the time I reach myself and go home, you won't be there, for you'll be minister at Llangogor or somewhere, and I shall be without a chum."

"You are not certain of that, Will," I remarked. "What do you think? (the train was about to start), I've had a call to the pastorate of Bethel church, and I do not now see there is anything to prevent my accepting it."

Will, smiling joyously at the news, said, "Fact? (the train was moving). Well, bye bye, and remember to be true to——"

I did not catch the other word, but I guessed what it was, for I had heard the phrase hundreds of times before. Had I known at the moment that that was the last time I should hear the voice and see the face of my friend, my heart would have been sadder than it was, for, in spite of all his failings, his wit, honesty and naturalness, combined with his great fidelity to me when I was a boy, had made him a place in my heart from which I could never oust him, if I wished to. And I miss him sadly still.

Speeding my way back, I made a strong effort to forget the past, and to think only of the future. My whole being had received such a shock, and my mind was so sore disturbed, that I dreaded seeing examination day come round. I knew I should take a lower place than if what I have chronicled had not happened. This was a source of great worry to me. I foresaw that some would be ready to say I had been lazy, than which I could not imagine a more odious accusation, nor one from which I was more free,whatever might be my other short-comings. Then I would think of my father in his deplorable condition. How fearful! And yet I felt some calmness of conscience at the thought that I had done my best for him ; and I fancied, if fancy it were, hearing a well-known voice saying: "Do not grieve, my son. You have done your duty, as I my-self did mine, by him. Between him and God be it, now."

A ray of light shot across my mind. Not in vain had been my journey to B————. I persuaded myself that my encounter with Will Bryan was a blessing. I had reason to believe that he was not left untroubled by serious thoughts about his condition. He gave me his word that he would go to chapel, and I knew Will did not consider the man who broke his promise to be true to nature. Besides, I felt I was eternally rid of the nightmare which had haunted me for so many years. Henceforth I could apply myself to the work of preaching with-out fear of my name being brought into disgrace.

What now troubled me most was the examination. I was certain I should cut a sorry figure at it. But I was spared. When I reached Bala I felt very queer. I thought the old town had entirely changed within the last two days. I fancied I had made a mistake, and that I had got out at the wrong station. I was thankful it was late, for my limbs trembled, and I feared people would take me for a drunken man. After much trouble I reached my lodgings. With a great doubt on the subject, I opened the door. But I was right after all, for here was Williams shaking hands with me heartily. I have no recollection of anything else.

Nine or ten days later I found myself in bed. It was day-light, and I tried to sit up, but could not. I saw Williams at my side, and heard him say, "Well, lad ; how do you feel ?"

To which I answered, "What is the matter? Who has been beating me ? Where have I been ?"

With a brightening face, he bade me be quiet and told me I had been very ill.

"What day is it?" I asked. "When does the Exam begin?"

"It is over, since yesterday," he replied. "So you shan't be at either top or bottom this time. You must try and keep still. You have been in a heavy fever, raving day and night about Will Bryan and some Sergeant. But you're on the road to recovery now, and I am heartily glad of it. Oh! here is Dr. H——. Well, Doctor, there's some sense to be got from him to-day."

"Has he got tired of talking of Will Bryan?" asked the Doctor. "It's about time he changed his story now."

Dr. H—— was a popular man, skilful and lively, with only one fault: he would never send a bill to a student. He joked with me a deal that day. I asked him when should I go home.

"You must first go to Jericho," he said, "and stay there till your hair grows."

I felt my head. Alas! My hair had been all sheared away. I mourned it greatly, being prouder than I thought I was. I inquired how long it would take my hair to grow so that I shouldn't be a fright to myself and to others. Weeks passed before I got strong enough to go home. Williams stayed a fortnight with me, behaving towards me with indescribable kindness. A few days before wishing each other good bye I gave him the substance of that long history which I have now nearly finished, which I believe no living soul knows except he and Will Bryan, and of which the facts, if they ever see the light, after I have gone the unreturnable way, will not be new to those two.

CHAPTER XLII.

THE MINISTER OF BETHEL.

I MUST now bring my Autobiography to an end, for the same reason, partly, as that which induced me to begin it. What was that? I will give it in a very few words. I have spent some years at Bethel in the capacity of a pastor. When I began to write, I intended the history of those years to form the most important part of my work. I now see that this is out of the question, and I am sorry for having taken so much time in speaking of less worthy topics. It was not without a great deal of serious reflection that I undertook, before I was twenty-three years old, the pastorate of the church I was reared in. It was myself I feared and not the church, for I knew every one of the members, who were easily-accessible, kindly people. I wanted no time to make myself at home. In going to Miss Hughes's to lodge, I was but returning to my old habitation. All that was new to me was the work. It is not for me to say what adapability I possessed for my duties; but I can say that my heart was full of them, and that my desire to perform them in the best way possible knew no bounds. I felt that my undertaking the office gave evidence of high aspiration, and often was self-abashed in consequence. But I think the responsibility thus cast upon me, induced me to pray more. If I was bound to fail, I determined it should not be by reason of indolence, careless-ness and self-sufficiency. I worked hard—possibly too hard—but I take no credit to myself for that—I couldn't help it. My stipend was small, but it was enough; my needs were not great. Indeed, I think I found consolation many times in the meagreness of my pay. It was not sufficiently large to bring me uneasiness of mind, and it was too small for anyone else to be at the pains of reproaching me. Had anybody done so, I fear I should have refused it altogether; there being a deal of mother's unreasoning independence about me. But no one ever did. I tried to do my duty; and I had in me an ambition, a principle, or something, to give satisfaction to those whom I served. The harder I worked the calmer became my mind, the easier I could sleep of nights. If I slackened my hands, my old enemy, low spiritedness, assailed me on the instant. I have not had much cause to complain since I am here; and even if I had, there were occasions enough for thankfulness to make me hold my peace. I was not overlooked by the Monthly Meeting, and was selected for ordination much sooner than I deserved. I got every assistance and encouragement from David Davis and " Eos;" every kindness from the church in general and the young people in particular.

About two years ago, I thought this kindness was becoming

more and more marked. If I had a journey of six or eight
miles to make, David Davis would insist upon lending me his
horse. Miss Hughes was more than usually careful that I
had enough clothes about me. Thomas Bartley was constant in
enjoining me to eat plenty of ham and eggs, while others exhorted me to take care of myself. The interest taken in me
made me think of inquiring into the cause. I knew I did not deserve all this. What, then, was the reason for it? I was not long
in finding out, and, having once found it, I could detect it
in the looks and the demeanor of all my friends towards me.
I was failing in health. I had never been strong, and although I
had for some time seen that my strength was declining, I had
not apprehended any danger. Others perceived it before I did.
When I realised the fact, my spirit sank within me. The doctor tried to cheer me by saying it was only a little weakness,
for which I wanted change of air and rest. Where should I go
to? I liked the sea side. No, I should not go there; it would
be best I went to Trefriw. I understood the hint. Yes, O, sea!
It is with thee I was compelled to begin the severance of my
earthly connection. The pang it was! Although thou always
made'st me sad, I loved to roam thy shores. I felt thy sound
to correspond to something in my bosom which I could not
define; that thou didst convey some message to me, from the
far off distances, concerning the Unknown! But I was now
prohibited from visiting thee!

At Trefriw I met several old friends, some of whom were foolish enough to express their astonishment at seeing me so much
better. They tried to comfort me, to rejoice with me and cause
me to forget myself; but, beneath their joy, I detected a serious
anxiety. How I envied them their sprightliness and vigour! I
got great benefit from my stay at Trefriw, and, before leaving,
was able to enjoy a little of the innocent fun which was carried on at the Well. From this I thought I had taken a turn for
the better. I cannot tell the satisfaction and the pleasure which
filled my breast, in consequence. When I returned to Bethel,
the friends there were surprised and delighted at the change
which had taken place in me. I preached on the Sabbath following without feeling the slightest weariness; and great
was my happiness thereat.

Weeks afterwards I found I had gone back to the old mark.
Thinking I had nothing to do but to re-visit Trefriw, and no
one being able to persuade me to the contrary, I went. As far
as I could see, I was the only stranger in the village. The
weather was cold and wet. I kept my room for four days before returning home, worse in health than when I left. I
feared the doctor did not understand my complaint, and fell to
searching the newspapers for quack advertisements. I secretly
spent much money before discovering that the announcements
were lies and the testimonials but creations of the advertisers'
fancy. I could not conceal from myself the fact that my health
and strength were declining, for I felt preaching to be getting
more difficult every Sunday. The occasional beginning of
service by some kindly deacon gave me an indication of my
real condition and depressed me greatly. At first I refused
the proferred kindness which I subsequently, however, grate-
fully accepted. It is over a year since I preached last; but I
think I would have gone on longer had I not consulted another
doctor who told me the truth, and ordered me to give up the
work at once. Should the truth be at all times told? This
is a truth I am bound to tell—I grieved a good deal that that
doctor did not keep the truth from me. It was a terrible truth
and one which sank my spirit into frightful depths. I had no
desire to speak to any one for some time afterwards. There
was aroused in me a fierce craving for life of which I had not
been conscious hitherto. I felt as if I had been deceived by
that on which I had most depended. For days and nights I
quarrelled, in my mind, with doctors, fate, Providence and, I
fear, God. I saw daily passing my window much older men
than I, sturdy, strong and broad-chested; some of them cursing, swearing and getting drunk; while I, poor wretch, had a
chest like a ricketty basket. Who was it ordered things
in this way? Was all but a blind, unreasoning medley? My
plans had been frustrated, and I felt keenly the force and edge
of the saying, "In that very day his thoughts perish." I had
by me several sermons on death, the other world, and similar
subjects; but how worthless they had become by this time!
How cold and how soul-less! If I had the opportunity, how
much better I could preach now than before! It took me

weeks to learn how to submit to the inevitable and to give in my resignation. How hard the struggle! By now, everything appeared in a new aspect. Those subjects in which I used to take the deepest interest—politics and literature for instance—lost all their charm, and I wondered having ever been delighted by them. The range of my studies diminished daily until my mind at last gave itself up entirely to matters which concerned my spiritual fate. No longer did those truths which I had once found the greatest pleasure in preaching do aught but sadden me and sink me down into depths of sorrow unspeakable.

But, by grace of Heaven, I presently mastered my melancholy. I got to feel readier to recognise God's hand, and to throw myself into His arms. I occasionally caught glimpses of ineffable happiness and flashes of light upon the order of the Gospel, which I had never experienced before I was afflicted. There were times when I went into silent raptures over my condition, and a powerful longing took possession of me for the perfection and glory of the spiritual world. Now and again I could contemplate my body and its weakness as something apart from myself, and laugh at both. I would afterwards subside into a pleasing peace, and reflect upon the disagreeable things from which I had been saved by this break-down of my strength by the way. Permitted to live, I might have been overcome by some temptation or other, which would have brought me and my calling into disgrace. Thinking of some I had known, what a mercy it was they had died young! Again there would come periods of dejection, of giving way to morbid and profitless brooding. During one of them, I was struck by this very strange fancy: If Providence was for taking me hence in the midst of my days, could I not compensate myself by living over again (in my own mind), the whole of my life, and so double it? Could I not, as my strength permitted, devote a few hours, every day, to going over the principal events of my career? This would keep me from stewing amongst unprofitable matter, and from eating myself up before my time. In one position I was pretty free from pain, and perhaps the writing of my Autobiography might do me good. The outcome of that fancy has been the present copious writing. It is the work of a serious man, though that may seem improbable to those who remember the various amusing incidents it contains. But there is nothing strange in that. If there be found here too much mention of Will Bryan, I flatter myself there are some things here, also, which every thoughful man—every man who has been awakened to the great questions of life—is bound to ponder. Were it otherwise, the fire would have been the fittest place for the manuscript.

I should have been glad to note something more definite and cheering with respect to Will Bryan. But I have not heard anything from him, for some time. In his last letter to me he said he had finished paving his father's debts, and that he continued to attend the Welsh Chapel, but that, as yet, he had not "reached himself." My last letter to him was returned marked—"left without address." It is months since then, and I never heard from him afterwards. Has Will gone out with the tide? No; I have a presentiment that at the last he will turn up safe.

My mother, as I have stated, charged me, upon her death-bed to requite the Bartleys for their kindness to her. But I never got the chance. The boot is on the other leg. The kindness of both towards me has had no end; their sympathy with me in my illness is beyond measure, and very precious. Their understanding is limited, and I have many times debated the object of their creation. And yet I envy them. Both are well, both happy and likely to live for many years to come. Even if they put their heads together they could not read a verse; but they enjoy religion, and doubtless possess its strength. So close is the similarity and union between them, that I almost believe they will die the same day. I do not see how Thomas and Barbara can possibly live apart.

If someone should go to the trouble of reading this history, it may be he will wonder why I have made so much mention of things connected with my family which are dishonorable; and perhaps he will ask, in Will Bryan's words, whether this is 'true to nature?" But how could the history be different and be true? And, after I have gone hence, who will be injured? No one need bow the head, because I am the last of my family.

In looking over what I have written, I see I have, from forgetfulness, left some things untouched which I would like to have dealt with; while other things have been purposely omitted. To all seeming, it is not likely I shall ever revise this account, because the writing of the latter portions of it has been burdensome to me; as, I fear, the perusal will be to others. If it so happen, the reader can do as I have done—lay it by when he has become tired.

THE END.

www.ingramcontent.com/pod-product-compliance
Lightning Source LLC
Chambersburg PA
CBHW030939110726
47900CB00004B/1058